Do you want to KNOW from whence
the PRESIDENT came?
This is the REAL stuff.
ONLY the NAMES have been
CHANGED to PROTECT the GUILTY.
ILLINOIS POLITICAL INSIDER

∗ ∗ ∗ ∗

CHICAGO CONFIDENTIAL

SENATOR ROGER A. KEATS

Heartland Press • Dripping Springs, Texas

Book Design by TLC Graphics, *www.tlcgraphics.com*
Cover by Tamara Dever; Interior by Erin Stark

Photo credits:
Chicago skyline ©iStockphoto.com/nazdravie
Blood spatter ©iStockphoto.com/sjharmon

ISBN: 978-0-9883194-0-0 (softcover)
ISBN: 978-0-9883194-1-7 (e-book)

Library of Congress Control Number: 2012950200

Printed in the United States of America

This book is dedicated to Captain Robert George Keats
United States Military Academy
WEST POINT, Class of 1965
1944-1968
Forever young

∗ ∗ ∗ ∗

"All that's NECESSARY for the FORCES OF EVIL to WIN in the WORLD is for enough GOOD MEN to DO NOTHING."

EDMUND BURKE

★ ★ ★ ★

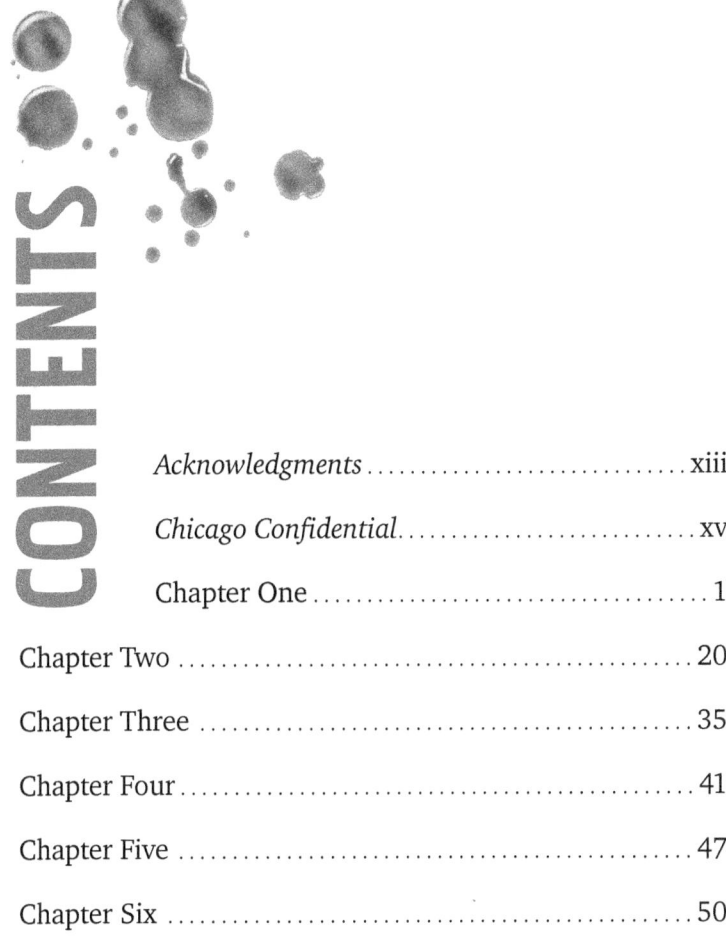

CONTENTS

ACKNOWLEDGMENTS

I AM A LIFE LONG SON-OF-THE-HEARTLAND AND A proud Big 10 man. I always assumed I would die in our home in the Chicago suburbs. My wife and I would then be buried at the Abraham Lincoln National Veterans Cemetery in Elwood, Illinois just South of Chicago in Will County. It took a great deal to get me to leave my family's home for essentially all of our lives. But finally the unbelievable corruption and obscene taxes made Tina and me decide, enough is enough.

To quote Davy Crockett when he left Tennessee "Y'all can go to hell. I'm going to Texas." He became part of Texas lore and died with his fellow Texans at the Alamo in 1836. Well I don't want my old friends to go to hell and I hope to avoid being killed in a battle at the Alamo. But I shared his frustration with my old home state and neighboring city, Chicago.

My wonderful wife Tina is the person who finally got me to write this book. I had some success with screen plays and real fiction. She was the one who finally got me to realize my imagination wasn't as good as the real life corruption going on in Chicago and Illinois: *Chicago Confidential* was born.

CHICAGO CONFIDENTIAL

THE IDEA FOR THIS BOOK CAME FROM SO MANY OF my friends telling me I ought to write about the goings on in Chicago and the State of Illinois. I know personally many of the renamed characters the story revolves around. Rather than writing a dry recitation of the foibles of the crooks that control Chicago and Cook County, I came up with this idea because in Chicago, fact is stranger than fiction. You can't make this stuff up any better than what is really happening.

For legal reasons, this book is a work of fiction. It is an amalgamation of true events wound together to form a unified story. In 2012, University of Illinois Professor Dick Simpson produced a study based on indictments and convictions to document that Chicago is, by far, the most corrupt city in America.

Long time Chicago area residents will recognize most of the events, the real people and the various story lines. I have simply changed the names to protect the guilty. The level of corruption in the Chicago political machine is so overwhelming the average person becomes numb to the constant drum beat of indictments, convictions and insider fixes. Crooked Chicago politicians are so inbred it is surprising to learn most of them have front teeth and aren't married to their kid sister. Chicago has shrunk from 3.66 million residents to 2.69 million residents. Maybe they can't stop the crooks, but they can leave. In the Epilogue I am more specific. Enjoy the story first and then see that facts are stranger than fiction.

Only the Federal Prosecutors occasionally pay attention and I do mean occasionally. That is why it is important who is in the White House. They appoint the prosecutors who follow the leads given to them.

The political insiders who control Chicago do not have a strong working relationship with reality. But that has not kept them from becoming seriously wealthy top one per centers. If they stole an extra fifty or one hundred thousand dollars, probably no one would care, or even notice. But they don't know when to stop. Many take home millions of dollars. It is all done by manipulating a corrupt system they built and they control.

Four of Illinois' last seven elected governors have gone to prison. Of Illinois' last nine elected governors five have been indicted. That is more than the other 49 states added together. It is hard to believe but Illinois has two former governors in jail at the same time! Big government always leads to certain amounts of corruption, but two governors in jail at the same time?

Attorney generals and state treasurers go to prison also. A Secretary of State and former Speaker of the House died while at the Mayo Clinic and left $800,000 in cash in shoe boxes, 49 cases of whiskey, two cases of creamed corn and one million dollars of racetrack stock on closet shelves in his hotel room. The total estate settled at four and one half million dollars. He had never made more than $30,000/year in his life. No one was indicted and his longtime girlfriend received the money.

Chicago has fifty aldermen and in recent years 32 have been sent to prison and a 33rd was just indicted. Chicago could hold a City Council meeting in "The Big House." In Chicago, "The

Big House" isn't Michigan's legendary football stadium, it is the federal penitentiary. According to the *Chicago Tribune* over 1,000 governmental workers have been convicted in recent years. Fact is stranger than fiction. You can't make this stuff up!

You would be made ill to see the Chicago zoning and permitting process in action! Virtually everyone in the permit department has been indicted and sent to prison.

Recently the Chicago City Council Finance Committee that oversees the City budget got caught with a huge new batch of "ghost payrollers". That is a term used for an old Chicago institution where the relatives and key political workers of politically connected big shots get paid by the taxpayers, but they don't actually work. In fact they don't even show up to NOT work. They stay home and not work. Or they go to bars to not work. Or, more often than not, they go to other jobs and get paid there also. In Chicago "ghost payrolling" is an honored tradition. There have been and are huge numbers of these ghost payrollers. Even newspapers as far away as the *New York Times* write articles about the institutionalized corruption. Yet the local prosecutors, aldermen and legislators are oblivious.

The corruption of "pin stripe patronage", where a guy gets essentially a no bid contract for white collar work (that may or may not be something that really needs to be done) and "ghost payrolling" in legislative commissions was exposed when I worked with legendary Chicago political reporter Dick Kay to uncover huge numbers of ghost payrollers in the legislature. They were just political operatives being paid with tax payer money to do political work. Dick Kay did such a fine job with the story he was awarded The Peabody for the best investigative reporter in America that year. Dick kiddingly nicknamed me his "Deep Throat" and we kept my involvement a secret for 25 years. We both knew there would be serious repercussions if some of my fellow legislators realized I had sent some of their favored political minions to jail.

Illinois isn't ranked 50th out of 50 states in fiscal policy for nothing! Or number one in unfunded pension liabilities by accident. Or the most governors and elected officials to go to prison by mistake. Only California has a lower bond rating.

If some of the action gets a little graphic, I apologize. But as we go to press, thirty-five and fifty-two people were shot in Chicago on back to back weekends! Nineteen were shot on just one summer evening. A guy was shot in the block of President Obama's home! Think of how many Government Agents are there and sadly someone got shot virtually in the President's back yard. This is becoming normal! The violence in the book is not overstated. There are gang related drug wars raging right now as you read this. It is so dangerous the Obama Administration is sending additional federal agents to his home town and the Department of Justice is increasing its support.

All that said Chicago is one of the world's great cities. I mention some history and also some of its finer points in the story. I don't exaggerate the corruption for the sake of the story. I actually skip over most of it. There is too much to fit in one book. No one who doesn't live in the Chicago area can truly comprehend just how corrupt the whole system is. The names and specific events are simply modified to protect the guilty. These are public figures and libel laws don't actually apply, especially since the libel is true! When you get to write about folks who have such a tenuous relationship with reality and think they are immune from prosecution, there is plenty to entertain.

This is why I remind you, this isn't really fiction. We have changed the names to protect the guilty. I have tried to make an interesting story amidst what is reality. When fact is stranger than fiction, why should a writer bother try to make this stuff up?

CHAPTER ONE

KESHAWN OKAMBO HAS EARNED THIS DEATH SENtence and he knows it. For years his Grandmother has prayed for him to break free of his gangster lifestyle. The drugs. The violence. The destruction of his soul. His grandmother's prayers have been answered, but that doesn't seem to matter to the leader of the Gangster Warlords, Akile Fort or his fellow gangbangers who are watching intently. The price for disloyalty in Chicago is high. Very high.

He tries to scream in agony. The thought of being dead in a few minutes is all he can hope for. He would scream if he didn't have so much duct tape holding his mouth shut. He trembles and shakes as the blood flows freely. Okambo looks in horror as he realizes the Gangster Warlord gangbangers have no intention of ending this any time soon. There are still plenty of body parts they intend to detach. The physical shock and blood loss will soon bring it all to an end.

The life of a Chicago gangbanger in the murder capitol of America isn't all that valuable. But Okambo hopes his new friend and confidant, Detective Rea will understand why this is happening. He knows his grandmother will. She never gave up on him. She never stopped praying for or loving her little grandbaby who had gone so terribly wrong. Okambo smiles internally as he thinks even a drug running gangbanger with no mother can count on the love of a Christian Grandmother. Funny, but true.

He knows it doesn't matter what he says or how he says it. They are going to kill him. Informing to the police always leads to a death sentence from the Gangster Warlords, Chicago's largest street gang. In the street gang world, there are just some things that aren't allowed. Informing to the police is number one on the list. But he knows why he did it and is willing to suffer the consequences.

Okambo can tell his old friend, Akile Fort, the leader of the Gangster Warlords, is speaking to him but he is having a very hard time hearing. Rapidly approaching shock tends to shut down most bodily functions. There is blood everywhere.

The Warlord behind him slaps his head several times to try to keep him from passing out. He feels no pain from the blows. He is past pain by now. Then Fort himself pours cold bottled water over his head. If Okambo really wants to remain conscience, he probably can. But it is time. He is at peace. He knows he is finally being called to account for all of the terrible things he has done. He just never expected it would happen at the hands of a man he had served and respected. At least not until now.

He might be about to die, but with the information he has given Detective Rea he hopes others will be spared the disastrous life he has led. Maybe this final act of repentance will give meaning to his wasted existence. In a new experience, he humbly prays it will.

Oh my GOD! Okambo thought he is now beyond pain! He is wrong. He isn't beyond feeling the pain. He can tell he is going into shock.

Keshawn Okambo closes his eyes for the last time. His final thoughts are of his grandmother who raised him after his mother died of a drug overdose at sixteen. He hopes someone will tell her of his sacrifice. He hopes she will finally have a reason to be proud of him. Certainly his life, until a few weeks ago, as a Chicago street gang member and drug runner was as utterly degraded as a human's can be.

Chicago's soft underbelly is neighborhoods like the "West Side" where Keshawn Okambo is about to die. There are large areas that have essentially never been rebuilt since they were burned out during the riots that followed the assassination of the Reverend Martin Luther King Junior in 1968. The public schools are at best a disgrace.

There are lots of big, empty parking lots and run down old factories for gangbangers and drug pushers to use for their business. This area was once the manufacturing heartland of America. Standing in one of those parking lots outside one of those abandoned factories is a big, muscular man, with wide shoulders and a powerful neck who Ieans on his unmarked patrol car, a beat up Dodge. He is nicely dressed in plain clothes, not a police uniform. He carefully surveys the surrounding area, a bleak landscape of desolation and despair.

His partner, a trim, nice looking, button down kind of a guy, Vladimir Kozak is ten feet away checking the lock on the inner parking lot where a large number of shipping containers are stacked.

Across the street in a small, not well-kept up park, a group of young children play. There is one elderly, grandmotherly looking lady watching them. Near them, way too near is a parked van with heavily tinted windows. The van's engine is running.

Near the gate Vlad is examining are some smudges on the ground. They look a great deal like blood.

The big guy with the wide shoulders, Detective Ross "Sunny" SunWarrior is the Chicago Police Department's unrepentant Comanche warrior. He is really only, at most, half Comanche, but smart people don't quibble about minor technicalities like that with Comanche warriors. There were plenty of reasons Comanche's were the most feared warriors on the Great Plains, so why irritate one of them. Sunny is more domesticated than most. But not much more.

Right now he knows he is getting near the end of his shift and wants to be thinking about heading home for dinner with his wife, Sheila. He kiddingly calls her his squaw. She doesn't mind. Who knows, maybe even a little something else after dinner. He loves to call Sheila the best dessert in town. She claims he is a pervert. Oh well, a nice evening with the wife he adores is a reward worth waiting for. Proud Comanche warriors like spending the evening with their wives. Comanches killed and tortured lots of settlers, but were almost cuddle bums when home with their own families.

But something here isn't right. He can sense it. The police got a 911 call about a break in at this container storage facility. The 911 caller, a woman, said there was electronic equipment in the containers. She said it was a group wearing black and crimson, Gangster Warlord colors so it looked like a gangbanger robbery.

Vlad and Sunny agree no one in their right mind will leave valuable anythings in as desolate a parking lot as this one. It makes no sense. They are here. There is no one else here and no obvious break-in.

This area is a study of bad government policy and how it can disrupt already wounded neighborhoods. The Federal government got bought off by 3,000 sugar producers and that destroyed thousands of manufacturing jobs in this neighborhood. All done by a tariff on low cost Caribbean sugar.

The West Side of Chicago was the national kingpin for the production of chocolate candies and most candies in general. Sugar tariffs and truculent unions make most Chicago candy noncompetitive. Now thousands of good paying, unionized Chicago candy making jobs are long gone.

All of these big plants just sit empty and make the neighborhoods look even worse than they are. A handful of sugar producers who know how to buy off Congress get richer. A bunch of union manufacturing workers get poorer. Many Caribbean economies are almost moribund because they no longer have sugar markets so no longer grow that much sugar cane.

Sunny SunWarrior carefully keeps an eye on the van. "Vlad you see that van?"

"Of course dipshit. You think I'm a crossing guard?"

Sunny laughs at Vlad's cynical response but keeps the corner of his eye on the van. "The van is too close to grandma and the kids. I think they are using them for a distraction. Behind those tinted windows I'll bet they're watching us as closely as we're watching them."

Inside the van six heavily armed guys in black and crimson jumpsuits sit and watch the two cops. They don't know they are Sunny SunWarrior and Vlad Kozak. But they know they are police detectives. It is obvious. What other White guys would be such idiots as to be wandering around in this neighborhood?

Their van is parked close to the old lady and the kiddy lot to make sure they are out of bounds for anyone to shoot at. But they can't leave the chained up parking lot with so much of their product locked up inside. They're armed for a reason and they're not leaving. Beside the body of the traitor in back needs to be dumped somewhere.

Vlad takes a closer look at the lock, "Sunny, come here. Either someone tried but couldn't get this open or we interrupted something. Maybe they knew we were coming?"

Sunny walks over to check the lock. "Could be. But if someone really wanted in, why didn't they just snip it? This isn't a heavy chain. Doesn't make sense. You keep looking...I'm going to go to the park and chat with granny. I don't want that grandmother and those little kids caught in a cross fire. It isn't our job to get little kids killed. I'll get closer on the other side."

Vlad nods. "Go get 'em big boy. I want to keep sniffing around here for a minute."

"OK. I want to sneak a peek because I don't like the looks of that van. Keep an eye on me and if I give you a sign, bring that Ithaca Mag-10 shotgun you've got under the seat, not the Benelli. That cannon is all the backup I'll need. OK? We just might be in the middle of some bad shit." Sunny walks away, but over his shoulder he mumbles "Don't go impaling that hole too."

"I heard that. Sheila is right, you are a pervert!" Vlad laughs but doesn't take offense. His nickname is Vlad the Impaler. Most people who know a little history think the nickname is a historical reference to his namesake from the 15th century, Vlad III, Prince of Wallachia. Prince Vlad was a hero for his battles with the Ottoman Sultans and a bit intimidating because of his frightening reputation for impaling his foes on large wooden stakes. But Prince Vlad is probably better remembered by his surname, Drakulya, or Anglicized to Count Dracula.

Actually Vlad Kozak's nickname has nothing to do with Count Dracula. He is a handsome bachelor and it is a reference to his very active night life. But Vlad, being a gentleman, always says he and his date had simply gone to dinner, a movie and home early. Statements to the contrary from eye witnesses were always dismissed by Vlad as simply hearsay or the unreliable, liquor induced ramblings of drunks.

Sunny approaches the elderly woman and turns so the sun will not be in her face. That makes him face the van with the tinted window. He nods as a friendly greeting and flashes his badge. "I'm Detective SunWarrior, Chicago PD. I was wondering if you have seen anything suspicious? Maybe someone trying to break into the lot across the street?"

Her face is stiff and afraid. "I ain't seen nothin' boy. Nothin' at all." But her eyes tell a totally different story. Her back is toward the van and she keeps shifting her eyes toward the van. "Everything is just fine Mr. Policeman."

The six Gangster Warlords never take their eyes off Sunny. All of them keep their weapons at the ready.

Sunny acknowledges her warning but remains casual. "Thank you, ma'am, sorry to have bothered you."

Just as he starts to leave, he turns back to her. "You know it is getting late. The kids should be getting home for dinner. Why don't you take the kids along now? Right now." Sunny then carefully places himself between the van and the grandmother and her brood.

"Yes sir. I think I'll do just that. Yes sir." The elderly lady rises and starts to herd the kids toward the corner and past the van. The meandering group of little kids is like herding cats.

Sunny is careful to keep himself between the noisy gaggle of kids and the van. He knows he is exposed but he needs to shield grandma as she gets the kids out of the way. He moves past the van and tries not to be too obvious by looking back at the rear of it. All he wants is a better angle if he needs to start shooting at anyone.

The six gangbangers follow his movements. They don't want the old lady to move, but they don't want to open fire until they are sure there is no choice. There is too much at stake.

Sunny casually lifts his cell phone and speed dials Vlad. All he wants to do is keep the van occupied until grandma and the kids are out of the line of fire. He speaks into the phone as if he were just chatting with a friend. "The old lady is fine. I'll be back in a minute. Do you see anything? I'm about to ask a few questions. OK?"

Just as the kids round the corner and disappear under a viaduct, Sunny hoists his badge in the air, grabs his revolver and quickly moves to the van's rear door. "Chicago Police. Please open up. I have some questions."

Right now, he wishes he had the Austrian Army Glock 9mm with an eighteen round clip. Chicago's political establishment doesn't want officers to have weapons the anti-gun critics complain about so they are very slow to put certain weapons on the approved list. That leaves most officers out gunned by gangbangers and drug pushers. Luckily the thugs usually can't shoot straight.

The City's lawyers are worried about liability not citizen safety. Since the notoriously political Chicago Courts are nationally famous as playgrounds for ambulance chasing, but politically connected lawyers, there is a point. Chicago often seems to think the police are more dangerous than the criminals.

Tires screech. The big van moves forward and a back window comes down.

A long arm reaches out with a gun and opens fire. Sunny's first two shots crash into the door with the open window and his third shot hits the rear tire. The van swerves and bumps along. The driver seems to be losing control of the hobbled vehicle.

Vlad, Ithaca Mag-10 shotgun on his shoulder steps into the street and with two pump action shots blows out the front tires and half of the front end of the van. Ithacas aren't city issue and in a liability conscious city there is a reason. They have the fire power of a small howitzer.

Mag-10s are called mini roadblocks, all by themselves. One cop with an Ithaca is like a couple of squad cars worth of guys with .38s. When you are firing one you need to be very careful to look at all of the angles because those Ithacas don't. They'll make a mess of whatever they hit, so it is important to not have them hit things you don't want hit. They tore up the van and could tear up just about anything short of an M-1 Abrams tank.

After firing, Vlad smartly kneels down behind a parked car and jams two more cartridges into the Mag-10. They usually hold three cartridges so Vlad wants to be sure it is back at full load. Because of the three cartridge load, some folks think they aren't that useful. They're idiots. Someone saying the Ithaca Mag-10 *only* holds three cartridges is like saying the Enola Gay *only* held one atomic bomb.

The City issues Benelli shotguns to detectives. Good weapons for gun fights. But if you are trying to stop a car, the old Ithaca Mag-10 is what you want. Of course you can't tell the city you have one. The lawyers would go crazy worrying about liability. Forget the victims, the point is don't offend the anti-gun folks or the criminals you are pursuing. They're the ones with the hot shot lawyers.

The car Vlad is behind is the only cover near him. He also uses it to brace his Ithaca to improve his accuracy. Not that accuracy is a big problem for a crack shot like Vlad using a mini howitzer like an Ithaca Mag-10.

Sunny slams his body against a tree to give him some cover and something to stabilize his aim. The van slides into the curb and comes to a stop. Its fancy wheel rims are bent from the weight of the van hitting the curb. It just sits there quietly. No more shooting. But also no open doors and no one exiting the vehicle.

Sunny holds up his badge so it is obvious. "Police! OK a holes...drop the guns and come on out. Hands up."

The van's back door flies open and three gunmen come charging out. Two run straight at Sunny and the third at Vlad. It looks like a charge organized by some crazy guy who doesn't realize he is facing two experienced, ex-military types who are crack shots and in protected positions.

The lead gunman fires at Sunny while he is running. Only a real expert marksman is able to hit a target protected behind a tree while the gunman is moving. These gangbangers are thugs, not expert marksmen. Sunny's aim is stabilized by the four point contact between the ground, his body, his gun and he starts firing. His first shot hits the lead runner in the chest and he stumbles. The following runner is right behind him so he almost trips over him. He has to stop and pause to avoid his falling comrade which gives Sunny the perfect shot. He takes it.

Sunny is not a thug. He really is an expert marksman. In fact from his Army days he is an expert with an M-16, an M-14, an M-1, an M-72 grenade launcher, a 7.62 mm machinegun, a .50 cal machine gun, an Army issue Beretta 9 mm pistol and some other weapons civilians never see and probably don't want to know much about anyway. For Sunny, hitting a standing still thug, while firing from a stabilized prone position, is about as difficult as scratching an itch on his chin. Too bad the gangbangers didn't take that into account before they decided to commit suicide by cop.

The third gunman runs straight at Vlad and never has a chance. He catches an Ithaca Mag-10 shot gun blast full frontal. His various body parts drop bleeding all over the street. It is really gross. A normal person would lose their lunch. Vlad just pumps the next cartridge into the chamber and stays behind the car.

Watching Sunny and Vlad handle the threat or in layman's terms, shoot the dumb shit gangbangers, makes it obvious who has military experience and who doesn't. Sunny and Vlad are cool and extremely accurate with their weapons. The gangbangers have no battle plans, no tactics, no interlocking fields of fire, no reserves, no exit strategy, no body armor and no brains to run straight at armed men in protected firing positions.

The gangbangers should realize a shotgun big enough to almost move their van backwards is nothing to argue with. The

Mag-10s are not new weapons and aren't even in production anymore. But even if they don't know what an Ithaca Mag-10 is, they should realize something destroyed the front of their van and did it with only two shots. Only something seriously big does that kind of damage.

You may not see the full Great White Shark in the murky water, but once you see the fin you should be bright enough to know getting in the water is a bad idea. There is very little good that can come from entering a Great White Shark's domain and doing it on his terms. There is very little good that can come from challenging a shotgun big enough to demolish the front of your van with only two rounds.

Gangbangers are not the sharpest knives in the drawer. That is why they are gangbangers not doctors, securities traders, teachers or salesmen. Actions like these make it obvious that drill sergeants do really beat some knowledge into their young charges. Listening to your drill sergeants does pay off. Sunny and Vlad are alive and well. The gangbangers are inert, ready for emergency surgery at Cook County Hospital or more probably, the county morgue.

Now the van sits at the curb. Nothing is happening. Just silence. Vlad carefully takes another shot at the one good tire and takes it out also. The big, heavy van just sits there on its expensive rims.

Sunny and Vlad aren't going to advance uncovered and the van doesn't seem to want to disgorge any more of its contents. The van can't move and the police have no intention of endangering themselves any further. Stalemate. It is quiet for the moment.

This is the side of Chicago that is hard to visualize because it is so hidden from America's most beautiful metropolis, which is a very livable big city. Nestled on the shore of Lake Michigan it has a skyline second to none. There are so many unique, downtown sky scrapers that a lover of architecture could spend months touring the lot. This is what you would expect from the town that invented the skyscraper.

There are lake front parks and beaches that extend uninterrupted for 20 miles. A wonderful assortment of bungalow based neighborhoods, 19th and 20th century town homes and a huge assortment of downtown apartment and condominium complexes give unlimited options to residents. Tremendous central location, unlimited fresh water, huge highways, rail lines, mass transit, several world class universities, the nation's largest fresh water port and busy airports make it a hub for everything.

It is wonderful to think of Chicago's beauty, but right now Sunny and Vlad are hunkered down in the forgotten underbelly hoping to avoid getting killed while they arrest some dangerous predators. They're doing their very dangerous jobs. It is hard to keep your head down while you do it.

Vlad calls in for backup but the dispatcher assures him help is already on the way.

"Let's see your hands, now! Come out, now! Don't make us come and get you," orders Sunny.

They just sit. The police assume they are more than happy to see if the police will be dumb enough to stand up and expose themselves to fire.

Police sirens start to wail. In a moment one car, then another comes around the corners and each parks to block the van's movement, forward or backward. The uniformed police officers jump out and use their doors as shields.

Sunny signals for the officers to just wait. Stay ready, but wait.

As they all wait three more police cruisers arrive and the van is surrounded by armed police officers with protection from behind their squad cars.

Seeing the odds now solidly in his favor, Sunny decides to lean out from behind the tree and yell, "OK guys. Time's up.

Throw your guns out the window. Come on out for a pow-wow."

The other officers, knowing Sunny's Comanche heritage chuckle at his pow-wow invite.

The van's windows come back down and several pistols and a shot gun fly out and land in the street.

"That's a good start. Now let's see you guys next. Hands up and face me over here."

Slowly three men get out of the van. They are all rough looking characters and wear black and crimson jogging suits. One is a little taller than the other two. He walks erect, his head held high. He is clearly in charge. While he does as he is told by the police, he never even deigns to look at one of the officers. He simply cooperates. He moves and acts with a certain level of dignity missing from his underlings.

Even when the big guy is told to lie face down, he does, but gets down slowly and at his own pace. No resistance, but also no attempt to do more than what he is told. The big guy is a cool customer with the dignity of a chieftain.

The big guy's three friends are still sprawled on the ground and are also in outfits that are accented by black and crimson. Something this action proves, as usual, is that the black and crimson outfits aren't bullet proof. Too many gang thugs think when they put on their colors they are invincible.

This stupidity is a little like the old Native American Ghost Dancers. By the time the warriors had finished with the rituals and wild dancing many thought they couldn't be hurt by bullets and some even seemed to think they were invisible. The problem was they forgot to tell the Cavalry's repeating rifles who didn't understand the warriors couldn't be harmed by bullets. Brave perhaps, but not the clearest thinking in the world. But at least they were optimistic. Just like the gangbangers lying in the street.

Once the survivors are all secured and given their Miranda rights they are moved toward a paddy wagon. The big guy looks at the arresting officer with a smile on his face. "I'll be out before you finish the paperwork. Why waste my time and yours with this stuff?"

The officer nods in agreement but still puts them in the newly arrived paddy wagon. They certainly become invisible once they enter the wagon. A large Black officer with arms that look more like pile drivers than biceps closes the door and looks over at Sunny and Vlad.

"Hey you nitwits...why are you messin' with your pals here? You have just forfeited your dinner invites at their momma's homes for the next week. The way Sheila cooks that is a really dumb thing to do."

Sunny and Vlad crack up as they recognize their pal, officer Harold Brookins. Sunny may love his wife Sheila deeply, but he is not above whining to friends about her lack of culinary skills. In fact her cooking sucks. She really seems to believe all of these trendy health foods taste good.

Sunny may be a muscle bound, Comanche warrior, but he is still too big of a wimp to mention to Sheila her health food crap sucks. Sleeping in a pup tent in the back yard holds no fascination for an ex-soldier who has spent many nights sleeping under the stars in Afghanistan. He just makes sure he has a decent breakfast and lunch while on the job and lets dinner go where it goes. Usually it goes wrong.

"Hey numb nuts" counters Sunny! "Who gave you permission to make fun of the SunWarrior family diet?"

Brookins laughs, "You callin' a man with three kids, numb nuts? Did you miss the sex ed classes in the juvenile penitentiary you grew up in? Besides, you did you idiot. You know I am always patient enough to listen to your sob stories of starvation and upset stomachs. If I have to listen to your BS, then I can editorialize about the truth."

Vlad looks at Brookins and then Sunny and shrugs. "The truth is its own defense."

Brookins waves for Vlad to come over. He speaks quietly. "All of that damage looks like your Mag-10. Be sure it isn't around if a lawyer or Internal Affairs show up. Don't forget lawyers run this place and all they worry about is the Warlords will sue us for damaging their van with an unauthorized weapon. In these crooked courts we'll end up paying them and apologizing to boot."

"You're right." Vlad nods and walks back to his car and dumps the Mag-10 out of sight in the trunk.

Two Chicago Fire Department ambulances role up and stop at the outer edge of the police vehicles. The paramedics from both vehicles jump out and hurry to the back of the ambulances to get their equipment.

Sunny grabs the head paramedic for a personal talk. "Do us a favor and get the fingerprints and send them out. I bet these guys names will come back fast."

"Why fast?"

Sunny smiles back. "The finger print data base is huge. So they prioritize it by level of scum the guy is. The first run-through is the FBI's most wanted list. Then the next list is a hundred or so of the next level of scum. Then probably a thousand or so scum. Those go real fast. They really want those guys. It slows down for the minor scum bags. These guys were riding around with the head of the Gangster Warlords. They are decent sized scum. They are going to have arrest records. So, the faster they are back, the worse a scum bag the guy is."

Brookins joins Vlad and Sunny, leans over to them and whispers, "You realize who the big guy is don't you?"

Sunny nods. "Oh yeah...that's Akile Fort, the head of the Gangster Warlords and some of his finest with him."

Brookins nods to acknowledge the answer. "That guy is pure evil. He does not have a soul and doesn't want one either. What the hell was he doing on some nickel and dime thing like this?"

Street gangs have ravaged whole neighborhoods in Chicago. Heck, not just Chicago, major cities all over the world. Middle class families living in the suburban belts or protected neighborhoods on the big cities outskirts that surround the inner cities don't spend hours worrying about criminals standing outside their doors and windows. There is no concern a stray bullet will come through the window and kill their young daughter sleeping in her bed.

Not that there isn't crime in middle-class neighborhoods, but it is nothing in comparison to what happens in the inner cities. If you live in Wilmette, North of Chicago and your daughter is a little late coming home from school you don't really worry she will never get home.

A car is occasionally stolen and a home is occasionally burglarized, but people go for long exercise walks on very dark nights without a second thought. Teenagers hang out at Gilson Park and wade into Lake Michigan in the dark without a moments fear. Sometimes the kids even have their swimming suits on. If a Wilmette resident leaves their door unlocked on their suburban home that is dumb, but it isn't going to be fatal.

It is almost impossible for those who live outside the crime zones to realize how dangerous it is for kids to be out at night on the West Side of Chicago. It is almost insane for a parent in the crime zones to let their kids out of their sight after dark. It is scary enough during the day time.

A star basketball player at the local Flowers High School was killed in a park while teaching younger kids how to play basketball. He wasn't the target of the bullet. The gangbanger was so incompetent when he shot he hit the basketball player completely by accident. The biggest killer of teenage minority boys is the violence that surrounds the gangs and their drug enterprises.

Most police officers view the murder of a gangbanger as a bit of a public good. The death is a terrible thing for a family, but probably good for the neighborhood. Many think if the mother really cared, she wouldn't have let the boy out at night anyway. She would have been sure he could read. She would have made him go to school and study. She would have helped him with his homework. She would have taken him to church and made sure he actually attended and listened during Sunday school. She would have gotten him into some of the activities at the park district field house.

When people think of gangbangers, they don't think of the father since only a tiny number of gangbangers have much of an idea who their father is anyway. Most people don't really think of the family either since these kids don't have families in the traditional sense. The gang is their family because their real family is usually dysfunctional.

Sadly, most of these gangbangers don't get many lessons about how to behave in public. Most of these guys are missing one or more of the essential elements needed to be successful human beings: A conscience being the element most often missing. A heart to allow them to have real feelings of affection for another human being and make them not want to hurt innocent folks just for the heck of it would help also.

One of the police officers opens the side door and leans into the van. "Oh shit! Get over here and take a look."

Everyone hurries to the van. In the back is a bound and gagged man, obviously dead. He is bloody and looks to be missing some key body parts. It is hard to tell exactly what body parts are missing with the blood all over him and the back seat.

When another officer opens the back he says, "Oh boy. Enough is enough. Don't even bother looking. Just hold what is left for the medical examiner. Oh my GOD, that must have hurt."

Vlad looks at Sunny. "I guess we know why Akile Fort was here. This poor son of a bitch must have led them here so we better get in there and see what is in those containers. I know some of our friends don't like us to admit it, but Akile Fort proves again, torture does work. GOD that guy looks bad! I don't want to think of the kind of pain he was in."

Sunny then looks at Brookins and the uniformed officers. "Better secure this lot and get a search warrant for the premises. Don't forget to mention we are here because of a 911 call. We'll go in and take a look once we have the warrant. No need to claim we were in hot pursuit. Nothing is going to go anywhere while we wait for the judge. Also let Internal Affairs know we had to perform some post-partum abortions on these non-viable shit bags that were lying in the street. They'll find the bodies in the morgue and they can call Vlad and me to whine about it at their convenience."

Brookins looks at Sunny with a tongue in cheek, surprised expression. "Thanks for the advice Einstein. None of us would have thought of that on our own."

Sunny just shakes his head and smiles at Brookins' humorous cheap shot. He takes an expression as if he is worried as he looks at Brookins. "Hey you look like you're in pain."

Brookins looks a little confused. "No I'm fine."

"You are now. You must have quit thinking about what to do. That thinking stuff really seems too painful for you on those rare occasions when you try to do it."

Brookins laughs and flips Sunny the bird.

One of the uniformed officers walks near the gate of the lot. He examines the smudges that look like blood and carefully follows a small trail of blood to the edge of the concrete. The ground cover looks a little bit like grass but more like just hardened dirt and weeds. The officer waves at the others and yells, "Hey! I just found the dude's body parts. Can't quite tell what some of these things were. But they're here." Several officers hurry over to see for themselves.

One young officer approaches, sees the bloody body parts, staggers backwards and pukes on his shoes. The rest of the officers laugh and make fun of him. But as every one of them looks at those still very fresh body parts lying on the ground, they realize what sheer horror must have happened here just a very short time ago.

As they walk back toward their cars, Vlad looks at Brookins and the other officers and says, "Glad to see you, but how did you get here so fast? I barely had a chance to call for backup."

"We got a 911 about shots being fired at police. Some lady said she was here. She said you helped her and got her kids out of reach before the gun shots?"

Vlad looks at Sunny, "Grandma must have a cell phone. We don't need her for questioning do we?"

Sunny chuckles to himself "A good deed is rewarded once in a while."

Both laugh at their help coming from a little old grandmother babysitting her grandkids and probably a few of the neighbor's kids also.

Sunny leans over to Vlad and Brookins, "Let's not bother with her as a witness for the moment. All it'll do is give the Gangster Warlords someone else to murder to keep her from testifying. We've got the 911 call for probable cause. Once we have the warrant we've got enough of a case."

CHAPTER TWO

AS SUNNY AND VLAD WALK BACK TO THEIR unmarked car Sunny's cell phone starts to ring. "SunWarrior... speak to me now or forever hold your peace."

The desk Sergeant smiles at the greeting. "Hey Sunny, a couple of the uniforms said remembering that Vlad and you are a pair of out of control, mentally deficient, scumbag detectives, they still thought you guys did an almost adequate job with the Gangster Warlords. Almost adequate."

Sunny chuckles at the half-ass compliment and continues to listen for a minute. Tongue in cheek he hassles the desk sergeant right back. "Why did you call me on the cell phone? We're cops you know. Despite the rumors, Vlad isn't really a crossing guard. He has a badge. He got it from a Cracker Jack box, but he does have one. We have a radio you know! Anyone train you on how to use it yet or is the skill set over your Neanderthal head?"

Sunny listens for another moment. "Oh yeah...I've got ya... Yeah, don't worry...I understand...We're on our way. Right now."

Most people are better off not hearing police officers talking with each other off the record. It is a little like street gang jive talk mixed with the relaxed, habitual disrespect of one alpha male for another alpha male. Police are Alpha Males, period. Even when a female officer is involved, the dialogue doesn't change much. It is just an alpha female enjoying some jive talk.

Men don't call each other honey and friend with sweet sounding pleasant familiarity; it is more like dirt bag, numb nuts, scum bag and dip shit. Woman rarely talk to each other the way men talk to each other. Something in the genes. But woman cops are more like men cops than other females. With cops, the difference is more like the difference between Levi Strauss, Wrangler and Lee jeans. Basically the same stuff, just a little different plumbing.

Sunny grabs Vlad by the arm and hustles him to their car. He says to Vlad, "Let the uniforms finish this one."

He then yells over to Brookins, "We just got a call for downtown. Finish up, OK? If you need anything, call me." Sunny gives Brookins the universal thumb to ear and little finger to mouth hand signal for a phone.

Brookins laughs. "Called downtown? Right at the end of day. Yeah, right. You sure it wasn't a call from your wife to stop off for Lou Malnati's salad special?"

Sunny laughs back and flips Brookins the bird. Vlad hurries with Sunny but quietly asks, "What's up?"

"Dead body in the river by the Apparel Mart."

Vlad chuckles, "Another homeless dude a little too tipsy to be that close?"

Sunny jumps behind the wheel and throws the car into gear. As they drive away he slaps the auxiliary light on the roof, flips on the siren and hits the accelerator. "It's a buddy of the Mayor's and Brennan X. Burke, State Chairman and the Speaker of the State House. The guy has a bullet in the side of his head and we're to keep the press from getting too close a look until we have time to get some more info. Do I have to mention the stiff was a co-chair of President Obama's Illinois campaign? "

"You don't have to tell me. I know who that crook Brennan Burke is, numb nuts. Another machine insider with ties to DC. That sounds like half the guys in Stateville prison. Oh shit. Sounds like a suicide with a bullet in the side of his head? I hate to work suicides."

"Maybe. But there is still this little top secret investigation of how the dead guy spent at least a half mil of taxpayer money that is still open. It appears to have been money from the school system and he might have used it for political stuff as well as personal."

Vlad chuckles. "Whoops, didn't know about that one." He then puts on a tongue in cheek look of amazement. "A Chicago political insider friend of Brennan Burke's might have been sleazy. Oh my God, I can't believe that! Does Burke have any friends who aren't sleazy? These dumb shit Chicago political hacks always think they can get away with that stuff. They're important so they can spend our money any way they want to. School money? Who cares? Screw the kids."

Sunny responds with his own tongue in cheek, cynical version. "You're right. It was only school district funds, so who cares? Less than half the kids graduate and of the graduates, about half are functionally illiterate anyway. Who cares if all these kids can't read so they can't get a job? No problem. If Brennan Burke and his buddies can keep them unemployable they will always need to get their livelihood from Burke. That keeps them loyal voters for his political machine. Why would he want educated, independent people who could take care of themselves? Keep his buddies and the school unions happy and the kids ignorant, barefoot and pregnant. Just being a smart Chicago politician. You got a problem with that?"

Vlad gives Sunny his best 'are you crazy look'. "Yeah, good point. Why would we want anything for the billions we spend on Chicago's schools? It is good for society to have a bunch more illiterate, unemployable, teenage parents running around with nothing to do but get in trouble."

"The guy was the head of the school board. GOD, why do these guys think this is OK? They're stealing from kids who have two strikes against them already. Nuts. Frickin' nuts!" Sunny shakes his head in disgust. "Then they give consulting contracts to their political buddies and outrageously generous contracts to the non-teaching union employees who work their precincts and contribute money to the party. Oh well, this is Chicago."

Sunny and Vlad speed through traffic while slowing, but not stopping at red lights and stop signs. They cross the Chicago River on the bridge going east on Lake Street and see the Apparel Mart just to their North, located on the river and right across Orleans Street from the Merchandise Mart. The *Chicago Sun Times* newspaper occupies a major portion of the Apparel Mart and they have a huge logo on the outside.

The massive, brightly lit Merchandise Mart is connected to the Apparel Mart by a sky tunnel over Orleans Street. Prior to the completion of the Empire State Building, the Merchandise Mart was the largest office building in the entire world. After WWII, Joe Kennedy, that family's alpha male was allowed to purchase the building from the War Department. He got a good deal, but it doesn't appear to have been an overtly crooked one.

 The Mart had become war surplus and Kennedy had the cash and contacts to be the first in line. Much to most folk's surprise, Joe Kennedy buying The Mart was probably a legit business deal. Knowing Joe, not too legit and a really good deal, but as pretty close to legit as Joe would do. Not one anybody needs to worry about anymore.

The Mart is now managed by Chris Kennedy, Robert Kennedy's eldest son. Joe's grandson. He is a well-respected businessman in Chicago and the Merchandise Mart has recovered its pizzazz under Chris's capable leadership. Kennedy is also a legitimate civic leader, having served among other things, as the Chairman of the University of Illinois' Board of Trustees. Although politically a Kennedy, he is still remembered affectionately by many Viet Nam vets, law enforcement types and conservatives because while he Chaired the Board he denied the retiring, former Weather Underground founder and domestic terrorist Bill Ayers, professor emeritus status. Yes, President Obama's Bill Ayers. Yes, the same Weather Underground terrorist bomber Bill Ayers. Yes, the leader of that group of radicals who bombed American buildings and tried to kill police and Pentagon personnel. Yes, the same guy who dedicated a book of his to many terrorists, one of whom was Sirhan Sirhan, who murdered Chris Kennedy's father, Robert Kennedy. The amazing thing was not Kennedy's actions but the fact that a major university had actually hired and given tenure to an unrepentant terrorist.

Even Northwestern University's Law School had given a tenured professorship to Ayers terrorist wife, Bernardine Dohrn and she didn't even have a law license anymore. Not that some universities have a political bias or anything.

Like some rich kids who inherited plenty of family wealth, Ayres has spent his life trying to undermine what America stands for. Being born with a silver spoon in his mouth, he never felt any need to earn anything the old fashioned way. He was never subject to a free market or needing to work to support himself. Actually many folks who fumed about Ayers having felony charges against him dropped for technical reasons, referred to his financial situation as being born with a silver spoon up his a**.

The charges may have been dropped for political reasons, who knows? Those charges might have ended up including manslaughter and maybe even murder. But the powers that were in the Nixon Justice Department, already embroiled in Watergate, figured they might buy favor from the Democrats by dropping charges against one of their heroes. What was the importance of the death of a few folks and the bombings of a few buildings? Nixon figured it wasn't really an issue any more. Time to move on? Another black mark on the Nixon legacy. Whatever.

Most people don't realize the Merchandise Mart is the Kennedy family fortune. The cash and almost all of the other assets have long since been spent. There are too many Kennedy family hangers on who need Chris to do the great job he does so they can remain financially comfortable.

There is already a small crowd gathered and the police are trying their best to not be obvious. But being totally incognito while fishing a dead body out of the Chicago River where it is meandering through the North Loop is not as easy as you might think. Especially when you realize one of Chicago's two major newspapers has windows that overlook the exact spot where the body is floating. You'd think a political hack might have been a little more helpful to his old allies and die in a less obvious place.

This area is just a matter of 50 yards from where the main branch continues East right through the Chicago River Walk restaurant, hotel and residential community. It is also where the river splits in a Y and one part turns to continue meandering to the North past the second arm of the Chicago River community. It goes past the famous Erie Café, with its great food and old time Chicago warmth that accents wonderful service. There is a small but picturesque city park on the point overlooking the river.

There are numerous prestigious residential addresses, The East Bank Club, hangout to the Chicago fitness "In" crowd and the *Chicago Tribune's* Freedom Center where the paper is distributed from.

Sunny's cell phone goes crazy. "This is Chief SunWarrior. What can I do for whatever mere mortal is interrupting me?"

Brookins cracks up. "Sunny you are so full of it. But you'll love this. Guess what?"

"I'll save you time, I give up."

Brookins laughs again. "We just recovered about a million tons of cocaine. Already cut and packed. Biggest take I've ever seen!"

Sunny thinks a moment. "That is what this was all about?"

"Yeah. Our drug freak officer says it is the highest quality he has ever seen. He actually did a double take on his quick field test because he couldn't believe the results. He said we've got millions of dollars of some really pure shit. He thinks this is something huge. Thought you'd want to know."

Sunny nods to Vlad. "Thanks I'll fill in the crossing guard here. You're right, this could be really big."

Vlad had been listening closely as Brookins and Sunny talked. "Don't bother explaining. We just screwed somebody big time. Only question is was it the Warlords or someone else farther up the food chain? And how mad is somebody going to be?"

Suddenly a commotion in the crowd draws both guys back to looking at the crowd and the dead body. Covering up the recovery of some big shot's body in this area is definitely an assignment for some serious master bull shitters. That explains why Sunny and Vlad were assigned the task to use their GOD given skills to keep this as quiet as possible. They have masters degrees in police BS.

Sunny groans when he notices the *Sun Times* Chicago beat reporter standing by the front of the crowd. She is a pleasant lady and a good reporter. Keeping her in the dark is not an assignment Sunny is going to relish. Especially since over time he has leaked several good stories to her. Sunny figures it is never a bad idea to maintain a viable relationship with a reporter as long as you respect them as decent folk with some common sense.

The *Sun Times* does some first-rate investigative reporting on many issues. The *Sun Times* has a very left wing agenda, but Sunny and everyone else knows that. It is old left media like most major media operations. No point getting worked up about it. He knows what it is and he is just going to have to find a way to deal with it. He has done it before, he'll do it again.

Sunny and Vlad approach the uniformed Officer, a Sergeant, who seems to be in charge. As they approach, the Sergeant recognizes them and comes over to talk with them in a hush, hush huddle.

"Don't know much yet. Knowing what we know, suicide is an option. Gunshot wound to the side of his head and powder burns around the wound. But…"

Sunny can see the uniform is not finishing the sentence and wondering if he should say more. He quietly asks as he leans into the cop, "OK. What is the but you're not mentioning?"

The Sergeant looks around and leans into Sunny. "No powder burns on the supposed gun hand. In fact none on either hand. The hole in his head is on the right side and I know who the guy is. I've been his police protection at community meetings in the past. I just happen to know our friend here is or maybe I should say was, left handed."

Sunny thinks a moment and quietly leans back into the Sergeant. "Good detective work. Not what the power structure will want the press to notice, so let's keep it to ourselves until we've finished the report and have a chance to talk to the Captain. OK?"

"Sunny, heads up. Before we say anything, remember they're sending over a political heavy to be sure we cover their ass. He'll tell us what to do. So be careful. You know they love your BS, but think you're maybe a little bit of a wildcard."

Sunny nods with a cynical look.

The cop smiles at Sunny and leans in again to say, "Hey, I'm with you. This isn't our problem. This is why the Police Chief and the Mayor's Press Secretary get paid the big bucks." All three share an insider laugh knowing they are about to pass this problem on to somebody else.

The Sun Times Reporter is signaling to get Sunny's attention, but he is ignoring her. Vlad leans into Sunny "One of us has to talk to her. You? Me? But one of us."

The uniformed Sergeant watches Sunny and Vlad decide who will talk to the reporter. "Guys...be real careful. This guy is probably dirty and he had friends who now don't want anyone to remember they were his friends. This stiff goes from city hall to the statehouse and all the way to the White House. If this wasn't a suicide there are some nasty, desperate folks involved."

Sunny and Vlad both nod to show they agree. Sunny puts his arm around the Sergeant's shoulder and they walk away from the small crowd that is watching. "That's why we're here. If they wanted this crime solved they wouldn't have sent us to help establish a cover. We'll do a little, but we and I suggest you remember, we're cops first. The guys we work for are crooks first. We all need to do our jobs, but watch our asses while we do our job."

Sunny walks back to Vlad and pulls out a quarter. He then nods at Vlad to make a call.

"Heads."

Sunny flips and it comes up tails. Vlad laughs and Sunny grimaces. Sunny heads to the reporter and flips Vlad "the bird" behind his back.

Sunny walks over to the reporter and in a quiet, conspiratorial tone tells her "We don't know shit. We just fished him out. Somebody blew his brains out. Maybe he did it himself. You don't want to see him unless you just want to blow dinner.

What is left of his face doesn't look too good. We'll have more for you later when we figure out something. OK?"

The *Sun Times* reporter points at a Cadillac parked near where the body was found. "His?"

"Maybe, but not sure yet. The caddy is leased to some company, so no name on the lease documents yet and the license is same problem. We'll know pretty soon. With no face, a fingerprint ID will take a few hours. OK?"

The reporter is obviously disappointed but knows Sunny's BS line is perfectly believable. So much for a big scoop. A disinterested observer can tell from that exchange why Sunny and Vlad were called in to kill time and keep the press at bay until the political powers that be in Chicago decide what their spin will be. Suicide or murder? A crook or just misunderstood? Somebody nobody really knew or a dear friend traumatized by untrue allegations? City Hall would decide shortly.

Losing prominent allies, even ones who might soon be looking at the inside of a jail for their future home, needs to be orchestrated properly in Chicago. It is a tense time. It isn't just City Hall and the State House that need cover, the guy was a friend and very public supporter of the President of the United States. This happens too often to pretend it is some isolated incident.

The FBI has just taken down another eighteen prominent Chicago insiders in Operation Silver Shovel where City guys were taking pay offs from waste haulers to look the other way while some seriously bad stuff was dumped in the wrong places. The Chicago City Council just had another six aldermen indicted in the scandal, including President Obama's personal alderman. They got machine hacks and even alleged independents. Didn't seem to matter much what they called themselves. They were still crooks. Six more aldermen on their way to The Big House. Spinning this latest guy is going to be another pain in the neck and a big issue.

Vlad walks back to the Sergeant "Get him out of here before anyone gets a look at him. Great job. Also, get that big caddy out of here also. Keep up the good work, pal." He then heads over to his car and motions for Sunny to join him.

A big black sedan pulls up to the curb and stops. The guy riding shotgun gets out and opens the back door to let the passenger out. The shotgun gopher is deferential to the passenger who gets out like he owns the town.

Just as they reach their car Vlad notices Stu Black get out of the back of the big sedan. Stu is the hired gun Press Secretary for Speaker of the House, Brennan Burke. "Oh shit, Sunny, here comes Stu Black. He is the biggest ahole in America. He wouldn't tell the truth if you tattooed it on his pecker in neon ink."

"I'll get him. I enjoy listening to him. Gooning him a little too. You can learn all kinds of BS you can use from him. The guy can spin Niagara Falls into a puddle after a light summer drizzle." Sunny walks to meet Black and shakes his hand."

Stu Black looks at the ambulance with a who cares attitude. He is a little rude and acts irritated about being there. All of this is beneath Stu Black. He's a big shot and expects you to know it and act like it. "Why did I get a call to be here? I'm busy you know. Some stiff in the river. Can't you guys handle this shit on your own?"

With a friendly, knowing smile Sunny nods back. He speaks quietly so only Stu Black can hear him. "Sure Stu, glad to. No problem at all. Sorry, no idea who called you or why. I just told the Sun Times reporter we didn't know anything yet. Should I go back and let her know I lied to her? The guy is really a big machine political fixer under investigation for stealing lots of tax payer money from young, innocent school kids. We aren't sure yet if he killed himself or if you waxed him to keep him quiet. And, oh, by the way, he was a big contributor and bud of the Mayor's, Speaker Burke, a West Side figurehead and enforcer for the President's campaign."

Stu Black is clearly getting irritated.

"Then should I tell her that guy over there is Speaker Burke's Press flak busting my chops because he's an Ahole. Why don't you go over and ask him some questions about his dead pal. Don't worry Stu. I'll take care of it for you as usual. You can say thanks later."

"Cut the crap SunWarrior. Keep his name away from the press until I tell you it is OK. I need a little time to work out a story to push him away from us."

"You could tell them the truth?"

"Fuck you SunWarrior. Remember who you're talking to. I don't have to tell the jackasses in the press shit until I feel like it. They can kiss my ass."

"Oh sorry Stu. I forgot how important you are. Here, bend over so I can kiss your ass also. Just like those two patronage flunkies who drove you here. What city or county agency pays their salaries so they can be you and Burke's ass kissers? What service are they supposed to be delivering to the taxpayers for their outrageous salaries?"

"Where do you get this crap? How long have you been on the force? I think long enough to know this disrespectful shit is bad for your career."

"Sorry, can't remember. I'm too busy covering up for your guys to keep track of stuff like that. I've spent so much time covering for you I have a master's degree in cover Burke and Stu's ass BS. Sometimes I think you think our only job is to cover the asses of you and your buddies. But in between I try to protect a few honest folks also."

It is obvious Stu wants to jump all over Sunny.

Before Stu can unload Sunny goes on. "You know where we just came from? You seem to know everything."

Black is disgusted. "I don't give a...you know you're day isn't all that important to those of us with real responsibilities."

"Thanks Stu. We just busted the Gangster Warlord's leader Akile Fort with what our guys think just may be the biggest coke bust we've ever seen. Not that it is important but Vlad and I had to kill a couple of Warlords who were trying to kill us. We protected your citizens. You're welcome. Don't worry about my day. Glad to be of service."

"Fuck you SunWarrior. Who gives a s...that is what you get paid to do. But keep your mouth shut about it until I have time to talk with Speaker Burke about the slant we want to play it from. I might do you a favor and say something nice about you, but don't count on it as long as you keep acting like a total jerk. You act like you're mister high and mighty. Playing for da Bears doesn't give you an excuse to insult Speaker Burke. Show some respect for people of his calibre."

"I do all the time while I'm putting them in handcuffs."

Stu Black is totally disgusted with Sunny and walks away. Then he changes his mind and stomps back. He gets right in Sunny's face. He looks small compared to Sunny, but since he is a big political guy he doesn't care. "What is it you're really after? Every time I see you you're disrespectful and nit picking every minor BS thing. What is your point? Do you even have one or are you just an asshole?"

Sunny does not back off in the slightest but speaks in a pleasant conversational tone. He is not at all confrontational. "After? I don't know. Maybe a little honest government? Concern for the taxpayer's wallet? Some BS like that."

"What the hell are you talking about? Are you saying we aren't honest? Huh?"

Sunny has a self-depreciating smile and Will Rogers type shrug. "Honest? I don't know. Haven't four of your last seven elected governors gone to jail? Aren't two of your big buddies, two former governors in jail, right now, kinda' at the same time? Have I got that number right?"

Black fumes at Sunny's insolence.

"Haven't 32 of the 50 Chicago Alderman gone to prison in the last few years? Doesn't that Include Speaker Burke's own Alderman? I think just about every one of the 32 were friends of Speaker Burke. Weren't they? All from his party organization?"

"You're an idiot, SunWarrior!" Stu tries to back off but Sunny stays right with him.

"Isn't Speaker Burke now a multimillionaire getting paid to fix property tax assessments in a crooked assessment system he controls? Kind of like payoffs, but since he is a lawyer it is called a legal fee not a payoff, right? Have I got all this stuff right? Is that minor enough BS for you? You know, I give respect where it is due."

"You're a jerk, SunWarrior! You know you're never going to be more than a detective with your bull shit attitude. I promise you'll never make lieutenant and one of these days you're going to go too far and I'll get your ass fired." Stu Black stalks away.

In his best imitation of Marlon Brando in *One-Eyed Jacks*, Sunny speaks in a lowered, soft voice that he knows Black will here. "You're just like a one-eyed jack, but I seen your other side. Nice seein' ya' Stu. Any time you need me to cover you or Burke's crooked asses, you just let me know. OK?"

Vlad walks over to Sunny but intentionally keeps a certain distance. "Just making sure I don't get hit by a near miss. You really enjoy gooning that ahole, don't you? You know he's Burke's shoe shine boy? Do you really want to get in a pissing contest with Burke's stooges?" Vlad starts to duck, bob and weave as he puts his arms over his head as if protecting himself from getting hit. He keeps looking around like he is expecting incoming fire.

"He and his boss are a bunch of crooks. I'll be damned if I'll cow tow to guys we both know belong in jail. He can threaten me all he wants. If I need Brennan Burke's help to be a lieutenant, I guess I won't make lieutenant. Not my style."

"You're choice. End of day. You've got dinner with Sheila and we both have a chat with IA tonight or tomorrow. This looks like a mess we don't need to be in the middle of. Before you get us both on a hit list, I'm outta here!"

Sunny looks very pleased with himself and just nods. "Wasn't it that Nobel Prize winning economics guy from the U of Chicago, Milton Friedman who said if you put the government in charge of the Sahara desert, in five years there would be a shortage of sand?"

Vlad nods. "With these aholes, it would only take three years."

CHAPTER THREE

SUNNY PULLS INTO HIS DRIVEWAY BY A LOVINGLY maintained bungalow. The street is quiet and lined with mature trees. During a summer day like this the sky is almost invisible because the leaves obstruct the view. Historians estimate the largest numbers of single family housing units in Chicago are bungalows. At one time approximately one third of all houses in the Chicago area were bungalows. Most were built between the two world wars with the first ones built around 1910.

There are associations dedicated to nothing other than maintaining the integrity of bungalows and the bungalow belt neighborhoods in towns like Chicago. It was in India, Bangladesh and the U.K. where the concept and name originated, not in Chicago as most Americans think.

Any bungalow freak would appreciate the SunWarrior home. The lawn is immaculate and the bushes by the house are carefully trimmed. The bottoms are lined with colorful impatiens. The pleasant, covered veranda, or in Chicagoese, the front stoop, runs the width of the house. It makes an onlooker think of the old neighborhoods where each evening the folks sat on their porches drinking lemonade, or whatever, and watched the neighborhood kids play stickball in the street.

There weren't the time-eating TV shows, or video games or the organized team sports. People talked with their neighbors and kept an eye on everyone's kids, not just their own. This is a bungalow in what had been a neighborhood like that. All of the wood window and door frames have been recently painted and the concrete entrance steps up to the veranda have clearly been resurfaced. Everything is picture perfect.

Sunny steps out of the car and simply enjoys taking in the view. His wife Sheila does most of the yard work with Sunny helping when it takes a little more muscle. He walks up the steps and hits his doorbell three times. That is his signal to Sheila he is home.

Then he unlocks the door and walks into a cottage that is as beautiful inside as outside. There is nothing out of place. Sunny just takes in the ambiance. It is fancier than average since he had made a few extra dollars during his days with da Bears, his time with the Army Reserves and his combat pay from Afghanistan. He could almost see Sheila in every detail of the warmth of their home.

"I'm home. The warrior has returned to his tepee and his squaw." He can hear the giggle in the kitchen at his macho entrance.

Sheila's warm voice calls back, "Did you do any good today? Or were you just out driving around the neighborhood trying to look busy with that reprobate buddy of yours, Vlad?"

All Sunny can do is laugh at her description of his work day. But he walks into the kitchen where she is still cleaning vegetables at the sink. He decides it is the better part of valor to not tell her if he eats any more vegetables he will turn into a turnip. Besides he had Lou Malnati's signature, deep dish, sausage and mushroom pizza for lunch. As a young cook at someone else's restaurant, Lou was an inventor of deep dish and his son Mark and the family who still run the restaurants haven't lost Lou's touch. There is no pizza like Chicago pizza and Chicago's best pizza is Lou Malnati's.

But Sunny thinks, enough about pizza, it is time to take a gander at his wife's impressive shape. Specifically her tight, athletic fanny. Her great legs and nicely rounded fanny are left over from her many years of competitive volleyball and the exercises and running that went with it. She remains a fitness freak and works out daily. Sheila never does anything half way. She doesn't just stay in shape. She takes her workouts seriously. She even lifts light weights. Serious stuff. It shows.

Sheila's attributes are obvious in her tight t-shirt and shorts and are highlighted even more by her light tan. Sunny walks up behind her and wraps his arms around her waist. He hugs her from behind and kisses the top of her head. Sheila continues to work on the vegetables in the sink. Under her bright yellow, spotless t-shirt Sunny notices she isn't wearing a bra.

Sunny decides to drift his hands up to greet two of his wife's best attributes. "How about a *hors devour* to begin with?"

"Careful lover boy, I'm holding a knife. You don't get to play with your dessert until after you eat your vegetables."

"I'm a gentleman and I'll behave. Honest injun! Bring on those vegetables! I'm ready to eat every one of them. But make it fast. A hungry defender of every man's right to safety and security needs a *hors devour* to hold him over before some nutritious dessert to replenish his strength."

Despite his assurance of good behavior, he puts his hands under the running water and then clamps them on Sheila's breasts and rubs them around. Essentially her t-shirt is now a wet yellow t-shirt and leaves nothing to the imagination. Sunny makes no attempt to release his hug or end his playful massaging of Sheila's breasts.

"Couldn't I just have a little nibble to keep my strength up? You know the Bellamy Brothers song *If I Said You Had a Beautiful Body, Would You Hold It Against Me?* You do and I'd like to show my appreciation."

Sheila doesn't really make much of an effort to get loose from his hug. "You know you really are a pervert. All you think about is sex. I don't know how I put up with you. Tell your brother Bellamy the answer is I'd try, for all the good it would do me."

Sunny tightens his hug and gives her a loving kiss on the cheek and a nibble of her ear. "You remind me of a beautiful and valuable book. As my brother Bellamy said, *Judging By The Cover I'd Love To Read The Book.*"

Sheila can't stop giggling as she speaks. "You're worse than hopeless. You're worse than a pervert. I do not know why I tolerate you."

Sunny's cell phone is ringing but he ignores it. "Ah yes, you reference my most endearing attribute. Remember, we're Catholic. In the book of Proverbs, Solomon reminds us that children are like arrows in a man's quiver. It is our moral responsibility to try to breed more and more fine Catholic children, remember?"

Sheila just groans at his somewhat accurate, but clearly self-serving interpretation of the Bible. "I hope your genes don't come through if we have a son or you'll raise him to be just as big a pervert as his father."

Sunny shifts his hands to move them down the back of Sheila's shorts and playfully pinches and massages her fanny. She gives up and turns enough to give him a welcome home kiss.

Just as their embrace and Sunny's hands are going somewhere his cell phone rings again. He is loath to put a stop to where he is going, but the phone won't quit ringing so he finally flips it open. "SunWarrior, this better not be a waste of time."

CHICAGO CONFIDENTIAL | 39

"It's Vlad. Brookins called you. Said he couldn't reach you. No one answered your cell. That little grandmother and her three grandkids are dead. Really nasty deaths in her apartment. No witnesses will ID anybody or seem to have heard or seen anything. They are clearly terrified. The murderers must have told them this is what happens to snitches. There was blood all over the apartment."

Sunny is shaken to the core. "My GOD..."

"Try this also; Fort is already back on the street. He was granted bail before the ink was dry from the fingerprinting. Don't know who the Judge was yet, but Fort's lawyer did. It went to their guy. Had the Judge's name on the bail petition and we didn't even know who the Judge would be!"

Sunny almost drops his phone. His face is a mask of horror. "What the ...? Who sprung him?"

"Alderman Larenda Bass and a lawyer were at the police station before Brookins even got there."

"Bass? Burke's consigliore on the South side? Talk about heavy clout! That bitch is serious, big time clout. Isn't she the President's Alderman?" Sunny shakes his head as he asks Vlad the question.

"Na...she's not Obama's. She is the next ward over from Hyde Park but she was a Committeeman and ally in his old State Senate district. The Judge granted the bail motion without even listening to the State's Attorney. Bail was only a hundred grand! For frickin' torture and murder by the boss of Chicago's biggest street gang! A hundred grand! The lawyer paid on the spot and they were out the door."

"How?"

"Fort must have called them before we even arrested the guy. That was probably what they were doing while we were sitting there watching the van waiting for backup. We should have moved in faster. He just calls the lawyer and some of his boys to break him out of jail and take care of granny while we waited."

Sunny groans and gives Sheila a hopeless look and shrug.

"The best part is Bass showed up with some patronage workers from Streets and Sans to vouch that Fort and the Gangster Warlords were seen in a park a couple of miles away so it might be a case of mistaken identity on our part."

"We arrested them on the spot?"

"Our word against theirs. Remember they had two eye witnesses when that Judge let the mobster hit man, Harry Aleman go."

"I'll take this one to the State's Attorney herself if they try that!"

"You mean the Crook County State's Attorney? The one they asked if she was for or against crime? That worthless State's Attorney?"

Sunny groans to himself. "Yeah, that one...yeah."

CHAPTER FOUR

IT IS A HOT SUMMER NIGHT AND ON ONE OF THOSE corners a group of guys are simply shucking and jiving. Just hanging out. There is laughter, booze, smoking and foul language. Some of the guys are clearly high or drunk. None look old enough for booze, but it is there anyway. Several girls hang out with them. The way the girls are dressed leaves very little question of their intentions. They are baby momma wannabes and making it obvious. None of them look old enough to be out this late or drinking either.

This type of crowd always makes you wonder where the parents are. Why do they allow their kids out at hours like this in neighborhoods like this? Especially dressed like these kids?

Just because you are poor doesn't justify being a bad parent also. Most poor folks try very hard to be good parents. But this group of kids clearly doesn't have parents that would fit under the term "trying to be good parents."

The South Side of Chicago contains the largest middle class Black community in America. There are a few wealthy areas, some very pleasant, middle class neighborhoods and some awfully gritty areas also.

The Chicago police assigned to tougher areas, especially the undercover cops, are known to be downright tough characters. You deal with some of the folks they do and you better be tough. The gangs and drug runners feel they have a right to the streets, especially after dark.

When you think of all of the violence on the border between Mexico and The United States it is necessary to realize those drugs aren't just "there", they go somewhere. The City of Chicago gets its fair share and the South Side is where large amounts of the worst narco crooks sell their wares.

The police do what they can to hold "the line" to offer their citizens a safe haven. But where there is demand, there will be supply. Where there is supply, there will be crime to allow the addicts to get the money needed to feed their habits. Those Mexican Drug Cartels haven't killed twenty five thousand Mexican citizens to make nickels and dimes in America. Blood thirsty criminals expect big money and a few dead bodies simply serve as a warning to stay out of the way.

Once we get sixty blocks south of downtown and in a bit from the lake front, there is one of the grittier sides of Chicago. Neighborhoods with names like Englewood that is the heartland of crime, gangs and drugs. Empty store fronts. Boarded up buildings. Overwhelmingly single parent households.

Most of the schools function as failure factories. A large majority of these kids do not graduate from high school and of those who do, many are functionally illiterate. Many of the school's standards are so low a kid can graduate and still be at the elementary school level as far as reading and math skills are concerned.

Gangbangers hang out on most corners selling drugs. They are usually visible because they are wearing sparkling clean white t-shirts. There are also poorly educated kids with no usable skills hanging out on the other street corners with little to do but get into trouble. The trouble with gangbanger wannabes is with this gene pool there is no lifeguard to limit who gets into the pool. That should remind us that it is the 99% per cent of gangbangers who give the rest of them a bad name.

Down the street from the gaggle on the corner two big SUVs park and four guys get out of each vehicle. They are all dressed in the black and crimson colors of the Gangster Warlords and they look ready for trouble. The eight fan out a little bit and walk toward the other crowd with a determined stride. As they get closer both groups hone in on the other and start shouting insults and threats. The groups merge into a gaggle of shoving and insults.

Just as things appear to be escalating beyond simply teenage boys doing the dumb things teenage boys do, a pickup truck with a Mount Carmel High School logo emblazoned on the doors screeches to a stop at the curb. Out jumps a clearly ageing and graying, white man who is obviously in excellent shape. His polo shirt covers some serious muscle and says Mount Carmel on the left chest front and Coach Burton on the back.

He runs right into the middle of the pushing and shoving gaggle. Coach Burton keeps himself right in the middle and keeps gently shoving the groups apart. He calls some of the boys by name and cajoles, not forces them to do as he asks. He doesn't yell or scream. Coach Burton just uses his humor and relationship with some of the kids to try to keep anything really stupid from happening. It is obvious many of the guys recognize him and almost all of them slowly start to follow his directions.

Just as it appears everything is quieted down one of the Gangster Warlords, one of the new kids pulls a silver plated hand gun from under his light windbreaker, steps up behind Coach Burton and shoots him in the back of the head. The coach staggers and then immediately collapses to the ground.

The crowd is stunned. There is literally a moment when everything seems to stand still.

One of the original groups screams, "Oh my GOD. My GOD. Coach Burton." He drops to his knees next to the body but it is obvious the coach is dead. Virtually every kid is stunned and no one seems to know what to do.

The guy with the gun is grabbed by two of the other Gangster Warlords who came with him. He is clearly high and feeling no pain. "Shit man...you don't realize who you just shot. Shit, I can't believe you just did that!"

The obviously high gunman responds in his best macho voice, "Some honky mo fo. Who gives a shit? None of his bizznes."

Police sirens can be heard in the distance and they are closing quickly. All of the kids look up and most start to run immediately. A few stand in dazed silence before they take off. On boy kneels by Coach Burton's body and puts his hand on the shoulder. "I'm sorry Coach...I'm so sorry." As the sirens come even closer he rises up and runs down a nearby alley.

The police arrive and two immediately go to the body on the ground. Two others go over to the Mount Carmel truck sitting near the curb with the door open and the engine still running. The officer who bends over the mortal remains of Coach Burton clearly recognizes the Coach. There is blood all over the back of his shirt, but Coach Burton is still readable.

He leans into his shoulder mike "Oh my GOD, the dead guy is Coach Burton from Mount Carmel. This is going to be a bad day for the Padres. Don't say anything yet. Give me a chance to swing by the school to talk with them face to face. GOD, I can't believe it. I played for Coach Burton. I'll go over to Mount Carmel. There are always some Padres there working late. Oh my GOD. I can't believe it is Coach Burton. This is not going to be fun visit. Shit!"

It is already the end of the day's shift. Sunny SunWarrior and Vlad are taking a minute to hang out at the police station with other officers and fill them in on the stiff at the Apparel Mart. The story hit the newspapers and TV and most of the officers knew Sunny and Vlad had been the guys assigned to tone it down. The coverage was light the first day because Sunny had been able to smudge the facts. But by day two, it was front page news.

There was a lot of interest in exactly what happened. Nobody among the officers believed the guy had committed suicide. He was a big-time political insider as both a real estate developer and one of the Mayor and Speaker of the House's point guys for the public school system. He also appeared to be a crook. Not unusual for a politically connected real estate developer and political point man in the patronage and con-tract heavy public school system.

The schools sucked but that didn't stop the political insiders from stealing all they could. What difference does it make if they steal a little extra? The schools have sucked for decades. The voters clearly don't care. They kept reelecting the same political insiders who keep the schools sucking. So they just keep stealing until someone gets mad and then they just hope they aren't the one who gets caught.

Sunny is working his way to his car. He knows Sheila will have dinner ready and he is looking forward to Sheila for dessert and is willing to suffer through the meal to show his good intentions. Eating her food was a little like foreplay. It made Sheila happy and got her in a good mood. Sheila liked to think the food was healthy and was making Sunny healthier. He thought it was killing him softly.

Just then one of the Captains motions for Sunny to join him away from the group of undercover police officers.

The other officers close ranks and continue to talk about the day and how things went.

Sunny and the Captain move off to stand aside by themselves. "Sunny, it hasn't been announced yet, but Coach Burton was shot and killed a little while ago. It wasn't far from Mount Carmel. A witness said he was breaking up what looked like some gang scuffle. Some gangbanger shot him in the back. No details, but it was definitely the coach and he is definitely dead."

It hits Sunny like a ton of bricks. He almost staggers he is so stunned. "Anybody ID the shooter?"

"He was in black and crimson but no ID yet. I'm sorry Sunny. I know you were close."

"Who will do the investigation?"

"Hasn't been decided yet. Nothing going so far. Alderman Bass already called to get info and be sure we know she is interested. So this is going to be a problem."

Sunny literally sits down on the curb and his head falls into his hands. Memories flood through his mind as he visualizes Coach Burton. This was the man who took an overgrown orphan and ward of the state of Illinois and put him on the path to a successful life. He saved Sunny from prison and gave him a big brother and a family he never really had. What had Coach Burton done wrong? He had been himself and was just trying to keep some other kids out of trouble. Life on the streets of Chicago with the gangs totally out of control.

CHAPTER FIVE

ST. THOMAS THE APOSTLE CATHOLIC CHURCH IN Hyde Park is filled to the rafters. St. Thomas is possibly the most multiracial Catholic Church in Chicago and is located in the heart of the University of Chicago community of Hyde Park.

Coach Burton and his widowed mother had lived in an apartment in Madison Park -a two-block long, self-contained community off Hyde Park Boulevard that is three blocks East of President Barack Obama's Chicago home. The Coach was not a priest, but he had never married. His thousands of students and the Mount Carmel community were his family and everyone who could pack into St. Thomas was there to honor what had truly been an exemplary life of service.

Sunny and his wife Sheila, dressed in their best conservative dark clothes, arrive early and enter the church with a man Sunny hasn't seen in many years, Judge Sean McCarthy.

The Judge is a bluff old guy with a shock of white hair and he takes Sonny by the bicep, just above the elbow, "Glad you turned out OK or I'd had Burton's ass for talking me into letting you off so damn easy."

Sunny chuckles at the friendly threat and introduces his wife. "Judge this is Sheila, my wife. She's glad you gave me another shot also."

"Aren't you the young lady he saved at the library?"

Sheila nods assent and takes the Judge's hand in hers. "Thank you. He isn't quite as bad as they say he is. Bad...real bad...in fact, downright lousy, but not as bad as they say." All three of them smile at her kidding comment.

As the three enter St. Thomas, Judge McCarthy leans over to Sunny "I'm sorry about the Coach. I know you were close. He was my friend also. But he died doing exactly what you and I would have expected of him. He couldn't just drive by. He had to help. That was just the Coach in him."

Sunny starts to tear up. "Where would I be today if it weren't for Coach Burton?" Sheila wraps her arm around his waist and they continue up the aisle. A very important era of his life has closed and he realizes it.

Sunny notices there are two empty seats on the aisle in the second row pew. He wonders who they are for since he can see all of the Mount Carmel leadership and the Coach's mother are already there. He holds Sheila's hand and quietly prays to himself.

There is a hush and Speaker of the House, Brennan X. Burke, his wife on his arm, walk up the main aisle to the two empty seats. No one walks close to them. Burke looks stiff and austere in his thousand dollar suit. He walks straight up with a disciplined step. He nods to the Mount Carmel leadership and a few other big shots but doesn't speak to anyone. He offers for his wife to enter first and then he sits down.

Sunny realizes the issue isn't his mentor, Coach Burton. This is a gathering of the Chicago Democrat elite. The Padres from Mount Carmel wouldn't see it that way, but this is a big, Irish Catholic event on the South Side. Speaker Burke and the Mayor are the patrons of the White, Irish Catholic Democrat elites. He is here as a symbol. He didn't know Coach Burton, but he is here to show his solidarity with his base.

After Burke sits down the church continues to fill to over-flowing. Tons of the guys look like old Mount Carmel football players in various stages of aging. Most look pretty respectable. Most have wives with them. The neat appearance is a testimony to Coach Burton's constant teaching that a man should look like a self-respecting person you would want to know and have live in your community, not some sloppy bum. He also praised the value of marriage, Catholic values in general, family and the obvious fact that most of the mourners are couples shows his admonitions had not fallen on deaf ears. The Coach would not have been embarrassed by his many former students. He considered them his family and from the looks of them, he would have been proud.

CHAPTER SIX

A NONDESCRIPT DODGE CRUISER WITH THE DRIVER leaning back, asleep, with his hat over his eyes, sits quietly in the limited amount of shade provided by one of the few trees on the mostly vacant block. An abandoned area like this always has several beat up cars with wonked-out druggies and hookers plying their trade. This denizen of sin solves a minor problem, because it excludes no one and allows no one to look out of place.

There are other cars with couples in them. In one recent model SUV, a powerfully muscled Black man in sun glasses seems relaxed as he leans back in his seat. The head of a woman bobs up and down over his lap. It is not obvious that behind his sunglasses he is keeping a watchful eye on the goings on up the street.

In this potpourri of illicit activity, even the new Lexus fits in as it moves slowly with the driver scanning the surrounding area. The Lexus finally stops and a burly, dark haired man with slicked back hair and his shirt untucked gets out and leans against the driver's door. He just seems relaxed and uninterested in the world around him. He is talking to the man in the passenger seat. The other guy stays in the car, but looks around as if he were not used to the area. His brown skin identifies him as a Latino. A citizen? Mexican? South American? Central American? Who knows? No big deal. This is Chicago, an international melting pot. There probably isn't an ethnic group in the world that doesn't have some member living in Chicago.

The burly guy looks Italian. When someone thinks of a mobster this is the guy they imagine. He is relaxed and looks like he feels at home in these surroundings. He ignores the late model, silver SUV with the flashy hub caps until it stops in front of him. The Lexus passenger lifts a heavy duffel bag off the front seat and hands it to the burly Italian. In turn, the burly guy hands it to the driver of the SUV who is dressed in black and crimson. He receives a large money bag in return. Then all hell breaks loose.

Taking a step back to yesterday, Sunny SunWarrior, received a call from "Carl" one of his most reliable informants. Now here is where Sonny is. When the event comes down exactly as "Carl" said it would, Sonny, the sleeping, wonked-out druggie knows he has a perfectly solid case and isn't going to waste time on the "due process" BS. He took a couple of quick pictures with his police issued camera and tossed it on the seat next to him. Sunny moves and he moves quickly. Gun drawn he charges out of the Dodge.

Even closer to the SUV and Lexus the two hookers and their "johns" come flying out of their junk cars and the decent looking SUV. A hooker with her skirt pulled up waving a police badge and running with a loaded pistol followed by her "john" with a shot gun is a rare sight, even in a neighborhood like this one. The "john" is Officer Harold Brookins minus his sunglasses. For a big man, he is hauling ass.

Sunny greets the cars with "Freeze!" "Drop your guns, assholes!" A greeting most policemen can emulate with all of the affection shown by a charging lion. It's a line they could repeat in their sleep. SunWarrior stayed alert, but he knew most drug runners, especially a mobster like this one, realizes he'll be back on the street faster than the cop can finish the paper work. They tend not to get too excited and start shooting when they are being arrested. The other guy in the car is the wild card. The police don't know who he is or what he will do.

But it is the exception that generally proves the rule because just then the burly guy drops to his knee and opens fire on Sunny. The Latino guy pulls a Glock nine millimeter and starts to spray rounds at Sunny also. This causes Sunny to stop and duck behind a junk car. With surprising agility for a big man the mobster jumps back into the Lexus and throws it into gear.

Sunny and one of the "johns" with the shot guns, who turns out to be Vlad Kozak, open fire on the Lexus and blow out the windshields. Vlad isn't using his favorite Ithaca Mag-10 or he would have blown out the entire back end of the Lexus. He uses his city-issued Benelli shotgun that certainly is appropriate for the job but isn't quite up to the firepower of his Ithaca mini howitzer.

The city lawyers didn't care about fire power or the safety of the cop, they just worry about liability. The burly guy, realizing he screwed up, drops the gun and raises his hands. The Latino looking guy also raises his weapon and sits quietly.

While most of the cops focus on the armed guys in the Lexus, the lady undercover police officer takes the big bag from the driver of the big SUV and rips it open. She looks in side and shouts, "Oh my GOD! This is the mother lode of cocaine."

All of the officers look up at her bag of cocaine. The SUV isn't moving and the driver has his hands raised. His big SUV is blocking the Lexus so there is no way the Lexus can get out anyway.

Four of the six police crowd around the Lexus and shout for the big guy to get out and hit the street, the other two watch the SUV. The cocaine is important, but two armed guys in a

Lexus is a little more here and now. The SUV driver, Brookins and his hooker policewoman keep one eye on the SUV while keeping the other eye on the four police officers. The lady is holding the bag on her shoulder.

The SUV's driver, do-rag, black and crimson outfit, gold bling and sun glasses realizes the lack of attention and floors the SUV. He grazes Brookins and the policewoman hooker as he goes by and grabs the bag of cocaine from off her shoulder.

Sunny sees his two fellow cops on the ground and opens fire. Vlad is behind the Lexus and simply doesn't have a shot so he hurries around the back to get a clear sight picture. Sunny's first round sends windshield glass flying everywhere. The second round hits the driver side tire and the blow out causes the car to pull out of control. The big SUV careens off the street and into Sonny's beat up old Dodge. The SUV isn't much worse for the collision. Sunny's car is a total wreck.

The undercover, lady cop playing the hooker with her skirt around her waist jogs over to the smashed cars and carefully, with gun still at the ready, looks in the window of the SUV. The driver keeps his hands up and is completely compliant. The police officer grabs the bag of cocaine back from the Gangster Warlord driver. She then turns to the crowd. "Sunny...you idiot...how much frickin' paper work is this going to generate? You just got City property totaled." All of the police, even Brookins and the lady on the ground start to laugh.

With a smile, Sunny shouts to the female officer, "Hey good lookin'...Two less aholes on the streets...I wanted a new car... two pigeons with one stone...what's your problem?"

"Paperwork! Oh my GOD, paperwork and you know it! I didn't see anything...nothin'! I didn't hear nothin'. I know nothin' about it. After that shooting you're going to have been around those idiot lawyers and IA so much most folks will think you've joined them."

Sunny is telling this story as he sits on the witness stand in the Criminal Courts Building at 26th and California on Chicago's west side. The people in the court room laugh as Sunny finishes telling the story.

The young State's Attorney asks, "Is there anything more to the arrest Detective SunWarrior?"

Sunny thinks a moment. "I suppose I could say something about the Mexican guy who wouldn't talk who was with the defendant. He acted like he didn't speak English so he requested the Mexican Consulate's assistance. But he jumped bail and disappeared. No one has seen him since. That is why he has not been part of this trial."

The State's Attorney nods with a pained look. Everyone was totally embarrassed when a Judge granted the bail request by the Mexican Consulate and the guy disappeared by that evening. Most of the police thought the Mexican guy was a major part of the crime, but they can't investigate someone they can't talk to. "Thank you detective. Anything more for the Judge?"

Sunny looks toward Judge Leoni and finishes his testimony by saying "No your Honor."

The State's Attorney reminds Sunny, "This is a bench trial. Are you sure there is nothing more for you to add?"

Sunny thinks a moment and then nods. "No your honor, that is the whole story."

Judge Leoni says "Thank you officer SunWarrior. You have been most helpful. If the defense doesn't have anything in cross examination, you may return to your seat now."

The Judge looks at the defense table where the burly, dark haired, mobster looking guy sits with a bored expression on his face. "Defense? Cross?"

The defense attorney with his slicked back hair, diamond in his ear lobe, thousand dollar suit and gold cuff links stands to address the judge. "Your honor," begins Sam Powers, "as we said earlier, my client is innocent. He simply gave the Mexican gentleman a ride because his car had broken down. I did not object when Officer SunWarrior inappropriately mentioned the stranger because it really shows my client being a decent citizen and helping a lost stranger in need. That said, my only question of Officer SunWarrior is this: before you made the mistaken arrest of my client, why were you there? You had no reason to hassle my client who was simply out for a pleasant drive. What was your probable cause?"

Sunny laughs at the defense attorney's line. "My best inform-ant. As you know, an individual with an impeccable track record called to let me know about the drug transaction. A known informant with a long track record. That is probable cause in spades. Case closed."

The attorney leans over to speak with his client in a whisper. "If you could actually produce this alleged...this nonexistent informant for cross examination I am sure we could clear up this mistake immediately."

Sunny guffaws at the attorney. "You want an informant to testify in a mob drug case? What the...

Informants don't testify in open court in mob cases."

"Your Honor, I object! I am offended my client, a well-respected businessman is being demeaned in this manner," protests Powers.

There is a long pause as Judge Leoni looks at both Sunny and the attorney. "You win the point counselor. Probable cause has not been established."

Sunny looks at the Assistant State's Attorney with an incred-ulous look on his face. The young man quickly rises. "Your Honor...probable cause was established by the long, well-doc-umented, track record of the informant that we submitted earlier as evidence."

Sam Powers just looks at the Judge for a long time. His voice almost sounds weary as if he is explaining some obviously simple point that everyone should understand. "Your Honor: No witness, no probable cause. We have the right to face our accuser. That is only fair."

Sunny and the State's Attorney wait as the Judge thinks.

Judge Leoni looks at Sunny and the State's Attorney. "You will need to produce the witness. The accused has a right to face his accuser. No witness...no probable cause...no case."

Sunny jumps to his feet. "Your Honor, this is a mob drug case. My informant wouldn't live a day after testifying in open court and we all know that."

Judge Leoni looks at Sunny with a condescending eye. "No witness...no case. Am I clear?"

"Your honor, this is most unusual. Informants don't normally testify in open court in mob cases."

Judge Leoni stares at Sunny. "No witness...no case. Am I clear?"

Sunny thinks a moment. "I have a solution. Your Honor, I'll bring the informant, disguised to your chambers. He'll answer all of your questions. Under oath, your Honor. Just the three of us. I have to protect him. This is the mob your Honor. They'll kill him if they learn who he is."

Sam Powers looks at Sunny with disgust. "Your Honor, there is no such thing as the mob and if there were, my client certainly isn't a member of this alleged group. That is just not acceptable to the defense."

Sitting in the back row, waiting to testify is Harold Brookins. He is in uniform and snoozing, so he missed the first part of the argument. But Brookins is smart enough to pick up the dispute very quickly. "Your Honor, I'm Officer Harold Brookins. I was at the bust also and was waiting to testify. I know this witness, or really informant, quite well. I will be glad to vouch for his track record and his expertise."

Judge Leoni ignores Brookins as if he weren't there.

Brookins is an imposing figure and walks toward the front of the court room. "Your Honor...your Honor..."

Judge Leoni thinks a few moments. "Sit down Officer Brookins. If I want your input, I'll ask for it." Then he turns back to Sunny. "Sorry Officer SunWarrior. No witness in the court room...no probable cause...no case. Is that clear?"

It is obvious Sunny is about to boil over but he holds his temper for the moment. "This isn't right. This is a well-known informant within the Chicago Police Department."

Sam Powers gives a greasy, shit eatin' grin, then speaks. He oozes sarcasm. "Mythical informants? Claims of some group of supposedly nasty people out there trying to kill your mythical witness. Are these groups of bad guys riding around on herds of unicorns?" Everyone laughs at the cynical comment.

Sunny loses it. "Bullshit you sleazy bastard!"

Judge Leoni smashes his gavel on his desk. "Order in my court! I will not warn you again Officer SunWarrior!"

The State's Attorney and Brookins hurry to Sunny's side but not soon enough. "This is bullshit. I'm not going to drag a respected informant in here to become a marked man, damnit! Judge, this is the frickin' mob! What is it about mobsters you don't seem to understand?"

Judge Leoni is red faced and obviously angry. "Officer Sun-Warrior you are pushing the limit. Enough is enough!"

Sonny explodes, "Enough is enough? Enough is enough? This is one damn dangerous frickin mobster you're turning loose. The son of a bitch shot at me and we caught him red handed!"

Judge Leoni screams, "One more word from you officer and you'll be held in contempt of court!"

"This is bullshit. You're the one who should be held in contempt!"

Judge Leoni points his gavel at the bailiff "Take this man into custody for contempt of court."

The bailiff looks stunned and confused. "Are you sure about this your honor?"

"You too? Take him into custody immediately! That means right now and if you don't you'll be sharing the cell with him damnit!"

Brookins steps in front of Sunny to block the bailiff, but the Assistant State's Attorney pulls him out of the way. The shocked bailiff walks to Sunny and delicately takes his arm. He mumbles under his breath "Sorry Sunny...you understand...it's my job...sorry."

Sunny quietly mumbles back, "It's OK...not your fault man. I'll be OK."

Sunny looks at the judge with total disdain in his eyes but allows the bailiff to lead him away.

"Your honor?" The young State's attorney asks with pleading in his voice. "You can't mean this. Send a Chicago Police Officer, a detective no less, to County Jail for contempt? My GOD! You realize how dangerous this could be?"

With fire in his eyes, Judge Leoni looks at the young man and says "Case dismissed."

The burly man and Sam Powers shake hands while sharing a knowing grin. They turn to leave the court room but Brookins stands in their way. Powers looks at Brookins, "Do you mind?"

With sheer malice in his voice, Brookins responds to Powers. "Yes, I mind. Walk your sorry, crooked ass around me scum bag."

Powers sizes up Brookins and decides walking around him is the better part of valor. The burly mobster bumps shoulders with Brookins, but he bounces off. He ends up walking around simply by having bounced off the big cop. He doesn't acknowledge Brookins and leaves with a smirk on his face.

The assistant State's Attorney hurries to Brookins. "Careful, that is Sam Powers. He was President of the Illinois Trial Lawyers Association two years ago. He's connected, big. He is one of the biggest machine fund raisers in Cook County and is on the Mayor's and Speaker Burke's finance committees as well as a bundler for the President. Walk lightly around him."

Brookins clearly isn't listening to the nervous but well intentioned young prosecutor. Politics isn't Brookins issue: Corruption is.

CHAPTER SEVEN

SHEILA SUNWARRIOR SITS IN A VISITOR'S ROOM AT the Cook County Jail across the table from her husband who is in a jail jumpsuit. She has tears running down her face and her makeup is a mess. Her shoulders shake as Sunny just sits and holds her hands. Between sobs, she says, "I can't believe this. How can some judge send you here? You're the good guy and he's the crook."

"Yeah...so? This is Crook County honey. He's a crooked judge. I called him and this is his response. Honey you know I told you there would be days like this. I work in a crooked system that is broke. The guys in charge like it that way. Shit like this will happen occasionally in this environment. I'm not going to change. What I'm sorry about is upsetting you. I'll be OK. I've got friends."

Sunny nods at Sheila and looks around the room. There are armed Cook County Sheriff's Police standing against the wall and by the doors. They are all alert and several seem to keeping a special eye on Sunny and Sheila. Sheila's figure would be enough to draw interest, but not as much as these guys are paying to the two of them.

All of the Sheriff's Police have heard the story of how Sunny got sent to County Jail and they are all pissed. They are part of the political system and understand there are plenty of crooks in the Cook County Judiciary, but are shocked to have the corruption so openly on display. Protecting a fellow law enforcement officer unfairly sentenced is in the DNA. For most of them this was a real life example of why their home county, Cook County is usually referred to as Crook County.

Sheila sits there and cries. Finally she looks Sunny right in the eyes. "I wouldn't want to live without you. Do you really think always challenging the sleaze balls is the smartest way?"

Sunny leans over and kisses the top of her head. "No it isn't. But what is my choice? Should I just ignore evil? These guys are destroying the opportunity for thousands and thousands of little nobodies. Who represents the little nobodies in Chicago if guys like me won't?"

Sheila nods in agreement. She isn't happy about all of this, but she is proud of her husband. She knows as a local guy made good, a former Chicago Bear and a war hero, it would be easy to take a pay check, kiss the right fannies and be a big shot in the police department. There were plenty of guys in town who had gone that way and lived profitable and comfortable lives. That wasn't GOD's calling on Sunny's life.

"Sweetheart, I'm no happier about being here that you are. What can I do? We weren't raised to look the other way, were we?"

Sheila sniffles but puts her chin up. "I don't think you should walk away. But do you always have to be the lead dog? Couldn't you let someone else take the bullet once in a while?"

Sunny laughs. "Good idea, but honey, there are plenty of folks with me. You know Vlad and Brookins are always there, but they aren't the only guys. We've got plenty of allies. I don't mean to be so out front. It just seems to work that way some days. Remember Samson took on the entire Philistine nation.

I've got less enemies than that." Sunny is proud of his Biblical reference to the great Jewish Judge of early Israel. Sunny and Sheila are doing a Bible study with their priest and they had recently discussed Samson in his role as Judge and leader of the Jewish people. He also knows Sheila will understand when it is put in terms of stark good versus evil. Will she like it? That is a different question.

Sheila tries a half smile. "You're forgetting Samson ended up dead? Could you try a different tactic?"

Sunny thinks, touché! "Honey let's pray. We could both use a little guidance." With that he takes her hands in his and they bow their heads right there in the middle of the county jail.

When they finish, Sheila looks at Sunny with questioning eyes. "How did it ever get this corrupt? How can you work for these people?"

Sunny smiles. "If you want to know I'll explain."

"I need to know how this could happen to our home."

"In the old days, New York and San Francisco were just as bad. Then in the 1920s, Al Capone and his mobsters made a pact with the Mayor of Chicago. The mob almost became part of the governing structure of Chicago. It just got worse from there. The tipping point we never recovered from was 1955 when the first Mayor Daley was elected. He beat the incumbent Democrat Mayor in the primary and made a lot of promises to get the support he needed. Remember Chicago had 3,665,000 residents then. We have 2,650,000 now. As he squeezed everything to pay back his supporters and keep his machine alive, he drove folks out. Once he won he needed every patronage job he could get."

Sheila nods as she follows Sunny's explanation.

"The biggest untapped source of new patronage jobs was the schools. So he appointed his political buddy, Sargent Shriver, the head of the Merchandise Mart to run the school board.

Shriver opened up all the contracts and jobs for patronage hiring by Mayor Daley. In 10 years a very good big city system had fallen apart and in 20 years it was an educational wasteland, financially bankrupt and had to be reorganized."

Sheila is just stunned at the explanation. It must be true. Sunny was telling her how it all happened. What she couldn't figure out was why no one was screaming bloody murder.

"It went broke under that incompetent political hack, Dr. Joe Hannon. By then the majority of the employees had nothing to do with teaching and the lowest paid group of employees were the teachers."

Sheila shakes her head. "Is Sargent Shriver the Kennedy Shriver?"

"Yeah. Remember the base of the Kennedy family fortune is the Merchandise Mart there on the Chicago River. A Kennedy is always looking after it."

Sheila looks stunned. "How can you run a city without a good school system?"

Sunny shrugs. "Maybe you need to ask the 1,000,000 folks who left. The funny thing is lots of folks opposed him and almost voted him out of office. His early elections were tough. So to build his power base he kept adding more and more do nothing patronage jobs to get more political workers. He stole more and more votes. He was the last real political 'Boss'. As corruption, vote fraud and the schools spiraled down his opponents moved out and it left him even stronger. It became like a Black Death Star. The more it collapses inward, the stronger it gets. "

"Wow. I didn't realize Chicago had shrunk so much."

Sunny shakes his head affirmatively. "The price of corruption. All of these guys think the survival of the Chicago Democrat Machine is more important than delivering the services expected at a reasonable cost. You know da Mayor was like Brennan Burke is now. They are politically brilliant but governmentally incompetent. To keep their power base they look the other way at all of the corruption, the mobsters, the crooked courts, the bonded indebtedness and the corrupt union bosses. They keep the murder and mayhem in the minority areas and blame the Republicans for it. They use up all the money hiring patronage workers and giving contracts to insiders and then blame the Republicans for not giving them enough money to deliver the services."

Sheila always had a feeling that Burke guy was a sleaze ball. What she hadn't realized was how bad a job he had done running the State of Illinois.

Sunny continues, "The Attorney General and Cook County State's Attorney refuse to investigate the political corruption and the vote fraud. They need the unions and ambulance chasers money to pay for the campaigns and the gangbangers for political work. Who else wants to volunteer to elect a pack of crooks and incompetents?"

Sheila just looks at him. "You want to work for these guys?"

Sunny shakes his head and looks Sheila in the eyes. "Who else is going to look after the little guys? If not us, who?"

At the same time, downtown, at the door of the office of Cook County Sheriff Steve Elway a group of lawyers, all young assistant state's attorneys huddle. The door opens and Marta, an attractive, bleached blonde with a huge chest and a short skirt gestures for the state's attorneys to enter. They all watch her beautiful way of walking as they follow her into Sheriff Elway's office and she closes the door. Marta, the Sheriff's personal assistant, is a woman who knows how to walk! She has stuff to strut and she knows how to strut it but do it in a way that seems almost innocent.

The Assistant State's Attorneys crowd around the Sheriff's desk. It is a familiar and friendly atmosphere. Most of the them feel like they know Sheriff Elway personally. He is a gregarious, old time politician competent at glad handing anyone and everyone.

The Sheriff also knows most of the State's Attorneys by face, if not by name. This is a group who views each other as allies. "Sheriff, you do realize this is a decorated Chicago Police Officer who is being dumped into your jail?"

Sheriff Elway remains seated. Despite his important position he is crippled and can't stand without his crutches. He is a big man. Not fat, just the big shoulders, torso and neck of someone who carried a lot of muscle in his younger days. He is obviously a former athlete. Actually he is a former Big Ten football player from Northwestern University in Evanston, on the North Shore.

"Guys don't worry. I know who Sunny is. Hell, he played at Illinois long after I played at Northwestern. There is no way I'm going to put him in with the general population. Don't lose any sleep. He'll be safer here than out doing his usual job. The city hired a contract lawyer to work with the Fraternal Order of Police's or FOP's lawyer to handle Sunny's case. We've got it covered."

The assistant state's attorneys don't look as assured as Sheriff Elway. One starts to speak, "sheriff Elway..."

The Sheriff raises his hand. "Guys...guys. I'm going to put him in a conference room 24 hours a day. Don't worry about it. I'm going to have guards with him at all times. I won't even let him go to the bathroom without guards. Remember, we're on the same team. OK?"

There starts to be some relief in their eyes.

"I already spoke with Superintendent Purcell. He's going to keep Sunny on payroll, overtime for weekends and treat this as duty time. Sunny was right, the judge was wrong. We've lost a solid case against a real gangster and the drug trafficking wing of the Gangster Warlords. The Superintendent isn't going to penalize Sunny. He shouldn't have run his mouth, but Sunny is Sunny. We're all set."

Most of the young state's attorneys look relieved.

One of the group says to the Sheriff, "I spoke with the State's Attorney herself about what happened with Judge Leoni. I told her because it was a bench trial I thought the fix was in and Judge Leoni was the fixer. I wanted to file charges in front of the Judicial Inquiry Board but she told me to just drop the issue."

All of the group quietly mumble in agreement to support the guy who is a little nervous raising such a touchy political topic with a legitimate County political heavyweight.

The young State's Attorney continues on in what all of them know is dangerous terrain. "We know Judge Leoni's father is a long time, powerful West Side Block Ward Committeeman who everyone thinks has ties to the mob. But he supported the State's Attorney in the primary so she doesn't want to ruffle any feathers or question anyone's integrity. He runs a strong ward organization. What do you think?"

"I think you are asking for trouble and getting in over your head. Don't mess with Leoni, his old man or your boss the State's Attorney. In a 99% white ethnic ward, did you notice the margins old man Leoni put out for the President all the way down to State Rep? He's untouchable. Don't make waves. She gave you good advice...drop the subject," said the Sheriff.

The young assistant State's Attorney looks totally crest fallen.

"You realize the lawyer was Sam Power? He is just as connected as Judge Leoni's old man. Don't get too far out on this limb."

"But..."

Elway cuts him off. "I was following the case. I know who that scum bag is and I know his buddy tried to run down two of Chicago's finest." Sheriff Elway grimaces as he shifts in his chair. It takes effort for him to move himself. His physical problems are getting more obvious as time goes by. "He should have kept his mouth shut, but still, a guy like Sunny SunWarrior has seen enough in his day. I can protect him. He'll be treated right. Don't worry. I know about Afghanistan and all of his military history. I even know about his time with da Bears."

Everyone laughs as Sheriff Elway refers to The Chicago Bears by their local nick name.

"Why do you guys always think I'm so out of it? You guys aren't old enough to even remember the real beginning. I bet you guys don't even know the story of when Coach Burton came in front of Judge McCarthy and asked that Sunny be given another chance rather than go to jail. He was probably eighteen but he was a big lug even then. Hell of a linebacker at Mount Carmel and Coach Burton treated all of his players like his own family."

It is obvious none of the young assistant State's Attorneys knew this full story.

"Guys like Sunny have their flaws. But Coach Burton never let the fact that his teenaged players were idiots like most other teenagers effect how he treated them or cared for them. I bet none of you guys know I was actually the assistant State's Attorney on the case. Judge McCarthy was tough, but he was fair."

The young guys are impressed by the story.

Elway continues, "He gave him two options…jail or the Army. Sunny made the right call. I was there. I saw it all. He was lucky it was old Judge McCarthy. He is a Viet Nam vet and always says if you haven't served your country you aren't really a full citizen. Sunny made the right call and the judge took it from there."

The atmosphere in the room improves markedly.

With friendly humor in his voice Sheriff Elway waves the guys out. "Get out of here and go convict some more scum bags will ya! I've got work to do and this is under control. Now scoot!"

Marta, Sheriff Elway's well-endowed and beautiful assistant appears again as if on command. As she leads them out, all of the young guys again get the pleasure of watching her walk. Most either look at her chest or her fanny, depending on their personal preferences, but try not to be too obvious about it.

She stops at the door and holds it open for the group. Marta, standing sideways holding the door accentuates her trim figure and impressive chest even more. She is very good at not noticing half of the young guys are mentally undressing her on their way out.

The last State's Attorney, too intent on watching Marta's shapely posterior and rounded chest walks right into the door frame and almost falls down. Everybody cracks up as the young guy turns two shades past beat red.

Marta catches his arm to steady him and the door slaps her fanny in a provocative way that gets everyone's attention. With a seemingly sincere naiveté, Marta asks, "Are you OK? You need to keep your eyes on the door. Sorry I was in your way. I know it is a little tight, but you can get through it."

They guy just blushes even more as his friends laugh even harder at his predicament. He is too embarrassed to even speak and just nods he is OK. The entire group keeps chuckling as they leave.

After they're gone Marta returns to the sheriff's office. "Are you OK? You're looking a little under the weather." She walks behind him and starts to massage his shoulders and neck. The sheriff is in obvious pain but relaxes as she massages his neck and shoulders. "By the way, your wife called. Just a reminder. You've got a dinner meeting tonight. A bunch of lawyers and activists who want to talk with you about conditions in the jail."

"Great. Another bunch of do-gooders worried our little charges aren't getting enough tender loving care. Yeah. I wish a couple of them would get mugged so they'd start to realize these characters aren't a bunch of Sunday schoolers who were just playing hooky from church."

"You sort of brushed off the young guy's complaint about the crooked judges. You know he has a fair point. These courts are crooked and all the insiders know. Heck, even the outsiders know. It is an issue you're going to have to deal with some day. Who is the lawyer the city hired to help with Detective SunWarrior's case?"

Elway simply sits and thinks a moment. He is relaxing under Marta's gentle massage. He speaks to her quietly and in a confidential tone. The way someone speaks to a trusted friend. "I doubt I will. There were crooks on the bench before I was born. There will be crooks on the bench after I'm dead. The bar associations and the voters don't seem to care. They know about the crooks. They seem OK with it. Hell our party is built on the ability to control the courts, contracts and patronage jobs. You know that Rakove guy titled his book, *Don't Make No Waves... Don't Back No Losers*. Good advice. I didn't get where I'm at by making waves. I'm too old to start now."

With a friendly scold in her voice, Marta keeps working on Elway's shoulders and neck. "You know, Mr. Sheriff, you didn't always think this way. I remember when you had a few more principles. I also notice you dodged my question about which worthless lawyer the city gave the contract to."

"I'm too old to remember that young fool. We didn't build this powerful of a political machine with independent thinking. With age comes wisdom...and the ability to forget. "

"You are telling me you haven't changed?"

Again, Elway sits and thinks before he answers. "You know, I'm not sure I really changed. I always thought about this stuff like this. My dad helped build this party and this is how they built it. The voters don't seem to mind a little corruption and that is what pays for the system. You think we would get the political contributions we do if we couldn't give the guy a little help now and then."

Marta listens attentively.

"I just never said it in front of you...or actually in front of anyone. I guess I have to say, I'm part and parcel of this system and it has served both me and my family well for seventy-five years. I'm not going to be some rebel now. It's too late. I have responsibilities to the guys who helped me get here. A few crooks don't really cause that much trouble and no one is getting hurt. Our guys get rich. My dad made a few bucks when he ran the ward. There is plenty of money to go around. No harm, no foul. That is just how it is. Besides this job is a bitch. You know what I go through to get our work done. But it is my responsibility to do it and I'm going to do the best job I can."

Marta smirks. "You dodged my question again. Which lawyer got the contract?"

Elway gives up. He knows Marta will get the information out of him. "Boboleski."

"Boboleski! He hasn't done an ounce of work for anyone in years. Didn't he have a contract from you for a long time?"

Elway basically mumbles a reply under his breath. "Yeah. Worthless. We paid him three grand a month for six years on a contract Alderman Blevins asked for. I gave it to him. What was I supposed to do? He is one of Blevins top precinct captains and raises some good money for the party and Blevins' ward organization also."

"You should have paid to send him to AA. You aren't doing the guy any good to let him get paid for drinking, voting senile people in nursing homes, shaking down local businessmen for political protection money and staggering around a precinct."

"I didn't give him the contract. You know it is Blevins's contract for all his ward does for us."

Marta laughs, "Remember no one forces you to do this job. When the Mayor slated you, you were more than happy to run for sheriff. Remember? You get no sympathy from me."

Elway leans back into her massage. Obviously enjoying the loosening of his tight neck and shoulders. "We Chicago Democrats have got the President, the Mayor, the Governor, the legislature and most important Speaker Burke. Please let me enjoy having it all. That took work you know. How come I never get a break from anybody? No sympathy from anybody. Geez!!"

Marta laughs as he complains.

The Sheriff relaxes and speaks over his shoulder. "You're great, as always. I don't know what I'd do without you, thanks. Oh, by the way, please give Sunny's wife, Sheila another call. OK? Let her know he isn't dead yet and he's already complaining about the bed. Funny, he's not complaining about the food. Tell her if he bitches much more I'll put him out with the work crews. Call them chain gangs to Sheila... Naw...No, come to think of it, don't kid with her. She is tense enough already."

Marta nods in acceptance.

"Give her some of your wonderful Marta TLC. She needs a little affection right now and needs to know I've got Sunny's back. Invite her out to lunch for a sisterly chat if you want. I'll get one of the lawyers to cover the cost, so don't be afraid to take her to a nice place you'll both enjoy."

Marta bends over closer and gives the Sheriff a stronger massage across his upper back. Then with a cute smile she rests her chin on top of his head. "Don't worry. I understand what you mean. So, whatever you say Mr. Sheriff."

Just outside the building several of the assistant DAs stand by the door and talk.

"Just getting to see Marta was enough of an excuse to see Elway."

"Come on. She's great, but we came to be sure Sunny is OK. I was worried when one of the guys told me names of the two lawyers who were looking after Sunny."

Several guys ask at the same time. "Who?"

"One of them is that drunk Boboleski. He's worthless. Sunny told me he has never even stopped by to talk with him."

"Duhhh. When was the last time Boboleski even showed up in court?"

"If the judge would be courteous enough to hold the hearing at a pub, Boboleski would be there."

"You're kidding yourself."

"Yeah, you're right. Boboleski would miss the judge if he was on the stool next to him."

"The other guy the FOP is sending is Carson Simmons. He's OK. Not the hardest worker in the world, but he's connected and he'll at least keep an eye on things."

The youngest of the assistant DAs pipes up. "Is it my imagination or do these city and school board contract lawyers sometimes not make it to their court dates? Last week I saw a judge grant a second continuance in the same case because the jerk missed both court dates. The judge was so pissed he called the school board to get the guy there. Don't know if he ever made it, but I couldn't believe the judge granted continuances that weren't requested. The other lawyer was fuming, but what could he do?"

Several of the guys give a cynical laugh. "Happens all the time. Those legal contracts are just pinstripe patronage. Just more political pay offs to the connected guys. If the taxpayers realized how much money we give to do nothing lawyers to miss their court dates, they'd scream!"

"Yeah."

CHAPTER EIGHT

ALL FOUR GANGBANGERS CAREFULLY MOVE TOWARD the darkened front porch. Jaron Fort leads the three Black teenagers, younger Gangster Warlords. As the field commander taking younger Warlords on what might be called a 'message' mission, he wants to be sure they accomplish their objective and learn their lessons well. He also doesn't want to make a mistake. The younger brother of Akile Fort, the leader of the Gangster Warlords has no intention of being embarrassed in front of his brother.

As the leader of the Gangster Warlords, Akile Fort began to realize there is going to be some big trouble very soon. His thought is to take out the spiritual leader of the one street gang that might be strong enough to ally against him. Remind them in advance of the consequences of messing with the Gangster Warlords.

Using the younger Warlords means he doesn't really care if he loses a few of them and if caught, he can blame it on their youthful macho mentality. If they succeed, it will be a major, major message. But important as that is, he needs to protect his deniability.

The four Warlords freeze as a light goes on in the back of the house. They huddle down below window level and wait a minute until the light goes out.

The fourteen year old kid in the middle sniggers, "Old fart had to take a piss."

That causes all of them to laugh and forces Jaron to slap the closest one. Not much military discipline but they all straighten out and look to Jaron to lead. Jaron signals for them to stay put for a moment while he moves closer to the door. Jaron is now separated from the other three by almost the entire width of the porch.

Just then gun shots start raining everywhere. There is no discipline to the gunfire. The bullets are going everywhere. It is a fairly good-sized house, a fairly good-sized lot and Chicago is a fairly good-sized city. The shooters are so inept and so determined to just blast away at the Gangster Warlords that most of the bullets miss the house, the yard, Chicago and maybe don't even hit Lake Michigan that is even bigger than Chicago.

Even though most of the shots don't hit anything, the shooters don't care. They are hunkered down out of sight and want to make sure whoever they are shooting at doesn't last long enough to shoot back. They figure with enough bullets, eventually some of them will hit something.

The thought they might hurt some innocent child sleeping in their bed in a nearby house doesn't mean anything to the shooters. Gangbangers don't' normally have well-developed consciences. Most of them probably don't have a conscience at all. Most of them come from the not very evolved wing of the family tree. They are still pretty doggone close to the amoeba in the mud. If you're a Christian and don't buy evolution, then this group of thugs probably were the kind of folks who were residents of Sodom and Gomorrah.

These guys are off to a bad start. Dad is a list of suspects. Really little more than a sperm donor. Mom was sixteen and a high school dropout when they were born and she almost forgot to go to the hospital for the delivery because she was high on drugs. The drugs probably affected their brains when they were born. At least that is a good excuse for their limited brain power and total lack of conscience.

Two of the junior Warlords grab for bullet wounds and go down. They are terrified. One of the wounded Warlords turns his weapon on automatic and blazes away. In his terror, he fails to think. He has no idea where he is shooting and all he does is waste his ammunition. His aim isn't any better than the attackers. He probably doesn't hit the yard, Chicago or Lake Michigan either.

Most gangbangers carrying weapons are so driven by macho they only worry about how they look with the weapon. The thought of actually taking target practice is simply not part of their world. They let the volume of bullets make up for the lack of accuracy. Most of the time, gangbangers are more dangerous to themselves and uninvolved strangers than to the folks they are shooting at. They are not usually the brightest kids in the neighborhood. Most are just cannon fodder for the gang leaders who are clearly the brightest guys in their groups.

All the flashes from the Gangster Warlord's shots do is pinpoint him for the five rounds that end his life. Easily another twenty rounds pour into the now inert bodies. Probably over 100 or maybe 1,000 rounds are fired at them. It sounds like a reenactment of the Blitzkrieg over London in 1940.

Jaron feels a bullet whip through his windbreaker and another crash through the window behind his head. He can hear shouting and in the dark just barely see shapes running but he can clearly see flashes breaking from the barrels of their guns.

He decides to dive for the edge of the porch and get out of the light. He low crawls into the hedge next door. It is near, but not too close to the porch.

Four gunmen run up the stoop steps. Several more stand back and cover the area with their guns. From the other side and behind the house Jaron thinks he can see two more coming up the side walk. Everybody is armed and still ready for more action.

Jaron is wearing the black and crimson colors of the Gangster Warlords so he does not stand out in the bushes or lying on the dark earth. There are no porch lights to expose him.

The group stands over the three bodies lying on the porch. All appear to be dead. There is a real big guy in charge and he speaks with a heavy Spanish accent "I thought I saw four? What'd you nigger lovers see?" The guy is physically huge, arms and shoulders like an NFL defensive lineman. His voice is deep enough it sounds like it is coming out of a 100 foot deep pit. Everyone responds to him with obvious respect. No one has to tell you he is the boss. It is obvious and he knows it also.

Despite the mumbles, it is also obvious no one else really knows how many Gangster Warlords had come to kill the Insane Jaguars spiritual mentor, Juan Carlos Allende. Inside the house, the old man makes sure the saint of death, Santa Muerte, their patron saint is fully honored.

The front door of the house opens and an old man with few teeth and wrinkled skin walks out. He is wearing a jeweled crown and a black and white cape wrapped around his shoulders. He face is painted black and the areas around his eyes are painted white. All of the Hispanic Insane Jaguars bow to him. Allende crosses himself and reaches his hand out to bless the Jaguars who have just saved his life.

"Santa Muerte is proud of you. Death claims more unbelievers and you have honored Santa Muerte and me by giving us their bodies. Bring them inside and leave them in the bath tub.

I will prepare them for sacrifice. They have betrayed and cheated our Southern brothers and we need to be sure they know there will be consequences."

The Jaguars lift one and drag the two other inert bodies inside. All of the Jaguars move into Allende's living room.

Juan Carlos Allende looks at the bullet riddled front of his house and shakes his head with a mirth filled smile. "Dumb motherfucking teenagers. Couldn't hit the broad side of a barn at two feet." He then carefully looks around but doesn't see anyone. He turns back into his home and closes the door.

In a neighborhood like this one no one calls 911 to get the police. Gun shots are common and people know to mind their own business.

In the hedge, Jaron Fort finally breaths. He can't figure out what Allende was talking about. Who were their Southern brothers and what had the Warlords done to betray them?

Jaron waits a moment longer and then low crawls to the hedge next door. The house is abandoned so he is able to avoid any light and continues to low crawl at the edge of the building. He realizes his left leg is starting to throb but he ignores it. If there is a problem he can worry about it later. This is not the time to look to see if he has been wounded or simply cut himself diving off the porch.

Once he is three houses away he gets up and tries to run. His left leg is blood soaked and not cooperating. But he just keeps on moving, hopping on his good leg.

As soon as he reaches the black SUV he pulls the key from his pocket, clicks the latch and jumps in the driver's side. He wastes no time getting moving. He turns the corner instantly and is gone from sight.

All Jaron Fort is thinking about is how had the Insane Jaguars known he was coming and what is this Southern brother's crap? Akile said their drug suppliers were pissed, but so what. What could anyone do to the largest street gang in Chicago, the Gangster Warlords? The three boys were just wannabes and don't really matter. He couldn't even remember one of their names. It was something like Labarkadeck or something anyway. It would be days before anyone would even notice they were gone. They didn't really have families.

Akile wouldn't be happy at failing to kill Allende. He'd be madder the Insane Jaguars were warned in advance. But that said, Akile had left his message. No one is safe if you cross the Warlords.

Everyone thinks Juan Carlos Allende is a little crazy. But this isn't the first time Santa Muerte's High Priest has seemed to know what no one else would have known. Weird. Santa Muerte, the patron saint of drugs, thugs and the dead ought to be more even-handed. Or maybe it is true, he is just another racist motha' fucka' like the rest of them.

CHAPTER NINE

SUNNY AND VLAD DRIVE EAST ON NORTH AVENUE IN the ultra-wealthy east Lincoln Park neighborhood. They are just west of Lake Shore Drive and its multimillion dollar condominiums overlooking Lincoln Park, the Zoo, the Lincoln Park Boat Club and Lake Michigan. They are going to make a quick stop to see a fellow who thinks he might have some information about a major burglary that took place in his neighborhood. Not their usual job, but the guy is a political heavy. He is a big ambulance chaser and Democrat organization fund raiser for the President, the Mayor and Speaker Burke. The police captain wanted to make a positive impression. The captain figured having a former Chicago Bear and war hero come by to get the information would present the right image. The captain told Sunny and Vlad to smooze the guy, get the information and just try to score some brownie points. If they ran a little late, they'd get overtime. The guy was no one to dismiss and should be treated accordingly.

Just as they are about to take a dog leg turn to the right to get to go over to Astor Street in the Gold Coast district of Lincoln Park they are stopped by a uniformed Chicago Policeman.

They know the guy even though he is new and just in traffic. That is the bottom end of the police department jobs. Officer Akito Harrano is brand new to the force. Sharp uniform. Shined shoes. Neat haircut. He knows his assignment today is serving the real royalty in Chicago, the Mayor, Speaker of the House and State Party Chairman, Brennan X. Burke and the big money trial lawyers. He's no fool. This is an opportunity to be seen and maybe noticed for a better assignment.

Harrano waves the car over to him. "Hey Sunny. What you guys doin' over in the zillionaire district?" He gives a nod to Vlad also.

Sunny gives him a smile. "We're just here to kiss some ass. Some big lawyer wants to give us some information but he is too important to come in or tell us over the phone."

Harrano rolls his eyes. This is Chicago. He may not have been an officer all that long, but he already understands a 'kiss ass' assignment. "Will you get a free dinner for the brown nosing?"

Sunny and Vlad crack up. Harrano's no fool. "It's Ruth's Chris tonight baby!"

All three guys laugh.

Harrano leans in the window. "I hate to inconvenience you, but I am under direct orders to direct all traffic not going to the fundraiser to go around. You can see the problem."

All three look down the street and see limos and fancy cars unloading or already double parked all up and down the street.

Harrano points to a big black limo. "That's the Mayor's." The driver and body guards hang out at the car. There is a small group around them chatting and just killing time. They all know they are on overtime and aren't in a hurry to go anywhere while they're getting double time pay.

Just then a big black SUV pulls up and two guys jump out to get the doors. One goes to each side. On the curb side, Speaker Brennan Burke's wife Sharon is helped out by a flunky/political errand runner. Mrs. Burke is very gracious and thanks the man with a big smile and squeezes his arm.

She is the Chair of the Illinois Arts Agency that distributes millions and millions of dollars to rich folks who want middle class folks to subsidize their high-brow enjoyment of trendy cultural niceties. The Agency employs a whole slug of patronage workers who spend a lot of time reminding rich people how lucky they are that Speaker Burke and his wife are such art patrons. Of course Burke is a patron with other people's money...a minor point best not to quibble about in a totally bankrupt state that hasn't balanced its budget since the last century. She waits for her husband to come around and take her arm.

On the street side, Speaker Burke steps out through the open door. He is pencil thin, ram-rod straight and dressed in a suit that easily costs well over a thousand dollars. He nods to the flunky but does not bother to speak. He simply walks over to his wife, takes her arm and grandly enters the magnificent mansion.

Sunny realizes the flunky is a Chicago Police officer named McGuire. He is well known as a political kiss-ass who is also on the board of their local Fraternal Order of Police Lodge. He hadn't done real police duty in years. He knew how to work the system to get the big money without lots of work. McGuire always said he liked indoor work with no heavy lifting. Sunny didn't really trust him but it didn't matter. They didn't have to work together. Every big police department has a few McGuires.

Vlad looks to Harrano. "Whose place is that? He must be some serious money."

Harrano nods. "Some big lawyer named Leonard Bernstein. Big connections but shady reputation."

Sunny leans a little closer. "Akito...I am sure you're right. But, I wouldn't be quite so candid about a money guy for the President, the Governor, the Mayor and the Speaker."

Harrano nods back. "Yeah, good point."

Sunny nods and pulls past Harrano to go around the street. It will be a little out of their way, but nothing to get upset about.

The problem to get upset about comes when they get to the lawyer's magnificent condominium on Astor Street and are told to sit and wait. Even though the lawyer set up the appointment he isn't there. His butler said he was at Leonard Bernstein's and expects Sunny and Vlad to wait for him.

As they sit in the beautiful living room, their tempers boil.

Vlad looks at Sunny. "Hey did you & Sheila remember to send Stephanie Brookins a birthday card? They're going to Greek Town to celebrate. She loves that flaming saganaki."

As Sunny and Vlad sit and fume, a big group of men stroll into the Parthenon Restaurant on South Halsted Street, South of Jackson Blvd and almost down to the Eisenhower Expressway. The Parthenon is one of many enjoyable, relaxed hangouts in Greek Town. The food is good. The service is friendly but relaxed. The drinks aren't watered. It is always crowded, but not packed to the rafters so it is easy to sit and talk while enjoying some of the best Greek food in town.

As the group enters, the clock on the Halsted Street Clock Tower reads a little past seven o'clock. The location is the West Loop a rapidly gentrifying neighborhood between downtown and The House that Jordan Built, the United Center. A destination area for young folks who move back into the City.

Not very long ago once you got West of Halsted Street and Greek town, this area was totally down and out and called the bowery. Until a few years ago, the Como Inn and Greek Town were a collection of wonderful restaurants that were essentially an oasis in the midst of almost total devastation. Greek town now thrives, but the Como Inn is long gone. It is now condominiums.

The Bowery contained some of the best Democrat voting precincts in Chicago. The fact that no one really lived here had no effect on the vote count. These were part of the River Wards that elected Jack Kennedy President in 1960. Everyone went to bed that election night thinking Illinois had voted for Richard Nixon. But surely as day follows the night many "misplaced", uncounted ballot boxes suddenly appeared. When everything was counted, with the River Wards voting many thousands of nonexistent bodies, at a rate of almost 99% for the Kennedy/Johnson ticket, Illinois had shifted from Nixon to Kennedy by 8,000 votes.

Some apologist historians claim the mob carried Chicago and Illinois for Jack Kennedy. That is just plain absurd. Mayor Richard J. Daley (Richard I) didn't need a pack of mobsters to steal votes for him. He could do it quite well without their help. He could add those 8,000 votes from two river wards and have forty eight wards left over if he really needed anything big. Heck, he could get more than 8,000 out of just one river ward. That wasn't much to steal in Chicago in those days.

This area, the near West Side River Wards, were some of his best. Sheriff Elway's father was a Ward Committeeman in this area. The average voter has no comprehension how many votes are cast by people who aren't alive, are alive but have no idea they are voting, are registered in more than one place, are voting in more than one place, or are in nursing homes and don't even know there is an election, let alone an outside world.

In the 1960 election there were even vacant lots that cast hundreds of votes per lot. Vote fraud is less blatant today, but anyone who thinks it doesn't exist is naïve. But to Chicago's embarrassment, the Wisconsin agenda, Milwaukee to Madison and back, with their same day registration with no real ID requirement, has pretty much passed Chicago as the vote fraud capitol of America.

Several of the group coming in together wear union jackets and several are in cheap suits. One guy is in a flashy suit and greased back hair. He is so obviously a lawyer that he sticks out like a shark fin protruding from the water near a pack of surfers.

One guy tries to look a little dignified. The way he carefully shakes hands with everybody, almost accepting homage, makes the casual observer think he must be a Chicago Alderman.

The group takes a big table in the side room near the bar. By the third round of drinks any observer thinks it is a band of brothers at a reunion. One of the Union BAs or business agents is doing the ordering and is clearly the man with the credit card.

None of the group pays even an ounce of attention to a powerfully built man sitting nearby with a laughing, friendly, pleasantly rounded and nicely dressed woman. Both wear plain, gold wedding rings. Officer Harold Brookins and his wife of almost twenty years, Stephanie, are celebrating her birthday.

The warmth and intimacy of their conversation hints that later they are going to have another way to celebrate such a wonderful event. But suddenly Stephanie gets serious and gestures for Harold to come close so she can whisper to him. "Honey, don't look over there. But are you overhearing that big group sitting over by the bar? "

Harold kisses her hand and replies, "I've only got ears for you babe. None of that group bore me three wonderful children. And I doubt any of them are here to help celebrate you're 29th birthday again. I'm off duty and the only thing I want to think about is sitting right in front of me."

Stephanie gives Harold a big smile but pulls his ear closer. "Ahh, 29, I love you. But they are talking about screwing with some commercial real estate developer because he hasn't hired Brennan Burke's law firm to handle his property tax work. They are going to get some cops to investigate the guy for some BS fraud of illegally using stolen material. They claim they'll have some of your brother cops doing the shakedown. I think one of them is that slime ball, Alderman Candyass Maldonado and at least another one or two are from the city permit department. I'm guessing the slimiest looker is one of their lawyers. The rest are union BAs who have guys working on the developer's site. The guy will be left hanging on his permits until he calls Burke. How rich does Burke have to be? Has he no shame?"

Harold kisses Stephanie's hand again and then just holds it. "Sometimes I think you would make a better cop than I do. But Maldonado using cops and city bureaucrats to shake down businessmen is standard procedure for him. It happens regularly. He sends the business to Burke to get brownie points."

Stephanie seems surprised Harold was so aware and gives him I can't believe it look.

"I can't listen to them with one ear and listen to you with the other. But what am I supposed to do about it. I can't arrest them for some trash talking over drinks and flaming saganaki. No judge in Crook County will give me a probable cause waiver. By the way, his first name isn't pronounced Candyass." Stephanie laughs. "Close enough and it is fitting, isn't it?"

Brookins nods and smiles. "That may be your Americanization of his real name. I admit, it is a weird name and he sure is a slimy bastard. Besides, if I tried to arrest every scumbag alderman, lawyer, patronage worker and dishonest union business agent, I wouldn't have time to spend with the loveliest lady I know."

Stephanie blows a kiss at Brookins. "You are one smart husband. You know where your bread is buttered."

"Besides, I know who they are. The guy with the credit card is secretary-treasurer of a carpenter's local, Martin Sheehan. It was Sheehan's kid, Kevin, a nineteen year old who got hired as a city building inspector when he was totally unqualified. He got in tons of trouble."

"I remember something about that. What happened?"

"Sheehan used his clout to get the kid hired. He was only nineteen and had to have five years' experience as a union carpenter to qualify for the job. No one could give any proof he was qualified for the job. But they were paying him fifty grand a year. Great work if you can get it for a nineteen year old who doesn't always even bother to show up. Don't be surprised at anything they say or do."

Stephanie nods.

Suddenly Alderman Candyass Maldonado, fairly drunk starts to tell a story. He is speaking way too loud. It is like he wants to impress all of the unconnected nobodies within ear shot. "Remember our old pal, Marco Morales-Simon? We got a message from him. After his cocaine conviction the kind hearted judge let him drive himself to prison and he never showed up. He is in Southern Mexico and living the big life. He says it is so much cheaper there. Remember he was supposed to talk to the prosecutors because he knew so much about so many, but he disappeared first. Well he was thanking us for getting his family the forty million in contracts from the Mayor. Says the contracts keep flowing and he keeps hiding. Guy is smart. He knows the system. Talk and you and your family get screwed or... Keep your mouth shut and your family will be just fine. You can live big in Mexico on the millions his family has sent him."

Brookins frowns at Maldonado's story. "Enough of these sleaze balls. I'd rather talk to my sexy wife about us, not them."

Stephanie just gives Harold her wonderful smile. "You're so smart. Honey, you know that cutie pie BS will get you what you want, every time. But open your ears so at least you know enough about them that if they do what they are talking about, you'll be able to back up whoever tries to turn them in."

"No one would turn in Brennan Burke. It would be safer for them to swim in a school of great white sharks with an open cut on their leg than stay in Chicago after turning evidence on Burke. A developer in Chicago knows he will need to pay off the boys or he won't get his permits. That is the system, period." Brookins is getting a little agitated. His disgust for the political leadership is obvious.

Stephanie is trying to decide if it might be a good idea to change the subject. She knows her husband holds most of these people responsible for the economic decline in Chicago and Illinois, the state they totally control.

But Brookins continues, "I really would rather not think about the crooks that run our town. As a policeman it is sickening to know about the corruption and know there is nothing we can do about it. Even if we arrested them their buddies in the Crook County Courts would allow a bench trial and find a way to get them off on a technicality. If we get them in the federal courts there is a prayer, but the federal prosecutor is appointed by President Obama and he isn't going to get his pals sent to jail. Not in the cards. So I want to change the subject. I just want to tell you how much I love you and appreciate all you have put up with to raise our kids the right way."

Stephanie is eating it all up.

"Maybe I'll even mention what I'm going to do with you after I get you out of that glamorous outfit. You are going to be too sore to walk by tomorrow. That is going to begin as soon as we get home. Unless we decide to reenact some of those good old memories. Remember those days? We'd slide the front seat all the way forward and it was amazing how comfortable and roomy the back seat seemed? I bet it is still pretty comfortable in the back seat. Wouldn't that be fun? We could act like newlyweds again."

Stephanie gives him a loving smile and a tongue in cheek nod. "You know Sheila SunWarrior claims Sunny is the biggest pervert in Chicago. You must be hanging out with him too much lately. If we tried some of the stuff we used to do you'd spend a month at the chiropractor just trying to learn how to walk again."

Suddenly the union BA doing the buying gets up and holds his glass of ouzo in the air. "To Speaker of the House Brennan Burke, the best friend our union ever had!"

Everyone slugs down a big gulp of ouzo.

The lawyer follows him and raises his glass. "To Brennan Burke, the best friend the trial lawyer's ever had!"

Everyone slugs down a big gulp of ouzo.

Alderman Maldonado gets up weaving a little on his feet and holds his glass for another toast. "To President Obama for his shovel ready stimulus trillion that bailed us out and paid all of our patronage workers and Chicago teachers. Thank you for saving the Chicago Democrat Party to fight another day! God bless him! He knows who made him!" The group cheers and makes a noisy mess of the place for a minute or two and then settles back down into the slightly tipsy haze of good friends, political allies and political BS.

The BA gets up again. "Alderman you are so right. To President Obama. Or should I say President shovel ready? He is a real Chicago guy. He knows how to pay his friends back!"

Another huge gulp of ouzo for everyone. The group starts to cheer wildly again.

Maldonado gets up still laughing. "And for all of us to remember to not get greedy. Remember a pig gets fat, but a hog gets slaughtered!"

Everyone laughs and pours down another shot of ouzo.

Brookins cracks up but nods in agreement and waits for the group to quiet down before he whispers to Stephanie, "You almost put me in the hospital on our honeymoon. Waiting until we were married was wonderful, but left us a little over ready to try a few things."

"You know that was our agreement. My father would have wrung our necks if his daughter, raised in the church, disobeyed him, sinned against GOD and our preacher's teaching."

"It was worth the wait. Think of all the fun things we got to try for the first time."

"Oh yeah. Don't you even try to bring up that trick we did on your Harley. To my undying shame, my girlfriend saw us and still kids me at how flexible I used to be. She embellishes the story even more every time she brings it up. Circus performers couldn't do what she claims we did! For your back's sake, let's just stick to the somewhat conventional. OK? Besides, I thought you said you wanted to play Boardwalk when we got home. I set the game out on the table so it would be ready."

Harold Brookins chuckles at her. "You are wonderful and you were wonderful and I bet you could still pull that one off if you wanted to. Remember they say lovers live longer."

Stephanie keeps laughing and just shakes her head. "For the sake of your back and my dignity, you've got to spend less time around Sunny. Remember I am a mother of three and should at least pretend I'm grown up by now. Actually capable of thinking of something other than sex. You have no excuse. A police officer is a defacto adult whether you like it or not. So quit thinking your perverted thoughts and start listening to those crooks over by the bar."

"I'll take notes on every word they say and keep them in my notebook to use when that one accidently honest city building inspector comes in to let us know about a plot to rip off a developer. I'll even have it date stamped on the way home." Then he leans forward and whispers. "But only if we can pull out the Harley."

Stephanie absolutely cracks up.

Brookins grins at Stephanie to see if she will take him up on his offer. He pulls out his note pad and a pen.

Stephanie gives him a mischievous smile. "You're incorrigible but you can keep your notebook in your pocket and your Harley in the garage." She leans very close to his ear. "I'm going to wring you out like a wet rag, until you're calling for mercy. But

I'll do it in a bed, under a roof and behind a closed door, not on the back of a Harley. "

Brookins looks like he is willing to let her try.

CHAPTER TEN

ALDERMAN LARENDA BASS DRIVES HER BIG, BLACK, leased at Chicago tax payer expense SUV into her reserved parking space next to her store front aldermanic office. She represents a depressed ward where gangs and drugs are as common as water in Lake Michigan. It is past noon on Tuesday and she is making her first appearance of the week.

The Alderman has the self-confident stride of someone who thinks they control power. Whatever that power might require, she feels she is ready. Just because her ward is a cesspool of drugs and gangs with some of the worst public schools in the country doesn't mean she has failed. After all, she is only one alderman. The Mayor is in charge of all of that crap, the little things like schools, cops, cleaning up vacant lots and being sure a notoriously nonproductive city work force does what little work they intend to do.

All she has to do is whine about racism causing the decay. It is racism that keeps the Park District from giving her ward good, clean parks for the kids. It is racism that makes almost 80% of her ward's families single parent households. It is because of racism that she has to protect the gangbangers standing on the corners selling drugs or something like that. Her real job? The only one that counts is to deliver a reliable vote for the Speaker of the House's candidates, the Mayor and the rest of her party's candidates. As long as she does that, she feels she has the right to make some extra money on the side. The perks of office in Chicago.

Brennan X. Burke, the Speaker of the Illinois House of Representatives, who is also the State Chair of her party, makes millions on the side with influence pedaling in the corporate property tax system. It is so open even an out of town newspaper like *The New York Times* writes articles about it. Everyone knows he controls a totally corrupt system, but what the heck, it isn't her problem. She has already helped to drive virtually every business out of her ward by doing nothing to protect them from the gangs, frivolous lawsuits and the city inspectors who stop by regularly for their pay offs. So what does she care about corporate property taxes. She doesn't have any corporations left in her ward.

Her main aim is self-enrichment as long as she is here. Eventually her voters will figure out what she is all about and replace her. So she might as well make hay while the sun shines.

The key for her is to not get too far over the line. In the time she has been politically active in Chicago, 32 of Chicago's 50 sitting aldermen have gone to jail. The insider aldermen like to say pigs get fat but hogs get slaughtered. One of her friends, the former Alderman from a neighbor ward, and now a County Commissioner just got indicted. He used to say he was the hog with the biggest nuts. How dumb could a guy be? When he goes to prison, as he surely will, that will be the 33rd recent aldermen who will have taken up residence in the big house.

Larenda Bass knows this fact as the raw face of Chicago politics and the Chicago Democrat Machine. Several more should have gone to jail also, but most of the other aldermen figure they are FBI informants or there is just no way they wouldn't be in jail also.

Open thievery is not her style. There are plenty of ways to make a few extra bucks without getting too high profile about it and getting the FBI too worked up. The byword for connected Chicago Alderman has long been the advice given by the late alderman and ex con, Fred Roti, "Pigs get fat, hogs get slaughtered." Bass knows she only has a certain amount of time before she is thrown out of office, so she better get to it. Plus she wants to be sure she sets herself up in such a way it isn't touchable. Hard assets that will survive if she ends up in trouble.

Bass remembers her friend and hero, former Alderman Ambrosio Medrano who refused to rat out his buddies and took the two and one half years in prison. She was stunned when Ambrosio got out of prison, yet was do dumb he got himself indicted again. But as long as he kept his mouth shut, he'd be OK. His relatives would get something from the Mayor or the other aldermen to keep them in the style they were accustomed. Loyalty and more importantly, silence is always rewarded by the Chicago Machine. Run your mouth to get a lighter sentence and there will be consequences and they won't be pretty for you or your family.

As a connected Alderman, Larenda knew it was important to know something about the other guy's corruption. In case she got caught she could keep her mouth shut, get a country club for a prison, take her prison time and know she'd be OK when she got back. She knew the code. As long as you don't take other folks down with you, you'll be taken care of.

Bass doesn't want to have to fall back on the largesse of the Chicago Machine and Party Chairman Burke, so she made sure she knew enough for them to buy her silence, if needed. Still she hoped to use these years to set herself up financially for life. Don't be a hog. Keep your focus on what is really important.

Bass walks into her ward office and sees a group of young men in black and crimson loafing in her waiting room. "OK boys. How're they hangin' today?"

They chuckle at her greeting.

"Aren't any of you studs going to do anything to make my life easier today?"

The leader of the Gangster Warlords in her office, Mustafa, stands up with a playful hurt look on his face. He bows at the waist like an old fashioned courtier. "Now what might the queen request of her servants?"

"Now that you ask so nicely, there are some things you can do for me today."

Mustafa, isn't just some gangbanger. He playfully bows at the waist like a courtly gentleman. He compliments here for everything she does. But he is really the guy who runs her political system. Not many people volunteer anymore in Chicago. Someone needs to ramrod the young gangbangers into action. It is a mutually beneficial relationship. Bass gets workers and money. The gangbangers have official protection. The residents get screwed. Eventually the residents get mad and they either move out of the city, as 1 million have or vote the alderman out of office. That is Chicago's city government in action.

"I need you to send somebody by the cleaner and pick up my dry cleaning. Also send one of the guys to Nordstoms on Michigan Ave. to pick up some dresses I bought." She hands Mustafa her car keys. "It'll take a while. Let a couple of them go. Take my car and while they're at it have your guys come on back later with an early dinner for all of us. Maybe Chinese tonight. Something a little different."

As the lead gangbanger, who is actually her assistant or sort of a chief of staff, Mustafa, takes the keys and gestures for three of the loafers to get moving. He hands one guy the keys, a big wad of dollar bills and the younger guys bow their way out the door. Mustafa goes out with them. The Alderman and the other guys chuckle at their leaders friendly and playful manner of responding to the Alderman.

Everyone knows she isn't going to pay for anything. That is why Mustafa handed a big wad of hundred dollar bills to the guys running the errand. Those Nordstoms dresses are going to cost a pretty penny but they are free to Alderman Bass. The early dinner will come from some restaurant and she won't get a bill. The car will be washed and the tank filled. These are a few of her ways to get something on the side. All in a day's work for one of Chicago's finest.

There are other benefits from being the alderman. She pays virtually nothing in property taxes on her home and she bought some apartment buildings with money lent to her by banks that do a lot of business with the City and the County. Nothing illegal about that.

Someone might call her holdings being a slum lord, but the buildings aren't worse and probably are a little better than the others on their blocks. The Warlords make sure the buildings aren't vandalized and the tenants meet acceptable levels of behavior. The Warlords collect the rents and serve as a bit of a security force.

Having the Alderman own buildings on your block is generally good for the block. She has also been smart enough to buy two buildings in North Side wards where the property values are better and the tenants less apt to be on public assistance. She hasn't told the Gangster Warlords about those ones. They are managed for her by a professional management company. The Gangster Warlords manage her other buildings for her.

Larenda Bass might not be a millionaire, yet, but she is setting up a way to make a very nice living once she is thrown out of office for being a do-nothing alderman. Her credo: Do as she is told by the Mayor and Brennan Burke; deliver a big straight party vote; make some money for herself.

She delivers a big straight ticket vote. From the top of the ticket to the bottom. Her ward also does a great job of voting the retention ballot for the judges. Big issue for the guys on the bench. She doesn't need to really deliver services. She just needs to show empathy for those having problems; Hold lots of public meetings and rail against the rich folks; Be sure everyone gets food stamps and whatever else she can find.

Bass relies on the hope that most of her constituents don't have enough education to really try to compete in the private sector, so she has them trapped in the palm of her hand. All she has to do is not get so greedy she alerts the FBI to her other activities. Those related to her ties to the Gangster Warlords and her assistance to their empire.

No arrangement is perfect and she understands the Warlords are careful not to make their ties to her all that obvious. Of course, bailing Akile Fort out of jail was a little higher profile than she likes, but there are going to be costs to protect her lifestyle. As long as Fort keeps his guys doing a good job helping her patronage workers for election get out the voter efforts, no one at the Party's county level is going to cause her any trouble.

Bass knows how to cover her trim fanny. The Cook County State's Attorney won her ward in a landslide and Alderman Bass has had her out to speak at some local events. Their relationship is that of girl-to-girl, friendly allies. She delivers the vote and does it well. The County State's Attorney minds her own business.

The Illinois Attorney General, Laura Burke is Brennan Burke's daughter. She also won the ward in a landslide. Bass has been careful to be helpful to her also. She organized a big ladies brunch at the South Shore Country Club, actually a really neat old facility right on Lake Michigan, owned by the Chicago

Park District. Laura Burke knows Larenda Bass tries very hard to be a helpful ally.

With all of those political ties to the people who could prosecute her, the rest of Bass' life is her business. Burke's dad gets rich. The insiders get rich. Bass...Fair is fair.

Outside, Mustafa pulls the three younger Warlords around him. "We had a little problem with a 43rd Street Kings dude yesterday. Disrespected one of our girls. Grabbed her after school, passed her around to four of his buddies and then sent her home naked. Do you believe that? That shit can't go unpunished. As you go north, be sure folks see the Alderman's car. See if you can find a 43rd Street King and mess him up a bit. Don't kill him. No lifelong injury. Maybe strip his ass and tie him to a light pole. Jam something up his ass. They didn't kill the bitch, so don't escalate things. They'll know what we're saying. Got it? Don't forget some Chinese food. Remember the Alderman likes Moo Shu Pork. OK?"

The three young guys look thrilled to have a chance to do some real work. "Done man. See you in a while."

Alderman Bass walks into her personal office and finds some beautiful flowers on her desk. The note reads 'Thank you, Akile.' She figures getting him out on bail is worth these flowers and the rest.

She sits down and checks her appointment book. She is going to be late to everything today but she will say she was tied up on ward business. Who would know the difference? She is never on time anyway, so why change today?

Her next appointment is with Hector Romero and Marvin Partee. She is looking forward to the meeting. She and her state representative got Brennan Burke to OK a new state legislative commission to study lowering the threshold for neighborhood gang interventions by the police. She doesn't remember the real name of the commission, but that doesn't matter. It isn't ever going to meet or report or really do anything anyway. It is just another way to stash ghost payroller campaign workers on the state payroll rather than the city's or the county's. It has an appropriation for $125,000 to hire staff but no real function for the staff to accomplish. The legislature has 40 or maybe even more of these worthless commissions stuffed with Chicago political workers who do nothing for the taxpayers to earn the money.

Romero and Partee were the guys she got her representative to have hired as part of the staff. Neither one knows it yet. The meeting is to let them know what she has done for them and what she expects them to do for her political organization to keep getting the cash from the state. Romero is a good talker and has been helpful getting more precinct workers from the Latino gangs north of her and Partee is a young lawyer who does some legal work for Warlords who are in jail.

She can use them for the higher skill political errands she needs done. The kind most of the Warlords just don't have the skills or vocabulary to handle. A drug dealing thug is fine for running a precinct and getting signatures on candidate petitions. But when she needs the absentee ballots for 100% of the people in the nursing homes in her area, that is another thing all together. Some of the nursing home operators are very touchy about being involved with such blatant vote fraud. Romero and Partee are better suited for that kind of work than a street thug.

After that some guy named Jensen, who owns some buildings that need zoning approval for improvements, will come in for her to lay down the law about how the system works. Since she is on the Building and Zoning Committee she needs to be sure some of these stupid landlords don't start thinking they can do what they want without paying the right folks for the privilege.

As she reviews the rest of her appointments, the Alderman can hear a loud commotion in her outer office where the young Warlords are. She checks her bottom desk drawer on the left to be sure her .38 pistol is there. You can never be too careful. She puts it in her pocket and walks to her door to see what is going on.

The young Warlords are in a circle around Jaron Fort talking in loud voices. They are clearly upset and threatening vengeance against someone. Jaron is leaning on a crutch and his left leg is clearly stiff because it is in a walking cast.

"What are my young gentlemen so upset about? Would you please fill in your Queen?"

Jaron quiets the group and speaks to Larenda Bass. "The Insane Jaguars killed some of ours and then skinned and mutilated them in some crazy rite with Juan Carlos Allende and the Santa Muerte cult crap. They left the bodies hanging on a fence behind the high school. It is a direct insult to us on our turf."

"Why do you think it was the Insane Jaguars? They're North of here. Were some of our boys in their area?"

Jaron shrugged. "We go where we want. No mo fokin'wet backs are going to tell us where we can or can't do."

"Maybe so, but you're not answering my question. Why are you saying the Jaguars killed your guys? Did you do anything to start a fight and they're just retaliating?"

Jaron shrugs again. "Nothin' out of the normal stuff we do. They don't deserve no respect."

Larenda Bass may not be Albert Einstein, but she can tell there is something going on that she isn't being told. This is her Ward and she doesn't want some pimply teenager to cause a gang war and maybe make a mess of her buildings or get any of her political workers in trouble. She doesn't want the police in here asking too many questions. She can push them away for most things, but not a gang war. That would be too big to ignore.

Just then Jarl Jensen walks in for his appointment. He is an hour early. It is obvious this is his first visit to an Alderman's office and he is nervous. He is sweating profusely and speaks with a heavy Scandinavian accent. "Excuse me, I am here to see the Alderman."

All of the Warlords go silent and just stare at Jensen. It is a bit like wondering how he has the nerve to interrupt them in a public office that belongs to an elected Alderman. Classic Chicago. What is this dumb tax payer doing here?

Bass looks at him and says with a bit of irritation in her voice. "You're an hour early."

Jensen looks humble. "I wanted to be sure I wasn't late."

Bass laughs and signals for Jensen to follow her into her office. She closes the door behind him and points to a chair. "Have a seat."

Jensen sits and looks like he expects to be executed.

"Mr. Jensen."

He nods as recognition.

"You want a zoning variance and a permit to do some work on your buildings? Right?"

"Yes ma'am."

"Have you hired an attorney?"

Jensen looks apprehensive. "Why do I need an attorney? I know what I need to do and I have some experience as a general contractor."

Bass just looks at Jensen with an are you an idiot or what look? There is a very long, very silent pause.

Jensen just sits there and sweats. "Do you really want your zoning variance and your permits?"

"Of course, ma'am."

Bass leans toward Jensen. "Look Mr. Jensen. Don't waste my time. There is a process, period. You want your permit, do as you're told, period."

Jensen just sits there and sweats.

"I'll be glad to give you the name of a respected attorney who can get the process rolling for you. Your buildings are in Alderman

Majerski's ward. He is not on the Zoning Committee, but you should make it a priority to meet him. Have I made myself clear?"

"I'm not a wealthy man. I'm embarrassed to say this, but the City inspectors have taken so much from me I just can't afford to pay still more."

Bass gives Jensen a look that could melt tungsten. "Are you alleging a City inspector has done something inappropriate?" Her facial expression is hard and blank and she sits there silently waiting for Jensen to answer.

"Ma'am, I'm not trying to cause trouble. I'm just trying to improve my buildings and add off street parking to save my tenants so many parking tickets. I don't want any trouble with anyone."

"Fine Mr. Jensen." She reaches across her desk and sets down a business card. "This is a well-respected attorney who works with the City and the Zoning Committee all the time."

"Ma'am. I'm not rich. I can't afford an attorney and all of the other costs also. Isn't there some other way to do this?"

"No. Hire the attorney I recommended and everything will go just fine. That is the system."

"If I can't afford to pay him, how can I hire him?"

"That is your problem, not mine. Follow the system we use or sell your buildings and don't do business in Chicago."

Jensen is clearly confused. He can't think of anything to say. He looks totally defeated.

"I'm very busy Mr. Jensen. I have told you what you need to do. Now call the attorney and everything will be just fine."

Jensen sits there with a hopeless look on his face. He doesn't get up to leave.

"I told you I'm very busy. Your appointment is over. Now goodbye and call the attorney today. He'll take care of everything."

Jensen gets up to leave. He looks like he wants to say something.

"I told you your appointment is over. Good day Mr. Jensen."

He decides to say nothing and simply turns to leave. No handshake. No thank you for your time. Nothing. He just leaves.

As soon as he is out the door, Bass picks up her phone and dials. She waits while it rings. "This is Alderman Bass. Jomo Washington, please." She waits a moment for Washington to pick up the phone.

"Jomo, you'll get a call from a guy named Jensen. He'll need some help in front of the committee. He is a serious retard. I laid down the rules, but he didn't seem to understand. Just do the usual and send me the usual. OK?"

Bass smiles as she hangs up the phone. She then dials her assistant in the front office. "Let me know when Romero and Partee arrive. Don't disturb me until they arrive." With that she picks up her TV remote and flips it on.

CHAPTER ELEVEN

SUNNY SUNWARRIOR SLEEPS FITFULLY ON A COT IN a dark and cramped conference room. Sitting by the door is a Cook County Sheriff's Police with a shotgun in his lap. The door opens a crack and another Sheriff's Police armed with a shotgun leans in. "I'm taking a quick trip to the boy's room. I'll be right back. See if you can handle this on your own for two minutes. OK?"

The guard laughs, flips him the bird and says, "Get out of here you jerk. Do you need any instruction on how to get it out? I hear guys like you haven't got much to work with."

"My problem is when I'm taking a leak the water in the toilet bowl is so damn cold and not deep enough!" Both laugh but it doesn't wake Sunny.

The guards are friends and enjoy the laugh together, but they do take guarding a fellow officer as an important assignment. They both know Judge Leoni, the jerk who sent Sunny to jail. Leoni has made more than one questionable decision, but never something like this. Leoni has quietly covered for the mob and some drug guys for years. Folks know that.

Sunny probably should have kept his mouth shut. The fix was already in and nothing Sunny said about the judge would change that. The judicial system is openly corrupt, but this time it went way over the line. They all know it, but what can a single sheriff's deputy do?

For years, Sunny continued to dream of the event that totally changed his life. Throwing that bastard out the third floor window crossed the line from dumb juvenile stunt to manslaughter. He still has occasional dreams about taking on the six of them. But with surprise, his size and strength and in Sheila's need, he overlooked the six to one issue.

An important thing he later learned in the Army was OK tactics done quickly, with an element of surprise and with real drive will usually beat a better plan that you spend too much time thinking up and don't get around to until much later. The element of surprise is worth many hours of tactical contemplation.

Sunny could still picture Sheila with the guy's hand over her mouth and most of her face, her blouse torn open and her skirt pulled up fighting to get free from those bastards trying to rape her. There was no give up in her. No tears. No whining. She was fighting them like a real Valkyrie. Right there in the library's third floor bathroom.

Sometimes he tried to mislead himself into thinking he didn't really mean to throw the guy out the window head first. The other guy he almost drowned in the toilet certainly deserved that or worse. The guys with the broken bones and the one with the concussion from having his head beaten against a urinal had gotten off easy. He couldn't have cared less about their whining. He should have done worse. He could have.

What saved the gangbangers from more injury was Sunny was more worried about getting to Sheila and calming her down. Deep down, he knew he did it all on purpose. Sometimes evil has to be dealt with and he did. His father raised him

Catholic and the conflict with evil and the necessity to defeat it was drummed into him from an early age.

Sunny didn't really lose much sleep over the dumb bastard getting killed when he hit the sidewalk head first. That three floor, head first drop wasn't planned, but also wasn't regretted. It had been pretty gory though. Bashed in head and his pants around his ankles made him look kind of pathetic. No open casket funeral for that jerk.

The police report showed it wasn't the dead guy's first rape and wouldn't have been his last. But he didn't live to rape Sheila and he wasn't going to rape anyone else if he was dead. Evil was defeated and dealt with appropriately. Tough luck if the devil was mad about it.

It always amazes Sunny these kind of guys, obvious gangbangers, usually get suspended or lighter sentences anyway. The dumb kid who just did something stupid but couldn't afford a connected lawyer seemed to end up getting a million years without parole. Not that gangbangers didn't go to prison, many did, but they were much more apt to get something minimal because they had connected lawyers on their payroll. In Crook County, connected lawyers can get an awful lot overlooked. Sunny always wondered if there wasn't more to it.

Sunny also worries about what is happening to young black maledom. The percentage that ends up in the various arms of the correctional system is overwhelming. Terrible inner city schools. Single parent households. Lack of academic achievement. Lack of positive male role models. Drugs. Gangs allowed to control entire neighborhoods and even some schools. White eye-witnesses who tended to think all teenaged Black males looked the same. He doesn't claim to have the answer, but he very well knows what the problems are.

A Black teenager in the court system without a connected lawyer is in trouble. It really is pretty true a young Black male is guilty until proven innocent. So many gangbangers have so poisoned the waters so badly that a White jury just assumes a Black guy is a bad guy. Being arrested is tantamount to a conviction. Fair? No one says life or the truth is fair. But this is getting to be a suicide pact.

He fears for the future of entire communities. It is a vicious cycle with no easy way out. He had been lucky even though he ended up a foster kid. His late father had tried to be a good Dad. He knew his Dad loved him. He worked hard to provide for Sunny. He took him to the zoo. He made sure he did his homework. They went to White Sox games and had hot dogs together in the upper deck.

When Sunny was little, his Dad read him bed time stories. He took him to their local Catholic church. He always contributed to the church and expected Sunny to put a part of his allowance in the offering plate also. Admittedly, his Dad tended to sleep through part of the services, but at least he was there showing Sunny there was a GOD he worshipped and something bigger than their little two person world.

There had been a real role model in his life who tried to be a decent one. No Mom, but he had a Dad he saw coming home from work, tired, but glad to see his son. Even tired they would go out and play catch with Sunny's football and shoot hoops at the park. His father didn't let Sunny waste his time watching TV. No TV but Fox Cable news on weekdays. Sunny figured he hadn't missed much by not seeing some meaningless sitcom. He preferred playing catch with his Dad anyway.

His Dad took him to Lake Michigan to fish. Smelt season was great fun. All the guys getting up in the middle of the night to be ready at some ridiculous hour. Then cooking the fish right there on the pier and sharing the catch with complete strangers who shared with them also. Sunny even got his first sip of beer by sneaking a gulp from one of the other guys cans when he wasn't looking. Tasted terrible to a seven year old. Too many kids had no role model to follow and remember. At least Sunny had a memory of a man who loved him and sacrificed for him to make a better life for them both.

But in the library he saw the opposite. The gangs would use the younger guys who could claim to be underage. Who knows, he probably was underage and wouldn't get worse than counseling and home detention. Those gangbangers rarely got what they deserved. Their gang lawyers knew who to pay and how much. Most of the gangs had ties into the city ward organizations and the political establishment. That meant they had ties into the judges, local aldermen and maybe even a few of the Cook County State's Attorney.

Rape isn't a big deal with these kinds of animals. It was probably a gang initiation or something anyway. Probably just teaching them how to rape properly. Rape isn't a sexual crime. It is violence and can be used as a tool. It can be used to maximize the terror and shame. Rape was one tool the gangs used to be sure decent folks, especially women, were intimidated enough to hear no evil, see no evil and not call 911 to speak about evil.

The library was Sheila's favorite hangout. She didn't have a real home or family. Sunny knew she lived with a foster family just like he did, but didn't know anything about how she got there. While he hadn't really known her before then, he knew who she was and she knew who he was.

Sunny was a big time football stud at Mount Carmel and most girls knew who he was. With his physique and his swagger, he was easy to pick out of a crowd. Besides, being a regular at the library told folks he probably was a decent guy and maybe a decent student. It was good cred with the smart girls.

When a seventeen year old girl looked like Sheila, every boy who saw her wanted to get to know her and he would feel like he sort of knew who she was. Not so much her beauty, because she was not really a spectacular beauty in the traditional sense. She was attractive enough for sure. But it was really her ambiance. Great body too! She always had a smile for everyone. She always had something nice to say to everyone. She always was willing to help everyone by letting them take a quick peek at her homework which was always done. Sheila was very academically disciplined.

She also played some mean volleyball for the Mighty Macs. Mother McAuley Catholic High School is a fine school and a real power in all kinds of things but especially volleyball. It is an all-girls school South and West of Mount Carmel where he went. But since they were both foster kids and scholarship kids, they didn't actually live that far apart. That was why he would see her at the library in the evenings when she was studying there.

He really wanted to meet her, but the battle in the bathroom wasn't quite the light hearted, romantic first conversation he had been rehearsing in his mind for months.

Judge McCarthy might have gone a little easier on him if that had been his first violent transgression.

Sheila attended every moment of the trial. Coach Burton, his football coach from Mount Carmel and the big brother Sunny never had, did all he could. Coach knew the Judge and he stood with Sunny every moment. Judge McCarthy and Coach Burton were Viet Nam vets, having met when they were there. They had bonded quickly when they bumped into each other again in Chicago and stayed friends over the years.

Both Judge McCarthy and Coach Burton had fought in the Tet Offensive in 1968. They understood each other. Tet was a huge American victory but at a significant cost. It was also a public relations disaster for President Lyndon Johnson's handling of the war. It demonstrated that Johnson really didn't have the faintest idea how to let his generals win a war. Both men had lost friends, fellow soldiers in that messy last gasp of the Viet Cong. After Tet the Viet Cong were out of existence and the war became the North Vietnamese Army and its Russian and Chinese allies versus the South Vietnamese Army and its American allies.

This was Sunny's third offense. Even reduced to manslaughter, the Judge probably didn't see Sunny quite the way Coach Burton did. But Judge McCarthy had called Coach Burton, the state's attorney and Sunny's attorney into his chambers and knocked heads until they agreed to the Judge's solution.

Sunny had a very good lawyer, one of the many Mount Carmel Caravan alums who had become a Chicago lawyer. Many of the kings of Chicago's court rooms were local boys who had attended one of the fine Catholic high schools in the Chicago area. Judge McCarthy himself was a Fenwick alum. Coach Burton was a De La Salle man.

Many of the lawyers were Old Catholic league football players and had either cheered for Sunny as Mount Carmel fans or booed him because they were loyal to suburban powers like Fenwick, Providence or Loyola or city powers like St. Rita, St. Laurence, De La Salle, Gordon Tech or Brother Rice. But if one of their own was in trouble, there was no shortage of good attorneys willing to help out.

Sunny had trouble with his rage over all of the unfairness that immature teenage boys feel is aimed at them. Not having a family. Being told his mother was probably a prostitute. His foster family were well intentioned, but they just weren't equipped to handle a boy as big, as strong and as angry as Sunny. His funny name. The fact that his father was part Comanche was what gave him the distinctive name. But like any teenager, he worried about the name because it made him different. Once he grew up in the Army, he learned to love the name because it spoke of heritage. His name gave him a heritage he didn't really have. An orphan often needs something to hang his hat on and a Comanche name like SunWarrior was a very big hat rack. That was all he had to hold onto.

His father's sudden death from a heart attack at work when Sonny was still a boy ended any ties he had to anything that could be called a family. He had been a skilled carpenter and a well-intentioned father who made a decent living. But with his death when he was barely forty, Sunny was left with nothing and no one. His almost blonde hair made him the first Comanche warrior since Quanah Parker to have such a light complexion. No one knew for sure, but his light complexion was probably why his father named him SunWarrior. His father was proud of his Comanche heritage, but unfortunately he didn't live long enough to pass most of it along to his son.

Someone had told him his mother had been blond. Rumor said she had been a prostitute. Had drug problems. Never married his dad. He was told she died of a drug overdose. Maybe it was true. Sunny didn't know. It was obvious she had no relationship with Sunny. He never knew her and had no idea if the stories were true. There were all sorts of mixed messages coming from Sunny's teenaged rages.

With his dad's death, their Parish Priest had taken Sunny to Catholic Charities. He bounced around a little with some families in his parish. Well intentioned people but with enough kids of their own and enough mouths to feed. He was essentially a ward of the state under the care of Catholic Charities. Not an easy life but he did have good Christian people who cared and kept him in church and Catholic schools. Eventually he became a foster child in a nice couple's home.

Luckily he had great athletic abilities. He also had dipshit friends who had as many dumb teenaged boy ideas as he did. Also, it turned out he was a pretty good student. His Dad had taught him to read by the time he was five and he had his own library card when he was seven. His Dad taught him to like learning new things. Being a carpenter they had great fun together building race cars for soap box derbies and forts in Sunny's room that he used to defend himself against attacks from those imaginary bad guys that all little boys love to vanquish.

The kid wasn't dumb so maybe the Judge figured an Army drill sergeant might have better luck cracking through his thick skull. Judge McCarthy's tough love turned out to be just the right answer.

Judge McCarthy did Sunny a huge favor. He made him grow up and grow up fast. Being an outstanding, muscle bound jock is one thing. Being a man is another. Drill sergeants specialize in making men, not muscle bound jocks. The Judge allowed him to finish his senior year at Mount Carmel and then off to the U. S. Army.

The drill sergeants that Judge McCarthy imagined would help Sunny learn to control himself did their job and did it brilliantly. A good drill sergeant helps a young man like Sunny realize the sun doesn't rise and set on their ego. No drill sergeant even gives a moment of thought to the excuses you used to think were so important. You are in the here and now and the past is irrelevant.

Becoming a reliable and trustworthy part of a team is far more important than being a star. You learn what to do and how to do it. You also learn to do what you are told and do it immediately. You cut the whining and moaning and feeling sorry for yourself. You realize they aren't being any harder on you than on the next guy. Drill sergeants don't discriminate. Drill sergeants treat all of you like shit.

When it is all over, you know you are part of something bigger than yourself and you're a better person for it. You're proud of yourself and you're proud to be part of the best trained and finest fighting force in the history of the world. And you're glad to get away from those drill sergeants who have used your ass for target practice for their boots for months!

Sunny and Sheila got to know each other and grew close during the trial and the last months of his senior year. Both being orphans and foster kids gave them a unique bond. They seemed to almost grow up together after all they had just been through. They had reached an unspoken agreement they wanted to know each other better.

But first it was off to Fort Benning, Georgia for Infantry Basic Combat Training. Then came Advanced Individual Training. Sunny volunteered for air borne and then ranger training. He graduated near the top of his class in every course.

Sunny had studied Latin and more importantly Spanish at Mount Carmel which was a big help as he advanced. He was in great shape and it turned out his language skills were another asset. Because he was good with foreign languages, he was allowed to volunteer for Special Forces training at Fort Bragg, North Carolina. Eventually he ended up a Staff Sergeant in the Special Forces. Life was good. His life finally had meaning and purpose. He had a military family where he truly belonged.

As a student majoring in elementary education at the University of Illinois in Urbana/Champaign, Sheila had waited for him as he worked off his debt to society. She dated but never met Sunny's equal. As a junior enlisted man during training, Sunny made just enough money to buy Sheila some airline tickets so she could come visit him a few times.

Marriage seemed to be the next step for their relationship that had blossomed. He had just about served his time and they were thinking of him returning home to Chicago when 911 struck. Next was the Defense Language Institute at the Presidio of Monterey and a crash course in the Pashto language. After killing as many Al Qaeda and Taliban as were dumb enough to come near him, Sunny got nicked by a couple of bullets and spent some time at Walter Reed Army Hospital. Once healed, Sunny now with a chest full of medals, decided it was time to return to Chicago, marry Sheila and become a solid citizen. Sunny knew he was eligible for the GI Bill as well as other veteran's benefits and decided college would expand his horizons. Just before he was released from Walter Reed, Coach Burton, leading a bunch of Mount Carmel students on Easter vacation in Washington stopped by for a visit. Sunny's injuries left no serious permanent damages and through physical training and just force of habit he was back in fighting trim.

Coach Burton was a loyal Illini and had sent quite a few of his fine players to Champaign. Next thing Sunny knew he was on the phone with the head football coach at the University of Illinois. The Fighting Illini had just won a Big Ten Championship and Sunny's soon-to-be wife was a huge fan of her beloved Fighting Illini. The coach recruited at Mount Carmel often and decided to take a chance that Coach Burton was right about an Army kid just back from service in Afghanistan. Besides it wasn't going to cost him a scholarship unless it worked out. The GI bill and Sunny's instate student status gave Illinois options to explore.

Sheila knew the coach since she was a very popular volunteer tutor for some of the players who needed a little extra academic help. She went with Coach Burton when he met with the Fighting Illini head coach.

It took a little while, but Sonny got back into top football form. He learned a lot more about how to be a Big Ten linebacker at the school that gave the world Dick Butkus and Simeon Rice, a fellow Mount Carmel Caravan. Sunny played for two different head coaches. Two fine men who kept Sonny on the straight and narrow. He started at linebacker for two years, was second team All Big Ten his senior year and got a degree in history.

From ROTC he was given a special commission as a Captain in the Illinois National Guard. Normally an ROTC graduate, even one with prior service, was commissioned as a second lieutenant. But Sunny's years of previous service, leadership skills in Afghanistan, chest full of medals for valor and competence and special forces training made him a little unique. The Army wanted to be sure they kept him in the reserves or national guard so they extended an offer based on his continuing in the service. Captain Sunny SunWarrior, degree in hand, felt he was now ready to face the world.

His marriage to Sheila was the happiest moment of his young life. But their honeymoon almost killed them both with a week of nonstop doing what honeymooners all over the world do on their honeymoon.

They didn't waste much money on food and didn't get much of a tan because they barely left their room. Getting caught skinny dipping in the middle of the night, not once but twice only added to the fun. That poor little old lady in the next room who happened to look at them on their balcony at the wrong moment almost had a heart attack. She had no idea two people could do things like that in that kind of a position. She was truly shocked. The bell hop who spotted them skinny dipping the second time was still dreaming of Sheila's body years later.

It was a week to remember and how every marriage should start off. For a few days Sheila was downright sore and walked a little funny. After that week, Sheila gave Sunny his nickname, Pervert. He was proud of it, but thought it best not to discuss how he earned it.

Sunny wasn't sure he was quite at the level of a pro football player, so he was all set to try something new when his old Fighting Illini coach, now the Bears offensive coordinator, decided Sonny might make it in the Pros and offered him an invite to the undrafted free agent workouts.

Sonny spent a year on the Chicago Bear's Special Teams and as a backup linebacker. He was way backup and didn't start a single game or play many downs. But between kickoffs, punts and other special team opportunities he got several tackles. He even made a game saving tackle on a punt return with no time left on the clock that had Sunny missed, would have cost da Bears the game. It was against the hated Green Bay Peckers, maybe it was really the Packers, but Sunny wouldn't admit the real name of their hated number one rival.

He enjoyed reliving his one opportunity to catch a kickoff. It was a bad kick on a very windy day, but who cared? Sunny, an up back, caught it. With some great blocking help from his teammates and a lot of luck, he actually returned the kick almost forty yards. He didn't fumble when he was tackled. He had both arms on the ball and held on like his life depended on it. The Bears' star kick returner, a really nice guy, kidded him that he wanted Sunny to give him some pointers on returning kicks. Sunny loved the kidding. Having an All Pro ask for advice, even if he is kidding is great fun.

The Bears had lost quite a few solid role players to free agency after they had played in the Super Bowl and that had given him a chance to have a year he would remember for the rest of his life.

Sunny loved being a Bear, but was smart enough to realize he wasn't quite at the level to make a career of it. A leg wound from Afghanistan kept him from having the top end speed a pro would need to really make it a long career. He figured he was still healthy and didn't want to risk a serious injury from four hundred pound Sumo wrestlers doubling as offensive linemen regularly smashing into his vital organs.

He talked it over with Sheila and they decided it was time to move on. Life was good. The Bears had been an unbelievable opportunity. He had memories for a lifetime. But it was now time to grow up and get a real job.

The Bears organization and players were wonderful to Sunny. They respected Sunny as a teammate and appreciated his heroic service in the Special Forces in Afghanistan. They accepted his decision and wished him well for his future. As a going away present they gave him a framed picture of him running in the midst of his one kickoff return signed by all of his teammates and the rest of the Bears' organization. It remains proudly displayed on his living room wall.

But many of the executives and players said if Sheila wanted to stay as an advisor or cheerleader, it would be OK with them. Everyone loved Sheila. It wasn't just her body, impressive as that was. Sheila just had the ability to make everyone feel important and special and like they meant something big to her. Because they did! Sheila loved everyone and thought well of everyone. Her name should have been Pollyanna.

Coach Burton had helped Sheila while Sunny was gone and Sheila had helped with the Coach's mother whose health was clearly failing. Sheila had been an athletic academic tutor at the University of Illinois and even helped a few of da Bears round off their educations. Her specialty was helping overgrown, muscle-bound galoots learn to speak well and interact with autograph seeking fans. Being big and strong doesn't always give you the interpersonal self-confidence skills you need to make you at ease when totally surrounded by crowds of fans. That was just Sheila being Sheila. Everybody loved her but she loved Sunny.

Sunny had learned to make the best of every situation. He had to. It doesn't get much tougher than when you are sleeping on the ground next to a dusty boulder in Afghanistan waiting for dawn so you can chase down some more Islamofascist murderers. Blazing hot during the day. Cold at night. Crazy Muslim

Taliban wackos all around you. You learn to make the best of it. That isn't optional.

As Sunny tossed on the cot his mind ran over so many of these details from his life. Everyone got nicked a few times. Heck, even Jesus his savior had some bad days! Sunny had made some mistakes, but had far more plusses than minuses in his life. His GOD, a wonderful character of a wife he dearly loved and a challenging job made for a satisfying life. He was content and happy. Of course sleeping on a cot in Cook County Jail, protected by County Sheriff's Police armed with shotguns because he was sent there by a crooked judge was one of the low points. There would be others, but a lot less than the high points.

CHAPTER TWELVE

SUNNY IS GREETED BY MARTA, SHERIFF ELWAY'S beautiful assistant. She is genuinely glad to see him and gives him a big hug.

"Sheila and I have gotten to be great pals and we talked every day so she knew you were doing OK. I took her to lunch just to be sure she knew the Sheriff had your back. She is a sweetheart. You have a wonderful wife. We didn't know it, but we both were Mighty Macs. Small world. I'm so glad you're here. The Sheriff is expecting you." She then got up to lead him through the door.

Even Sunny couldn't ignore someone who walked as competently as Marta. He would have felt guilty if anyone saw him perusing her shapely bottom and over-stuffed blouse. But hey... GOD put beautiful women on the earth to be admired and appreciated and he was just doing his Catholic duty of admiring and appreciating one of GOD's shapeliest creations!!

Sunny turns to Marta "Thanks. You've been great. Sheila appreciated your support."

Marta gives Sunny a friendly wink and leaves the room.

Sunny knows Sheriff Elway is crippled so he hurries over to the desk to shake his hand. "Thanks Sheriff. I appreciate your help."

Sheriff Elway reaches over to shake Sunny's hand. "I had that long chat with Judge Leoni. He is still pissed off at you but he finally relented. I'll have the guys get you out of here by noon so you can have lunch with Sheila. Marta called her and she'll be out front waiting for you."

"It will be nice to see her through something other than a thick glass window. By the way, your guards couldn't have been greater guys. Every one of them. But you might have warned me they were sharks when it came to playing Hearts. Those guys were good players! I'll be paying off my debts for months!"

Both guys chuckle at Sunny's attempt at levity.

"Sunny, let me give you some advice. When your lawyer, Coach Burton and I met with Judge McCarthy those years ago, the Judge was worried about you acting before thinking. You just spent two weeks enjoying the County Jails food and Hearts tournaments for talking when you would have been better to walk away."

"But Judge Leoni..."

"Sunny, Judge Leoni is a Judge. He and his father are important members in good standing in the Cook County Democrat Party. You don't need to trust or like him. He is still a well-respected Circuit Court Judge. He will remain a Judge as long as he wants to. That will be for quite some time. He is what he is. Don't forget he can destroy your life."

"Yes, but he is a crook with ties to the mob and the drug traffickers. We can't survive as a society when people in powerful places are corrupt. We need to attack the problem."

Elway smiles. "Fine, if that is what you think. Just remember, as long as you keep your thoughts to yourself, you're a free man. If you want to keep bad mouthing him you can rejoin the

Hearts tournament at our luxurious County Jail. The guards enjoyed your company and taking your money. Now, is that clear to you?"

Sunny realizes trying to get a stalwart of the most corrupt political machine in America to want to change it is a waste of time. Elway's father was already a leader of the Democrat Machine when Al Capone was the King Pin in Chicago. His father became a millionaire from his political machinations. Elrod couldn't be a nicer man, but a reformer...? Sunny decides this isn't a discussion where he can convince anybody who has been born and bred in the Chicago Democrat Machine to see the world differently. He gives in. "Yeah."

Elway cracks a big friendly smile and waves Sunny off. "Now go get cleaned up so you'll be presentable to take your beautiful and worried sick wife to lunch. That is an order! Now get going."

"Thanks." Sunny shakes Elway's hand and retreats out the door. Sunny is from Chicago and understands perfectly well what he has just been told. Shut up or there will be consequences! He doesn't like it, but there isn't really another option if he wants to get out and stay out of jail.

Now that Judge Leoni has relented and finally let Sunny off on his contempt charge, it is time to get back to the real world. But the Judge refused to reinstate the case against the mobster and also refused to allow the case to be moved to another judge, thus killing the prosecution. Sunny has to shut up to get out of jail. Talk...back to jail. Sunny is dying to talk to someone about Judge Leoni's corruption but for the time being that is not a practical option.

Sheila and the Police Superintendent, Phil Purcell, convinced Sunny he was more valuable on the street. Purcell, always the suave diplomat, told Sunny if he didn't get back on the street pronto he was going to use a cattle prod on Sunny's behind while staking him out in the desert sun naked on top of an ant hill while he was covered with honey. While Purcell knew that may have born a resemblance to a favored tactic of Sunny's Comanche ancestors to use for entertainment on a hot Texas evening, it held no historic fascination for Sunny.

After reading *Empire of the Summer Moon,* S. C. Gwynne's excellent book about the great and also the last days of the Comanche nation, he knew way too much about how his ancestors treated prisoners. If Purcell had read it also, Sunny was going to be in trouble because it explained several more of the Comanche's favorite means of entertainment. None of it seemed to be a lot of fun to Sunny so he decided the better part of valor was to do as he was told and get to work.

He had nothing macho he needed to prove. He wasn't quite that much of a Comanche! Getting back to the street seemed like a far better idea. Besides, Purcell had been a tough street cop in his day and Sunny wasn't all that sure he had been kidding about the cattle prod.

The day Sunny got out of Cook County Jail, the FOP lawyer, Carson Simmons, a nice enough guy with good political connections came to see him. Carson had been told to deliver a message from the powers that be in the Chicago Democrat Machine and Speaker of the House Brennan Burke. Sunny was getting to be a little too high profile for some nobody street cop. He needed to learn his place in life. No more pissing off Stu Black. No more pointing the finger at corrupt Crook County judges. Live and let live in the system Burke controlled. Or there would be consequences. Sunny asked but Carson didn't know what those consequences would be. Still the message was delivered, again.

Sunny asked if Boboleski would be by to check in with him also. He had never even seen Boboleski during the two weeks he was in jail. Not even once. Oh well, Sunny knows what pinstripe patronage is and really asked the question to confirm what he already knew. Simmons admitted Boboleski had received a six month contract for $30,000 to represent Sunny. Another worthless Chicago machine hanger on did his usual nothing to earn the tax payers money he received. Nothing unusual about it.

Carson Simmons reinforcement of the message may not have been well received, but at least it was heard. Sunny had seen good cops get their careers derailed by being too aggressive in areas the Chicago power structure didn't want exposed. Pissing off the big time trial lawyers like Sam Powers, asking about ghost payrollers or noticing the open theft of tax dollars were always bad moves as far as the machine guys were concerned. Your next assignment could be as a crossing guard in Timbuktu.

Sunny thought about it a minute and dismissed the advice he had just been given. It was well intentioned, but... He worked for the citizens of Chicago, not the Democrat Political Machine. He wouldn't go out of his way to get in trouble, but he would never forget who his real employer was. If he never made Captain...well then he'd never make Captain. He'd killed terrorists in Afghanistan to defend his country. He wasn't going to be intimidated by the sleazy Brennan Burkes, Stu Blacks and Judge Leoni's of the Chicago machine.

Sunny returns to duty but has been moved back to uniform patrol. Spending time in the County Jail, even if it is for a good reason had the Internal Affairs Office reviewing his file. Then add the shooting of two gangbangers, even with legitimate grounds of self-defense, had Internal Affairs following up to be sure Sunny is being careful. So just to be safe, Sunny returns to street work for the time being.

Vlad Kozak is also back in uniform and on the street remaining as his partner. Vlad told IA since he had only shot one gangbanger, they should concentrate on Sunny who shot two and leave him alone. As usual, the IA folks had no sense of humor and put Vlad through the same inquisition they were using on Sunny. Nice try, but...

Behind their back, Vlad refers to the IA investigator as Torquemada. A good historian would remember Tomas de Torquemada of Castile as the first Grand Inquisitor, or officially the first Inquisitor General of Spain, during the era of the Spanish Inquisition that started during the later years of the fifteenth century. Torquemada was known as a loving and reasonable man willing to believe the best about the people he questioned over tea and crumpets while sitting in a pleasant outdoor garden. That isn't really true, but that is probably how the Inquisitor General saw himself. Vlad made that up to make fun of his IA inquisitor. Torquemada, known as the Hammer of the Heretics probably preferred other less friendly methods.

A little known fact is that Brother Tomas de Torquemada was actually a bit of a fifteenth century penal reformer. He cleaned up the notoriously filthy Spanish prisons and made it a requirement that prisoners be fed and given adequate clothing. His reforms were so popular that regular criminals in normal jails constantly petitioned the Inquisitional Courts to have their cases transferred there from the common courts so they could be under his authority.

When torture, mangling limbs and major abuse seemed to be an improvement, I hate to think of what the common Spanish prisons and courts were like. True history be damned. Torquemada's reputation as a reformer seems to have faded so much that by 1832 his tomb was ransacked and what was left of his earthly remains stolen and burned to ashes. As Vlad used to say, dust to dust and ashes to ashes. Or maybe it was man to fertilizer or something like that.

After the two of them had enjoyed some of those fun arrests for drunken assaults, drugs and other violent behavior, Sunny was spending some time at 26th and Cal, short hand for the Criminal Courts building, as a trial witness.

The area around the courts building at 26th Street and California Ave. was not the best neighborhood, but in broad day light it was pretty much OK. He had the great new Brad Thor book in one pocket and a spell binding Vince Flynn book in the other. He was set for the trials. If it took a few days, he had some of the best action fiction available and he would just hunker down and read it out. The last thing on his mind was about to be dropped into his lap after someone else tried to knock him over.

Walking down the hall, Sunny almost bumps into Terry Hake, a former Cook County Prosecutor he has worked with. Terry is a great guy and had been a top prosecutor. Now he is a criminal defense lawyer. Sunny couldn't figure that one out. He had more than one chat with Terry about how corrupt they both thought the Cook County, or Crook County as Terry and he called it, Courts were.

The problem was it wasn't just the crooks in the court system. It was the outside influences that protected the crooks also. The Bar Associations who claimed to evaluate judges on their performance never seemed to notice the ones taking cash under the table. Heck some of them took it over the table. Some even had their bailiffs collect it for them out in the hallway. One even sold art work painted by his wife to lawyers who appeared in front of him. The prices were astronomical!

The judges were selected by the local Democrat machine ward committeemen and slated by the county organization. The elections were almost rigged based on who was allowed to run and where. Getting your name on a ballot is unbelievably difficult in Crook County. If the machine doesn't want you on the ballot, you won't be. The Bar Associations would then get the word about who to find unqualified to undermine independent opposition. A totally rigged system and all of the insiders knew it and said nothing. Sunny use to call it Chicago and Crook County's hear no evil, see no evil and speak no evil court system.

Two cases that Sunny remembered well involved organized crime. Chicago is one of the cities the criminals are still well organized in! In one case a known mob hit man had been identified by two eye witnesses literally at the murder scene and the judge released him in a bench trial.

In another, a body builder mobster got off after he had almost beaten a female cop to death for having the nerve to stop him for drunk driving, regardless of the fact he was wandering all over the road and endangering innocent other drivers. It was another bench trial.

In lesser sins, some of the judges spent almost every summer afternoon on the golf course. Many attended big, all day golf and gourmet dinner events paid for by the lawyers who appeared before them and joined by clients who were appearing before the judge and were being represented by those lawyers footing the bill. Of course most people knew the lawyers would bill the client for face time with the judge. Then there were the party bosses who put the judges on the bench and then expected them to help a friend every now and then.

Sunny and Terry were both committed to getting the scum off the streets so the decent folks could feel safe. Sunny just couldn't figure how Terry had become a criminal defense lawyer. "Terry, I heard you had changed sides. Man. What are you doing?"

Terry blushed at Sunny's question but still smiled and shook his offered hand. "Hey, even the scum bags deserve a lawyer and they pay better."

Sunny just didn't believe a first rate guy like Terry Hake could have lost his principles for a few extra dollars. Assistant State's Attorneys didn't get rich, but it wasn't minimum wage either and the health insurance and pension were first rate. "Maybe, but not as good as a guy like you can give them."

"Thanks Sunny. I know what you mean. Hey, how true is the story about Judge Leoni and you?"

Sunny looks all around and then leans in to Terry so he won't be heard. "You didn't get this from me. I've been warned to shut up. But just for your ears...yeah, you heard right. The crooked SOB sent me to County jail for two weeks for calling him on fixing a case. Remember I didn't say a word to you about it."

"That's what I heard. All true? 100% stuff?"

"True as I never missed a tackle or got a penalty when I played for da Bears. You know we should have been back in the Super Bowl!"

Terry, like most Chicagoans, is a fan of da Bears and just laughs at Sonny's often repeated critique of his athletic abilities. Terry pauses and seems to think for a moment. Then he refocuses on Sunny. "Can a friend of mine and I buy you a dinner? Both of us know Sheila's cooking will kill you some day, so before it does, this gives you an excuse to eat your last meal. Besides it might be at Ruth's Chris Steakhouse."

Only a true friend could kid about Sheila's cooking skills. Besides, truth could be its own defense. Sheila was wonderful, voluptuous, vivacious and would break her arm to help a complete stranger. But cook? Health food freaks like Sheila were dangerous. "Ruth's Chris? Do I have to kill anyone to get there? You sure? For the filet and creamed spinach side I'd even kill a few extra scum bags. But you know I'm a cop, so I'll need to limit the pile of bodies to a manageable level. So what's the catch?"

Just as Sunny is thinking he has to call Sheila to let her know he has a business dinner and his mouth starts to water as he thinks of a Ruth's Chris petite filet he can hear a commotion behind him. Terry's eyes pick it up immediately and he half pushes Sunny around to face an armed gangbanger sprinting down the hallway with three out of shape, doughnut aficionado bailiffs in slow pursuit.

The crowds part, heading for the walls to get out of the way. But some aren't that alert or are old and don't move very quickly. In general, the hall way is a mess.

The difficult situation is all to the advantage of the younger, stronger, faster gangbanger. His black and crimson jogging suit flaps open in the breeze caused by his speed. He shoves people out of his way but into the way of the slow moving bailiffs. He is increasing his lead. So far he is actually careful not to hurt anyone and he certainly hasn't shot anyone either.

Sunny, with Terry right behind him, step to the side of the path of the escaping thug and just as he gets close, Sunny ducks his head and makes a perfect, knee high tackle from the side. If he had on a helmet and shoulder pads da Bear's defensive coordinator would have given him an A for form and effectiveness.

Because of the gangbanger's momentum, the two of them go down in a heap and slide a long way across the marble like floor. Unfortunately the gangbanger does not lose his grip on what looks like a Sig Sauer P220. That is a serious piece of armament to have gotten past security. Big gun. Heavy hitting bullets. Dangerous to be on the wrong side of. Not the usual cheap gangbanger piece of crap that was reasonable cost, not that accurate and covered with chrome and stuff to add to its macho effect.

Unfortunately, Sunny slides into an older couple and the three of them end up in a heap with the lady almost on top of Sunny. The gangbanger is luckier. He slides into the wall and only hits a cute young woman who moves quickly to seemingly get in his way. They do a bit of a tango before they can get separated. Sunny is hopelessly tangled for the moment with the older lady who is two inches short of hysterical.

As the gangbanger separates and turns to run the cute young woman quickly moves toward the lady's room.

The bailiffs are lost in the crowd and can't get through very quickly. The gangbanger is on the move as he gets out of the confused crowd. Just as he is about to start running again Terry Hake grabs him in a bear hug from behind. The gangbanger is bigger, younger and stronger but Terry is able to hold him long enough for Sunny to untangle himself from the lady grab his pistol and jam it into the gangbanger's ear.

"Move you son of a bitch and I'll redecorate the wall with that little pea of a brain of yours. Now hand me the gun. Now!"

The three bailiffs arrive. Two have their weapons drawn but the third is unarmed. By now the commotion has drawn the door guards, actual armed policemen and they arrive also. Their weapons are also pointed at the gangbanger.

The young gangbanger quits thinking about his options and relaxes. He is still being held by Terry, but gestures with his hands that he doesn't have a gun and he is submitting. He is being totally cooperative and making no attempt to antagonize the police. Sunny looks at the guys hands and there is no Sig Sauer P220 to take. Sunny looks around quickly but doesn't see anything or anyone who looks like they have the gun. Then Sunny turns back to the gangbanger and starts to recite the Miranda warning. One of the door guard policemen joins in as he slaps handcuffs on the gangbanger in the black and crimson jogging suit.

The bailiffs come close and are huffing and puffing. The crowd gathers around to see what is happening. The other two door guards start to move the crowd back a little to be sure there is room for them to sort out what just happened. The guard who put the cuffs on the gangbanger shrugs at the bailiffs with a what's happening look.

In between huffs and puffs a bailiff steps up to Sunny, Terry and the guard. "He popped up from the crowd and was about to waste one of the witnesses in a Gangster Warlord trial. I saw him, shoved the witness behind the bench and pulled my gun. The guy was about to take me on when someone, don't know who, screamed don't shoot, run. The guy took off like a rabbit." He pointed at the other bailiffs. "The guys heard the commotion, came out to look around and then helped me chase the guy. Now we're here. Right now, that is all we know."

While slowly raising his hands so everyone can see them, the gangbanger in a calm and even voice says "I don't have no gun. I was just pointin' at the witness to say hi. She's an old friend. That's all."

Sunny looks at the guy who looks to be the lead guard. "His gun is missing. Why don't you take him to a lockup until we figure out what happened." He hands the guard his card. "I'm just here for witness duty, so give me a call when you need me. OK?"

The bailiff who chased the gangbanger out of his courtroom also hands the cop his card. I need to get back to the courtroom. It is probably a mess. I'm in 305. Let me know when you need me and I'll come right over."

The cop asks. "The judge OK?"

The bailiff chuckles. "He's a criminal court judge who handles gang crap all the time. He keeps a Smith & Wesson Model 386 Night Guard in his top drawer. He's old military. Don't you worry. Nobody is going to take him out with that cannon in his hand. It's the crowd I'm worried about."

The door guard nods. "Mack, bring the guy with us. Charlie, you head back to keep the door covered. I'll get back to you as soon as I can." He looks at Sunny and the bailiff, "We'll get back to you. Thanks. As soon as our guys arrive, please direct them to look for the weapon."

The door guard yells to get everyone's attention. "Anyone who saw anything, please remain here. I will have other officers here in just a minute to get your names and stories. Thank you for your cooperation. Do not leave this area."

The guard then turns on his shoulder microphone. "We have captured the suspect. His weapon is missing. Need immediate assistance, repeat, need immediate assistance to question the crowd and search for the weapon."

The three police officers move off and the bailiffs round up the crowd.

The attractive young lady who the Warlord gangbanger had bumped into is back from the lady's room and watches as he is led away.

Once the crowd moves off into groups to huddle with the folks who didn't see anything so they can tell their descriptions of what happened, the bailiff looks at the two other bailiffs who helped. "Hey, thanks guys. As soon as the police arrive, you go ahead back. I need to talk to this guy for a moment.

The two bailiffs move off. The third moves to the side with Sunny and Terry. "Hey guys. You know I'm sincere when I say thanks. That could have been a mess if he had to try to shoot his way out of here."

Terry looks confused. "Why was he trying to take out a witness in the court room? Not an easy play. Didn't they think of waxing the witness before that?"

"Witness protection. They couldn't get at her before then. Besides, if you're a Warlord, think of the intimidation factor of blowing away a key witness sitting in the witness box. You'd never get anybody willing to testify against them again."

Terry shook his head. "As a former prosecutor, I know what you mean. I wasn't thinking about witness protection. God would that have stifled any attempts to get a Warlord conviction. But trying to take out a witness here at 26th and Cal. Boy that is as ballsy as I've heard in a long time."

Sunny takes the bailiffs arm. "I don't mean to ask a dumb question, but two of you are armed. That third guy wasn't. Huh?"

The bailiff chuckles. "A real hard core patronage guy. If you ever saw his record, you'd know why they won't give him a gun. He'd never pass the background check. So they keep him in courtrooms that probably won't get dangerous."

"What the hell is he doing here?"

The bailiff chuckles again. "The best precinct worker in the 26th ward. Hey you've been around a while. You know. Some of us get here on the merit list. Some are like him. What can I say? At least he tried to help. I got no beef. None of my business and you know what I mean by that."

Sunny leans in to the bailiff again and speaks almost in a whisper that Terry can barely hear. "I heard one of the shift Captains for the Sheriff's Police doesn't even have a driver's license. Too many DUIs. Yet she's still a Captain and has two county cars issued to her. Drives 'em without a valid license. True?"

The bailiff shrugs again. "She was a big shot in the old Hispanic Democratic Organization before the Feds broke it up. She got the job then with Victor's rec behind her. She's a political heavy. You know in those days Victor got what he wanted. None of my business either."

The police have arrived and are organizing the crowd and getting everything in order. They know what to do and are doing it.

Sunny and Terry give the bailiff their cards and then shake hands with him. "When you need us, we're around. Just call. OK?"

"Thanks. You know we'll have to be back to you. Again, really, thank you. Big Time." The bailiff goes over to talk with the police and then heads back to his court room.

Sunny laughs with a sort of gallows humor ring. "Hey! A little excitement at the office. Still on for dinner?"

"Trust me. I'll pick you up at the parking lot at five."

Sunny said, "See you there. I'll call Sheila to let her know I'm broken hearted to miss that healthy stuff."

Sunny grimaces. "Maybe she'll save me a little."

Sunny may not have been happy about Terry having gone over to the dark side, but he sure was there today when he was needed. But he thought so highly of Terry he figured it would be worth hearing what he was doing and why. Besides, Terry had hinted at a free Ruth's Chris petite filet with a side of creamed spinach and for that Sunny would have thought it well worth listening to even Jack the Ripper explaining the fine art of picking up girls on the street.

As any good detective knows, it is their job to do all the grunt work. All the nasty stuff. Interview the perps and perverts and slime, condense it and give it to the Prosecutor. If the detective did a good enough job of crawling around in the mud with the scum of the earth getting all of the evidence, the people win the case. Then the prosecutor looks like a hero at the press conference without even getting a little dirt on his shoes.

Most detectives understood that and didn't really mind as long as the prosecutor bothered to say thank you. That was their job description. A cop volunteered for the job. It was not a glory job. OK. What Sunny liked about Terry was he got the conviction and was the first guy to call the cop and say thank you, you did a great job. The city and county are safer today because of guys like you. You could tell he really meant it and that made it even more satisfying. That was why Sunny would always give Terry Hake the benefit of the doubt. Of course being bribed with a Ruth's Chris petite filet helps also!

At the restaurant, Sunny and Terry are joined by a guy who looks like a marine drill sergeant. They are sitting in a booth in the back corner of a Viet Namese restaurant on North Broadway. Ruth's Chris was just going to be too high profile a place for this type of meeting.

Sunny is kiddingly working Terry over. "You know Terry, false advertising to a cop can be a criminal offense. Maybe even a capital crime. I'm still looking for the Ruth's Chris Maître D'. Heck, I'd settle for Gibson's. It is first rate also. You know Smith and Wollensky would have kept you off my S list. But instead I'm sitting here playing with my chop sticks. This is a no-no."

Sunny then looks at the new guy and nods. The fellow is trim, wiry muscles, sinewy looking but still powerful in appearance and close to, if not quite six feet. The guy had a square jaw, short hair, almost a flat top and a disciplined manner about him. "I finished with my last drill sergeant a few years ago. Don't want to meet any new ones. By your look, you're ex-military. Your physique looks like Special Forces or Seal or a special operations type. Or maybe a real hard ass drill sergeant."

The new guy smiles, "Yep."

"What branch?"

"Army."

Sunny nods with a smile. "Then not a Seal. When did you get out?"

"A while ago."

Sunny smiles again. "Can't talk about it right? So not a drill sergeant. Ranger? Air Born? Any languages?"

"Farsi."

"Ohhh...big time stuff. Anything else that would impress me?"

The crew cut guy gives Sunny a funny, crooked smile. "Do you have a need to know?"

Sunny chuckles at the classic military non-response. No matter how high your security clearance is, if you don't need to know the information, you won't be told. It wasn't a put down, it was simply a military way of saying it was something best not discussed in public or maybe not at all. If it was classified at that level, you knew it was not something the public would want to consume.

Sunny then nods, "Nope, no need to know."

Terry's friend smiles in return. "What were you? I would say at least a ranger, right?"

"Need to know?"

Terry's friend laughs at the friendly, get even response. "That tells me you have a Top Secret Clearance also. Language?

Sunny nods back to acknowledge the Top Secret. "Pashto and Spanish."

Terry's friend nods with approval. "Special Forces...ranger... air borne...Afghanistan veteran? Probably lots of medals and nasty stories. You're bigger than the average SF. But with Pashto language training you would have been SF. I'll guess you must have been part of the early waves in based on language and how long ago it would have to have been that you went. You've been out long enough to have been a big time Illini and even the Bears. Anything you can tell me without having to kill me?"

Sunny gives a smirking nod. "Nothing I can talk about without making your wife a widow. But, it's da Bears, not the Bears. That shows you're not a native Chicagoan. Accent says the South West. Demeanor says Texan."

"The Hill Country between Austin and San Antonio. Nice little town called Dripping Springs. I admit I cheated a little. Terry told me you were a star with the Illini and played for da Bears. Before my time here. The rest is observation by experience. How old are you?"

Sunny laughs, "Don't know exactly. I wasn't big enough at the time to remember the exact date. Besides it was long enough ago not to matter anymore."

Terry looks at the two of them. "OK guys...enough of this macho military BS. It is obvious you both know enough to be dangerous to some Islamofacist scum. Dinner will be cold by the time you finish showing each other how smart you are. Now let's eat and be macho over dessert."

Both laugh and nod to show they agree.

Sunny says, "OK, no more of this shit for me. So what is this? Some CIA recruitment thing?"

While they all chuckle, there is an underlying tension. The drill sergeant look-alike reaches out his hand to Sunny to shake. "I'm Special Agent Ray Fromm of the FBI's Chicago office."

Sunny laughingly says, "Oh shit, I didn't do it."

Fromm doesn't laugh. "Actually you did and that is why we are here."

Sunny looks at Terry with a 'what is going on here' look.

Agent Fromm looks Sunny in the eye, "You were right about Judge Leoni. He is a major target of our investigation. We believe you can help us."

Sunny is stunned but listens. He detests Judge Leoni and the open corruption he represents. "OK. What investigation? I'm listening."

"Terry is now an FBI agent working undercover in the Cook County Court System. We believe as many as 10% of the judges and a huge number of lawyers are operating a justice for hire ring. The code name is Operation Greylord. We need to have an insider with ears to help cover Terry's back. We also need an insider with many friends to support Terry's cover. We wouldn't mind if that insider was a police officer who could listen to his fellow officers talk about questionable decisions in the courts. Terry tells me he thinks you just might be the guy we need."

Sunny looks at Terry and gives him an approving nod. "This is long overdue. Who knows what?"

"Outside of Terry, the FBI and some senior guys in the Justice Department? No one."

"Will the Superintendent know I'm involved?"

"No one and that includes your wife."

"Sheila is like my second skin. She's me. She is everything to me. That puts me in a tough position."

Agent Fromm pauses and just looks at Sunny for a short while before responding. "You won't be doing anything out of the ordinary for your wife to question. Terry is the mole. You are simply you. We need you to reinforce Terry's cover. You spread a rumor or two about your frustration with Terry going over to the dark side. Listen if anyone says anything about Terry. When questionable decisions come down, you just bitch to the cops involved about getting screwed like you did with Judge Leoni and then listen to what they have to say. That is all you need to do. When it is over, your name won't even come up unless you want it to. You're not going to be mentioned anywhere unless you want to be. You'll be protected and your career won't be harmed."

Sunny looks at Terry "Is this why you left the State's Attorney?"

Terry nods. "I simply couldn't take it anymore. You know what it's like. You weren't in the courts as much as I was, but you have seen plenty of it. They're passing money in the hallways. It is almost like there is a printed pay off sheet. It costs this much to get off for that."

Sunny leans back in his chair and thinks a moment. "Are you going after that mob hit man who got off even with two eye witnesses? You know it was a bench trial? That damn judge is retired on a pension I pay for, living in Arizona right now. The word is the guy he let off is both mob and union muscle."

Agent Fromm smiles, "We know the case well."

Terry looks at his hands for a moment, "That is one of the cases that put me over the line. When mob hit men can kill with impunity, it is time for the good guys to act outside the box."

Sunny smiles, "I should have known. Sorry for giving you a hard time."

Terry puts his hand on Sunny's powerful forearm. "I'm out here alone. I need someone people trust to help build my cover. Someone I know can keep their mouth shut. You know that is what you and I have talked about many times. Will you help?"

There is a long pause. Just silence. Finally Sunny looks at Terry. "You got the tough job man. But I'll cover your back." Sunny smiles and reaches out to shake hands with his new partners.

Terry says, "One of our war time Presidents, I forget which one, said if your enemy is trying to destroy himself, you should get out of the way and let him do it. These crooks are trying to destroy our legal system. That we won't allow. But we'll get out of their way until they have dug their holes so deep they can't get back out. That is the time for us to get in the way and shut these bastards down. These guys are idiots. This system has been crooked for so long these slime balls think they are untouchable. You know the bar associations and the media have been bought off. They think they're immune. They are so open you can see some of the bailiff's actually collecting the cash in the hall ways."

Sunny nods at Terry, but then with a twinkle in his eye, Sunny looks straight into Special Agent Fromm's face and says, "Next time its Ruth's Chris or I'm outta here man!"

CHAPTER THIRTEEN

SUNNY AND VLAD ARE DRIVING ON NORTH AVENUE with the radio talking at them, both guys are listening.

"Alderman Maldonado has requested police at Humboldt Park. There is a big back to school fair going on and he says there is some kind of disturbance. He wants some help keeping it from getting out of hand."

"10-4"

Alderman Maldonado is talking with two officers. One appears to be a big Latino guy named Gilberto Reyes and his partner, a Black woman named Darnell Madison. They are one of those Mutt and Jeff teams. Reyes, big and muscular and Madison short and trim. Sunny and Vlad pull up to the curb on Division Street and join the threesome. They pretty much know Maldonado and nod to the other two cops who are old friends.

"Listen I called for you guys. I need some help. There are a bunch of Puerto Rican volunteers here with that Republican guy who is running for President of the Cook County Board. Israel Vasquez and that pain in the ass Debbie Gordils are with him. Republicans got no business being at a Puerto Rican event in my ward. I want them out of here!"

Reyes looks at Maldonado and then at his partner, Madison. He looks ready to talk but looks at Sunny and Vlad for backup. His partner, Sunny and Vlad nod they're with him. "Alderman... this is a public park. It is reserved for this back to school rally by a huge church so it is technically up to them if the Republicans can be there. Have you talked to the minister?"

Maldonado is getting irritated. "I don't need to talk to no stinkin' minister. This is my ward. This is my park. Attorney General Laura Burke and Governor Quinn are both here. I don't want no stinkin' Republicans near our candidates. Speaker Burke doesn't like Republicans around his daughter. Something embarrassing could happen. I own this territory! Get their asses out of here!"

The four cops all look at each other with that 'what do I do now look'?

Sunny takes the lead. "Alderman, we'll go talk with him and see what we can do. What do you want us to do if he refuses to leave?"

"Threaten him with arrest if he doesn't leave. If that isn't enough, arrest him. Put them in cuffs and take him out of here, now!"

All four cops look like they have been asked to charge hell with an empty bucket but take off in the direction Maldonado is pointing.

Madison nudges Reyes in the ribs with her elbow and giggles. "I'll talk with the guy. I'm on the FOP's political action team. I know who he is. A bunch of the FOP guys are quietly giving him a lot of help. The Lodge won't endorse him for fear of retribution from Burke, but we know him. Good guy but Burke hates him. He got the better of Burke when he put together a coalition of all the Republicans, the Black Caucus and the one Latino. Beating Burke and embarrassing him about

Chicago machine corruption will make Burke a life-long enemy. I'll handle it. You guys just back me up, OK?"

Everyone nods as the Republican candidate comes into view. He is a big, blonde guy wearing a bright yellow shirt with his name on it. He is standing there talking to Governor Quinn, the Democrat incumbent running for reelection. It is a friendly chat.

The Republican is accompanied by ten or more volunteers. The four cops spot Israel Vasquez who has a name tag. Nice looking guy. They spot Deb Gordils in her yellow shirt. She is a firecracker and thoroughly disliked by the Puerto Rican Democrat leadership for pushing Republicans on Democrat turf. She was a cheerleader in high school and has that kind of bouncy, friendly but aggressive personality. Her cute, grade school daughters are with her and they also have on yellow shirts.

The guy Maldonado wants arrested must be six feet five inches or more. He says a friendly good bye to Governor Quinn and starts shaking hands and chatting with lots of mothers and handing literature to them and stuff that looks like candy to the kids.

Madison gestures for the other three to wait while she walks up to the big guy. "Sir, are you aware you are not supposed to be here?"

The big guy nods at Madison with a friendly smile, "No. Free country. Public park."

Madison knows he is right but has to do her part. "This is a private event and you weren't invited."

The big guy smiles back at her. "Public Park. The Pastor who has reserved it knows we are here and it is fine with him. I'm an evangelical and he is an evangelical pastor. I've been to his church. But, if you'll throw out Attorney General Laura Burke and Governor Quinn, I'll leave with them."

Madison knows she is pushing up hill but needs to at least look like she is doing as Maldonado asked. "Are you sure this won't cause trouble? "

"Not my problem. Arrest me if you want. I'll only go if I am in handcuffs. But if you're going to arrest me let me know now so I can call Fox News so they can have a camera here to record it." That is a polite, but firm response. He gestures toward the huge crowd. "I've got to get back to campaigning. I know Candyass sent you. Tell him I politely said I'm staying. Beautiful day. Big crowd. Need to get back to campaigning. Have a great day officers." With that he nods to the police and walks off surrounded by his volunteers.

Sunny, Vlad and Reyes all quietly laugh at Madison. She did what she could. She knew she was wrong but in Chicago you don't intentionally buck a Democrat ward committeeman and alderman on his home turf. She had done all any of them were prepared to do.

Reyes gives her an elbow in the ribs. "Good job, twit. A midget like you really scared him, didn't you? You looked like an ant next to him."

Sunny and Vlad give her friendly shoves like school kids walking away after getting caught doing something they shouldn't have been doing at recess. All four chuckle as they approach Maldonado to get their behinds chewed. They had done their part. Sunny knows he works for the citizens not the Democrat power structure, but after his Leoni incident he wasn't about to start a shouting match here at a public park with the alderman.

Later, Sunny and Vlad are having lunch with a bunch of police officers, Reyes and Madison, McGuire, Burke's driver and escort guy and Patrick O'Donovan, the President of their FOP Lodge. The discussion is heated and is based on the underfunding of the police pension fund and the general lack of integrity in the overall governance of Chicago and the state of Illinois.

O'Donovan raises his hand to silence the group. "Guys... Guys...enough is enough. Aye, we know what we have to do. But I hate to do it. I always feel sleazy havin' to deal with them crooks. That Brennan X. Burke, the Speaker of the House in Springfield never does anything for free. The man has no soul. No principles. No integrity. The right thing means nothing to him. For him, government is his business and he expects to be paid just like he was sellin' a product. That is what it is like."

One of the younger officers breaks in, "Patrick...don't tell us you're payin' those bastards. We know it is Chicago, but we're cops, we don't do that kind of stuff."

"Oh no. If all Burke ever wanted was simply cash, it'd be a lot easier. He wants our souls. He wants me to hire one of his staff attorneys to become our lobbyist to be sure our FOP guys only endorse and support his guys in the primaries and the general elections. He'll make sure on election days we don't monitor certain precincts. If the election judges in the precincts call in, we don't go to investigate. We all know what he's goin' to do in those precincts. That is the type of payment Burke wants. Total subservience."

"Patrick...we're the police, remember? Why do we need one of his weenies to be our lobbyist? Why do we need political direction from Burke? Isn't that your job?"

"I know. GOD I know." Patrick O'Donovan makes the sign of the cross on his forehead and chest. "But Burke is the devil himself. Monty called him the bad twin brother of the Anti Christ. You sleep with him or he rapes you and then slits your throat. He controls everything. Not one of his State Reps will stand up to him. Not one! It is embarrassing to watch. It is like they are all eunuchs."

The group knows what Patrick O'Donovan says is true.

O'Donovan continues. "Illinois is ranked 50th for fiscal policy. We're number one in failing schools. Number one in unfunded pension liabilities. Number one in governors and judges going to jail. We sell state bonds just to cover day to day operating expenses which is unconstitutional but no one says squat. All that and no one does anything but kiss his ass. Who is going to stand up for us if we piss Burke off? If you've got an idea on how else to deal with the crooked bastard, I'm all ears."

"Why don't you give him the business on some of the property tax appeals on buildings some of us own on the side? Maybe let him do the appeals on property the pension funds own. That's really where he makes his personal money isn't it?"

O'Donovan just shook his head. "I suppose I should mention he already has any of them he wants. Some of 'em aren't big enough for him to fool with. That is sort of the minimum. Besides he saves us taxes."

Sunny interrupts "Yea, but he shifts the property taxes from his clients to all of our homes and the rest of the Cook County home owners. He doesn't help the pension fund, he just takes the money out of our pockets. Then the son of a bitch puts one third of the savings in his own pocket. What a crook. How the hell did you guys let Chicago and Illinois get so crooked that a man everyone knows is a crook has almost total control? "

The whole group chuckles at Sunny's kidding reference that they were the ones, not him, who let this stuff happen. No one really bothers to respond because none of them really want to deal with the issue that many feel they are working for an evil empire. It is a legitimate moral dilemma and they all know it.

McGuire breaks in. "Hey guys. Don't get carried away. Burke could hurt us if he wanted to. He leaves us alone and helps when he can. Quit acting like he is the enemy."

All of the officers smirk but no one responds directly. They all know McGuire is Burke's guy and he is just trying to intimidate them into silence.

Patrick O'Donovan just looks at the table. "Don't forget we went to the wall to get his stepdaughter, Laura Burke elected Attorney General. She is so worthless it is hard to believe an Illinois Attorney General could look the other way as often as she does. Here we live in the most corrupt big city in the most corrupt state in the country with two of our former governors in jail at the same time and she doesn't do any public corruption investigations. Her Daddy put her there to make sure no one makes any waves. GOD have we failed."

Sunny, trying not to look too eager asks "Guys are always telling me her assistants are laying down on cases, but I don't follow them that closely. Can you guys think of some case she's thrown or some obvious crap she pulled?"

O'Donovan smiles, "Oh if it were only that easy. She makes the final decisions. She never puts that sort of stuff in writing. Unless you've got something we can implant in her empty, crooked head to read her mind, you can't catch her. She is her daddy's daughter. She thinks just like him. Never write anything down. Keep it all in your head. Remember who owes you and what they have you want. She lives the Chicago system."

"I was about to ask about the Cook County State's Attorney, but I let my mouth move faster than my brain, sorry. If she were anymore worthless they wouldn't pay her salary. Remember that Republican guy running for President of the County Board said we need to ask her if she is for or against crime. Based on her record it isn't obvious whose side she is on. " The whole room breaks out in guffaws.

As they all laugh, one of the other guys said "Remember when he said in the war on crime, she's on crime's side?" Everybody laughs even more.

McGuire cuts in again. "Guys, let's be fair. Her job isn't chasing dumb shit, crooked aldermen. She is supposed to convict gangbangers and stuff like that."

Again, no one challenges McGuire. Why waste time arguing with a machine hack? He isn't going to listen anyway. They are blind to the corruption all around them.

A retired officer, Evangelino Luis Cortez, who had been a member of the FOP pension fund board cut in. "Hey it is fun to laugh at the crooks, but you guys have forgotten how hard it is to say no to Burke's guys. One of Burke's and the President's money guys, Tony Rezko, pushed us hard to hire one of their big contributors to manage $100,000,000.00 of the pension fund's assets. He tried to make an end run around our consultant. His track record just didn't merit us giving him the money to manage. It was a big fight. We ended up giving him some money to manage for the pension fund just to get that Rezko slime ball off our back."

Officer Darnell Madison, still a little sheepish about the embarrassing fiasco at the park with the big Republican guy pipes in. "Isn't Rezko the guy who helped the President get that huge mansion of his in Hyde Park? Wasn't he also our convict Governor Blagojevich's biggest money guy?"

There are plenty of smirks but no response. Everyone knew it was just a rhetorical cheap shot at the crooks running the city and state.

Finally, Cortez chuckles and adds, "You mean the guy in the cell down the hall from Governor Blagojevich and Governor Ryan?"

O'Donovan looks up and winks to Madison but does not respond to her comment. "Oh yeah. You forget the city appointee on the board aggressively suggested we get the money managers to contribute to their list of candidates. We weren't happy about that and didn't do it."

Cortez frowns. "Maybe not, but remember the city guy shook down the money managers on his own and got the contributions out of them? Remember that BS?"

"They said that is how the State and County pension funds operate and we should also. None of our board members got indicted, but the State Teacher's Retirement Fund sure did. They got screwed big time by some board members appointed by Governor Blagojevich who blackmailed money managers to give Blago the contributions and took care of themselves also. It was that Rezko guy again. Wasn't he Obama's big money man in his early days when he was just starting out as a state senator?"

Several guys speak at once. "Yeah."

"Is there nothing they won't stoop to? I was sick to see Governor Blago's guys ripping off a bunch of little old lady retired school teachers. We fight them, but they are on us constantly. Burke's guys never quit. They want a piece of everything. Nice thing is Blago's guys got caught and all of them went to jail. But Burke is immune. I always wondered why he is immune while there is slime all around him?"

Cortez nods but cuts in. "Remember Blago's number one guy committed suicide before they sent him to jail?"

The group nods. The guy was a crook. But the thought of suicide to avoid prison was a tough option.

O'Donovan gets serious. "This is Chicago in Illinois. What do you expect? But the real issue is when did we, the law enforcement folks, become the protectors of Chicago's crooked political class? Anybody who has a brain knows these guys are stealing us blind, but who can we get to stop it? The city is broke and the state is in worse shape. Our pension fund is broke, but it isn't as bad as some of the others."

"Patrick, you're our political guy. Screw the money issues. We're already screwed on that. What do we do to change the way things are going?"

O'Donovan shrugs with a hopeless look on his face. "Any voter who could read knew Blagojevich was a crook and under investigation in 2006 when he was running for reelection. He had a competent primary opponent and an experienced Republican who had won three state wide elections as Treasurer and the voters reelected him knowing they were voting for a crook. How do you change things when the voters of Chicago and Cook County give such massive majorities to openly corrupt candidates? There aren't enough voters down state to overcome the Chicago majorities."

Cortez waves the group to silence. "You know the Democrats in the State Senate went 100% with Blago. Every one of them did his bidding and the voters still reelected them." Cortez sips his drink and in a conspiratorial voice continues. "Remember when Barack Obama was a State Senator. He voted with Blago 100% of the time. That is unless he was asleep and his seatmate voted him present. Chicago voters don't care. Hell, America's voters don't either. They elected him President and he never even sponsored a bill of any significance in Springfield or Washington."

The whole group grumbles, but they all know O'Donovan and Cortez are right. Anybody who paid any attention knew Blago was as crooked as a dog's hind leg. But he still won by big margins.

Cortez continues, "The funny thing is the only reason they finally cracked down on Blago was because he tried to sell Obama's vacant Senate seat. Hell, Burke has been selling judgeships, legislative seats and special interest favors for years. Why be offended by Blago? What did he do that the rest of his buddies weren't doing?"

The whole group sniggers. No point in answering. They all knew it was true.

"I heard Burke had one of his guys put in a special amendment so the lobbyist for the Chicago Teacher's Union could be in the Teacher's Retirement Fund without being a teacher and not having been a member before. One day as a substitute teacher and he is in for life. He vested immediately. One frickin' day! Over the years, he'll draw a couple of million from the fund but Burke doesn't care. His attitude is when it all goes to hell he'll be retired. He's a multimillionaire. He's stolen enough he'll be financially fine. He doesn't care about his government pension. It won't happen on his watch."

O'Donovan nods. "It's true. He did it and then acted like he was shocked it happened!"

McGuire interrupts again. "Hey, don't blame Speaker Burke. He didn't sponsor the amendment. The Chicago guys wanted it. It is not his fault. He was just helping out the Chicago guys."

Again, McGuire is ignored with smirks.

From the back another older guy asks in a very gruff voice. "Patrick do we have anybody in our fund we don't know about?"

There is a very long pause.

This time there are several voices. "Patrick? Answer the question."

Another long pause.

Patrick finally answers. "Yeah, we do. Not as bad as that. The union officers and some guys who aren't cops anymore are in even though they are supposed to be on a union plan, not the city police plan. The city plan gives them a chance to maybe double dip a little. I'm not sure how it works. That is happening."

The whole table groans.

"The union guys negotiate our union contract and got the city to allow it. Nobody ever talks about that stuff. But Burke's guys in Springfield had an amendment that would have over ridden the city contract anyway if the city hadn't done it first."

Another round of groans.

Sunny cuts in to ask a question. "Who fed the corruption stories about Brennan Burke to the New York Times? They ran that whole series about him and his fixes in the property tax system. The articles showed how Burke and his buddy, Juan Cordova on the property tax appeals board were driving a truck up our asses. Burke is making millions screwing the people he is supposed to represent. Yet nothing happens. It's not like the New York Times would write an entire expose about a Democrat unless he was really filthy. They wrote it. Yet, still nothin' happened."

McGuire doesn't give up easily. "Burke is a business man. He is a lawyer and he is smart. Are you saying he doesn't have the right to make a living?"

Again, McGuire is ignored by everyone.

O'Donovan nodded, "You notice no one picked up on it. Not the Attorney General or the State's Attorney. Burke is just too vicious for anyone else to challenge him. He is so petty if you cross him nothing you want will ever pass in Springfield, ever. They don't come any tougher. We all know it. Have you noticed Burke never appears on TV or the radio. He always sends some flunky to spin for him, usually that ahole, Stu Black. He feels he doesn't have to answer to anyone."

For the first time Vlad pipes up. "Ask Sunny about Stu Black. He loves to goon the sleazy jerk."

The whole group laughs. Most of them have heard of some of Sunny's attempts to bring the machine big shots down a little to the level of mere mortals.

Even McGuire chuckles about Stu Black. Everyone knows he is an obnoxious jerk.

"Patrick you're forgetting the Attorney General is his daughter and the State's Attorney owes her election to him. He is vicious but he also knows how to stack the deck."

"True."

Gilberto Reyes pipes in. "Petty? I got a call from Alderman Candyass Maldonado's office to take some guys to Humboldt Park and kick some Republican out of the park. It was a big festival thrown by a local mega church and the machine pols were there campaigning. This Republican guy had the nerve to be there with a bunch of supporters, just like the Democrats and Maldonado wanted him out. Sunny, Vlad and Madison were with me."

Cortez cracks a mischievous smile. "You had 2½ helpers?"

The whole crowd guffaws. Everyone likes Madison, but she is really short and regularly catches tons of friendly grief about her size. She looks at the group with a big smile and flips all of them the bird with both hands. The group keeps laughing.

Finally one of the guys gets serious and asks, "What'd you do?"

"We went. We talked to the Republican. We tried to muscle him. He was nice but told us he had no intention of leaving a public park unless we threw out the Democrats also or the Pastor told him to leave. He wouldn't go unless we arrested him. The Pastor was fine with the guy and we weren't dumb enough to ask the Democrats to leave. What could we charge him with? We had to leave the guy and his supporters alone. What else should I have done?"

"You chicken. If you're going to be a political pimp, at least do your pimping without peeing down your pants leg." Everybody has a good laugh at Reyes expense.

With a smile on his face, Reyes explains, "Look he was talking to Governor Quinn when we came up to him. How was I supposed to kick him out when he was standing there talking to the Democrat governor?"

"So? What'd Candyass do?"

"Candyass was livid. Said Burke would be mad as hell for us not doing our jobs since his daughter was there campaigning and he didn't want any Republicans near her. Someone might raise the issue of why she never went after corruption in Chicago. She is a total wimp about official corruption. Hates to be challenged about anything like that because everyone knows she has no answer other than she is one of them. She hates debates and ducks them if she can. Terrified to answer tough questions. What were we supposed to do? Those guys are unbelievable."

"Remember her dad owns everything and everybody. Just ask his guys. He even picks most of the judges, has full control of what they get paid and what their pensions will be. So even if we had a prosecutor, what difference would it make? He owns the judges. How the hell do you stop him?"

Sunny shrugs. "Speaking of prosecutors, did you guys see Terry Hake quit to become a criminal defense lawyer? I can't believe it. I always thought he was a decent guy. I jumped on him about it and he said it was better money. Man...that was a shock." Sunny said nothing more.

"Yeah. I hear ya. I was as shocked as you. Sunny, that is kind of like you and Vlad going and joining the Gangster Warlords as field commanders. You guys in black and crimson jump suits and do-rags on your ugly, shaved heads!"

A collective groan goes up as everybody in the room thinks of Sunny and Vlad in do-rags.

Patrick O'Donovan smiles at the thought. "Sunny, you'd look good in black and crimson."

Sunny flips all of his pals the bird with both hands.

Another round of laughter.

O'Donovan gets serious again. "But think about it. The gangs use guns, but don't steal one hundredth as much as Burke and his lawyers and his political buddies do. Burke wants us to pay his weenie $100,000 and he'll be part-time lobbyist! At least the gangs didn't make the schools useless or raise the income tax 67% or bankrupt our state's pension funds or drive so many companies out of Chicago. That was Burke and his political buddies. I'm not all that sure the gangbangers are worse than Burke and the politicians."

As they all leave, McGuire catches Sunny and Vlad just outside the door. "You guys aren't being fair to Speaker Burke. Running Illinois is a tough job."

Both Sunny and Vlad look McGuire in the eye and just nod. Neither speaks. They just move on toward their car.

McGuire watches all of the cops leave. He is standing alone by the door. No one makes any attempt to be friendly or to chit chat with him.

CHAPTER FOURTEEN

SUNNY AND VLAD WALK INTO THEIR CAPTAIN'S office. They both doff their hats and do grandiose bows like French Musketeers of the 17th century.

Vlad straightens up, snaps his heels together and comes to a stiff attention position. "Herr Commandante, your peons await your every command!"

The captain laughs at them and just shakes his head. He is used to the playful disrespect. "OK you worthless pond scum, I have someone you both need to meet. She seems to have found some stuff about the Gangster Warlords drug transportation system running through Des Moines. That is in Iowa for you illiterate twits."

With a broad smile, Sunny intentionally looks confused. "Iowa? What's that?"

"All right morons, enough of that crap. It will be tough, but could you both please pretend you are competent police officers and don't embarrass Superintendent Purcell and me. OK? She is Detective Tiffany Burroughs-Rea. You'll get along great with her. She is ex-military. The Des Moines Chief said she was in Afghanistan at the beginning. Now get out of here and pick her up at Lt. Dornan's office."

Both guys looked stunned and turn around to leave. Nothing said.

"Remember try not to embarrass us. The guys in Des Moines didn't need to reach out to us. They are trying to be helpful. They mistakenly think you may be competent. Act like real police officers, OK?"

As soon as they are out the door and close it, Vlad grabs Sunny by the arm and pulls him aside. "You've got to handle this. I'm not feeling well. I'll catch up once you are done."

Sunny looks almost as distraught as Vlad. "I can't, you've got to take it. I've got a meeting. Call me when you're done."

Both just look at each other.

Sunny's face makes him look like he is in pain. "OK Vlad, what is your problem? This is serious, I can't be involved."

Vlad just looks stricken. "Remember I told you about that really helpful three week long drug trafficking seminar in DC I went to a while ago?"

Sunny nods affirmatively. But he still looks very nervous.

"The one I thought was so helpful. Maybe I forgot to mention I had this, ahhh, this friend there. We had a lot of fun. You know just some dinners, museum visits and movies on the middle weekends. Nothing much, really...just friends."

Sunny cracks up. "You mean Detective Burroughs-Rea was your, ummm, how do we say it, your friend?"

"She was just Officer Tiffany Burroughs from Des Moines then. She was single. I swear it. We were both ex-military. Both Midwestern. She had a great personality."

Sunny starts to laugh. "You dipshit. Caught in the act. No chance at denial."

Vlad looks embarrassed but nods.

Sunny chuckles and says, "You're as big a dipshit as I am. We have the same problem. Remember I told you about this really fun Intel Sergeant who was my, ummm, pal in Afghanistan. The one with the serious knockers and some amazing moves that could wring it out of you? Don't forget Sheila and I weren't even engaged or anything so it was OK."

Vlad starts to giggle. "Oh my goodness, Sergeant Tiffany Burroughs? That's right, she had been in Afghanistan. She did have some great moves. Oh yes she did! What a body."

Both guys just stand there and laugh. Sunny leans on Vlad as they both are shaking they are laughing so hard. "We are up shits creek. Without as much as a paddle."

Vlad keeps chuckling but manages to talk. "We might as well go meet the lady. She actually was a neat lady. Real sharp. That was what attracted me to begin with. It wasn't just, what did you say, the serious knockers? Maybe she remembers both of us kindly? We had a lot of fun together."

"Keep a straight face. As I said, I really did think she was neat and a fun person to be around. But if you say one word of this to Sheila, you are dead meat. Dead, you hear me? One word and you'll have to eat Sheila's cooking for a year."

Vlad chuckles at the thought of a year of Sheila's terrible cooking, but nods. "There are some things a gentleman does not speak of in front of his partner's wife. Period!"

The two pals head off to Lt. Dornan's office and knock on the door. Inside, Dornan, in his mid-fifties and balding, but still trim and official looking waves for them to come in.

Sitting in front of his desk is an attractive, strawberry blonde woman who looks around thirtyish. She stands up. Taking a long look at her athletic frame is clearly worth the time. As Sunny said, she has some serious knockers. It is obvious she is a lady who can catch a man's attention if she wants to. But she is also radiating a reserved, demure message to say look, but that is it. She also is wearing a very obvious wedding ring.

As Sunny and Vlad walk in the woman breaks into a huge smile that almost covers a deep blush.

Detective Tiffany Burroughs-Rea reaches out her hand to shake Sunny and Vlad's. "When I realized who I would be working with I can't tell you how excited I was. I figured it had to be you two. Where could I find two more professional gentlemen?"

Sunny and Vlad look totally relieved at her friendly, but professional response and both shake her hand with warmth and familiarity. She clearly remembers them with fondness, as they also remember her. The relationships had been hot and heavy for the time involved. But neither of them or her either had taken advantage of the other. They had fun times together in a faraway world where they thought they would never see each other again.

But that was then and this is now. Everyone smiles and it is clear Detective Burroughs-Rea is carefully setting everything up to be professional and friendly, but that was the limit. This is to be now and nothing else. A very professional overture in a compromised situation for all three of them.

It is obvious to Lt. Dornan the three know each other. "OK you thugs, tell me what is going on? You all look like there is some little conspiracy going on here. Keep your lieutenant up to code here."

Tiffany turns to Lt. Dornan and says, "Sunny and I met when we were in the Army in Afghanistan and Vlad and I attended a drug trafficking school together. They were both quite sharp and left a positive impression on everyone who met them."

Sunny and Vlad look more relieved than a Western gunfighter just granted a reprieve from the hanging noose.

Lt. Dornan just shakes his head. It is obvious he doesn't really want to know any more. "Whatever. Why don't the three of you take the East conference room? Detective Burroughs-Rea seems to have come across some stuff that might be very helpful."

The three officers nod and turn to leave.

Dornan continues, "Hey, since you two jug heads have been pretty much point on a lot of the Gangster Warlord stuff, this seems to be a match made in heaven. Now get to work. She has some great stuff that will be very helpful and you're going to need to respond. The Captain said you guys can work through dinner if you need to and it is on us. But Sunny, don't give me that Ruth's Chris crap. Try China Town or if you want, Greek Town. You know we have friends at the Greek Islands and the Parthenon, but don't get carried away with the tax payer's money. Flaming Saganaki is OK, but no Ouzo."

Sunny nods. "Thanks Lieutenant. You are just too generous. If you want we'll just do Taco Bell and drink water from the fountain. You know, I like the Chalupas? Or maybe just some stale bread with the water from the bath room sink will hold us?"

Lt. Dornan laughs and waves them off. "Get outta here before I throw you out."

The three retreat, giggle and head down the hall to the conference room. Vlad opens the door for Detective Burroughs-Rea and bows at the waist as he holds the door. When Sunny tries to go in, Vlad hands off the door to Sunny and laughing says, "What, you think I'm your slave?"

All three sit down and there is a pregnant pause. Detective Burroughs-Rea smiles and finally speaks. "OK, it's Tiffany and I can't believe my bad luck the two of you ended up partners. I have wonderful memories of both of you. But that was long ago. That was one great husband and one darling little boy ago to be exact."

Sunny and Vlad smile at the friendly, but clear way she establishes a professional boundary.

"Ditto and for me that is one wonderful wife ago also," Sunny says. He pokes his thumb at Vlad and with a laughs says, "For him it is zippo. He still hasn't grown up to face reality. Same old reprobate."

Vlad shrugs with a cute, self-depreciating nod.

"Sunny, let's see, last time I saw you was just as they were loading you on your way to the medevac plane back to Ramstein. You didn't look very good. Don't look much better now." Everyone laughs at her friendly insult. "Obviously you recovered. I had heard you were OK. I never thought some Taliban twerp could do you much harm. By the way, I always assumed that sorry linebacker with Illinois and inept special teams guy with da Bears was you. Right?"

Sunny laughs. "Spoken like a true Packer's fan."

Tiffany looks hurt. "How could you question a good Iowa girls loyalty to da Bears? Screw the Pack! And I'm a proud Hawkeye now. Thank you to the GI Bill. I even saw your pathetic efforts on the field against my Hawkeyes!"

Sunny sits up straight in his chair and playfully puts his nose in the air. "I think I remember something like a ten tackle game with a quarterback sack against those buzzards!"

"Just luck. Most of them were just my guys tripping over your prostrate body lying in the way! You were so slow the quarterback was just taking a break for lunch when you bungled into him. Sheer luck. But, you know, I actually enjoyed seeing you play. Brought back some nice memories. To my chagrin and the shame of a loyal Hawkeye, I actually cheered for you."

All three smile with a distant pleasant memory type of look on their faces.

"I heard you were both detectives but some judge gave you the opportunity to spend more time on the streets as uniforms again. The judge seemed to think it was an insult to be called a fixer judge? Lt. Dornan said you will be back as detectives soon.

CHICAGO CONFIDENTIAL | 159

He said it will be a sorry day for mankind when you are returned to detective status, but there was nothing he could do about it."

The guys laugh at the Lieutenant's jest but nod in agreement.

Tiffany takes a long look at Vlad Kozak. "Vlad, I won't call the vice squad on you. That is as far as I'm willing to go!"

All three just laugh as the ice totally melts.

"But I am here for a reason. If either of you are as sharp as the Lieutenant says, which I doubt, I think I have a real breakthrough. I was following some fairly big drug shipments into Des Moines and as far away as the college towns of Iowa City, Ames and Cedar Falls. We didn't just want the drugs and the delivery boys, we wanted the suppliers. Next thing we know I have caught up with some guys in black and crimson from Chicago. Some seriously bad guys."

Vlad nods, "Ah yes, our beloved Gangster Warlords. We always knew they were involved in bigger stuff and in a bigger arena, but there is so much here, we really hadn't had a chance to follow them West. Now you do know we busted Akile Fort for Murder One, right? But another of our judiciary's finest put him on bail."

Sunny adds, " Some lady Alderman and his lawyer swore Fort was the only means of support for his aged, Alzheimer ridden mother. A million dollar bail for him would have been pocket change, but the judge only asked for a hundred grand! Do you believe that? A hundred grand bail for murder one. His lawyer had him out before I was home for dinner."

Tiffany nods. "When I couldn't find a guy, a reliable and in-the-know informant we really liked, I put together the fellow minus the fingers, nose and ears as our key informant. As his fingerprints probably told you, his name was Keshawn Okambo."

Sunny and Vlad nod to acknowledge the facts.

Tiffany continues. "Actually a pretty decent guy. Deserved better. He had been a really bad actor, but was seriously trying to clean up his act. We were going to get him into witness protection with the FBI once we put together all of this stuff outside of Iowa. Unfortunately, your Gangster Warlords beat us to it. It tore up his poor old grandmother. She had prayed over that boy for years and when things where finally going her way she was overjoyed. She had her entire church and her pastor praying."

Vlad agrees. "We try to never give up on these guys. All of a sudden, one day it dawns and... Never know when or why."

Tiffany nods, "Maybe the key, I don't know, but maybe was when he met the guy his grandmother claimed was his biological father. The guy had just gotten out of prison on parole after 20 years. He was a new man. Became a Christian from the Kairos Ministry. He assured Keshawn he could start over. GOD did really forgive. He made Keshawn a believer in second chances. It was really an amazing event."

Vlad looked pained. "Wow! Great story, but believe me Tiff, you are glad you didn't have to see his body. It was brutal. Several of the guys blew lunch looking at him."

Sunny agrees, "As bad as I've seen since Afghanistan"

Tiffany grimaces. "I couldn't believe how much he changed. Once he made up his mind to get out of the gangbanger life, he really turned it all around. I was kind of proud of the guy. I really hoped he could make a new life. But, that said, we think he was on to something and that's why they took him apart. The Warlords wanted to know what our guy knew and who he had told it to."

Sunny's face lights up. "So that is why the big kahuna himself was there." Sunny nods to Vlad who also realizes this could be a breakthrough. "Multistate! Maybe we'll get Ruth's Chris out of this yet! We get the FBI in and they have a budget for this type of information sharing."

Vlad looks at Sunny cross wise. "Ah, we hit on the chink in the armor. If you ever ate his wonderful wife's cooking, you would know why he is fixated on Ruth's Chris steaks."

Both chuckle but then get serious. "You know we took a ton of their really good stuff out of some shipping containers on the West Side. It was already cut and all packed up and ready for delivery. That is where we found the various parts of your poor informant's remains. I don't know if you heard, but the little grandmother who called it in and her grandkids were brutally murdered for letting us know about the stuff."

Tiffany pulls a file out of her briefcase, puts it on the table and opens it. "Sorry about the lady. Whew. These are bad guys and I'm not surprised. But, yes you did take a bunch of their best stuff and there were ripple effects all the way back to our little burrow of Des Moines. But from what I've dug up, I think you got their hors devours and you pissed off the big dogs by stealing it. What our guy was on to seems to be tons of this stuff coming up a pipeline out of Mexico to your boys here to distribute. But it is kinky."

Tiffany turns the file for Sunny and Vlad to see.

"The word is there is some kind of a profit back guarantee. It is supposed to be so pure it is worth multiples of normal. The cartel is shipping the rest of it at a discount but want a premium once it is sold. Supposedly it costs so much the Warlords didn't want to come up with the cash up front to cover, so the cartel extended credit. But they have to get the cash back to Mexico within a week or two or the boys will come after it. I think we're looking at a possible drug war and you guys just bungled onto the first part of it."

With humor in his voice, Sunny clarifies Tiffany's comment. "Bungle? It was spectacular detective work by the modern day Sherlock Holmes and Doctor Watson."

Vlad isn't in to the humor and looks less than pleased. "Oh oh. This doesn't sound good."

"You just took the cash out of the cartel's pocket and they're pissed. They may not know your names yet, but they will. After they mangle a lot of Warlords to make their point they usually come after the police to raise the intimidation factor. You're the guys they'll be looking for."

Sunny just nods as he looks at the ceiling. "Great. Just great."

"Remember those 'Fast & Furious' guns that crossed the border and the idiots at Obama's Department of Justice let them go without a trace. You may be about to see some of them make a return trip in your good old home town. We've got a week or so and then they'll be here asking where their money is. The Santa Muerte Cartel are not nice people, they have Fast & Furious guns and they will want to ask you a few questions about what they think you stole from them."

Vlad looks at Sunny with a quizzical expression.

Tiffany says it again. "Maybe you're not hearing me right. We think they are going to be looking first for the Warlords. That is why your kissin' cousin Akile Fort was personally involved in the dismemberment of Keshawn Okambo. Based on what the guy told us, once the Santa Muerte Cartel finish with the Warlords, they like to go after the police. Sheer intimidation."

"That is unusual"

"Yes, but why do you think all of those Mexican cops and army types wear balaclava masks to cover their faces? They'll go after the guys and then their families. These Santa Muerte guys are missing lots of the essential parts that go with being normal human beings. I can't stress that enough. Once Santa Muerte finishes with your gangbangers they will want to look you up. Intimidation is their biggest tool. You know they have scattered thousands of bodies, yea, thousands and they have scattered them around Northern Mexico to make a point. They like folks to know they are not people to mess with and you just messed with them."

Sunny smiles at Tiffany. "I appreciate you being the messenger. Any time you want to rain on my parade, please give me a little advance notice, OK?"

Vlad thinks a moment. "I have no one to worry about. But should Sunny get Sheila to go visit a friend in Alaska for a few weeks while we sort this out?"

"When we got this info, I didn't know who the Chicago cops were who were involved. That is why I am here, to give a warning. I didn't really care which of the Warlords they were pissed at. They could kill them all for all I care. Let me assure you I was as shocked as you are to realize it might be you they will be looking for. That was when I heard you were married. Sunny, getting your wife out of town might not be a bad idea. Let's start to look at how we get ready for their arrival."

Sunny is deep in thought. "I want to say I'll be able to protect Sheila, but knowing these guys reputations, maybe I better take your advice and get her out of here."

CHAPTER FIFTEEN

CHICAGO SUN TIMES REPORTER MASON HUNTLEY IS going to be late to work and he knows it. He had been covering a late night local meeting with the alderman. He waited until the end to talk with Alderman Suarez. The alderman said he hadn't had dinner and why didn't Mason join him for a "dog" at Michael's, some of the best dogs in a town famous for great dogs. Unlike many of the aldermen who wouldn't be trusted as crossing guards, Alderman Suarez was very helpful and a fun guy to talk with. But getting home way past midnight, full of hot dogs, fries and beer was just too late. Mason had left a message for his editor and said he'd be a little late.

As Mason walks to the "L" train he passes a gas station. In the parking lot are two trucks just idling. Mason wouldn't have thought anything of it except both had signs saying they were part of the City of Chicago Hired Truck Program. Sitting in the trucks were two sleeping drivers with doughnut bags on the dash boards. Mason pulls out his cell phone, calls his editor and tells her what he wants to cover. Next thing he knows he is on assignment and he'll be even later than he is now.

Across the street is a Dunkin Donuts and Mason decides he will have an apple fritter and some good coffee. He will just see how long it takes for the trucks to do anything. He writes down all of the pertinent information about the trucks including their license plate numbers and the Hired Truck Tags.

Not bad. On assignment and having an apple fritter and an extra-large coffee at Dunkin Donuts. This is the good life. Mason pulls out his *Chicago Sun Times* and settles in to wait.

Two hours later Mason realizes this might be an all day job. One of the drivers still isn't awake yet. He calls his editor again and asks her to review the rules for how trucks get hired and what they are supposed to be doing.

She gets back to him to confirm the program was set up to save Chicago money by not having to buy so many trucks that would just sit around. The city can always lease the trucks when needed. It let the private business folks take depreciation which the city can't do which reduced the costs. Plus a guaranteed contract with some of the firms could supposedly be a way to save even more. The trucks are paid over $50 an hour at a minimum.

That might be reasonable if they are actually doing something. After six hours of sleeping and eating doughnuts in the morning and sub sandwiches for lunch, Mason asks his editor to send out a photographer and he begins to wonder what these trucks are actually supposed to be doing for their $50 plus bucks an hour.

As Mason ponders the utility of taxpayer funded trucks idling all day doing nothing, he sees Detectives Ross "Sunny" Sun-Warrior and his partner Vlad Kozak stop their car across the street and walk into a building. Mason knows Sunny and Vlad to be straight cops and decent guys so he walks out and waits for them to come out of the building.

In about 20 minutes Sunny and Vlad come out. They look a little worse for wear. Mason walks up, "Hey you guys look like

you just got your asses kicked by some out of sorts housewife."
Both guys laugh and shake Mason's hand.

Vlad straightens out his bullet proof vest and says, "I wish it weren't that obvious. She had her husband locked in the hall closet and she was threatening to remove parts of his body with a kitchen knife. A domestic situation and we had to sit her down and ask her to behave."

Mason laughs and asks "Did the enraged lady not wish to cooperate?"

Both guys laugh and say in unison "No shit."

Vlad continues, "GOD I hate these things. You never know when one of them will pull a gun or knife or he's high on PCP or who knows what. What a pain."

"I'll let you two recover your shattered dignity on your own if you'll give me a piece of info."

Both look at Mason and Sunny says. "You know everything we know is very valuable information and it might be illegal for us to tell you shit." Both chuckle and Sunny follows up with, "But if you throw in an apple fritter for each of us, we'll think about telling you what we can."

"Fair enough." As they walk to Dunkin Donuts Mason asks "You guys know this area like the back of your hand. Are there any city construction projects around here right now? Streets and San', sewer work, park district or anything else? "

Sunny looks at Vlad and both think a moment. "No. Nothing I can think of. But let me make a quick call." Sunny calls in and asks his dispatcher. "Nope, nothing."

Mason pays for the Dunkin Donuts and says "Thanks...you've been a big help." As Sunny and Vlad head for their car Mason dashes back to a table in the Dunkin Donuts. He quickly sits down again and notes there are no city projects anywhere near the two trucks that have not moved in almost seven hours. After writing his notes he heads for the L train and his office.

As they drive away Vlad turns to Sunny. "I wish to hell we hadn't bumped into Mason. I really would prefer there wasn't a witness. Especially a reporter. You think he bought that domestic violence line?"

"Sure. You looked like shit anyway. You really did look a little like some PCP deranged lady had been beating on you."

Vlad grimaces at the reference and rubs a sore spot on the side of his neck. "Yeah. That son of a bitch caught me a couple of good ones before we finally got the cuffs on him. I didn't think our Warlord informant would be up and around this long before dark. Guess that proves he isn't a vampire. He could have just given us the information and saved himself the pain."

Sunny nods. "Yea, but look at what we got out of him. I think Tiffany is right. That guy is clearly afraid of something. What I didn't pick up on immediately is his reference to the Insane Jaguars. Are you thinking what I am? The Jaguars have some ties into that Mexican cartel and will be part of the retribution?"

"I think you might be right. This just keeps looking worse. Warlords and Jaguars don't like each other. Both think they're the big bangers in Chi town." Both think for a moment. "But let's give Mason some help to keep him from wondering what we were doing."

Sunny thinks a minute. "Good idea. Tracing a few trucks for him won't be that big of a job."

The next morning as Mason walks toward the L train his cell phone rings. The number on the caller ID looks familiar, but he doesn't quite recognize the number so he just takes the call. "Hello, this is Mason Huntley."

"I know who it is dickhead."

Mason cracks up. He knows the voice but decides to play dumb. "And who is this pleasant gentleman who insults me this early."

"Thank GOD you're not a cop with a memory like yours. It's me, Sunny."

"Now why would I have the privilege of being insulted by one of Chicago's finest so early this morning?"

"There are two trucks delivering asphalt for a private driveway and back yard basketball court. I'm watching them unload as we speak. They're getting ready to go back for more to finish the job."

Mason wonders what the point was. "Now why do I care?"

"Geez, if I do all of your work, shouldn't I at least get half your outrageous paycheck? Both trucks have signs saying they are part of the City's Hired Truck Program and they just picked up the asphalt at a city garage. I'm watching the driver take cash for his load right now. It is stolen city property and Vlad and I are about to slit the thieving crooks throats and haul their asses in."

Mason is so excited he almost jumps through the phone. "Sunny, please don't do that. I'm working on a story. Where are you, I'll be right there." Mason turns around and runs back down the street for his car. "How did you know I was taking a look at the Hired Truck Program?"

"Geez Mason, we're detectives remember? You think Vlad and I couldn't figure out what you were doing yesterday after your question? Hey! We're two of Chicago's finest. To quote my dumb shit partner, we're not crossing guards you know. Give us a little credit will ya'?"

"Please don't say a word yet...please."

"Don't worry pal. Everybody's got to earn their rice bowl once in a while. We'll cover your sorry ass but it could cost you a couple more apple fritters." Sunny laughs as he thinks a moment. "You know Mason, we just might be able to help you with a few of these trucks. We are around the city yards and planning engineers all the time so we'll keep our eyes open. Keep your cell phone on. When you win one of them big Pulitzer Prizes for this story, Vlad and I want to be sitting in the front row."

"Thank you. This means a lot to me and my career."

"Mason, don't take this wrong, but you forget, we're on the same side. Different positions but the same team. We don't like all this corruption any more than you or your editor does. We know the City and County won't do anything about it. I'm a tax payer just like you. Sometimes you forget, I'm a cop. Catching these guys is what Vlad and I do. We volunteered for this job because we don't like crooks either."

"Thanks. You know, sometimes we reporters forget what the other guys are trying to do also."

"Yea. Now get your shit together and get over here or we're going to bust these crooked schmucks right now and send their asses to jail where they belong." Sunny hangs up.

Sunny and Vlad share a smile at Sunny's informal rant at their friend Mason Huntley. They like the guy. He is a good reporter. A guy they can leak things to and not worry about reading their name in the wrong place.

Vlad's cell phone ring startles both of them. "Kozak." He listens. "Gosh honey, I'm really sorry. I'll need to see who belongs to whom, but I should be able to help. OK? We're just finishing something; I'll be there in about twenty minutes. He closes the phone."

Vlad looks at Sunny. "Sorry I need to make an unscheduled stop."

Sunny covers his face like he is hiding from a camera. "Is she pregnant?"

"No dipshit! I'm not that dumb."

Sunny wipes his brow like he is relieved. "Whew, thought the impaler had really screwed up this time."

"You're hopeless. We enjoy some good food, jazz, a little dancing and old movies together. She loves to dance and she is good at it. Nothing big. We get home early. You know my friend, Judy Schurz. Nice lady. She has been rehabbing that neat old brownstone near Hyde Park? You and Sheila had dinner with us there a couple of weeks ago."

"Sure. Good kid. Cute. Way too smart for you. Actually talks like she has an education. Probably reads books that aren't mostly pictures."

Vlad flips Sunny the bird. "Thanks, ahole. She finally finished the brownstone and went to get her city occupancy permit. The inspector came out and tried to shake her down for a bribe to give her the permit. She refused. Probably said some things she shouldn't have. The inspector got huffy. He says she's never going to get an occupancy permit until she apologizes and pays the going rate. Then he stalked out."

Sunny has a cynical expression. "An honest person, but pretty naïve. She is so naive she thought an occupancy permit just goes to people who meet the code? Didn't think she'd have to pay? Not as bright as I thought she was."

"First I'll need to figure out who the inspector is. Then I'll find out which ward organization he is out of. Then I'll figure out who is the real boss...the committeeman, the alderman or the legislator or Burke directly? Finally I'll have to go see who ever the boss of her ward is and get them to pull the guy back some or I'll bust his ass."

Sunny laughs. "Let's just kick his ass for the fun of it."

Vlad frowns. "Great idea. Eventually someone will come and do a legit inspection. Then and only then will Judy be issued her occupancy permit. Finally Judy gets to move in for real."

Sunny makes an X rated gesture. "Then Vlad gets his reward."

"You are every bit the pervert Sheila says you are. Maybe even worse."

"Yeah. Is that a problem?"

Vlad laughs. "You're hopeless. Can we make a quick swing by Judy's office? She's in the North Loop."

"Sure. We'll have her problems solved in no time. You realize she is probably in the 5th Ward or else she is just over the line in Larenda Bass' ward. There is a lot of gentrification going on in Hyde Park and Kenwood as folks fix up some of the old housing on the edge of Bass' area. Lot of nice old stuff that will be spectacular when it is rehabbed. Also a couple of very pretty boulevards run through there. If Bass would get out of the way her ward would really start to take off."

"Get real. Would Bass want constituents who can read and don't live off public aide? Her power like a bunch of the aldermen and the Chicago Machine is based on holding down and limiting any growth from educated folks. There is a reason Chicago has shrunk from 3.66 million folks to only 2.69 million in the last census. Bass wants to keep her folks dependent on her and her generosity. If she had voters who could read and get a job she'd be toast."

Sunny acknowledges Vlad's point. "Her and thirty more of those idiots she serves with. How many of them have been indicted in this last year alone?"

"Oh come on. This wasn't a bad year. I think they only got four of them. That's nothing!"

CHAPTER

SIXTEEN

JUDGE LEONI IS ENJOYING HIS LUNCH IN THE MAYOR'S Row restaurant across Dearborn Street from the courts building, the Richard J. Daley Center. Food is good. Lots of lawyers to stop by and pay homage and always at least one willing to pick up the tab.

Finally he sees Stu Black walk in and look for him. The Judge just sits there and lets Black look until he finds him. It is beneath the dignity of a Cook County Circuit Court Judge to wave his hand or stand up to get someone's attention. Even for an important guy like Stu Black, Brennan Burke's key media aide and political throat slitter. Leoni appreciates Black coming to lunch, but with Black's reputation as a brutal hired gun and effective media leak back stabber, you have to be careful what you say. Just in case he ever turns on you. The problem today is Leoni needs something he can't get without Black pushing Burke to take care of it.

Leoni waits for Black to find him. He can just look until he does. Leoni isn't going anywhere. He is easy to spot. Dignity is important to a judge like Leoni. Honesty, now that is another thing.

Stu tells the guy at the cash register what he wants and tells him which table to have it delivered to. He reminds the guy to put it on the Judge's tab. Stu knows whoever is getting the Judge's lunch isn't going to complain so he can take care of this one too. The clerk knows who Stu is and knows for sure he isn't going to pay any more than the judge will. This is Chicago. This is Mayor's Row. This is how things work. Then Stu walks over with his big shit eating grin and shakes hands with the Judge.

Old friends, relaxing and enjoying a good lunch on someone else's tab. That is the way the big dogs live in Chicago. It is a good system if you're one of the big dogs. "Always nice to see you Judge. Sorry I'm a moment late. I got caught in a meeting with a guy from the Carpenters Union. Wants thanks for doing Speaker Burke a favor by sending some major law business. We didn't ask him for it but he still wants a chit anyway. Screw 'em."

"No problem, I was early so I ordered but I'll have dessert with you."

"My pleasure. You know I never had the chance to tell you how much I enjoyed you sending that jerk, Sunny SunWarrior and his big mouth to the can for a few weeks. It made my week. Heck, it made my month. He has never learned his place in the program."

"You can't let those guys get out of line. Next thing you know they start asking questions that are none of their concern."

"I'm with you. What can Speaker Burke do for you? I am sure he will be glad to help."

"I appreciate that Stu. It is just a small thing. My boy is a senior at Oak Park River Forest High School and would love to go to the University of Illinois in Urbana/Champaign. A father needs to look after his son."

"Smart idea. Great school. A public ivy! What's the hang up?"

"Well Francis was rejected by the admissions department. I would love to have them take a second look."

"Speaker Burke always keeps the channels with the University open. You know they are forever whining about their budget and he keeps a good grip on their nuts to be sure they remember who controls the purse strings. They will do what we recommend. They know if they follow orders their life is definitely easier. What was Francis' problem?"

"I wish the boy would do a little more homework. He isn't always as hard working a student as he should be."

"Give me a feel for his grades or class rank. Oak Park is a good high school so there is wiggle room. The university tries to limit admissions to the top ten percent. You know they are a premier university and the competition to get in is brutal. Is he in the second ten percent?"

"Not quite. A lot closer to the bottom of the class. We're hoping his grades get better this year to bring him into the third quartile."

"Ummm, Judge...this is the University of Illinois. We may keep a tight grip on their nuts, but this is one of the top colleges in the world. I can see their problem with a kid from near the bottom."

"Oh Stu. He's a kid. He'll do fine once he decides to apply himself. You know how that works."

"Is he an athlete so we can maybe say he is being recruited? There is more leeway there."

"Not really."

"Any activities we can talk about?"

"Not really. I had the convictions expunged from his record, so he is clean there. He would have been a football player, but the football coach wouldn't let him back on the team after the arrests."

"Arrests?"

"Oh, just little stuff and they have been expunged. No one ever proved the drug thing so it never came up as an arrest."

"What's little?"

"You know the kind of stuff all kids get into. A little car theft. A burglary. Probably a little too frisky with a girl who was coming on to him. The DUI didn't count since he didn't take the breathalyzer and we got the hospital to lose his blood test."

"Judge, you know how highly the Speaker thinks of you. We'll get him in, but this will take more than just a friendly chat. We'll have to put him on the Speaker's 'cannot refuse' list. That will be the only way. The University is going to kick and scream, but they know when to hold 'em and when to fold 'em. This will be one they'll have to ask the admissions guys to fold on. It might take a while to get them to take a kid with Francis' grades, but we'll get it done. Don't worry."

Stu Black starts to think of how mad the university is going to be to be forced to take a dead beat kid with a track record that just did not belong in a premier university. Kid probably doesn't even belong in a third tier college, let alone a top rated school like the U of I. Kid probably needed some jail time to get his act together. Oh well, tough luck. The University of Illinois just needs to remember who is in charge. They want to play tough? They'll need to be reminded no one can play tougher than Speaker Burke.

But Judge Leoni asking really took some chutzpah. The kid is obviously a loser. If he wanted to be a good dad, he might have tried doing it earlier and kicked the kid's ass a little more when he was younger and it would have made a difference. Clearly the jerk kid deserved a good ass kicking. But when he was on the bench the Judge knew what to do without having to be told and loyal lackeys were just part of the dead weight the leader of the party had to carry.

"Believe me Stu, I really appreciate this. A dad needs to help his kid when he can. You know I'll remember. I always do."

"Yes you have."

The two keep eating as they talk. The Judge is particularly enjoying a piece of warm pecan pie.

"Oh, Stu, by the way...Alderman Larenda Bass is bugging me about some young guys the prosecutor seems to think are Gangster Warlords. They appear to have grabbed some kid who police think was a gangbanger also. They said something about 43rd Street Kings or something? They stripped him naked, tied him bent over to a light pole and jammed something up his tail. Also some stuff about robbing a Chinese takeout restaurant, stealing the food and rousting the clerk. He wasn't in the hospital all that long. She assures me they aren't Warlords. Just some kids who got caught on a mistaken identity thing. You know DWB."

Stu looks at the Judge. "DWB?"

"Yea, DWB. Driving while Black. It really is an actual problem. She says they are some excellent precinct workers and she would really appreciate me giving them the easy road. What do you think? Is she someone I want to help?"

"Oh yes. She is one of our best ward committeemen. I don't know if these kids are Warlords or peaceniks. Don't know. Don't care. But we know she gets a lot of precinct help from nontraditional sources and they do a first rate job. She has one of the highest turnouts in the city and one of the best margins for everybody, up and down the ticket. She helps out in other wards with weaker organizations. We think very highly of her."

"Sounds fair. You know I like to help a kid when I can. Goes with the turf of being a judge. I inherited the case from Judge Madigan. Seems our lady friend is a little busy on the golf course and touching up her tan this summer and she has been sloughing her cases off to those of us who don't play as much golf as she does."

Black nods in acknowledgement. "Glad it is you, not some guy who wouldn't recognize it as an important case."

"I try to keep my docket moving but it is hard when you keep getting so many cases dropped on you at the last moment. I can't figure why these others seem to think summer is a perpetual vacation to be spent on the golf course. I'll bet a quarter of the Judges basically take off a couple of weekday afternoons all summer to keep their handicap down or some to improve their tans."

"That is an issue we may have to deal with some day. The courts are so back-logged and clogged we can't have so many dead beats on the bench. We've added something like 100 associate judges and it hasn't helped the back log. What are there, five hundred plus judges in the county?"

"Something like that. Most work hard, but we have some real embarrassments too."

"I'm not sure what or when, but at some point some reporter is going to pick up on the work habits of some of your fellow judges and start making waves. It will probably be that damn Fox News or that pain in the ass, Andy Shaw over at the Better Government Association. Those guys don't have any common sense when it comes to what not to report. What a bunch of jerks. But still, it will be embarrassing. No question about it."

"I agree. You won't be embarrassed by my work habits. By the way, how's that steak sandwich. It is one of my favorites."

"Great as always. Even better when someone else pays."

"You got it. It is against my principles to pay for lunch."

CHAPTER SEVENTEEN

LIEUTENANT DORNAN LOOKS AT SUNNY AND VLAD. "What the hell did you guys do to our Warlord informant? I dropped by to see him and he looked like you had used a cattle prod in his ear and a baseball bat on his nose. He was very upset and wanted me to string you guys up."

Sunny and Vlad look at each other and shrug. Vlad looks like an angel says, "Looked fine to me when we went to see him yesterday."

Dornan laughs at Vlad's purported innocence. "You guys have more nerve than a high wire walker. I know we're worried about this Mexican connection, but that doesn't justify tearing up an informant who is usually pretty helpful."

Both guys shrug. Sunny pulls a notebook out of his pocket. "He did give us a lead over at the Building and Zoning Department. These Mexican Santa Muerte Cartel guys will need to stay somewhere and I doubt it will be the Ritz Carlton. The Insane Jaguars have a bunch of buildings they control over in Little Village. They're shitholes and I have never been able to figure out how they ever got occupancy permits. But there are permits posted on the front window. We'll go there for a start.

OK if we bring Brookins along. There are often a bunch of the Jaguars there and we wouldn't mind a little extra back up."

Dornan shrugs. "Brookins is just as apt as you are to start World War III. He can't do much more harm than you guys will do on your own. Well, probably not much more, but that isn't saying very much."

"Thanks for the vote of confidence."

Sunny and Vlad exit Dornan's office and Sunny calls Brookins. "Hey. We're going to play nice with some Insane Jaguars and Dornan said you won't do any more harm than we will, so he OKed you coming with us."

Brookins responds "What a vote of confidence."

"That is exactly what I just said to him! I also want to take a peek at how they got those occupancy permits. You know what those places look like."

"A payoff. How do you think dummkopf? But let's check whose name is on the permit."

"I'll see you there. I'll wait at the corner just North until you get there."

Vlad drives past Brookins' car and Sunny waves. Brookins puts the car in gear and follows. The three cops and two cars see a group in front of some slightly rundown buildings that don't really look like legit slums. They look much better than Sunny remembered and seemed to have had some work done on them quite recently. Out front there are some recent model SUVs and several large motorcycles. There is also a City of Chicago car parked by the SUVs. Surprisingly, across the street are two trucks with Chicago Hired Truck program signs on them and a pair of Streets and Sanitation Department trucks.

In front of the crowd is a City of Chicago Inspector talking to a big Latino guy. The rest of the crowd surrounds them. It doesn't look like the friendliest meeting. The Inspector is pointing at his open hand. It is getting very hot. So hot none notice the cars go by. Brookins is in a police car and they don't even notice it. The inspector's voice can be heard over the crowd even if his words aren't intelligible. He doesn't look like he understands what is happening around him.

The three of them keep going and swing around the corner out of sight. Sunny and Vlad get out and signal for Brookins to stay where he is, but keep his weapon ready. As the two come around the corner they see the big Latino backhand the City guy. The Inspector hits the ground like someone just dropped an Oak Tree on his head.

Vlad yells for Brookins to follow them and then he follows Sunny at a trot. The big Latino guy kicks the Inspector in the ribs and then grabs him by the back of his shirt collar and hoists him like he is a wet rag. With his other hand he starts slapping the Inspector. The thwacks can be heard all of the way to the end of block. The knot tightens around the foolish city inspector.

The rest of the crowd looks an awful lot like Insane Jaguars who intend to leave the remains of the city inspector in a trash container. They crowd around the big Latino and start to tighten the knot. This does not look good.

As Sunny jogs toward the group he raises his badge and shouts, "Police! Drop the guy and keep your hands where we can see them." Right behind him Vlad is jogging along brandishing his Ithaca Mag-10. Right behind him is Brookins, a moose of a man and he is brandishing Sunny's city issue Benelli shot gun.

The big Latino shrugs and drops the Inspector. He looks at the three cops with an ambivalent look and no real hostility. He speaks with a heavy accent and a deep base voice. "Glad you're here. This crooked piece of shit inspector is demanding we pay him so folks can live in my building. I already paid him once and his buddy also. When is enough enough? I'm just a landlord trying to make an honest living. These guys are bleeding me dry."

All three cops stop in shock. They recognize the big, powerfully-built Latino as Arturo Ortega, a major Insane Jaguar General. This is one real big time, bad ass guy. The last thing they expect is for him to complain about corruption. They are totally disarmed. Ortega is about as big as you can get when it comes to Mexican oriented gangs. None of them had ever met him but all of them had seen pictures of him. He was no dummy. All three of them were pretty sure he had no arrests and certainly no high profile criminal activity.

Brookins speaks first. "What? What's the problem?"

Ortega points at the Inspector huddled on the ground with blood dripping from his nose and mouth. He is going to have a serious shiner by tonight and probably some broken ribs. "This crook is trying to shake us down for a bribe. He is with the City Building and Zoning Department. These guys always have their hands out. It is hard enough to own and maintain a building in the city and pay the taxes, but the pay offs are just getting to be too much."

The three cops remain stationary with their mouths open and just look. They simply can't believe the scene unfolding in front of them. An Insane Jaguar General complaining about corruption. This is the very definition of chutzpa.

Ortega looks back. "What's the problem? Don't tell me you want something also. Give me a break!"

Sunny finally gets his wits back and walks over to the group. There is no hostility. The Insane Jaguars act like put upon citizens with a grievance. "This guy is soliciting a bribe?"

"That's what I said and I'm willing to press charges if you'll arrest him. There are plenty of witnesses and it isn't the first time. What is this city coming to when a landlord can't even make repairs on his building without making a payoff?"

Vlad walks over to the Inspector. "Have you got anything to say?"

The guy is obviously terrified and just shakes his head, no. So Vlad reads him his Miranda rights and arrests him.

"Harold, go get your squad car will you please?"

Brookins nods but doesn't move. He wants to see how this plays out.

Sunny walks up to Ortega, introduces himself and gives him his card. There is a look of recognition in Ortega's eyes.

"Aren't you the cop who used to play for da Bears?"

Sunny thinks miracles will never cease. "Yes, I did. But it was a few years ago."

Ortega extends his hand to shake and introduces himself. "Arturo Ortega. A pleasure to meet you. I own all of these buildings and I'm trying to fix them all up to code so my tenants will be more comfortable. They need work but I can't get these damn City Inspectors to give me the necessary permits to get the work done without paying them an arm and a leg."

Ortega gestures toward the rough looking characters surrounding them. "These guys are my crew and they were ready to start work today until this crook stopped us."

Vlad was thinking the crew looks a lot more like Insane Jaguar hit men then carpenters, painters and laborers, but who knows?

Sunny asks "Mr. Ortega, do you want to fill out the forms to press charges? I'll need these filled out. Maybe this is a dumb question, but would you be willing to come to the station to fill out and file the charges?"

Ortega smiles pleasantly back at him. "Can I come down later today or tomorrow?"

"Either is fine. If I'm not there I'll make sure the desk sergeant has what you need. Thank you."

The three walk back with the Inspector in handcuffs.

"Vlad, take his keys and you drive his city car. He'll go with Brookins."

All three are shell-shocked. This is the last thing they would have ever dreamed of when they visited the heartland of the Insane Jaguar's. They are so shocked they totally forget to see whose name is on the occupancy permits or wonder why there are trucks there that appear to be on the city payroll.

CHAPTER EIGHTEEN

BROOKINS PLACES HIS HAND ON THE CITY INSPEC-tor's head and pushes him gently into the back seat of the squad car. The guy is in obvious pain and isn't very mobile. Brookins acts accordingly. Then he gets in the front seat and takes off.

As he drives, Brookins talks over his right shoulder. "Do you realize who the hell you were trying to shake down?"

The guys just hangs his head and bleeds on his lap. It is obvious the pain isn't diminishing. He might even be in a little shock. He is lucky to be alive and maybe he is just starting to realize it.

"Those guys are the Insane Jaguars. They eat guys like you for lunch. The big guy is Arturo Ortega one of their biggest generals. If he says you're dead, you're dead. Are you crazy?"

The guy looks up. The pain in his face is obvious. "Thanks for the advice. Where the hell were you when it would have done me some good? I wasn't shaking them down. I was just trying to get them to understand they needed help from a consultant."

Brookins chuckles as he drives. "A consultant? Yeah." There is a silence for a while. "You're damn lucky we came by or your body would have been recovered from a trash container in a week or two. Probably half eaten by rodents and crows. You don't realize how lucky you are."

"I do, now. But I'm not a crook. I was just trying to be helpful."

As Harold Brookins pulls in at the front of the Police Station he sees Sunny waiting for him by the door. Brookins stops at the curb and opens the window. "Are you standing here soliciting or were you looking for something? If you are soliciting and look like this, you're not going to get much business."

Sunny flips Brookins the bird and then gets in the car. "Drive to the McDonalds at the corner. Let's have a heart to heart with our friend in the back seat."

They pull into the McDonalds lot and get out. Sunny opens the back door and takes the hand cuffs off the City Inspector. "I'm going to buy you a coke. This may be your last coke. If you live to get out of jail in the next ten years, Arturo Ortega will find you when we aren't there to protect you and he'll take you apart. Piece by piece. It will take a little while so he can be sure you know you screwed up by fooling with him. This is kind of like a last smoke, only we don't smoke so we thought the coke might be more enjoyable."

Sunny just stares at the guy who is now even more terrified than he was before. "Let's go in." The three of them go in and take a table in the corner.

Sunny reaches out his hand to shake. "I'm Detective Sunny SunWarrior and this lug is Officer Harold Brookins. What's your name?"

The guy uses napkins to finish wiping the blood off his face. He looks like he isn't sure he wants to join in this conversation, but finally reaches out his hand. "I'm Jerry Katorski and I don't like these threats."

As Brookins shakes his hand he holds it for a while. "What threats? Not us. You still don't get it. Those were the Insane Jaguars. Between them and the Gangster Warlords that accounts for about half the murders in Chicago that don't get solved. Arturo Ortega is going to come in, file a complaint and get you put in County Jail where several of his little darlings are already there on gangbanger vacation time drawing three squares a day. They are bored to death because they are too dumb to be able to read a book. That makes them just waiting for something to do and when he puts a kill order on you things will move quite quickly. Are you so dense you haven't figured this out?"

The guy looks shocked.

Sunny comes back with three cokes. "You really haven't figured out you're a dead man walking have you?"

"I was just trying to help them out."

Sunny looks at Brookins. "Let's finish the cokes and take him to the lock up. He won't ever get it." Sunny then looks Katorski right in the eyes. "This is serious shit you're playing with!"

"OK. OK. I don't want to die. I've got a wife and a kid. I'm just trying to make a few extra bucks. Everyone in the Department does it. You help us, we help you. Everybody does it. Don't act like I'm the only guy trying to make a living."

Brookins looks back at Sunny. "I love that phrase, you help me, I help you. How do you think the prosecutors will interpret that? Especially with a bunch of Latino witnesses all claiming you are destroying their opportunity to earn a living."

The three sit there and enjoy their cokes.

"Do you want to live or not?"

"Of course I want to live. I've got a decent job. A family. I'm just trying to make a little extra. Everybody does it."

Brookins pulls out his wallet and looks at it. It isn't very thick. "I have a wife and three kids. A mortgage. One about to leave for college and another getting ready to go right behind him. We have a tight budget, but we keep to it. My wife can't really work with three kids. We decided raising the kids right is more important than just making a few bucks extra. I'm not doing it, as you describe it. Don't act like the rest of us are soliciting bribes. We aren't doing it. Maybe you and your buddies at Building and Zoning are, but not all of us are. You got that?"

"I didn't mean to offend you, but you're on the street. You're a cop. You're different. We at the City, we work five to six hours, do a good job in the precincts and make a little on the side. That is just what it is like to be a City Inspector. With the extra cash I buy some political fundraising tickets from Brennan Burke, my Alderman, the Mayor, the County Board President and the State's Attorney. Keep the rest for myself. Life goes on. I'm not doing anything hundreds of other guys aren't doing. This is how the system works."

Brookins looks disgusted. "I'm just a plain old cop. Maybe not the sharpest knife in the drawer. But I know this. You're a dead man walking. Maybe you don't care, maybe you do. I carry a gun. You don't. You get to County Jail I give you 36 to 48 hours. At best 48. Maybe you never get past the initial lock up."

Katorski still doesn't look convinced.

"You don't get it. Arturo Ortega, an Insane Jaguar General is voluntarily going to come to a police station to fill out your death warrant. You know why? Because then every City Inspector knows not to screw with his crews. He gets to send a message to hundreds of guys and the postage is free. All it costs is your life. The rumors take care of everything from there. Do you think he gives a shit about your wife and family? Not his problem mon."

Sunny scratches his chin and just stares at Jerry Katorski for a while. "Have you got much life insurance? Enough to take care of the wife, the kid, the funeral and the mortgage?"

"Why?"

"You can't be as dumb as you're acting. You're dead and you're not even planning ahead to take care of your family. You aren't worth a shit as a husband and father."

"I can't believe that guy would hurt me over a misunderstanding. Just a couple of bucks."

Sunny and Brookins look at each other for a while.

Sunny talks as if he is communicating with an idiot. "The Insane Jaguars killed maybe twenty folks in the last year. Maybe far more. We don't know the exact number because most of the crimes go unsolved. Why bother to look for a gangbanger who killed another gangbanger. We view it as helping clean up the city's gene pool. One less ahole on the streets."

Brookins nods in agreement. "You would be a little different. You'd go unsolved because jail house killings all fall under the don't snitch rule. Doesn't matter how many witnesses. There'll be none who'll talk to us. Tell me Jerry, is that how you want your wife and kid to remember you. A dead crook. Killed by some gangbangers in jail. You won't even be able to defend yourself against a bunch of thugs. It won't be one guy coming to see you. They'll rape your ass in front of plenty of witnesses to make the point they aren't guys to be messed with. You'll just be a dead wimp lying on the floor in a pool of blood with your pants around your ankles when the guards find you."

Sunny just shakes his head. "To boot you won't leave enough insurance so your family will lose their house and your wife has to go work some night shift to pay the bills? They'll have to leave the neighborhood and your Parish because they'll be so embarrassed about the dead jerk who used to be their husband and dad."

Jerry Katorski starts to cry. His face is a mess. The blood was mostly gone but as he wipes his eyes with the back of his hands the cuts start to bleed again. It is obvious he will have one heck of a shiner by tomorrow. He is sitting funny because his broken ribs are killing him. His lips are swollen from getting smacked by the backhands. He looks pathetic. He just sits there and cries.

Brookins shifts to Jerry's side of the booth and pats his arm. "Do you want to avoid all this? You want a viable exit strategy? You want to keep your job and get all this hushed up?"

Through the tears Jerry Katorski looks at Brookins like he is Jerry's risen savior. His port in the storm.

"How?"

"You're serious?"

Jerry is almost blubbering. "I don't want my wife and son to see me like this. I can't go to jail. It would destroy her. She is active at our school and with the Parish. She's a decent lady. I'm lucky to have her. She has no idea I do stuff on the side. All she cares about is our family, our home and the church. That's her whole world. She doesn't deserve this. What? What can I do?"

Sunny writes a name and phone number on a slip of paper. "This is a Federal Prosecutor. She'll call you and set up some place for you to meet in secret. You tell her everything you know. You don't go to jail. You keep your job. Your family survives. If she tells me you didn't cooperate and tell her everything... Well, back to scenario number one. Is that completely clear?"

"No one finds out? No one? I keep my job? I don't lose my pension?"

"Yep."

"How about Arturo Ortega? What will he do?"

Brookins chuckles. "That will be the hard part."

Sunny nods in agreement and thinks for a moment. "I'll have to take care of him. He'll be upset. Real upset. I suggest you keep away from any of their buildings and maybe warn some of your buddies to keep away too. He's got bigger fish than you to fry. Eventually he moves on to whatever murder and mayhem is next on his platter. But don't forget. Be sure he gets all of his permits. All of them. And don't bother him again. Am I clear?"

Jerry quits blubbering. He looks like he can almost see the light at the end of the tunnel. "Yes. I'll take care of all of that."

Sunny and Brookins look pretty satisfied. "You won't regret this. But just remember. Don't start feeling sorry for yourself. This is a door you chose to walk through. You don't have any other way to go. But you still are walking this path voluntarily. Got that?"

CHAPTER NINETEEN

THE NEXT MORNING, ARTURO ORTEGA WALKS INTO the Precinct. He is as friendly as can be. You would think he was a solid citizen, not a General in the Insane Jaguars. He stops at the Desk Sergeant and asks for Sunny or if he's not there, the paperwork that he needs to fill out. He cracks a joke and has the Desk Sergeant guffawing all the way back to find Sunny.

"Sunny, an Arturo Ortega for you. Should I bring him back?"

"Thanks. Bring him to the conference room. I'll meet him there in one minute."

The Desk Sergeant takes care of bringing Arturo Ortega to the conference room and gets him a bottle of water. Ortega is in a short sleeved white shirt and neat slacks. He is nicely dressed and looks just like a business man landlord should look.

Sunny walks in and Arturo rises to shake hands. "Nice to see you this morning Mr. Ortega."

"Pleasure is mine Detective SunWarrior." Arturo Ortega looked like a big man on the street, but in a small conference room he looks more like Hulk Hogan or The Rock. He is one big guy with shoulders, arms and hands that look like a power lifter. His biceps fill the short sleeved shirt and the muscle definition is obvious. Sunny couldn't believe he hadn't noticed yesterday. No wonder that back hand made such a mess of Jerry Katorski's face.

Sunny opens his bottle of water and spreads the paperwork on the table.

"Please call me Arturo. I followed your time with da Bears. I've got season tickets with some friends in a Sky Box. I remember the time you almost returned a kickoff for a touchdown. We were screaming our heads off for you." Ortega still has his accent but it doesn't seem quite so pronounced today. His voice is still about as deep as Jacob's well, but in this more refined atmosphere it isn't quite so intimidating.

"Call me Sunny." Sunny thinks miracles will never cease. A General with the Jaguars has a Sky Box at Soldier's Field for da Bears. The guy remembers when he caught the kick off and ran it back forty yards. He is just blown away. If he didn't know who Ortega was he would believe the guy was simply an honest landlord trying to maintain his rental property in a tough neighborhood. It was all he could do to keep his game face on.

Both relax and settle in.

"Arturo, I'm going to need to ask for a favor. After we took your pal Katorski in we did a little digging. He is up shit's creek without a paddle. You will need to wait in line to press charges. And it is a long line. A very long line. Is there any way you could see to just let this sit for a while? Not drop it! Just let it sit. Fill out and sign the paperwork. I'll hold it if it is needed. But Katorski is in so much trouble I don't think they'll get to this for quite a while. I talked to his boss and he has committed to me you will get all your permits, yesterday! Anything you need from them will be walked through immediately. Here is the card for the guy who is personally responsible to be sure you are treated properly and for free. Arturo that is one sleazy operation over there." Sunny slides the business card across the table with the name and number of Arturo's go-to guy.

Ortega looks at the card.

Sunny smiles as he tries to find a way to ask the next question. "Yesterday there were some Streets and Sans trucks as well as some that looked like the Hired Truck program vehicles across the street from your buildings? Did you see the operators? Were they doing anything?"

Ortega laughs. "You really don't want to ask. It is an answer that will just complicate your day. You don't want to know."

Sunny decides things are going too well to muddy the water. He'll tell Mason Huntley about them later if it doesn't cause problems.

Ortega thinks for a very brief moment more as he looks at the business card in his giant hand. "I'm glad to cooperate. I don't have a dog in this fight. I just want to be able to upgrade my properties without being hassled. I'm a businessman and like most businessmen, all I ask is for the government to leave me alone and I'll be fine. I'm buying more rundown properties around the outer edges of Little Village and will be bringing them up to code as quickly as possible. You know there are many immigrants coming to Chicago and they need decent housing. I also plan on opening some more small Mexican oriented restaurants to go with the Taco Trucks we send to job sights and the parks."

Sunny keeps getting more amazed the more he listens to Ortega and what he is up to.

Ortega slips a business card across the table to Sunny. It is for Aztec Properties with Arturo Ortega as Principal. There is an address and various phone numbers to go with an E-mail.

Sunny looks at the card. "Thank you Arturo. If he slips up, I'll be back to you in a heartbeat."

"Always glad to be of assistance. If I can ever do anything for you, let me know. We've got friendly ties with Brennan Burke and his guys. I send some of my work crews over to help with precinct work at election time and to collect petition signatures to get his candidates on the ballot. My guys are mobile so we can help him in a lot of areas in the city and in the Latino areas in the suburbs. I've even got some first rate guys out in Aurora, Carpentersville, Elgin and Joliet. We're also good for a slug of tickets at his fundraisers and those of his key peons. That's why I'm so mad about this Katorski jerk. We follow the rules. We support the powers that be. We don't make any waves. We expect to be treated fairly."

With that Sunny walks Arturo out the front door of the Precinct and they shake hands on the steps. Arturo cracks another joke and has Sunny laughing all the way back to his desk.

While Sunny walks back to his desk, chuckling, he has a long lost look in his eyes.

Vlad comes over and smacks Sunny on the shoulder. "What's up? What happened? It looked like you guys were best buddies."

"Vlad, he couldn't be any more cooperative. Essentially Ortega just told me how the Jaguars launder their drug cash. These guys are nobody's fools. They're building a real estate empire that can be their money laundering machine. Plus they are going to add more restaurants and I told Ortega we would be sure he got all of the permits he needs. Cripes, it is like I am almost helping him launder his drug money."

Vlad laughs. "A real solid citizen?"

Sunny almost laughs out loud. "Geez, it is right under our noses and as close to legal as you can get if you're laundering illegal money. Guess what else? He helps Brennan Burke with precinct workers! Not just in the city but out in the collar counties also. Talk about connections. Doggone it, Ortega is sharp. I'm impressed."

"Brilliant. It is like they are just modifying the old method the mob used to us. They liked to own movie theatres, especially control the porno theatres and restaurants. On paper they could hire their guys for cover as ushers and waiters and that took care of them for income tax purposes. The guys were legitimately employed at real businesses. The business' were heavily cash, so easy to launder money through them. No strangers there to ask dumb questions. How were you going to argue how many people were in a theatre, or there at work or ate at a restaurant? Some pervert in a porno house wasn't busy counting the number of ushers, guys in the projection booth or other patrons. Worked well then. Probably still does."

Sunny nods in agreement. "The other thing is the tentacles. They will use some more of their own guys as suppliers and have another layer to launder. Once they have filtered their cash through the IRS, it is all legal. That kind of money laundering is so slick it is still hard to catch. How is the IRS going to prove who and how many live in his buildings or eat in his restaurants? Try checking the cash flow of a Taco Wagon. In places like Little Village, that stuff is all cash. Heck, its cash everywhere."

Vlad and Sunny think a minute. Sunny continues, "People think all these guys are just dumb drop outs. The average gangbanger is mentally about a rock. Some no better than a pebble. But the leaders are getting more sophisticated every day. They have crooked lawyers and crooked accountants who don't mind being paid in dirty money. They make a lot and it isn't hard work. You have to sell your soul, but most of these guys think that isn't such a big price. These crooks keep getting smarter."

Vlad nods in recognition so Sunny continues. "People forget most crooks don't mind paying a little in taxes. Just like the mob. As soon as they pay some taxes, the cash becomes legit. Great cover. Their guys have jobs and alibis. They even pay social security and Medicare taxes. Can use it when they get out of jail and then they can retire on our nickel. Some taxes are a small price to pay to make big chunks of their cash legit. Remember, making the cash isn't that hard. It's drug money, some gambling and hookers. Ready market. Making the cash legit, now that is some serious skill."

Vlad chuckles, "Use when they retire? What gangbanger lives long enough to collect social security?"

"Yeah, good point. I got carried away."

The average citizen doesn't realize how many slimy lawyers and slimy accountants there are who specialize in helping crooks launder illicit money. They make a good living. But somewhere in their psyche where the remorse gene should have been, it has simply gone missing. It just isn't there. AWOL. Somewhere there should have been an internal struggle to justify what they do, but they never visited that somewhere. They do what they do. They make a lot of money. They drive fancy cars. They wear expensive suits. Diamond earrings stuck in their left ear lobe. They live in the suburbs or in a fashionable condo by the lake. They go to charity events to look like decent folks. They eat at the right restaurants. They go to the fancy health clubs.

The consequences that other people face from their crooked clients is not an issue. Other people simply do not factor in to their equation. Their life is a me, myself and I world. These are not guys with a real close relationship with the reality other people live within.

Outside, Arturo Ortega gets into his big, dark blue Lincoln Navigator. He feels the meeting couldn't have gone any better. A good days work done and it isn't even lunch time yet.

CHAPTER TWENTY

SUNNY STANDS OFF BY HIMSELF BEHIND A TREE AND talks on his cell phone. He is with Vlad down the street from Alderman Larenda Bass' office. They are there to have a chat with her about one of her precinct captains. The guy is a city inspector, the one who tried to shake down one of Vlad's girlfriends, Judy Schurz for her occupancy permit.

On the other end of the line is Terry Hake, the former prosecutor turned FBI informant. "Terry...good to talk with you. I've got to give you some info real quick. We were talking about the Warlords after the Lieutenants meeting and I picked up some info. The Judge who sprung Akile Fort after we picked him up on the West Side is a guy named Harrison. He is out of the nineteenth ward and has ties to the usual list of suspects. I also hear he made a kinky decision about a couple of Warlords picked up for auto theft about a month ago. The other guy is a Judge named Wolfson. He is taking a bunch of cash on drunk driving and other seriously bad driving stuff."

Sunny listens to Terry tell him something. "Yea, Wolfson. He was so blatant the Head Judge, Harold Commerton, yanked him out of the traffic court to get his attention. Once he promised to be a little less obvious, Commerton put him back in. My guy said anyone who looks at his cases from about a month ago on back for a while can't miss the patterns. His bailiff is dirty also."

Again Sunny pauses to allow Terry Hake to write down the names and issues. "Heck the Head Judge, Commerton has to be dirty also. He knows why he yanked Wolfson and why he put him back. He's as dirty as Wolfson if you ask me. That's all I've got for now, but they tell me the Warlord Judge will really look hot if you do any digging. Tell that drill sergeant buddy of yours I'm nearing my Ruth's Chris outing, OK? Talk to you later."

He folds his cell phone and the two of them walk into Alderman Bass' ward office. They have an appointment. Sitting in the reception area are several younger guys in black and crimson outfits. They look surly but are more interested in snoozing than causing trouble right at the moment. As soon as they close the Alderman's front door a nicely dressed black man walks over to greet them. He is very precise, very measured and looks athletic. He has a military bearing.

"Hello, I'm Mustafa. Detectives SunWarrior and Kozak? You're here to see the Alderman, correct?"

"Yes, thank you. We have an appointment."

"Please follow me." With that he opens the Alderman's door and lets them in. He does not enter with them and shuts the door behind them once they are in. He is courteous almost to a fault.

Alderman Bass stands up to shake hands with Sunny and Vlad. She is very well dressed and has her reading glasses perched on the end of her nose. "Detectives. My pleasure to meet you. What can I do for two of Chicago's finest?"

Vlad shakes her hand and sits on one of the comfortable chairs in front of her desk.

Sunny stands. "Do you mind if I stand? My back is bothering me from sitting in that stupid squad car so much." What he is really doing is using his imposing physical size and somewhat menacing presence to help establish an image of strength to support Vlad playing the nice guy. Good cop, bad cop.

"Feel free. Can I get you anything to drink?"

"No thanks." Vlad says agreeably. "We apologize for bothering you, but there has been a misunderstanding we wanted to clear up."

The Alderman's face immediately perks up. Misunderstanding is Chicago code. It is a nice way of saying one of the crooks got caught. He is your crook so we're here to give you a heads up to clean this up before we have to jail the jerk.

"Oh my goodness. Thank you for letting me know. What can I do to clear this up?"

Using all of his charm and discretion, Vlad explains. "A city inspector named Lucius Monroe seems to have left the impression, with a lady who had just completed a rehab in your ward, that he expected a gratuity from her if she wanted to get an occupancy permit. I am sure it was a misunderstanding so we thought we would give you a heads up."

"Thank you so much. I know Lucius quite well. I am sure it was just a slip of the tongue. Do you happen to have the lady's name and address?"

Vlad gives Larenda Bass a slip of paper with Judy Schurz's name, address and phone number on it.

Bass looks at the name and address to be sure it is her ward and she doesn't know the person. If she knew her it would be embarrassing. She doesn't know Judy Schurz. Name sounds like a White woman, so she has to live in the Northeast corner of the ward where some White folks are doing rehabbing like this Schurz lady. "I'm sure you are right. Just a misunderstanding. I'll take care of it. Thank you for giving me the heads up."

Vlad and Sunny get ready to leave. "We appreciate your attention to this minor detail."

"Of course. My pleasure." Bass pushes a button on the side of her desk.

The door opens and Mustafa steps in to show them out. Everyone shakes hands and exchanges smiles as the detectives leave. As Mustafa shakes hands he bows slightly at the waist with an otherwise stiff countenance. He is very precise but not standoffish. Just courteous, very neat and almost military.

As soon as the outside door of the ward office is closed Bass's composure changes completely. "Get that imbecile Lucius Monroe on the phone. Tell him to haul his dumb and sorry ass over here right now! I said right now and I mean right now! Get him here."

Mustafa signals for the lady at the reception desk to do as she is told. He then looks at Larenda Bass and shrugs.

"The idiot tried to shake down some cop's main squeeze. Great! Not the visibility we need. Kick his ass when he gets here and get this cleared up. Immediately!"

Mustafa acknowledges the directive. He knows Lucius is an idiot. He'll be sure Lucius understands he made a big mistake.

Later that evening, Akile Fort, Mustafa, Alderman Larenda Bass and a flashily dressed guy, who is obviously a lawyer, relax at a table in the corner. It is a very nice restaurant and everyone is dressed for a big night on the town at a fancy restaurant.

Fort sits with his back to the wall, facing the door. Fort enjoys his glass of wine and leans toward Larenda Bass. While he is smooth and talking in a relaxed manner, there is a little edge of nervousness in his voice. "The last thing we want to do is cause complications for you. But something has come up. We have a business arrangement that appears to be going the wrong direction."

Bass is quite mellow from the wine and maybe something else. Maybe a little high from something she smoked. Who knows? "Akile, you know I will do everything I can to help your guys, but I don't want to know anything about your day-to-day business arrangements."

"I appreciate that. But when armed gunmen show up at your ward office, I think you will want to know in advance."

Bass' eyes grow large. "What are you talking about?"

"We tried an innovative way to transship some products that belong to some Mexican businessmen. Actually lots of product. They offered us credit with easy repayment terms. The problem is the police seized some of the Mexican's goods. Thus we didn't sell them. Thus we are short of money. Thus they are mad. Thus they say they plan on a visit to Chicago to get their property back. Thus their reputation for overkill is worth noting. They don't seem to understand the police won't just hand it back to us if we ask nicely. They don't seem to understand this isn't Mexico where the arrangements are a little more fluid."

Bass' eyes get a little larger. "Where do I fit in?"

"They seem to feel you are the go-to person in Chicago. They seem to think you can fix things up for them. They view you a little bit the way they view some Mexican politicians."

If Bass' eyes get any bigger, they will pop out of the sockets. "Me? Why do they think that?"

"We may have mentioned to them you have helped us over time."

Bass looks like she is about to have a heart attack. She now realizes she may have to pay a price for her Faustian bargain. It all looked easy when she first met Akile Fort. She had moved from Arkansas to teach in Chicago. She was an ambitious, moderately attractive young lady who wanted money and power. Fort had both. She had a good reputation, was an occasional church goer and very much a social animal. She taught first grade in the Chicago Public School System. Fort was known as a dangerous and powerful drug lord. A menacing figure. She still wanted money and power. He needed someone to cover for him.

At first, their relationship was secretive and fun. They took some long weekends together. No one at school or at Trinity United Church of Christ knew about him. Then she met their local alderman. He was ageing and lazy. Fort knew Larenda loved politics and thought up the idea of her running against him. She loved the idea. While she was ambitious, she had no real political experience. With Fort's drug money and foot soldiers she overwhelmed the lazy incumbent. Over time her relationship with Fort had become more one of business associates. But, she still wanted money and power. Being an alderman gave her power. Then she turned to making the money. She didn't really like to see it this way, but she was where she was because of Akile Fort. Faust had done the same thing.

Her mind returns to the conversation. "You told them what?"

"You have been very helpful."

Bass is having a hard time breathing. "I never...I never...I never agreed to anything like this."

"It may be a little late to worry about the exact wording in the contract."

Bass looks lost and speaks in a small quiet voice. "What contract are you talking about? We don't have any contract."

"Not our contract. The verbal contract between the Warlords and the Santa Muerte Cartel. They are very easy to work with until they're not. We are a little surprised they are so upset. We can't control the police. When one of our guys met with them to explain we would make this right over time, they were much more upset than we expected."

Bass is on the verge of hyperventilating. "Upset? What do you mean upset? How much do they think you owe them?"

"Well they weren't in a negotiating mood. They sent Rodney's head back to us in a UPS box. There were other body parts in there also. He's not going to be needing them anymore anyway. They neatly put everything in sealed plastic bags. I think they may have taken the parts off while he was still alive. I'm going to miss Rodney. I wish he hadn't gone in such a difficult way."

Bass struggles to get her words out. She realizes she hasn't seen Rodney recently. He often stopped by the Ward Office just to be friendly and usually brought her a very nice lunch. He was always entertaining and she thought he was really her favorite Warlord. "You didn't answer. How much do they think you owe them?"

"That is the difficult part. I think they are estimating a little high."

"How much?"

"By their count it is a little over four million dollars. That is their calculation of half the profits from the street value of the product the police seized from us on the West Side that day I was arrested. I think we could make them happy with a decent down payment."

Bass slumps in her seat. She looks like she is about to pass out. "How much are you looking for? How are you going to get that down payment?"

"I'm glad you asked because I think we can do it fairly easily."

Bass goes from almost comatose to just looking suicidal. "I get this feeling you think I am involved. Where do you think I'm going to get money like that to help you?"

"The advantage of my boys helping you during elections has made you very popular with the powers that be in Chicago and Illinois. Remember our party is in control of everything in the City, the State and the White House."

Bass doesn't answer. She just sits there with a terrified look on her face.

Fort looks at his lawyer to be sure he is saying this correctly. "Our attorney here, Mr. Bernstein, assures us your friend and ally, the Speaker of the House Brennan Burke has some discretionary funds available. He appropriates various sums of unallocated money to certain state agencies. He also squirreled away some of the stimulus funds the President sent for Chicago and Illinois' shovel ready projects."

Attorney Leonard Bernstein nods in agreement to support Akile.

Akile continues, "Burke has people in those agencies to be sure the funds go to their friends and allies. Obama's stimulus stash still has hundreds of billions of dollars sitting around to give to his pals. Illinois is important to the President and Speaker Burke as State Democratic Chairman is an important political pal. Ain't we his pals and supporters also? Perhaps we could get a grant to perform some social services in your ward or the greater South Side area. State or federal stimulus funds, doesn't matter."

The whole table realizes this might be a way out.

"They never follow up on state funds or federal grants, so they won't be missed. He allocates millions of dollars every year that go to friends of his. The state budget is something like fifty or sixty billion dollars and has no one who really monitors grants that Burke personally has distributed."

Everyone, especially Bass are following the idea closely.

"We think four million dollars or some major portion of that is not an unreasonable sum to get for the South Side that gives him such huge pluralities. The stimulus money is even less closely monitored than state money. It is just sloshing around waiting to be claimed by President Obama's allies and we are his allies, right!"

Bass' terror factor drops with the idea. She knows how Burke does things. She also watched the stimulus money pour into the hands of Chicago machine allies and the union leadership that controls their political money. She has gotten several grants for organizations before. Nothing like four million dollars. But hundreds of thousands with no real strings attached.

They probably did a good job with the money. She has no idea and doesn't really care either. She just knows they owe her now for the free money they got.

She knew Burke didn't know either. Neither Burke or she really cared anyway. They were too busy shoveling the money out to friends and allies to actually follow where it went. Keeping the best political organization in the country greased took lots of money. Much of it never really accounted for. Especially the 'walking around money' Bass used so extensively on the South side. Compare that to almost a trillion dollars of stimulus money. Accountability? Yeah, right!

She has her mind in gear by now and is especially thinking of the grants Senator Dickie Hersher got for some after school programs in his district on the West Side. Because he was such a high profile lightning rod for corruption a reporter had actually looked into them. Not one of the programs seemed to be functioning. None had any afterschool activities anyone could find open. But no one had to pay the money back.

After the splash from the *Tribune's* stories some legislative committee held hearings. But nothing ever came of it. The money had disappeared down the sewer and life went on. There were no follow up newspaper stories. Everyone knew Senator Hersher passed out tax payer money to his friends like it was his own. But nothing ever happened to him. He was reelected easily. Another Chicago crook just keeps rolling along. Bass thought about that point.

Brennan Burke's daughter, the State Attorney General, Laura Burke and the Cook County State's Attorney just ignore the obvious and open corruption. No one in the press even asks them why they turn a blind eye to the theft of tax money. The misuse of tax money in the Chicago machine is a bit like water through the Grand Canyon. Say what you want. Do what you want. The river is still going through whether you like it or not. The electorate doesn't seem to care.

Maybe her Faustian bargain with Mephistopheles isn't going to come due today. Not that she looks hopeful, but at least she looks like she can comprehend a solution.

"Who do they have here and how long do we have?"

"Well that is a bit of the downside. It appears the Insane Jaguars are sort of annexed into our Mexican friends. They handle some of the product in their area also. They chose not to use the creative financing method we experimented with so they aren't under any pressure I know of. That said, our guess is our Mexican friends will be here to talk in less than a week."

Bass sinks back into despair. "A week?"

"Probably less than that. But we can move quickly. Burke is in town right now. You could go see him tomorrow. We have already prepared paperwork and set up a bank account to receive the money." Fort looks at his lawyer. "Right?"

The lawyer nods yes.

Bass starts to think like a Chicago Alderman. "Don't we need to have someone we can trust on this board? An address? Some function the group will supposedly perform? Some track record?"

"The address we have. A fabricated track record was easy. Even some endorsement letters from nonexistent community groups to be put in the file. We made Rodney the Chairman of the Board. No one but us knows he's dead. So if things go wrong, we blame it on him. No one will be able to find him, so he'll be a safe place to lay the blame. Rodney stole the money and disappeared."

Bass knows this could work.

Akile looks at Bass. "You're on the board also, but not an officer so you have no liability, but you add credibility. If you can get more than the four million out of Burke, once the money disappears, maybe you should keep what's left over. You know the last thing President Obama wants is for someone to hand him some of the stimulus money back. You're doing him and Burke a favor by helping the money stimulate."

Bass brightens up when she realizes she might make a buck and not have to account for it. Too bad about Rodney, but this scheme sounds pretty good. Then it dawns on her, she is on the board. "Wait a minute I shouldn't be on the board. They might come to me and I won't be able to answer the questions about what happened."

"Number one, no one is going to ask questions you will need to answer. Number two, if you're not on the board, Burke might be more hesitant to give you the money. Number three, we need your help and this isn't the time to get all weak kneed. We have been there for you and made you a player in the party. Life is a two way street."

Suddenly Bass starts to see Mephistopheles at the door again.

"The Insane Jaguars killed a couple of our guys the other day. I think it was a special delivery message from the Santa Muertes in Mexico. We will retaliate, but we think it best to wait until this is all worked out. Don't want to raise our profile right now."

Bass thought back to Jaron Fort, Akile's younger brother, in the office with the cast talking about the kids who were skinned and hung on a fence behind the high school. She had been right. There was something they weren't telling her.

Now she realized it was something she really didn't want to know about. A gang war between the Gangster Warlords and Insane Jaguars with backing from a Mexican cartel using high powered weapons they probably got from the Operation Fast and Furious fiasco was more than a nightmare. A war between the two biggest gangs, Black and Hispanic, would be a nightmare for the entire South Side of Chicago. Both gangs were notorious for not really caring about collateral damage.

Who knew who might win that one? She knew the loser would be a bunch of South Side folks who happened to be in the wrong place at the wrong time. But when she added in a blood thirsty Mexican Drug Cartel, short four million dollars and armed with Fast and Furious weapons, it was obvious the Warlords chances dimmed very quickly. She could see why Fort seemed so bent upon coming up with the money.

If Fort was right and the Santa Muerte Cartel wanted to teach some folks some lessons, she and her buildings could be torched in the middle of the night. They didn't have anything close to the fire code required warning devices. But she still had time to get fire insurance on them, so she'd be OK. Maybe she could have a kid keep an eye on the buildings and if there was a fire he could sound the alarm. She'd have to think about that because it might make it too obvious she knew there could be a problem.

Her mind kept moving at warp speed. Her life wasn't quite flashing in front of her eyes, but she was seeing some frightening snippets. Even a brief summary of your life flashing before your eyes is not a reassuring thing. Faust may not be standing there handing Mephistopheles her soul right on the spot, but Mephistopheles clearly has hold of her skirt.

The pause was getting a little long so Fort continued. "Our attorney, Mr. Bernstein here, can go with you. He will be able to lay out some of the additional information. Your real key is to carefully remind Burke what percentage of the vote he gets on the South Side and how much this assistance will mean to his most reliable voters. Avoid anything too specific. He has given more than four million to North Side and South West Side stuff. Especially for their parks. You might want to remind him about that. He gets a lot more votes from us than those white bastards. It's not his money, so what does he care. It is just free money from him to his supporters. We carry his ass every election. It is time for some payback."

Bass has trouble speaking. "I have never asked him for something this big."

"That's the point. They are shoveling the stimulus money out the door by the wheel barrow load. Burke gives away money from his stashes in the various bureaucracies all the time. We need to ask. He figures people are afraid to ask him so he can just keep the money for his little band of banditos. We're not getting our fair share of the spoils of victory. Elections matter. We win those elections for him. He needs to do a better job of paying for our votes. It isn't his money. He took it from some rich guys now give it to some guys in need. We need it and we need it now."

Bass is very nervous. "What if we get caught?"

"The bigger issue is what if we don't get the money? Don't look at it from our side. Look at it from there's. They can't lose this much face. No way."

Bass is calculating the risks in her head.

"Don't think of the down side from Burke. Think of the down side from the Santa Muerte Cartel. If those cops hadn't answered that old lady's 911 so fast, we wouldn't be in this problem. So it is their fault not ours. They stole our product from us. If we had gotten to sell our stuff there wouldn't be a problem. It is the city's fault."

The lawyer in the fancy suit nods in agreement to support Akile's take on the reason all of this is a problem now. At what he is being paid, he would nod in agreement with Akile if he were explaining why Adolph Hitler, Mao Tse Dung and Joseph Stalin, the three greatest mass murders in world history, should be given the Nobel Peace Prize.

"Rodney gave the Cartel the names of the cops who stole our stuff. Don't think the Cartel isn't going to stop by their homes and let them know messing with the boys from Santa Muerte is a no-no. They're going to be the example. A message delivered by the Cartel to anyone who tries to interfere with business. It has worked in Mexico. It'll work here."

She may be terrified but she can't seem to think of any option. It isn't her money and if Rodney gets called a crook, so what. He's dead. He won't care.

Fort can tell Bass is slowly coming around. "This may look bad for you and us. The Chicago police cheated us and stole our product. That happens sometimes. We end up looking bad."

The Alderwoman seems to clearly be buying into his story.

"We need to look at it from Santa Muerte's perspective. It's worse for them. If the word hits the street they got cheated in Chicago and didn't do anything about it. Other folks might think it is open season to rip them off. They can't afford to let this go. They have to act. We need to make them whole and then keep our mouths shut so they don't lose any face. It will be OK for all of us then."

The look on Bass' face makes it obvious she is hopeful, but not a fool. This is a risk. This could be jail time. But jail beats getting killed. She knows if they did to Rodney what Akile hinted they did, jail wouldn't look as bad as that. Faust is going to have to hold her cards close to her vest until she can find some other way to solve her dilemma.

CHAPTER TWENTY-ONE

SUNNY AND VLAD ARE EATING IN THEIR FAVORITE lunch spot, Lou Malnati's pizza out at the corner of West Ogden and Cermak in one of the toughest areas on the West Side of Chicago. In the mid-1990s the Malnaties put the restaurant there in conjunction with Rev. Wayne Gordon's Lawndale Community Church. The Malnaties are successful businessmen and devout Christians.

The Lawndale community was badly singed in the riots after the assassination of the Rev. Martin Luther King, Jnr. After the riots, the area became a restaurant desert. Malnati's restaurant serves as a wonderful training opportunity for folks there in a very tough neighborhood and the food is excellent in this relaxed environment. It was probably also the only sit down restaurant in the entire community when it opened. The restaurant isn't far from where Sunny and Vlad took down the Gangster Warlords drug operation a few weeks earlier. Great food and lots of nice folks working there and eating there, so it isn't obvious they are cops on a lunch break.

Both are chuckling as Vlad recounts a story. "It took less than four hours for some guy named Mustafa to show up at Judy

Schurz's office. I think Mustafa was the pleasant guy we met at Bass' office. He had an occupancy permit for Judy, in hand. In hand, baby. Four hours and delivered with an apology for the misunderstanding. If Judy had any other problems she was to call Mustafa personally. She was flat impressed with our work."

"Another day, another problem solved. We really are good aren't we?"

Vlad puffs up his chest. "You bet! We da best! And the best lookin' too!"

"Don't get carried away. Best, no question. Good lookin'? You? Don't push it."

Playfully, Vlad flips Sunny the bird.

Sunny's cell rings. "SunWarrior, speak or forever hold your peace." He listens and then responds. "We're in Lou Malnati's on Ogden. Can't talk. You talk, I'll just listen." Sunny nods to himself but doesn't say anything. Just keeps listening and nodding. He looks at Vlad. "I'll fill you in once we get to the car."

They pay their check, leave a nice tip, wave to the manager, the cooks, the cute waitress who has been all over Vlad and he certainly has been eyeing her also for the entire lunch and then out the door. They get into their car.

Once in the car Sunny opens up. "Listen up dipshit. That was LaTonya, the Federal Prosecutor we hooked Jerry Katorski up with. She was so excited I thought she was going to wet her pants. With Katorski's help they can plant a mole among the facilitators who rep the builders and contractors and really pay the bribes and work the system. Katorski agreed to direct the right guys to the right spots. He's living up to his end of the bargain."

Vlad nods in approval.

"Based on early results, LaTonya says there are eighteen inspectors and every one appears to be a crook. Do you believe this crap? Everybody who works there she thinks is on the take. They will get at least fifteen and maybe all eighteen of them on tape and will send them to the Big House. I'm not talking about Michigan's Football stadium, the real Big House, dipshit. By the way, an amazing stadium. Got to play there in front of 107,000 crazy fans. What an experience. Sorry, I digress. You know when you were a star athlete like me, not a dip shit seventh string reserve water boy like you, you get to go to some impressive places to strut your stuff."

"Yea, strut your stuff while you lose 99 to 0. I'll stick with the water bucket." Vlad feels pretty good about his flippant comeback. Sunny is a good friend, a great partner and an even better guy, but he can, even though it was meant with some humor, get on Vlad's nerves about his achievements. Real and imagined achievements.

Vlad didn't get to play college sports. When he got back from the army he went right to work doing security out in Rosemont. The late Mayor Don Stephens was always good about hiring a bunch of part- time cops for all of the shows, hotels and huge business conferences at the Rosemont Convention Center. He went out of his way to hire veterans and just guys and gals who wanted to go into law enforcement. That first job in Rosemont allowed them to get some experience, made them eligible for additional training and was worth some good money also. Stephens built an amazing town. Almost all business with virtually no residents. Of course immediately abutting O'Hare International Airport didn't hurt. Realtors talk about location, location, location. Rosemont has location!

The Donald E. Stephens Convention Center is something like the eleventh biggest in America and was done by a local government with private funds. Rosemont only has a little over 4,000 residents but purportedly has over 5,000 part-time cops to go with multi thousands of hotel rooms and hundred plus restaurants. Really an impressive entrepreneurial enterprise by the late Don Stephens. Working there was a great experience for a young guy fresh out of the Army who hoped to be in law enforcement.

Vlad's folks were able to sneak out of Ukraine when it was dominated by the Russian Soviet dictatorship. They were comfortable as peasant farmers and minded their own business until they accidently walked into the middle of someplace they didn't belong. They were ethnic Ukrainian slavs with a little Cossack thrown in. They were not communists or Russians and were smart enough to stay out of politics. They had saved a little money and decided to take a weeklong vacation at a Black Sea Coast resort. The third night they were in their own little world, walking hand-in-hand along the Black Sea when they stumbled onto a group of what were probably Communist soldiers or maybe KGB agents beating some helpless man to a pulp. They had no idea who these people were and tried to turn and run, but were caught. They tried to explain they were just tourists, but it didn't help. Both were badly beaten and Vlad's father, Bogdan was shot while trying to defend his wife. His mother, Katya was raped and abused by these men and they didn't even know why.

Bogdan and Katya told no one anything. They claimed to have been robbed. Once they had recovered they spent the next months planning how they were going to get free of this communist tyranny. Eventually they were able to get across the Black Sea to Istanbul, Turkey where they went to the American Consulate and asked for asylum. From there it was to Chicago, with its huge Ukrainian population, where Vlad was born and then they moved to an agricultural area in west central Illinois near the town of Galesburg. It was a wonderful place for Vlad to grow up. They never had much money and often struggled, but neither parent ever complained. They just worked hard and helped Vlad and his sister Valya get a decent start in life.

When Vlad and Valya asked why they left Ukraine, their parents eventually told them what had happened. They never told Valya about her mother being raped and abused. As good Orthodox Christians it didn't seem appropriate to tell a girl such stories about her mother. Vlad never told her either. But hearing of the treatment of his parents made Vlad grow up wanting to be a soldier and eventually he added police officer to his ambition. He wanted to be able to protect people the way someone should have protected his mother and father. As could be expected of most Eastern European immigrants, Vlad shared his parents negative view of too powerful government. He often compared the corrupt and abusive communists to the corrupt and abusive Chicago Machine. Not a totally accurate comparison, but definitely kissing cousins. At least the Russians had long since quit pretending they were there to help!

Vlad didn't finally earn his college degree until he had been on the Chicago Police Force for two years. But he had gotten there the old fashioned way. He busted his butt and with the help of the GI Bill and reached his goal. Maybe not a star linebacker but a classic American success story never the less.

After Vlad's first rate retort, Sunny looks a bit dubious but ignores the cheap shot. Illinois led into the fourth quarter but they had lost. They beat Ohio State that year, but not Michigan. Vlad has a point. It is Michigan, the winningiest football program in the history of college sports. Oh well. Besides Vlad gets a lot of friendly crap from Sunny and Brookins who are faster wits than Vlad. He almost never takes it personally.

How could an alpha male cop take crap from other alpha males personally? Too much, too often to even worry about. Just part of being male. But in a tight spot, Vlad was the guy you wanted next to you.

"Anyway, LaTonya is pretty sure they'll get a bunch of the facilitators also. They're the bag men. She was so excited I thought she was going to offer to build a monument to us."

Vlad nods with one of his tongue in cheek, self-promoting smiles. "All in a day's work of protecting the little guy from the overreaching hand of corrupt government."

Sunny laughs at Vlad's self-promotion. "Listen, LaTonya said she got a quiet heads up from a friend that you and I ought to be a little lower profile. Making waves isn't the Chicago system. I thanked her, but, hey...it's our job."

Vlad nods but looks serious a minute. "I didn't mention it, but when I was in the gym the other day, McGuire was there also. You know him, he's Burke's guy. I helped spot for him while he was bench pressing. McGuire's a weasel, but he said a little of that lower profile stuff also. Like he was trying to be a friend and helpful. He's a jerk. But a lot of folks seem to feel we are out on a limb."

"It's our job, buddy. We don't work for Burke or his crooked buddies."

Vlad nods but then raises a question. "But what are the facilitators for? How are they the real bag men?"

"Geez, if you hang around me long enough you'll actually know something about Chicago. The Building and Zoning Department sleaze balls don't want every Tom, Dick and Harry knowing they're on the take. Too dangerous. So they make the contractors and builders hire connected guys they call Facilitators. It is the Facilitator's job to get all permits and OKs. They know about rules and zoning and know who to talk to and who to bug to get stuff. They charge the contractor a fee. Big job, big fee. Little equals little. Then they pay off the sleaze balls at Building and Zoning and buy the political tickets from the alderman, Burke and the Mayor. Good old fashioned Chicago politics in action. Gotta' love it."

Vlad realizes he should have figured out that on his own. Chicago is so corrupt they even have feigns to cover up the obvious. Vlad never ceases to be amazed at how smart and ingenious the crooks get to be. When you have an entire political system on the take, with a worthless Crook County State's Attorney and Burke's daughter, the Attorney General, helping to cover it up, it becomes a playground for entrepreneurial crooks.

"Most of them probably work precincts in the ward organizations also. It is just more patronage jobs the city doesn't need to pay for. Brennan Burke and the Mayor's fundraisers love the system. Gives them more guys to shake down and the city doesn't need to pay their salaries. Just another system set up to steal under the table. Nothing out front. All of it handled by guys in the system and loyal to the system."

Vlad shakes his head. "If I didn't know you knew what you were talking about I wouldn't believe anything could be that corrupt. These guys are as crooked as a dog's hind leg. "

Sunny laughs. "You know Vlad, some days you are a real cupcake. It is really obvious you grew up in a small town, not Chicago. There ain't nothin' straight in Chicago. There ain't nothin' on the level. You just have to ask who wants what and then who is getting what and work backwards from there. Always be sure to keep Speaker of the House Burke's interests involved and his political contributors and you'll eventually figure it out."

"Those crooked bastards."

"Yeah. This is Chicago. What's your point? By the way, LaTonya will keep our names out of it and told Katorski to forget he ever met us."

"Hey is LaTonya the one with the cute fanny I was hustling the last time we were there? Maybe I should give her a call to allow her to express her appreciation."

"You're being a serious dipshit sexual predator again. She weighs two hundred pounds, has glasses three inches thick and has more brains than your entire family. She can actually hold an intelligent conversation. Not your type."

Vlad the Impaler catches a lot of friendly grief from his so-called friends.

CHAPTER TWENTY-TWO

AS THEY DRIVE, THEY FIRST DECIDE TO TRAVEL SEVeral blocks north on Pulaski to get to Madison Street so they can go through the shopping area near Pulaski. It might be one of the toughest areas in Chicago, but several good informants hang out near there, over in Garfield Park and also near the Conservatory.

One key guy was a custodian at Providence St. Mel's School right off Garfield Park on South Central Park Ave. The school is a kindergarten through high school beautiful educational oasis in the heart of a learning desert.

The late W. Clement Stone, the largest Republican campaign contributor in history had played a key role to help save the school when the archdiocese gave up on it as no longer viable. In the 1960s, Stone was one of the wealthiest men in the world. During his life time the ever optimistic Clem Stone gave over $275 million to various charities. That was during the 1950s, 60s and 70s and 80s. Easily double that in today's dollars. He gave Richard Nixon around ten million in his two winning presidential campaigns.

Stone was Mr. PMA: Positive Mental Attitude. The license plate on his big caddy limo was PMA. Stone started from nothing. He dropped out of high school to sell insurance for his mother's agency. The company he founded in 1919, when he was only seventeen years old, Combined Insurance, eventually merged with Pat Ryan group to form the AON Insurance Company in 1987. They took over a chunk of the Standard Oil Building, one of the five tallest buildings in America and had it renamed the AON Building.

All this is pretty impressive for a guy who dropped out of high school to sell insurance door-to-door. AON remained one of the world's premier insurance companies for years and Pat Ryan like Clem Stone is an unbelievable generous philanthropist. Stone was already 85 years old by the time of the merger, but still active as a businessman and philanthropist. He was a legendarily generous figure who helped thousands of kids through his long time support of The Boys and Girls Clubs.

He was a small, rounded man who loved to dance, smoke aged Cuban cigars and drive his own limo while his chauffer sat in back with Jesse, his wife of 75 years. He lent his massive, lake front chateau in ultra-wealthy Winnetka to President Nixon's daughter for her honeymoon. Servants, private beach, chauffer and all. People like W. Clement Stone are very few and very far between.

By the early 1980s, Providence St. Mel school had come so far that President Ronald Reagan visited it two years in a row to highlight the fine job it was doing in a very depressed area. The attention he generated helped the school get more contributions from wealthy Republicans who were not residents of the depressed West Side and wouldn't have known about the school's achievements without a popular President pinpointing them.

Next, Chicago's own beloved, Oprah Winfrey kicked in a million dollars of her own. It is still a tough fight to keep the school going, but the support from outside the neighborhood has been instrumental in undergirding the local efforts.

Sunny and Vlad figure once they get to the Madison and Pulaski area, they can always roust one of their informants, slap him around for cover and see if they know anything about what the Insane Jaguars are up to. This was North and West of the Jaguars, but there were plenty of Latino gangs East of Garfield Park and if the Jaguars apparent collusion with a Mexican Cartel, the Santa Muertes is already known here, that means it is already big news. That means it is bad news.

As they drive east on Madison Street they don't see any of their usual informants, but do see several trucks parked in the lot near the corner with Pulaski. This is the local shopping district and is always crowded. The trucks have signs on them that say City of Chicago Hired Truck Program. They are empty. There are no city building or repair projects anywhere to be seen.

As they continue East they enter Garfield Park and decide to turn North on Central Park Ave. to go by the beautiful Garfield Park Field House with its famous Spanish Baroque Revival architecture and topped by a brilliant golden dome. The huge, surrounding park is from the Jens Jensen school of prairie-style landscaping. There are lakes and ponds and gazebos and then two blocks farther North is the Garfield Park Conservatory. In the midst of violence and poverty is a park that seems to have floated down out of heaven to offer a lovely break from the humdrum of everyday poverty.

As they pass the Field House they notice several more trucks from the Hired Truck Program in the parking lot. Again no work being done anywhere they can see and no drivers near the trucks.

The famous Garfield Park Conservatory is next and it is an oasis of horticultural beauty. A wonderful place to spend a summer afternoon. Enjoy the Conservatory, maybe see one of its special shows, then sit outside in the huge back yard and enjoy a picnic. The good life. Immediately East, across the boulevard is Flowers High School and there are several more trucks sitting at the curb. This time there are drivers near them, but they are smoking and joking with attractive high school girls from Flowers.

Sunny turns to Vlad. "Shit, I can't take it anymore. How many trucks have we seen on the taxpayer's dime doing no work?"

"Too many. Why don't we give Mason Huntley a call?"

Sunny dials his cell phone. "Mason! It's Sunny. Drop everything you're doing. Get your ass out here to Garfield Park. Half the trucks in America seem to be on our pay roll and none of them are doing shit! None! Get your camera man and get out here!"

"Oh my gosh, Sunny, thank you! I'll be out the door with a photographer in one minute."

"One minute is all you get. Get moving boy. These shots will be half your Pulitzer Prize. Go to the parking lot north side of Madison and Pulaski on Madison, the Field House and Flowers High School by the Conservatory. Don't forget, Vlad and I get to be there in the front row."

Sunny shuts his cell. Both guys get a good laugh at the thought of Mason flying out the door with his photographer in tow. But Mason is going to love them for these pictures. They are as good as gold for his story about how corrupt the Hired Truck Program is. The taxpayers are getting screwed out of millions of dollars by the usual list of politically connected Chicago machine insiders.

"Sunny look right. There's Jose la Boca by the corner. He is almost alone. Let's go grab him and chat."

"Great. You slap the cuffs on him and I'll push him around and shove him in the back seat. OK?"

"Perfect."

Sunny speeds up to the corner, they both jump out and grab Jose la Boca by the scruff of the neck. Jose isn't a real big guy, but he has that gangbanger strut to him. He is a walking advertisement for gangland tattoos. He has them everywhere. Probably even has one on his butt. His hat is sideways. He wears his gang's colors and he's got attitude for everyone. He looks like he is ready for a scuffle until he sees the guns and the cuffs.

Vlad cuffs him while Sunny, wielding his gun, screams insults at him and shoves him around enough to look like this is for real. They both shove Jose into the back seat and the car takes off. The whole scene takes about fifteen seconds. Way too fast for anyone to respond.

The two Latino gangbangers standing in the door way of an adjacent building barely have time to quit ducking and looking for gun fire before the car is gone.

"Henrico! Hell happen?"

"I got no idea. No idea. But they got Jose. We better call it in. I got no idea at all what they wanted but that big dude slappin' him and wavin' the piece seemed awful mad. We better make a show so he don't get beat too bad. We'll track him and back him up."

Two miles away in the area of another gang, The Black Almighty Monarchs, the car pulls over and Vlad climbs in back to take the handcuffs off Jose. "Sorry man. Just the usual."

Jose la Boca rubs his wrists and smiles. "Damn if I didn't know you guys I be peein' in my pants by now."

All three of them chuckle.

Sunny picks up a tin foil package. "We've got some left over Lou Malnati's. You want it."

Jose looks at the tin foil the way a beggar looks at a steak. "The best pizza in the world. Thanks. I'll help you by eating it so you don't get fat."

Again, all three chuckle. Vlad looks out the window just to be sure no one is watching them.

"Hey Jose. Have you heard anything about an Insane Jaguar alliance with some Mexican Drug Cartel called the Santa Muertes?"

"Sheet man! That's all anybody been talkin' 'bout the last couple of days. The Jaguars claim to have got some of those Fast and Furious guns those jerks in Washington shipped down to the cartels in old Mexico. Got 'em from the Mexicans they-selves. Big honkin' pieces. They claimin' they goin' to take down the Gangster Warlords."

"That isn't what we want to hear. But that does confirm what we are hearing."

"You hear about them killin' and skinnin' a couple of dem junior Warlords and hangin' dem bodies on the fence behind the high school? Somethin' about those Santa Muerte guys comin' up to settle some score. Sheet, they mean man. Real frickin' mean. Them guys are real evil. Don't know more. Just bits and pieces. It has all come down just the last days. Want me to keep listenin'?"

Sunny and Vlad look like they were just kicked in the gut. They both realize their old friend, Des Moines Detective Tiffany Burroughs-Rea and the Warlord informant they roughed up a bit were right. "Yeah, keep listening. But what you just told us confirms some things we have heard and wanted to check out."

"Sorry guys. This goin' ta get nasty. Hey give me a pop on the lip so it bruises. I'll finish the pizza while you take me back to drop me off. Just East of Flowers be fine."

Sunny drives back East as they both think about what Jose said. Jose just munches on some great pizza and enjoys looking out the window.

Vlad pulls his fist back. "Sorry man. But this was a big help." He then back hands Jose twice.

Jose laughs and holds the side of his face. He humorously snaps at Vlad. "Sheet! I said a fat lip not knockin' out some of my frickin' teeth. I got a date tonight. Gots to look good."

Vlad climbs out of the back seat and pulls Jose behind him. Jose slowly rolls out of the car and collapses on the sidewalk as Vlad slaps him across the back of his shoulders and appears to kick him in the ribs. The car drives away without looking back.

Jose rolls over on his back and lays there for a couple of minutes. He keeps a hand on his face and moans a little. He is finishing chewing his pizza so he doesn't want to get up and look like he is eating. Finally he rolls over on his hands and knees. Slowly he gets up, looks around and walks gingerly down the street.

Sunny and Vlad drive East in silence. Finally Sunny looks over. "I better get Sheila out of town. Just to be safe. It shouldn't be too long. Do you think we ought to tell Brookins to get Stephanie out of town also? I don't know the Mexicans will think of him the way they think of us. Maybe just to be safe."

Vlad thinks a moment. "We owe it to Brookins. No point in taking a chance. He's one of the good guys. Actually he's one of the very best of the good guys. He's the kind of guy you trust coaching you're a- little-too-grown-up teen age daughter's gymnastics or swim team. He is the kind of guy you trust to be sure your widow and family get all of the stuff you planned for them to have."

Sunny laughs. "Don't get so carried away. He's not an angel. Yet, anyway. But let's be super safe with the girls. Besides if Stephanie ever found out we left her hanging she'd mangle us. Mangle us bad."

Vlad cracks up. "You're right, I'm not messin' with Stephanie. The two of them safe? Sheila and Stephanie together on a road trip. It'll be Bonnie and Clyde and you'll have to bail them both out of jail before they hit the Indiana line."

Both chuckle as they think of the two lady pals motoring down the road to some hideout in the North woods of Wisconsin or in the Upper Peninsula of Michigan.

The two playing cards. Drinking ouzo. Sheila trying to get Stephanie's well rounded figure on the floor to do all her crazy exercises. Stephanie trying to do the cooking so she won't die of health food overdose. The two of them laughing and cracking even more of their crazy jokes until two in the morning. Stephanie telling tales about their early kinky sex life on the back of Brookins' Harley. Brookins glad he's not there to defend some of the truly weird stuff Stephanie alleges they did. Sheila blushing and laughing so hard she gets the hiccups about getting caught skinny dipping twice on their honeymoon. Maybe even telling about thinking she was going to have to do CPR for the poor old lady who happened to look at them on their balcony at the wrong moment on their honeymoon.

Vlad laughs at Sunny. "Maybe they'll be glad to have Santa Muerte in town. So much fun they'll make it an annual event?"

Both keep smiling until Sunny talks. "Clean up your mind you pervert. One positive thought is Stephanie is a pretty good shot with that M9, 9mm Beretta 92F Harold brought back from the army. That mother has anything from a ten round to twenty round magazine. I guarantee you, she would hurt you before you hurt them. It is nice to know they won't be defenseless."

"But be sure they don't tell you where they are going, don't call so they can't be traced and don't come back until they read in the news or see online we've killed the bastards."

"Yea. Be careful how you tell Stephanie. She'll kick your ass and Brookins' too if she isn't happy. As Brookins' says, if momma ain't happy, nobody's happy and Brookins ain't gettin' laid."

Both laugh at Brookins' stories. He is just a funny guy who is more apt to make fun of himself than he is of others. The butt of almost all of his jokes is himself. A mountain of a man with a chest and shoulders like a pro wrestler who does exactly as momma says and does it immediately. He often lectures young cops who are getting married. He reminds them there is little worth arguing about with your wife and getting your ass kicked for the next month because of it. Let her have her way and you'll both be happier and you'll get laid. Brookins was a true expert at the art of saying "yes honey".

"You're right. I'll call Brookins if we don't bump into him at the station. I better talk to the Captain also. Tiffany briefed him so he should be OK. Might even send someone with them. That'd be nice."

CHAPTER TWENTY-THREE

FOUR YOUNG WARLORDS IN THEIR COLORS ARE drifting past their local high school. They know they aren't supposed to be so obviously out in public right now. But they're tough. They're armed. They're horny.

Of course, they're teenaged boys. They're always horny.

It is early for gangbangers to be out of bed, so the guys figure nobody else is out and around. Thought they might pay their respects to some young ladies here at school and then go back underground. Maybe have the ladies stop by later for a second round.

Since they are thinking with the wrong head and acting macho they don't bother to look at anyone other than the couple of cuties they are homing in on. They don't notice a skinny Latino kid on his cell phone around the corner and behind a parked car.

Warlords don't bother to pay attention to skinny Latino kids unless they are looking for some ass to kick. That is all a guy that skinny is good for. They only have eyes for well-rounded girls who are impressed by armed studs with lots of tattoos, in gang colors and wearing their hats at a funny angle.

They stop their SUV in a no parking zone. Warlords don't have to follow the law and they want it to be obvious. The four of them lounge around the SUV and signal for the girls to come over to them. They flash gang hand signals and some pornographic ones also. It is obvious what they want. The girls know they should be in school, but they aren't going to bother to learn anything today anyway, so they might as well have a little fun.

Six girls approach the four guys. It is a friendly and familiar gaggle. A little bit of talking. A little bit of touching. Somebody lights up some joints. "Yo dude, take a toke and pass the joint. This is some seriously good shit." Everybody takes some tokes.

Two of the Warlords get in the SUV with two girls and the others back off to give them some privacy. Not much privacy. It is obvious everyone is sneaking a peak at the action. The Warlord in the front seat playfully hangs the girl's bra on the rear view mirror. The back seat couple stays too low for much to be seen. The SUV rocks a bit and the four girls and two guys start to clap to the rhythm.

Forty minutes later the group has had its fun. The girls use the SUV's mirrors to check their makeup and hair. Everyone agrees to try to get together again after school. The Warlords promise to have some really great "stuff" for all of them to try when they get back together. The girls mention they might bring an extra friend or two and the Warlords assure them that will be just fine. The girls then head back to school. No one seems to have missed them.

The four young Warlords are feeling no pain as they get back in their SUV and slowly drive down the street. None of them notice they are now being followed by a small car. It is kind of a junker. It is the exact kind of car no one would notice.

The driver has her cell phone to her ear. But in that neighborhood every young guy and gal has a cell phone at their ear, so who would think it meant anything. The junker follows the SUV for the six blocks back to their apartment hangout.

Once the SUV stops and parks, the junker pulls up next to them and the girl rolls down her window. "Hey, you studs got some dope to share with a horny lady?"

Since all four are still a little high and mellow, they give her a few obscene comments they think are macho and check out what she looks like. She is a pretty cute Latina, so they agree she is welcome to join them upstairs.

"Wait for me here, I'll park and be right back." She drives half way down the block to park. All four Warlords watch her park. She makes sure they can see what she is doing. She takes a couple of minutes to touch up her makeup and her hair.

The four guys stand around their SUV and act macho. They discuss what they will all do to this young Latina once they get her good and high. This looks like it will be a great day.

Slowly the girl gets out of her car and even slower walks as seductively as she can back toward the four Warlords. She is doing plenty to keep their attention on her. About twenty feet from them she stops and pulls her tank top up over her head. She is naked from the waist up and it is a view worth enjoying. She playfully entertains the four of them and tells them what she intends to do to them once they are upstairs. All they need to do is supply the dope.

None of the four even notice the armed Insane Jaguars sneaking up behind them. Four, high, macho, horny, teenaged Warlords enjoying a suggestive show from an attractive, half-naked Latina are an easy mark.

They are down before they even know there is anyone there. The Jaguars at first use silenced weapons and then baseball bats. They quickly handcuff and gag the Warlords. Next they stuff two of them back in their SUV while a white van moves up next to them and the other two are tossed into it. The Jaguars take the keys to the Warlord SUV out of the pocket of the kid who was driving and the two vehicles are joined by two more and the four of them are off. They give their gang hand signals to the attractive Latina who is still standing there topless.

She waves back and then puts her tank top back on. She scurries around to be sure there is nothing left behind to show the Jaguars have been there. She picks up a few things and is satisfied. She then hurries back to her car and is gone.

The entire operation from her first conversation with the Warlords by their SUV to the cleanup took a little over five minutes. Half of that was taken up as she killed time in her car getting her makeup ready. She needed to give the Jaguars time to get there and get into place. She did a great job.

She parks behind an abandoned warehouse. The other four vehicles are already there and have been joined by five others. The driving beat of some heavy Latin music reverberates through the walls of the building. This looks like it might turn into a real party.

The attractive Latina opens her trunk and pulls out a bag. Sticking out of the top is what looks like a knife handle. She puts the bag over her shoulder, closes the trunk and goes to the door. She knocks on the door and is admitted. Inside there is already a big group and they have already started drinking and shooting up.

The four teenaged Warlords are lying on the floor, bleeding, bound and gagged with duct tape across their mouths. There are several more women in the room. She is welcomed by all.

There is a fifty gallon drum cut in half in the middle of the crowd. It is full of charcoal and is burning brightly. There is food barbequing on top of the drum and a beer keg surrounded by mattresses, over turned cups and chairs.

An hour later the group is thoroughly high, thoroughly drunk, swaying to the music and now in the mood to pay attention to the four Warlords lying on the floor. The attractive Latina is now more than topless, she is stark naked. Almost everyone in the room is naked. This is an orgy that is about to turn into a torture chamber.

The naked Latina squats down over the first of the Warlords. His eyes are wide open. She takes a knife out of her bag and holds it where the guy can see it. She cuts off his clothes and leaves him lying there naked. Other naked women do the same to the other gangbangers. The crowd is clearly excited and kicks and abuses the wounded and bound gangbangers.

The crowd encourages the naked women to rub their bodies all over the Warlords and then start to cut off body parts. They start with ears and fingers and work their way from there. There are pools of blood and body parts everywhere. Some of the body parts end up on the grills.

The music, the drugs, the naked bodies and the dancing turn the steamy old warehouse into a vibrating room of shaking bodies, partying thugs and dancing girls. They use the Warlords for entertainment. It is brutal beyond a mere mortal's imagination.

CHAPTER

TWENTY-FOUR

THE NEXT MORNING SUNNY DRIVES PAST THE PRO-
posed site for a new Walmart in Chicago. It was a
blood bath fight to get an OK. The Chicago City Council turned
them down twice, but finally a coalition of Black community
groups, Black Alderman, Chicago businessmen, Republican
politicians and the Mayor prevailed.

As Sunny drives by he sees Insane Jaguar General Arturo
Ortega watching the crowd picket. It is probably an entertaining event. Lots of colors. Lots of commotion. Moving parts
going various directions. Sort of a festive atmosphere. Clearly
the paid picketers are enjoying the nice weather and free food.

Ortega wears reflective sun glasses. The kind that make it
impossible to see his eyes. He is relaxed, just lounging
against his car, a big dark blue SUV. Ortega is sipping an
orange juice and nibbling on a Dunkin Donut apple fritter.
Boy that fritter looks good. Sunny is tempted to stop and say
hello and see if Ortega has another one in the bag. Then he
thought better of it and decided he should mention it to Vlad.
Why is an Insane Jaguar General out this early just watching
anti-Walmart pickets?

The opposition to Walmart was led by a coalition of unions who claimed they were opposed because Walmart didn't pay enough and didn't offer fancy health insurance policies like other big companies did. All of the unions are closely affiliated with the national AFL-CIO, an overwhelmingly Democrat group. The thing the Democrat unions are careful not to mention is Walmart is one of the most heavily Republican companies in America. They are very hard core defending free markets and international trade. They don't have unionized workers. They give a lot of money to Republicans. Who knows, maybe those facts had nothing to do with AFL-CIO efforts to screw Walmart.

Some people kid Walmart is really America's most successful foreign policy initiative. They buy products from all over the world. Little seamstresses in Bangladesh know some American, somewhere in that giant country of America is buying the shirt she sews. They know they have never made this kind of money before and the only reason they are making it is because an American is willing to buy this shirt at a Walmart and give the money to this little seamstress living in a tiny house. But this tiny house is a lot better than the hovel she lived in before she got the job making shirts for Walmart to sell across the ocean.

The seamstress and her family are living better than they have ever lived before and better than any of her parent's generation had ever lived. She thinks well of that American shopper she has never met. He isn't giving military aide to an allied government. He isn't giving foreign aid to some corrupt government who will never use it to expand economic opportunities that help the poor people in their country. He is giving her family the money to allow them to eat better and live better than they ever have before. Because of Walmart, America has a better image in Bangladesh, Honduras and Sri Lanka and the other developing countries that sell Walmart things for Americans to buy.

The Black community groups supporting Walmart reminded everyone that Walmart's pay was better than the zero the unemployed potential Walmart employees were making. The Black politicians split almost right down the middle. This is a textbook example of who thinks being a loyal Democrat is more important than helping their Black and Latino constituents get jobs. Who wants to get big union money for their campaigns and who is willing to put their constituents ahead of union bosses.

The health insurance issue really doesn't matter. The person is getting their health care free from Cook County Hospital now. If they get a job, they will continue to get it there. But now they will be paying taxes and copayments that would help offset the cost of that free healthcare and eating better, so hopefully that would make them healthier.

The buildings will be built by union contractors because in Chicago nonunion contractors will never get a permit they need to work, so they are not allowed to work. The unions own a majority on the Chicago City Council. They and the big personal injury and criminal defense lawyers are major contributors to Aldermanic races.

But that union controlled majority includes all of the Black and Latino Aldermen who are making it very clear they want Walmarts to be built in their areas. Many of these areas are called food deserts because there are virtually no grocery stores there and virtually no fresh foods. Walmart being the largest grocery store in the world will fill that void.

Outside the fence that surrounds the site, a band of paid demonstrators, paid by the unions, continue to picket the Walmart site. All of the demonstrators are just paid folks with no real tie to the unions. But they appreciate Walmart also. Walmart got them their present job walking a fake picket line. They make a little over minimum wage and get two free meals and all the free coffee, Gatorade and snacks they want. It is easy work.

Sunny is distracted after getting Sheila all packed up and off on the road with Stephanie Brookins. The Captain had asked one of the female officers to go with them. She was one bad ass lady. A former Army drill sergeant and before that an MP during the Persian Gulf conflict. She was a 20 year military veteran with plenty of experience. When she talked with Sunny and Harold Brookins she made it clear she understood this was similar to witness protection service. She had done that before on several occasions.

To add to the protection, Stephanie wasn't a bad shot and she was armed. She was a daughter of the South Side. No one in their right mind would go out of their way to mess with Stephanie. She knew what crime was and knew plenty of people who had been victims. She knew what she had to do to be sure she and her kids didn't become victims also. She wasn't afraid to hurt you if she needed to. The best defense is a good offense and Stephanie could play offense.

Of course they couldn't admit Stephanie was armed since Chicago has a handgun ban. The Supreme Court declared it unconstitutional, but Chicago doesn't care. What relevance does the U. S. Constitution have when compared to the political will of the left wing anti- gun activists, the Mayor and the City Council?

All that is irrelevant for the officer since she is a cop, she is an excellent shot and she is definitely armed whether the anti-gun activists like it or not. Sheila doesn't know the grip from the barrel, but has packed a ton of healthy snacks, some chilled V-8, some tofu crap to nibble on, a bunch of popular novels and several decks of cards.

Of course the girls aren't happy about leaving their husbands behind to face a well-armed Mexican Drug Cartel, but they know if Sunny and Harold with all of their special operations training can't handle the Cartel, no one can.

They might be afraid for the seriousness of the problem. But they know perfectly well that Sunny, Vlad and Brookins are ready to deal with it. There are some very well-trained officers and SWAT team members on the Chicago Police Department and they know that also. But police wives still worry. It is in the DNA.

Sunny gets to the Police Station still wondering why Arturo Ortega is interested in a bunch of hired pickets wandering in a circle. Maybe he is just renting out some of his gangbangers as protesters and on site protection. Who knows?

There is a huge commotion in front of the Captain's office. Sunny is on time, but that is late for him. He is always on Army time, which means five minutes early. "Hey! What's going on?"

Vlad quickly comes over to Sunny. "They found the bodies of four Warlords early this morning. They aren't just dead. Whew! They're mauled. No IDs yet. No fingers left for finger-prints. No teeth left for dental records. Also no private parts if you know what I mean?"

Sunny is stunned. "How do they know they were Warlords?"

Another officer leans toward Sunny and Vlad. "They had crimson and black strips from their running suits tied around their necks."

Sunny groans. "Oh shit, it's starting. Thank God Sheila and Stephanie are gone. What else? When do we implement the Captain's battle plan?"

"The Captain wants all of us to meet in a half hour. He isn't in too big of a rush just yet. So far, they are just killing each other. He's not sure that is a bad idea. The Warlords have gone to ground. It looks like there was a gun battle about 2:00 AM and both sides lost a few. But the Insane Jaguars and the Mexican Cartel took their guys bodies with them so counts aren't exact. It looks like the Cartel or somebody set fire to a couple of buildings on Warlord turf."

Fifty minutes later Sunny and Vlad get in their cruiser. Vlad has his Ithaca Mag-10 shotgun under his feet and several boxes of extra shells in the glove box. He keeps it hidden. Having unauthorized weapons is not something the Police Department approves of. Of course the liability terrified lawyers for the city of Chicago worried about everything. If it were up to them the police wouldn't be armed. Too much liability risk. They always think like lawyers which means they think about whom they can screw or who can screw them. Warped view of the world. No help at all when your job is to protect people from slime balls.

Both guys wear their body armor under light coats so it isn't that obvious where it is. The lawyers probably worry about the liability of body armor. If some scum bag shots a cop he might sue because the body armor keeps him from achieving his state of nirvana by murdering a cop. Thus in the lawyers world the scum bag is treated unfairly. His psyche will be damaged for life. He'll find some lawyer willing to take the case. Shakespeare borrowed it from Solomon, but either way, they're both right. First kill all the lawyers!

Vlad's cell rings and he answers. "Kozak." He listens. "Shit! That was Mortonson at the fire department. They set fire to my apartment building. Three people were hurt."

Sunny looks at Vlad. "Shit they probably got mine also. It is locked up, but that won't stop a fire. Call the Captain and let him know we're going to check out my house."

Arturo Ortega had carefully watched Sunny's car go by. Sunny couldn't tell he was watching because of the reflective sun glasses. This was the route Sunny used most often. As a smart detective should, he varied his routes, but there were only so many possibilities. He opened his cell phone and speed dialed. "His house. Now."

Ortega chews the last of his apple fritter, swigs the last of his orange juice and carefully tosses the bag and bottle into a trash can. He then wipes his lips with a napkin and throws that in also. Only then does he get into his SUV and pull away from the curb.

Sunny and Vlad pull up the driveway next to his immaculate Bungalow. Everything looks fine. No obvious problems. Looks just the way he left it.

Vlad opens his door. "You sit. I'll look. I know what I'm looking for. You're too old and crabby to be any good walking around anyway."

Sunny flips Vlad the bird, but stays in his seat.

Vlad gets out of the car, stands up to look around. He takes one step and all hell breaks loose. Bullets are flying everywhere. Vlad is hit multiple times. He staggers and shakes from the hits, but is able to drop himself back into the car.

The unmarked police car is hit by at least ten bullets. The front and back windshields shatter. Glass is everywhere. Two Molotov cocktails are thrown and land one in front and one in back of the car. The bullets keep slamming into the car. The flames from the Molotov cocktails leap up to surround the car.

Sunny ducks low and grabs Vlad by the shirt collar. He pulls Vlad back farther into the car. Sunny slams the car into reverse and floors it. The tires screech as he flies back out of the driveway right through the wall of flames.

He obviously can't see much so he goes too far and rams a parked car across from the end of his driveway. The collision causes Vlad's door to swing wildly but it ends up slamming closed. Luckily Vlad is sprawled on the seat and the floor so the door doesn't break his leg. Sunny spins the wheel and floors the car again back down their street

Another Molotov cocktail bounces off the hood of the car and ignites into flame as Sunny smashes against a parked car. He can't see a thing through the fire and smoke and keeping his head down to avoid the gun fire. As the car accelerates, a bullet hits a tire and it blows. Sunny swerves and fish tails.

Since his head is still low down, he can't see very much and he is running on only three good tires. The unmarked police car slaps into two more different cars as it fishtails down the street. The car is leaking gas, two hub caps come flying off and shattered glass sprinkles all over the street. But Sunny keeps the accelerator floored.

"Vlad...Vlad...you OK? I'm going straight to the U of C hospital!" Sunny slaps the flashing police light on the top of the car, stomps on the brakes so he can swerve around a corner and then stomps on the accelerator again.

He grabs his radio to call in a distress call and get more police headed back to his house. He isn't sure who was behind the attack, but he knew Arturo Ortega's morning vigil at the Walmart site must have been related.

Vlad's eyes are a little glassy but he is conscious. His voice is groggy. "Your driving will kill me before the bullets. Careful dipshit. There are a lot of beautiful ladies who are depending on you. So don't do anything crazy. I'll hang in there until we get to Billings."

Sunny breaks a smile as Vlad demonstrates his ever present sense of humor.

A second tire is nearly flat and the car is almost impossible to control. Just as Sunny looks up he sees a police cruiser turn on its light and siren, U-turn in the middle of the street and start a full speed pursuit of Sunny's car.

He realizes the cop must be wondering what the heck is going on with the blown away car. He hits the brakes, brings himself to a stop at the curb and jumps out holding his badge above his head. "Help! Need to get an injured officer to the emergency room."

The police cruiser swings sideways to block traffic and the officer comes out on the far side of his car with his gun aimed at Sunny. As soon as he sees the badge and hears the explanation he holsters his weapon and rushes to Vlad's side of the car. There is blood everywhere but a groggy Vlad smiles at the cop as he looks in.

"You think we look bad, you should see the other guys."

The cop laughs and pulls the door open. "Leave this wreck here. Can you get to my car or should we carry you?"

Sunny hurries over and the two of them help Vlad hobble to the police cruiser. Vlad signals Sunny to come closer to hear him. "Don't forget the Mag-10."

As the officer gets Vlad settled in back, Sunny hurries back to their car, grabs Vlad's Ithaca Mag-10 and the boxes of ammo. He then reaches through to turn off the engine, slams the door and heads back to the police cruiser.

He takes one last look at his car and is stunned. All the windows but one in the back seat are blown out. The paint has been scorched on both the front and the back ends. Both front and back windshields are destroyed. There are probably 50 bullet holes in the car. Gas is leaking onto the street from the shattered gas tank, two of the tires are flat and two hub caps are missing. The car looks like it just came back from a war zone in Beirut.

Sunny settles into the back seat next to Vlad to try to help with some emergency first aide until they get to the hospital. The uniformed officer turns on the flashers and the siren and then jams the accelerator to the floor. "Hang on, it'll be about five minutes to the U of C emergency room. I'm calling ahead now and then I'll call HQ. I wish we were closer to County, they've got the best treatment for burns and gunshots."

Sunny mumbles "thank you" and starts to wrap some of the emergency bandage the officer has tossed into the back seat around Vlad's leg and then moves to the arm.

Four minutes later, the officer skids to a stop at the Emergency Room Door as two gurneys and emergency personnel rush to the back seat. The doctor and nurse quickly get Vlad on the gurney and head back inside.

The other nurse and orderly help Sunny out and try to get him onto the other gurney.

"Wait, I'm fine. Don't worry about me."

The nurse looks at Sunny like he is mentally defective. "Come on, let's cooperate and get on the gurney."

Sunny is having a hard time seeing her because there is some kind of a red sheen in front of his eyes. When he tries to lean on the gurney his arm gives out and he collapses on the ground. The orderly, a big, well-muscled Black guy, scoops him up in his arms and gently sets him on the lowered gurney. Sunny leans back and rests his head on the pillow. He is just going to close his eyes for a second to refocus.

CHAPTER

TWENTY-FIVE

ALDERMAN LARENDA BASS AND THE GANGSTER Warlord attorney enter the district office of Speaker of the House Brennan X. Burke. It is a middle class or maybe really a mixed working class neighborhood on the South West side of Chicago.

A police officer named McGuire meets them at the door. He looks them up and down. "You have an appointment?"

Bass would be offended by some flunky stopping her, but knows it isn't worth worrying about.

The whole neighborhood is very neat, the streets are very clean, the trees planted on the parkways are in very neat alignment and the alleys with a fifty gallon drum for a trash can behind every garage are spotless. Brennan Burke knows where his powerbase is and is careful to be sure they know he appreciates them.

He figures he can take whatever he wants from Cook County and the State of Illinois as long as he makes sure the hometown neighborhoods are happy. He lives in a very nice home, the nicest in the ward. But it is not too ostentatious and does not get additional City services the way most of the other political

244 | SENATOR ROGER A. KEATS

big shots homes in Chicago do. He doesn't really need it. Like all ward bosses he appointed the ward's sanitation superintendent. As important as Burke is, he gets first pick of the up and coming city workers and he hires sharp young guys. What young guy wouldn't want to be under Burke's wing? Problem taken care of.

When you have been your party's State Chairman for over a decade and Speaker of the House for thirty years as Brennan X. Burke has been, you figure you can pretty much do as you please. You essentially appoint your stepdaughter as the state's Attorney General knowing full well she is well-trained at your knee to know not to ask tough questions and never deal with public corruption issues.

You don't even feel any real need to speak in public or do interviews. You don't even feel a need to speak to members of the other party. By the time you have become a multi-millionaire by using your influence to get massive tax breaks for your clients, you are as insulated financially as you are politically.

You know anyone who comes to see you is probably too petrified to do anything but kiss your fanny so you don't have to deal with unruly taxpayers or voters. Besides the money you are giving away isn't yours. It costs you nothing. So you might as well use it to build your political machine and your personal influence. If the taxpayers don't like it, who cares?

You have gerrymandered the state so thoroughly you can elect an ax murderer or child molester from your own party in most of the districts. Half of Burke's State Representatives aren't much better than that. He doesn't want sharp, top flight legislators. He wants duds who still can't believe they are there and will do anything to stay there. Burke is their ticket to a long political career with a double dip patronage job and a big pension. They'd sell their kid sister's virginity to keep those seats. They know they could never do half as well on their own. That is the secret to Burke's power. Be sure your underlings don't have the brains or guts to challenge you regardless of what outrageous things you do. Every now and then politically kill off someone who asks too many questions so everyone knows that is a bad idea.

Burke knows the system all too well. He grew up the son of a Chicago Democrat machine minion in the neighborhood of the late Mayor Daley, Richard I. He worked all of the political campaigns and quickly aligned himself with the Daley/White Irish led party. He was a smart kid, carried water for the donkey and did what he was told. In the early days he was a friend and ally of the 2nd Mayor Daley, Richard II. Fresh out of law school at the age of 26, Richard I made Burke and Daley's son, Richard II delegates to the State's Constitutional Convention. At 28, Richard I made Burke a State Representative.

Burke did what he was told and followed the Chicago Machine rules: Build up chits and don't make any waves. Richard I rewarded hard work and loyalty. Burke worked hard and he was ultra-loyal. Most of the machine legislators are just hacks so a bright young guy with brains moves up quickly. Da Mayor as Richard I was called made it clear he didn't want too many bright people in office. A few to run the show, the rest to be irrelevant back benchers doing what they are told. At the young age of 34, Da Mayor appointed Burke as his number two in the legislature. The guy he would call to deliver his directions. Suddenly Da Mayor is dead and the Democrat Speaker of the House is defeated and guess who is in charge of it all at the age of 38? By 40 he is the Speaker of the House and 30 years later he still is.

It is always better to be lucky than smart, but Burke was politically smart to go with his luck. Burke was in the right place at the right time. The death of Hiz Honor, da Mayor left a vacuum and the South Side White Irish Democrat Machine moved quickly to fill the void. There were plenty of older Irish-men in the Senate, the City Council and in Cook County office. But at that exact moment, when da Mayor died so suddenly, the only bright Irishman in the House was a kid named Burke.

Burke decided what needed to be done for him to emerge as the unchallenged leader. He then built alliances with unions and ambulance chasers. Next with brutal discipline, intimidation, union thugs and union money, ambulance chaser money and military precision he worked to strip everyone else's power. Burke gave no quarter and slit throats freely. Between back stabs, indictments and deaths, Burke eliminated all challengers. Suddenly he was the last man standing. The politics are brilliant.

Burke is a genius at influence peddling and has become a multi-millionaire. He is also a political genius, as far as winning elections is concerned. But, at his real job, governance, he is hopelessly incompetent. Burke has turned Illinois into an economic basket case buried in debt, high unemployment, terrible schools and allegations of corruption. Of course there were plenty of convictions of key allies to show the corruption allegations were true. But what the majority of Chicago and Illinois votes being what they are, corruption and incompetence doesn't matter and 30 years of economic decline continues.

Larenda Bass doesn't care that Burke is destroying the economic viability of the state. She just wants to be sure she gets hers. She is well aware who she is coming to see. She also knows there were gun fights and some buildings burned in her neighborhood last night. People she knows were killed. She knows time is not her ally. She also knows Burke has access to millions of dollars whose only purpose is to keep his political organization rolling along. Principle be damned, win the election. Bass knows she plays a key role in winning elections.

There is one solution, convince Brennan Burke to hand you over four million dollars of the taxpayer's money. You know he has the power. You know he has the money sitting there under the control of people he appointed to their jobs. You know there is millions and millions more of President Obama's stimulus money just sitting around. You need to be humble but you need to be clear. You want the money and you need the money. It will be used to calm the waters on the South Side, the most important voting block for Brennan Burke's party in the State of Illinois.

The Alderman knows that Burke knows on the South and West Sides the gangs are all pervasive. They are almost everywhere, Black and Latino areas. Only a handful of neighborhoods don't have some gang activity. Virtually every public high school has gangs. Anywhere there is a concentration of broken homes and single parent households, there are lots of gangbangers. Over 85% of Black kids and over 70% of Latino kids in the public schools come from single parent households, the breeding ground for the gangs.

The police have told Bass and Burke there are 70,000 to 125,000 gangbangers in Chicago alone. Over 100 different gangs with various alliances. Most are all but illiterate so they don't ask big policy questions. A huge controlled group and many are old enough to vote. All are old enough to do political work. Just what a Chicago political organization needs: big groups that can be easily controlled by a central authority.

Bass also knows it would be impossible for Burke not to know most of her key political workers are gangbangers or have ties to them. All he has to do is read the newspapers and he knows that. They work precincts. They work the polls. They work as election judges and run a tight ship in the polling places. They buy tickets to political fund raisers and show up to make the size of the crowd look good. They can cause trouble when they want. They can calm the waters when they want.

She knows she has to be careful how she says things. It has to all be in code. But Burke knows who her key people are. He knows her political issues are different than a lot of other of his state wide and regional consigliores. He knows her organizations deliver his biggest vote. They get tons of absentee ballots and nursing home ballots. Whether the people know about it or not, they do vote.

Burke is way too smart to ask too many questions. It isn't his money, but it is his political organization. Besides, she knows that Burke can just call President Obama's Chief of Staff and the money will be sent from DC as supposedly part of some made up stimulus program. So the money is free. Who cares, it doesn't really cost anyone anything anyway. Bass knows in her ward, less than 25% pay any income taxes at all. So the money really is free to the ward.

Bass and her allies don't ask for pinstripe patronage. They don't demand millions of dollars of pension fund money to be managed by some ally of hers. She doesn't have a single constituent in the municipal bond business so she isn't looking to get one of them made the senior manager. She wants patronage jobs and her political performance has earned them. But in today's climate they are hard to get. So she takes care of her own political workers. Or to be more exact, Warlord leader, Akile Fort takes care of her political workers. She is normally easy for Burke to work with. All of that is great, but she needs something and she needs it now!

She needs to be sure he understands he doesn't want gang wars to wrack the neighborhoods. He needs to know the money will be used to work with the teenaged boys in the danger zones. She knows the money will be used to make a payoff, but that is merely a technical detail. It is not Burke's business. He might not care anyway, as long he is insulated from blame. Especially, if it comes from DC via President Obama, it won't be traceable to him anyway. She cannot take no for an answer.

To her surprise, McGuire the cop comes out to lead her into Speaker Burke's office. McGuire greets them in a very friendly way and ushers them into the Speaker of the House's and Democrat State Chairman's office. It is a little like being led in to an audience with the emperor. Just this emperor isn't as friendly or as honest. Bass takes a deep breath and goes in.

McGuire closes the door and Speaker Burke slowly rises to greet his guests. He smiles but does not speak. He walks around his desk to shake the hand of Leonard Bernstein, the Gangster Warlord's attorneys. Nothing said. They know each other.

To Bass' surprise Burke walks up to her and gives her a light hug and a kiss on the cheek. They have never done more than shake hands before. He then offers both of them padded office chairs. Not fancy. Very utilitarian. But comfortable.

Bass and the attorney sit facing Burke's desk. He returns to his seat and settles in.

"Alderman. Mr. Bernstein. It is my pleasure. What can I do for you?"

Talk about all business. One quick smile. No offer of coffee or water. Right down to business. This is a busy man who has granted you a couple of minutes of his time, so get on with it.

Everything about the office screams utilitarian. Sparse furnishings. Nice but not fancy wall decorations. No picture of President Barack Obama or Governor Pat Quinn. A family picture on the credenza behind the plain desk. Burke knows he represents a middle class ward of mixed blue collar and probably lower management executives. There are also plenty of government employees from the State of Illinois, the county of Cook and the city of Chicago. A large dose of unionized workers. Hard working, practical people. They would not want their State Representative and Ward Committeeman to sit in a $1000 office chair behind a big mahogany desk. Everyone knows their guy is the biggest of the big guys in Illinois and they like that. He can call the President and the phone will be answered. But they also expect their ward to be spotless. It is. There are trees planted on the parkways and no homeless people in the way. Burke is not loved, but he is respected. By everyone. Especially his opponents.

CHAPTER

TWENTY-SIX

DRIVING IN THE INDIANAPOLIS 500 WAS A DREAM come true. A wonderful experience. Sunny was leading by a tiny margin. He had the accelerator floored. The margin was slowly expanding. He was great on curves and here came another one. Just as he pulls out of the curve the second place car somehow manages to swing inside and come even. As Sunny looks over he sees the driver has a gun in his hand and is aiming it at him. What the...?

Sunny can hear a little bit of bustle around him. Funny there seems to be some sort of soft beeping near his head. He is quite comfortable and wishes people would quiet down and just go away and let him sleep. SLEEP! What the devil is he doing sleeping?

He had just been in a one-sided gun battle at his home with some people he hadn't seen. One-sided isn't an accurate description. Neither Vlad nor Sunny even got off a shot. They were simply mobile targets for someone who clearly wanted to kill both of them. The embarrassing part is Sunny isn't even sure who it was shooting at them. After getting thoroughly whipped in the gun fight, Sunny had rushed his badly injured pal, Vlad to the hospital. Well maybe not him, this other cop was nice enough to help. Wonder where he is?

Sunny is feeling someone or something fussing about him. They are shuffling his pillow and his sheets and even his arm. What is going on?

Slowly his eyes open. There is a firmly built, blonde lady in her fifties smiling at him with some kind of a clipboard in her hands and she is looking intently at him. She is wearing a white outfit. What is she doing here? Wait a minute, she is a nurse and that is some kind of a medical chart she is filling out.

"Who are you? What are you doing? And what am I doing here?"

The friendly nurse smiles at his question. "I am Lyudmila Skynovich, a nurse in the ICU. I am checking your vital signs. You are in the ICU at the University of Chicago hospital and you are here because you got in the way of some bullets, a fire and also decided to smash your chest into your steering wheel. Your vest shielded you from any real damage. The cuts on you face seem to be from flying glass. The burns aren't very serious. More specifically, you're here because you drove in the ICU's front door. Are those enough answers for you?"

Sunny's head begins to clear. "Yeah. I guess. How is my partner, Vlad Kozak?"

"He was entertaining the nurses in the pre-op section last time I saw him. He is a real charmer. I assume by now the doctor has knocked him out so he can take a few bullets out of him. He will be OK if he does not try to make a career out of being a mobile target for guys who aren't really good shots but have lots of bullets. His vest stopped several of those bullets but they still gave him some very sexy bruises that will serve as a very macho decoration for some time."

"You're sure he'll be OK?"

"Positive? Let me put it this way. You don't need a parachute to sky dive. You only need one if you hope to sky dive twice."

Sunny's head isn't that clear and he has a confused look on his face.

Lyudmila gives him a friendly chuckle and takes hold of his arm to check his vitals. "That translates to saying he'll be OK if he decides not to stand in front of guys with loaded guns again. He got away with it once. Twice is a bad idea."

Sunny tries to lift his head and shoulders to get up to look around.

Lyudmila gently restrains him. "You don't want to do that just yet."

"Yes I do."

Lyudmila still gently holds him back. Her charming smile brightens up Sunny's area. "The last thing I want to do is hurt you. But it is still on my list. So do as you're told, or else." Her smile is gentle, friendly and reassuring, but her hand on his shoulder is a definite deterrence.

"I give up." Sunny settles back on his bed, closes his eyes and lets the world leave his area in the ICU.

Just outside his area, one standing and one sitting, are two alert, well-armed Chicago Police officers stand watch.

In the next building and up three floors, twins of the officers by Sunny stand outside the Surgery Room doors protecting Vlad.

While Sunny snoozes, Harold Brookins is with a team of ten heavily armed police officers inspecting Sunny's house. Taking into account the Molotov cocktails, assault rifles and H & K MP5 machine gun fire, the house doesn't look as bad as Brookins expected. Nothing that couldn't be fixed. But with the shattered windows as well as the burned lawn and bushes, it definitely did look a lot worse for wear at the moment.

Brookins looks carefully to see any clues. He has been to the house many times so is very familiar with what is there and

254 | SENATOR ROGER A. KEATS

what shouldn't be there. Even after the ambush, the house has a calming influence. It is a home, not just a house. The place has dozens of wonderful memories attached to it.

The crime scene crew has come and gone with tons of shell casings, what little was left of the Molotov Cocktails and some of the bullets dug out of the brick and trees in front of the house. They even found some finger prints. Whether they were Sunny and Sheila's or the attackers hadn't been determined yet.

The AK-47 7.62mm shell casings littering the ground are expected. Whether they come from the Fast & Furious weapons the Federal government had stupidly given to the Mexican Drug Cartels or are just bought on the black market doesn't matter. They are expected and fairly common for gangbangers using long guns.

It is seeing 9mm shells from H & K MP5s that is not something the police want to find. These are legendary machine guns with thirty round magazines. Not always completely accurate in the hands of nervous, teenage gangbangers, but with thirty rounds they don't need to be perfect. That said, they were still plenty accurate for what this group needed.

The 9mm parabellum shells they fire are like NATO rounds. They could do a lot of damage and do it quickly. A German manufacturer had essentially borrowed a Latin phrase to use as the name of the bullet. Parabellum essentially comes from the translation of *If you wish for peace, prepare for war.* The Gangster Warlords, Insane Jaguars and Santa Muerte Cartel were clearly preparing for war. Whether they actually wanted peace was a different question, as yet, unanswered.

Lieutenant Dornan climbs out of his car and gestures toward Harold Brookins. "Brookins! Come here. Good news and bad news."

Brookins joins him and shrugs as if to ask what?

"The good news for you is Vlad is in surgery but not in any life threatening danger anymore. They stopped the bleeding and found the bullets. His vest saved him from six direct hits near his heart, lungs and throat. Most of the rest were spread around his arms and legs. But he did have a wicked looking nick on his forehead that bled all over, but didn't do him much real harm. All that blood was what made him look so bad."

Brookins has a pained look on his face but nods. "They say we're all born naked, wet and hungry, then things get worse. This is Vlad's worse. At least he survived."

Dornan laughs. "Yea maybe. Sunny is asleep and with a head as hard as his, he probably did more harm to the bullets than they did to him. He'll be OK and out of the hospital in a day or two. Nothing serious, a few burns, lots of little nicks and a bunch of near misses. His vest absorbed some crap also.

Brookins shrugs with a smile. "With Vlad in the hospital for a while, at least he can't go chasing those poor innocent nurses with all of those holes in him."

Dornan chuckles at Brookins. "I guess that is a positive from our point of view. But think from the nurses point of view. They might not agree with your perspective."

Brookins chuckles back. "You're right, I hadn't thought of it that way."

"But, the bad news is some of the rounds have been traced to the guns those idiots at the Department of Justice sold to the Mexican drug cartels. That means we don't think it was the Gangster Warlords."

"Not the Warlords, I guess that is some kind of good news."

"We are assuming it was the Insane Jaguars. While I might guess it was the Jaguars, we do know for sure whoever it was, they had guns supplied directly by the Santa Muerte Cartel and indirectly by the Obama Justice Department and the ATF. The gunman may even have been assisted by Santa Muerte thugs.

That means they are in town and they know who they are mad at. Maybe the Santa Muertes did the whole thing? Not sure yet. How Obama's Justice Department was dumb enough to allow those thugs to get thousands of the most modern armament in the world, with their help, is beyond me."

Brookins acknowledges the info. "Whoever said the federal government is on our side?"

Dornan nods in agreement.

Brookins looks quizzical. "Any more dead gangbangers or more about the Warlord/Jaguar feud?"

"Three younger guys bodies but it looks like two are Jaguars. Might be Santa Muertes, but can't tell just yet. They both look Mexican and we don't have fingerprints on all of them."

"Makes sense. Is City Hall still telling us to soft pedal the gang war? Call these unrelated shootings?"

"Of course. But we think three other killings are collateral damage, family members for either the Warlords or Jaguars. No one has seen anyone we can identify as Santa Muerte Cartel thugs, but they would look an awful lot like a Jaguar so who knows? It is quiet at the moment."

Brookins nods and thinks a minute before he speaks. "You know Lieutenant, this gang war won't determine who is right or wrong or whether the Warlords made a bad deal with a cartel. All it will tell us is who will be left. I might bet against the Warlords because of the outsiders that have come in here, but I am more worried about the totally uninvolved folks who get caught in the crossfire."

Dornan nods in agreement.

CHAPTER

TWENTY-SEVEN

AKILE FORT AND MUSTAFA DOUBLE CHECK THEIR clustered group of Warlords. All of the others are pretty young looking. It makes Mustafa think of the proverb about the Fountain Of Youth: we have plenty of youth...where the hell is the fountain of smart?? All he hopes is they really did listen to him and they really do understand what they need to do.

Everyone is in very dark clothes and well-armed with both shotguns and big handguns. The alley is almost as dark as the guy's clothes. A box of Molotov Cocktails is passed around among four guys who double check the wicks. Everyone looks prepared.

Most street gangs are a pack of low IQ thugs. Others just lack common sense. Some of the leaders are actually fairly bright, but don't always put the best interests of their gang members at the forefront. As Akile Fort proved when he sent three of his Warlords to rush Sunny and Vlad on the West Side. With no training, all he did was get two of them killed and the third would never walk without a limp and the hitch in his shoulder would be painful. But that was Akile. He was the leader, not the tactician.

On the other hand, before joining Alderman Bass' staff, Mustafa had served in the Marines fresh out of high school. He was not the most competent Marine. He wasn't the quickest learner in the Marines. He never advanced above the rank of Lance Corporal. He had never been selected to be anything but a member of an infantry team. But he had been smart enough to listen to the tactics instructors.

He knew he would never be a general. He knew he would always be an infantryman. If he wanted to survive and carry his own weight, he needed to know what to do in combat. How to prepare the battlefield. Cover and concealment. Interlocking fields of fire. How to use surprise. Hand signals and others means of communication on a battlefield. When was the best time to attack.

Mustafa was about to demonstrate to Akile, the Insane Jaguars and the Santa Muerte Cartel why having an actual military veteran set up your assault was a very good idea.

A single Warlord and Mustafa stood to the side dressed in black like everyone else. He took the ignition switch from Mustafa and after checking to be sure it worked, put it in his pocket. The two talk quietly. "I'll repeat. I hear you Mustafa. I do. If neighbors, the police or firemen arrive first, just abandon the stuff and get back to the headquarters. If more Jaguars or Santa Muerte guys get there first, wait for them to approach the building and then set it off. OK? I got it."

Mustafa smiles to himself and claps the Warlord on the shoulder. They share gang hand signals and a knowing nod. Then the young Warlord hurries off into the darkness and goes around the block.

Mustafa was actually proud of having been a Marine. It was the one thing in his life he had done that had been good for society. He didn't really consider being the faithful right hand to a crooked and not very bright Alderman as something good for greater society. It wasn't much better than being a Warlord commander. Actually being a Warlord might have been better. After all crooks like Larenda Bass did far more harm than good and she was the shield for far too many street gangs and drug pushers. He was caught helping someone he really neither liked nor respected. But that was his Warlord assignment and he would do it to the best of his abilities. Being a Marine had been his one positive moment. Sometimes he thought he made a mistake getting out after his enlistment was up. But he knew he was never going to advance very far.

The other guys were more gung ho. They all seemed to study the field manuals more than he did. Many were better shots. But he liked being part of a team. It was good to have someone always covering your back. But he just wasn't made to handle the discipline or the academic part of the job that required him to learn new skills and work with updated equipment. The advances in technology got to be too academic for him. Also, it was just more structure than he could handle.

His late grandmother, who had essentially raised him, was very disappointed when he got out. She knew having him come home was not a good idea. She had been right.

He came home. Got in trouble. Spent time in prison. Learned lots of bad habits. Joined the Gangster Warlords in prison. Became a half-assed Muslim. Changed his name. He didn't really believe that Muslim stuff, but it had been helpful in prison. It gave him a bigger identity and more guys to cover his back. In prison, guys covering your back is a big deal.

All that said, he still smiled at the Marine boast. There is no such thing as an ex-Marine. Only a Marine no longer serving on active duty. Tonight or more accurately this morning he was going to be sure the Insane Jaguars and the Santa Muerte Cartel learned that motto had real meaning where Mustafa was concerned.

Akile speaks to no one in particular. "There won't be any police for at least the next half hour. That is our window of time. We can't stall, so let's go." The Warlords took up their assigned positions.

The two, three-story buildings they surround clearly do not have fire alarms or sprinklers and the front and back doors simply hang on their hinges. There are plenty of places for breezes to blow through to enhance the flames.

Akile signals his team is ready at their building. Mustafa returns the signal and the four assigned Warlords with the best throwing arms walk toward the silent buildings. Two in front and two in back. On a signal from the old Lance Corporal the four Warlords throw a bunch of Molotov Cocktails at windows on the second floor and then run back along the first floor throwing them through windows on the first floor.

All of the Warlords start screaming "Fire! Fire! Fire!! Get out of the building. Everybody out."

The fires and the screaming cause mass confusion. As the people, many of them Insane Jaguars with girlfriends and even a few kids come running out the doors, they tend to huddle into groups. Clearly girlfriends, not wives and the guys are best called sperm donors. These are not families. They are just horny young folks hooking up. No commitment, just sex and kids who will grow up to be fatherless losers like the girl and sperm donor. As soon as the groups get big enough, Akile and Mustafa signal for the Warlords to open fire on the crowds milling around.

Only a handful of the Jaguars had been awake enough to grab weapons, so few are armed. They are mixed into the groups with their girlfriends, some kids and other tenants of the buildings.

The noise from the fires masks the initial shots, but after a moment as the shot guns blast and the .357 Magnums open fire at almost point blank range the mayhem is fearful. Bodies fall everywhere. Blood spatters on the walls and the ground. The Jaguars have no place to run or hide. Gangbangers, girlfriends, innocent bystander tenants and screaming kids are scattered all over the blood soaked ground.

There are three Santa Muerte Cartel gunmen staying with a cousin of theirs who is a Jaguar. They are the last ones out of the Southern building. They know what Molotov Cocktails are and how to use them. They also know when someone is throwing Molotov Cocktails, to not go out without their weapons. These are experienced thugs and killers. They may not be kids their mothers are proud of, but they're no fools.

The flames finally force them out and they manage to walk right into two shotgun blasts by a Warlord a mere ten feet away behind a wrecked car. The Cartel gunmen know what to do and how to do it. But as luck would have it, they are in the wrong place at the wrong time and don't have a chance to offer any resistance before they are cut down at point blank range. They are no loss to society.

The now dead Cartel gunmen are a major target. The Warlords knew they were there. But the bigger target was to send a message. If the Insane Jaguars want to help the Santa Muerte Cartel, then prepare for the worst. The Cartel gunmen are dead. If a Jaguar wants to help them, join the body count.

A second message was sent also. There were two apartment blocks very nearby that would have been much easier targets, but they weren't hit. There were no Santa Muerte Gunmen there. You don't have to be a friend. But don't be a foe.

After little more than five minutes, Mustafa signals for his Warlords to withdraw and they join Akile's group as they all jump into Black SUVs and disappear down the alley and into the dark.

The Warlords are gone before anyone has even called the fire department. No one in a neighborhood like this one is going to call the police.

In the beat up, abandoned building across the alley from the fires raging in the Jaguar's buildings, the Warlord Mustafa had coached earlier is hunkered down so he isn't exposed to the heat from the flames and the light they cast on him. He waits to see who arrives first.

In a matter of only a few minutes, several half asleep Jaguars or maybe Santa Muertes jam on the brakes and skid their old and worn SUV to a stop by the back of the building. The Warlord patiently waits. The thugs are well armed.

The Warlord takes one last peek. He can just make out the new arrivals. They look better organized and better armed than Insane Jaguars. But he can't really tell if they are Jaguars or Santa Muertes. He checks the pace of their advance and carefully ducks down behind the brick wall to be sure he has plenty of protection in front of him.

As the Gunmen, holding their weapons at the ready, cautiously walk from their SUV to get a better look at the building the bomb goes off. The entire back of the building comes down on top of them. Flames, bricks, window frames and parts of the back stairs fly into the air. There is noise, smoke and flames everywhere. The Gunmen are buried under the pile. There are briefly some screams of agony but they fade quickly.

The Warlord takes a quick peek again to be sure everything has gone as planned. It would be hard to see anything specific in the dark and with all of the dust in the air, but with the flames he gets a clear picture of death and destruction. That is all he needs to know. He then hustles out of the building, into a small black car and is gone before anyone even knows he has been there.

Message delivered with lots of blood. We aren't afraid of you and we aren't going to be easy to abuse.

According to TV reports twenty nine were dead, twelve were seriously wounded, six had lesser injuries and three, all children, were unharmed. In the mayhem, the kids had been knocked to the ground and folks had simply ignored them. No one had tried to find them or help them. They just lay on the ground, screaming, curled up in horror with their arms over their heads and as dead or wounded adults fell on them, they were protected.

Both buildings were total losses. The Reporters said it appeared this was a surprise attack by one street gang on another. What was different was the military precision and obvious organization involved.

In addition to the fires and sneak attack on the survivors, there appeared to have been a secondary explosion. No one was sure yet if it was just something in the buildings, ammunition stored somewhere or an additional bomb. The tactics appeared similar to those used by many Muslim terrorists. First a bombing to cause death and destruction. Then shortly later, when help arrived, a second bomb to kill the first responders and cause more death and terror. Whether that was the actual tactic wasn't clear yet, but it sure looked like a well-organized operation.

The police would hold a press briefing that day at four o'clock once they had time to digest the facts and evidence from the site.

Lieutenant Dornan was surrounded by police officers, evidence techs and just interested staff from the Mayor's and Aldermanic offices. They are poring over the facts gleaned so far from the wreckage and the bodies in the morgue.

The Lieutenant, an Army veteran of the Persian Gulf War in 1991, said to no one in particular. "This was the best organized and implemented gang attack I've ever seen. If I didn't know better I'd think it had been planned and carried out by some paramilitary group or at least guys with military training."

An aldermanic aide asked. "Do any of these gangs hire mercenaries?"

"Don't think so. But forget the viciousness. Just look at the tactics. A classic pre-arranged ambush. The fires forced the dead right into the ambush and with interlocking fields of fire, no one was safe and no one had any place to hide. The use of Molotov Cocktails was ingenious. We think the Jaguars used Molotovs on Detectives SunWarrior and Kozak. Now it looks like the Warlords turned around and used them on the Jaguars. Imitation is the supreme compliment."

The aide listens to every word. "Is this an escalation or...?"

Dornan shrugs. "Ask me that in a week. We'll know better then."

The Mayor's aide looks at the gathered reporters and crowd and says, "Nothing here conclusively proves this was a gang war. Don't jump to conclusions until we have more information."

Most of the crowd looks away and scoffs at such a blatant attempt to cover up the obvious.

A detective in jeans and a sweat shirt comes up to Dornan. "Hey, Boss. Got an observation for you. Maybe more of a question. There are other Jaguar apartments around the corner and a couple of blocks over. The buildings are older and have more flammable material. Why hit these? What made these a better target?'

Dornan's expression is serious. "Good frickin' point. Let's talk with the morgue and see if we can figure out what was here they were looking for."

CHAPTER TWENTY-EIGHT

IT IS FIRST THING IN THE MORNING AND SUNNY, still not 100%, is leading a convoy of five police cars to the buildings where he had last seen Arturo Ortega. Sunny could easily get rehabilitation time or sick leave or something else, but has too much to get done to malinger. It is first thing in the morning because gangbangers tend to still be asleep at this hour in the morning.

The police are armed with shotguns and surround the buildings. Sunny gets out in front where he had first seen Ortega beating up Jerry Katorski. Sunny still has bandages on his face and arm, his skin is still pretty red from the burns and he limps slightly. But taking into account he was almost killed, he looks pretty good.

As soon as Sunny gets out he is joined by Brookins and another well-armed uniformed officer. He then walks up the sidewalk toward the building. Arturo Ortega and two of his Insane Jaguars come out of the building and meet Sunny, Brookins and the other officer half way to the building. It is almost as if they were expecting the police.

"Sunny, glad to see you're OK. I heard about the attack and was worried about you." Arturo reaches out his hand to shake.

Sunny is again amazed by Ortega. The guy has no shame. First he tries to kill him and then tells him he's glad he's OK. But he shakes the offered hand. "Are you sure you're glad? We saw you at the Walmart near my home."

Ortega looks a little hurt. "We rented some of our guys to the unions to be protesters and walk a picket line. I stopped by to be sure it was all going well. They pay good money. They were passing out free Dunkin Donuts apple fritters. How could I resist?"

Sunny isn't sold.

Ortega speaks quietly so only Sunny will be sure to hear. "Sunny...think about it. Did you screw the Warlords? Did you screw the Santa Muerte Cartel? Did you screw the Jaguars? Who has reasons to want you dead?"

Sunny nods as he listens. He clearly isn't sold.

"The Warlords owe you one. Don't pretend they aren't mad. You think Santa Muerte has a short memory? What do the Jaguars gain by killing you? I'll let you ponder that one"

Then he gestures for Sunny to join him away from the group. They stroll over by some bushes. "Sunny this isn't our fight. Not mine, not yours. This is a fight between some guys from Mexico and the Gangster Warlords. They want the Jaguars to be involved, but it doesn't make sense for us to get in the middle. A few of our guys are relatives of the Mexicans and are helping on their own. I'm trying to stay out of it. You should too. Let whatever happens happen. I don't have a dog in this fight and if you're smart you won't either."

Ortega manages to stun Sunny again with his openness and his candor. "How do I not? We're the police."

"This will blow over quickly. If your guys aren't in the way, it will blow over faster than if you try to intervene. I'm a businessman. I'm sticking to my business not some else's. You're the police, protect the innocent and let the guilty face the consequences of their own actions."

"The Mexican's have a habit of threatening people's families, not just those involved."

Arturo Ortega looks around and is clearly thinking. "You think I didn't know about your wives? I saw them leave. I have a bug on their car. I know where they are. I let them go. Santa Muerte wouldn't be happy but I won't tell them, so who's to say anything. The fight is the Santa Muerte Cartel versus the Gangster Warlords. Your wives aren't either and I protected them. They aren't part of this fight."

Ortega pulls something from his pocket and drops what looks like a tracker on the ground and steps on it. "Now they are totally safe. They aren't part of the fight. Keep them out of it."

Sunny simply has no idea what to say. Ortega clearly understands what is at stake and he still punts.

As they stand there a moment a car squeals to a stop at the curb. Several guys who could be younger Insane Jaguars jump out and hurry to Ortega. They seem unfazed by and ignore the police. Sunny can clearly hear the conversation.

The Jaguars are excited and angry. "Four o'clock this morning they hit our buildings on Cermak. Fire bombed them and then shot the people as they came out. Our guys, women, kids, everybody."

Ortega goes white with shock. He looks around at the police. "I'll be at the cafe in a few minutes. Now go." He sort of shoves the young guys back toward their car.

Sunny shrugs. "I'm sorry. We came here to tell you about it if you didn't already know. That is why we're here. We just didn't get that far yet."

"You understand. I tried to keep us out of this. I'm a businessman and I tried to keep the peace. I tried. Any Jaguars involved were on their own. We've got guys who have friends and relatives in Santa Muerte. Won't stop a man from helping his friend. But the Jaguars were doing almost nothing as a unit. This is a declaration of war on the Jaguars. The fight was Warlord versus Mexicans. What am I supposed to do now?"

Sunny couldn't think of anything to say. He was still thinking about Arturo dropping the tracker on the ground and stomping on it. The guy had knowingly and intentionally protected Sheila and Stephanie. He had no idea what he should tell Arturo to do. Arturo is a Gordian Knot to him. He is supposed to be a blood thirsty, drug running, and violent gangbanger general. But he is either not what he is supposed to be or he is a great actor.

Arturo goes back toward his building and signals for the two other Jaguars to join him. "I'm sorry, I need to go." That was all he said and he was gone.

Sunny walks back to Brookins and leads him to the car. He signals for all of the police to get back in their cars and follow him. Sunny is quiet as he drives. Brookins sits with him.

"Sunny, I didn't hear every word, but enough to get the drift. I'm with you. I can't figure this guy out at all. Is he for real or is he a total fraud? I don't know either. But I saw him stomp on that tracker. I wish I had time to look at it. But if that really is following a bug on the girl's car...really is...what do we say? I have no idea what to say or do about him."

"I'm with you. I don't know why, but I believe him."

"One way or the other, the Warlords hitting those buildings was a brilliant military move but a really dumb stunt if Ortega is right that the Jaguars have been a bit on the sideline. GOD, I just don't know. Remember you're the big, smart detective. What the...?"

"Brookins, they are about to reap mayhem in Warlord territory. We need to do something even if we think it would be smarter to just walk away."

"No shit. Let's get back to Dornan and regroup."

As they drive back they go by the local high school named after a famous figure in Mexican history. The building is only a few years old. It really looks like it could be a nice environment if it weren't for the gang graffiti near the building and on the walks surrounding buildings. It is still a half hour before classes will start. The building looks almost vacant. There are only a handful of cars in the teacher's parking lot.

The police detail that surrounds schools in most of the troubled neighborhoods is just starting to arrive and get organized for a morning of metal detectors and gang insults directed at kids in rival gangs. It is a world that is hard for the average person to understand. Large numbers of the kids come from broken homes and the gang is a way to have a surrogate family. Albeit a drug running, well-armed, violent and embarrassingly ignorant family. Still more of a family than they find at home.

When parents, or really a parent have done such a bad job that their own children join gangs to imitate family, somebody needs to look in the mirror ask themselves some tough questions. Of course they don't and that is why their kid is in a gang.

Brookins looks at the school. "Isn't that the school that young kid who got killed the other day was supposedly attending? We investigated the death."

Sunny thinks a moment. "The kid in the alley at ten o'clock at night, on a school night? The one with the mother who claimed he wasn't in a gang but she still let him out at that hour so he could stand around in an alley everyone knows is a gang hangout and where drugs are sold. That kid?"

"Yeah...that kid. You know the thing about that one that so stuck in my craw was the mother claiming he was an honor roll student. Never been in trouble. Good kid. All that stuff. Then the *Sun Times* reporter checks with the school and asks if that was true and it turns out the kid hadn't even been to school in over a month and clearly had never been within a country mile of the honor role. You want to say to the mother, don't make it so obvious what a terrible parent you are. If you keep your mouth shut it won't be so obvious you don't have the faintest idea who your kid is."

"I remember interviewing the mother," says Sunny. "I probably shouldn't have, but I talked with the reporter who wrote the article. The reporter and I talked about what makes both of us frickin' nuts is no one ever mentions the father. Not PC. It is like all of these kids were born by immaculate conception. The Mom is supposed to be a saint. No Dad role model. No one helps with the bills by sending child support. No Dad at the funeral. A boy that age could really use a role model. A guy coming home after an honest day's work.

The reporter wanted to raise the issue but he knew he'd catch hell for bringing up the 1,000 pound gorilla in the room. Everybody knows virtually every one of these kids is from a single parent family. No fathers. 90% of the guys in prison come from families with no father in the house. We all know it. But you make the feminists mad if you mention kids with fathers, especially fathers that work, tend not to be found dead in alleys where gangbangers hang out."

Brookins nods in agreement.

Sunny keeps railing' on. "Somebody to give a shit if he's dead or alive. Somebody who ought to check to see if his homework is done. Ahh, forget it. Depresses me. What is it about these guys they feel no responsibility once they pull their pants up?"

Brookins couldn't agree more and just continues to nod in agreement.

Sunny is on a roll. "Wonder what's the matter with society? This is Lyndon Johnson's Great Society in the real world. Johnson and the idiots around him didn't think having a father in the home meant anything. They were rich, Ivy League social engineers and so frickin' smart. Well here it is baby. The brave new world of the Great Society live and in color. Unfortunately the color is red blood left on the sidewalk."

"Stephanie and I just decided she wouldn't work," Brookins replies. "We thought raising our kids right was more important than an extra car. Paying Catholic school tuition isn't easy, but what is the choice. We have to live in the city."

"Sheila and I never miss Mass. She usually goes every day. Don't let me be serious about stuff, but I wonder where I would be right now if our Priest hadn't taken me under his wing after Dad died. Catholic Charities and Mount Carmel truly shaped me and my values. I attended Catholic schools and got my butt kicked regularly by sadistic female leprechauns disguised as Nuns. Of course I probably deserved every butt kicking."

The two friends share a laugh. Anyone who ever attended Catholic schools has at least one hilarious story of some tiny Nun in her habit giving them holy hell for being godless sinners heading straight down the primrose path to Hell. The Nun was usually right and it terrified the kids into remembering what they were being told by the Priest and the Religion class instructor.

Sunny turns to Brookins and asks, "Since when are you Catholic? Sheila and I are, but I thought you were some of those crazy holy rollers! "

Brookins laughs at the portrayal of their religious faith. "Up yours. We're not Catholic. Most of the Black kids in the school aren't either. Thank goodness the archdioceses doesn't get too hung up on that. I suppose they view it as proselytizing. Besides, we are what is called Evangelical you ignorant twit. Holy rollers are something else. Not really all that crazy, just a little more excitable then us. They are not like you Catholics who worship by sleeping in the pews."

Both guys share a laugh at Brookins' friendly insult.

Brookins keeps at Sunny. "The last time I saw a Catholic awake during a service was when Stephanie and I went to St. Sabina with friends. That was Father Michael Pfleger's church then. He would wind up the crowd. Now those are your Holy Rollers. You wouldn't know Pfleger is Catholic. Of course the Archbishop wasn't so sure he was either. He drove the Archbishop nuts!"

"Sheila and I have been there a time or two. Father Pfleger is not your average Priest. Probably the Cardinal is glad about that too. Cardinal doesn't need too many pains in the neck. Pfleger can be a bit of a trouble maker. But he's OK. He usually makes trouble for the guys who someone ought to make trouble for."

"St. Sabina has a pretty good Catholic school. You know, Stephanie always says institutional racism isn't all that crap you hear about, it is really forcing all these inner city minority kids into these terrible public schools where there is no hope of them getting a good education. The good kids are surrounded by the thugs and druggies and it is almost impossible for them to get an education."

Sunny agrees. "No education. Guaranteed failure."

"Right, that is institutional racism in the flesh. In Detroit and Milwaukee something like 35% of the kids graduate and no one says a word. Here in Chicago the Secretary of Education called this the worst school system in America a couple of years ago. Now they have the dropout rate down to around half and they act like that is really impressive. So the guys who run the school tell us to just shut up and we shouldn't ask questions about the billions we give them. This is BS."

Sunny considers what Brookins said. "Never thought of it that way, but I think she's right. Now forget all this deep thinking. What are we about to do to keep a bunch of these uneducated, fatherless, over sexed, drug addled thugs from killing each other?"

CHAPTER TWENTY-NINE

ALDERWOMAN LARENDA BASS AND THE GANGSTER Warlord's attorney pull her huge, black SUV into the parking space beside her Aldermanic office. They lock up the SUV and then unlock the office. Inside is Gangster Warlord Commander, Akile Fort, her aide, Mustafa, also a major Warlord leader and two heavily armed young Warlords sporting their black and crimson colors. All of the Warlords are still in the essentially black outfits they wore the night before for the raid on the Jaguar apartment buildings.

Akile sees Larenda and gives her a big, warm smile. He looks ready for good news.

"We got it baby!" Bass screams and does a cute little dance all over the office. Everyone joins in with her and they all dance and whoop and high five each other. "He took the completed application and corporate papers and said his guy will cut us a check tomorrow. It is coming from Obama's stimulus funds that Illinois got. His guy will have to walk it through the Comptroller's Office to get the check quickly. She is being a bit of a pain in the fanny since Illinois is broke and not paying billions of dollars in bills. She has been holding up checks because the state doesn't have any money. They'll have to finesse her a bit. But we've got the money!"

Mustafa pauses and thinks. "I don't follow this stuff, but what did you say about Illinois being broke and can't pay its bills? How is the government broke? Can't they print money or something?"

The lawyer carefully responds. He doesn't want to offend Mustafa. "Well, broke is a relative term for government. Now a state like Illinois can't print money. They only do that in Washington."

Mustafa still looks confused. "But you say they broke. Don't broke mean broke? Like the Warlords are broke right now until we get Burke's cash. Are they like that?"

"Sort of. But remember it is Obama's cash. Burke just directed it to us. What Illinois does is just not pay people, like doctors, the universities, schools, the pension funds, pharmacists or people who have done things for the state."

Mustafa looks more confused. "Why would the dumb motha' fukkas' do work if de weren't goin' to pay 'em?" As the conversation goes on and Mustafa becomes more confused, his vocabulary becomes more ghetto. He is not figuring this out.

The lawyer looks a little frustrated at Mustafa not understanding. When he would talk to Mustafa, he seemed bright enough to grasp the points. "What the state does is borrow money to pay their bills. The state hasn't had a balanced budget since the 1990s. They just don't pay bills and borrow to cover their immediate term cash needs. Since they don't have any cash, they borrow. But because everyone knows Illinois is broke they pay the highest interest rates of any state in the county and have the lowest bond rating of any state."

"You mean like a guy gettin' a pay day loan? He's a bum with bad credit so the pay day guy charges him a lot to make taking the risk worth it?"

"Basically yes. That is a good analogy. The Governors were George Ryan and Rod Blagojevich and they just kept spending and borrowing. The new Governor Pat Quinn does the same thing. They didn't seem to care there wasn't any money to pay the bills they were running up. They'd say they wanted to spend the money. Then Burke would shove it through the legislature. Those guys more than tripled the state's bonded indebtedness in just a couple of years."

"Wasn't Obama in the Illinois Senate then?"

"Yes."

"Did he vote to spend money he didn't have?"

"Of course. He voted for all of it. Just like he's doing now as President. That's how we're getting this money. But in Washington he just prints the money. Ryan and Blagojevich had to borrow it."

Akile looks at Mustafa. "Remember we worked for both of those guys, Ryan and Blagojevich or however it is pronounced. We worked precincts and got out the vote for them. We met with Ryan one time when he was just running for governor and he gave us a grant to help with reading programs in our neighborhood. Maybe it was anti-drug education too. I don't really remember exactly what, but he gave us some money from his grant fund. But he wasn't governor, he was a secretary of something. Then we worked for him to get him elected Governor."

"Yeah, I remember. Boy he was a dumb shit. Believed everything we told him and then he gave us a bunch of money. We met that Blagojevich guy too." Mustafa gestures for Larenda Bass. "We took a bunch of our guys to a fundraiser you had for him, didn't we? I remember we had to do something to get checks from a currency exchange because he didn't want all the money in cash."

Bass nods yes. "You gave him $25,000."

Akile smiles back. "You know I liked both of them. Ryan reminded me of grumpy from Snow White and the Seven Dwarfs. Blago took me back to bein' a kid. He made me think of Mickey Mouse. I haven't seen them in a while. How are they doing now?"

There is a very long pause. Finally the lawyer says. "I think maybe you missed some of the news. They're both in prison now."

"No shit! They were governors. How'd that happen?"

The lawyer speaks carefully. "Blago kept claiming he was innocent. He kept saying that is how business is done in Chicago and Illinois. He has to be upset at getting hung. He doesn't think he was doing anything different than all the guys around him. Speaker Burke. Most of the Chicago Aldermen. A bunch of the lawyers in the legislature and City Council. The City Council zoning committee. He sort of has to think, why me? Who did I piss off? I'll bet he has a clear conscience. But it is the result of a pretty fuzzy memory."

Akile nods in agreement. "Too bad, I liked them."

Alderman Bass knows they are in jail. It never dawned on her the Warlords didn't follow the news at least a little bit, so she did not answer their question. But she stumbles over her words as she answers. "You know I love you Akile. But if you like some guy, that might not be a great character reference for them in front of a grand jury. I don't mean to offend you, but you see life a little different than the average guy."

Fort isn't offended. He thinks about her statement for a moment. "Yeah, you're probably right. Well, too bad. They were good guys. OK, but how do we get our money as soon as possible? The Mexican guys and the Jaguars are going to be pissed about something we did last night, so let's get them the money and get them out of town."

Mustafa's mind finally returns to the rest of the crowd. "Hey, the guy at a restaurant we protect said something about they had this big tax increase. He was complainin' up a storm. Right? So how they broke?"

The lawyer is again searching for a delicate answer. "They did raise the income tax 67% but they ended up spending even more money and had a bigger deficit with more money."

Mustafa looks as confused as ever. "They must really be dumb. You give Akile and me more money we don't end up with less."

Akile walks back to Mustafa. "Yeah, they must all be real dumb. That Brennan Burke runs it all and he must really be the dumbest one or really crooked to keep spending all that money he doesn't have. Look at all the money he's giving us. Really no questions asked. I don't like doing business with guys like that. You can't trust 'em. They're too crooked. No loyalty. They just think they can buy people off."

The lawyer turns his back and coughs to try not to laugh out loud at the naiveté expressed by these wanton killers, pimps and drug pushers. He knew they were right, but thought it best to just keep his mouth shut. They clearly didn't understand Chicago politics. The place is run by crooks. Deal with the crooks or you don't deal with anyone.

Akile turns back to the lawyer. "You OK?"

The lawyer nods. "Something in my throat."

"OK. Tomorrow you and Larenda need to go get that check. I'll be sure to alert our bank guy we'll need four million in cash by tomorrow. You know, the usual old bills and stuff. I'll tell our guys to stay low until then. I'll call a meeting with the Mexicans and give them the cash. If they go along, we end it. If not, we'll have some guys ready to finish them off while they're in the open."

The lawyer looks at Akile. "I didn't know you had a banker."

Akile laughs at him. "Not the kind of banker you're thinking of."

Now Larenda Bass looks a little confused. "You think everyone will just walk away if you give them the money?"

"Sure. Why not? It isn't personal. It's just business."

CHAPTER THIRTY

VLAD SITS UP IN HIS BED IN THE SPECIAL RECOVERY
unit. It is something like a standalone, miniature hospital that simply handles folks recovering from surgery. Once
they are out of danger, but still in need of hospitalization, this
is a cost effective way to handle the recovery process.

The nurses monitor his diet and pain levels. The unit also
has physical therapists that come around and hassle patients
like Vlad to move, walk a little and do some basic exercises to
speed their recovery.

Vlad is still too sore to be excited about moving and walking.
He does some, but he is not ready for anything major yet. By
the time a surgeon takes six bullets out of your body, the internal trauma doesn't go away overnight. Outside his room are
still two well alarmed and alert Chicago Police Officers.

The doctors, physical therapists and nurses don't know Vlad
has a weapon under his pillow. But he is always a policeman,
even in a hospital bed. The cops on guard know he is armed,
but pretend not to know.

This is one of Vlad's old favorites. He would rather bite off his
finger than give up his weapon, a 9mm Steyr GB pistol. It is the

first choice of Special Forces types. Widely carried by them and totally trusted. It has no safety catch. It just takes a hefty double action pull for the first shot and then eighteen more in the magazine. Very accurate for a pistol. Vlad is always ready. Always.

Visitors are intentionally limited, but Vlad convinced them to let Judy Schurz visit. She was still bubbling about getting her residency permit for her rehabbed brownstone and Vlad's help. She didn't really understand what had happened and figured she was better off not asking too many questions. Vlad took care of it and that was good enough for her. She was shocked at how bad he looked. Six bullets in various parts of your body and several more direct hits to a bullet proof vest rarely leaves a person looking their best. Vlad appreciated her help and support. Of course he didn't mention she was only one of several who had wanted to visit. He didn't think that would score brownie points with her.

Vlad isn't really dozing, but he isn't exactly all there either. He hears the commotion that sounds like it is coming from the front of the building. Lots of shouting and maybe furniture being knocked over. The shouting gets louder and then he realizes one of the voices comes from a police guard outside his room. Next thing he knows there is gun fire, screams and what sounds like automatic weapons fire.

Vlad is now awake and the SIG Sauer GB is in his hand. Even though he is attached to an IV, wires, monitors, drips and assorted crap, he knows he wants to be behind the bed, not propped up in the middle of it. He may not know what is going on, but he was sure gun fire in a recovery hospital is not a good thing. Why be a bigger target than necessary? Vlad drops to the floor, knocking over all kinds of valuable equipment. His heart monitor sounds like his pulse has just doubled. He doesn't even want to think how much money he has just wasted by breaking all of these monitors.

Even if Vlad didn't know exactly what was going on. He did have a feeling it had to do with him being there. Some people had wanted him dead. It was safe to assume they still did. This was not a good sign.

As bad as he feels about breaking all of that equipment, he is more upset at having knocked over the plate of cookies Judy had baked for him. Forget her many other fine attributes. She could bake and enjoyed doing it. Vlad had gained several pounds since they had started dating. He thinks a moment and wonders why he is worried about cookies. There are armed thugs out there trying to kill him and a few lost cookies aren't really an issue. He is amazed his brain is still a little addled from the drugs and sedatives at a moment like this. He is a warrior and knows he needs to be able to concentrate.

He can hear more screaming and weapons being fired. He thinks he can hear bullets thud into his exterior wall. The door bursts open and one of the Police backs into the room pumping his shotgun as he comes. He ducks behind the door jam and looks for something else to use as cover. He knows the wall isn't going to be able to sustain much automatic weapons fire.

"Vlad stay down."

Vlad aims his Sig Sauer at the door. "I am. I'm behind the bed and I'm armed. What just happened."

The gunfire and screams continue. "It looks like some of your Mexican friends aren't satisfied. I think they want you dead! Or maybe they want you alive but in their possession."

"In their dreams. We'll hold them off. How are the other folks?" For the first time Vlad notices the Policeman has blood on his arms and leg and is dripping even more blood on the floor.

The Policeman pumps more rounds into his shotgun. "Not good. I think several of the front desk folks are down. Couldn't tell if they were shot or just getting out of the way. Dansberry is behind a metal cart across the hallway. He gives us a better field of fire because we can support each other."

Vlad knows what he means by supporting fields of fire and knows Dansberry is an experienced Police Officer. Good thinking. What he is really worried about are all of the innocent bystanders in the recovery hospital. There is a momentary pause in the gunfire, but the screaming goes on.

"We're trying to protect everyone, but back in the corner like this, they got to some of them before we could react. Being in the back corner has pluses and minuses."

He blasts two more shotgun rounds at a guy who is trying to run at them. Both rounds hit him and he staggers. As he drops, he skids almost right up to the door. He lies there quietly, leaking blood all over the floor. He looks well past just dead. The Cop pumps more shells into his shotgun and pulls his pistol.

Vlad pushes his bed toward the door. It gives quite a bit of cover. He is still a little groggy from all of the medicine in him. But with all of this excitement he is perking up pretty fast. Vlad pulls tubes and drips and monitors from his arm. He chuckles as he tosses them on the floor. "I know my nurse will be pissed, but I think she'll understand."

"Not her problem anymore. She was at the front desk. I saw her get hit in the first charge."

Vlad is shocked about his funny, friendly nurse. "Shit. How many are there?" He thinks he sees movement and opens fire. There is a scream, but nobody falls out from behind the file cabinets.

Vlad empties his magazine into and around the spot where he heard a scream after he fired. No scream, but this time he can see a hand and part of the forearm of someone lying on the floor. The arm is dark with tattoos. He quickly slaps a new magazine into his SIG Sauer.

The Police Officer fires next to the area Vlad hit. He speaks over his shoulder without looking back. "Didn't see them all, but a bunch."

A loud voice with a heavy accent comes through the open door. "Listen up, Kozak. We have prisoners. Either come out now or we start shooting the prisoners. Now!"

The Policeman looks at Vlad.

The thunder of a single shot from a large pistol explodes into the room. Probably a .357 Magnum or something of that size. There is shrieking everywhere. The gunman shoves a nurse out from behind the shelves they are behind and tosses her limp body toward the doorway. Half of her head is missing and there is blood everywhere.

"We said now! You have ten seconds."

Vlad and the Policeman look at each other again. Neither knows what to do. They don't know if he's bluffing or serious and haven't the faintest idea if he has other prisoners.

A second thunderous blast breaks the air. The mangled body of the file and billing clerk is shoved out from behind the file cabinet and lands near the dead nurse. The nurse is face down. The clerk is on her side. Her face isn't any more recognizable than the nurses.

Police sirens wail in the distance. There are clearly several, not a single one.

Dansberry yells at the gunmen from behind the overturned metal cart. "I called you in. Half the Chicago Police Department will be here in a matter of seconds. Now drop your weapons and surrender!"

"We'll find you! We'll get you next time!" The whole building shakes with machine gun and hand gun blasts. Everybody ducks. There is a breaking of bottles and flames start to shoot across the room following the trail of the spilled liquid. Nothing can be seen, but it sounds like people running out the door. Then everything but the wailing police sirens is silent.

Vlad's guard continues to cover his door, but Dansberry carefully advances on the front desk area. He has his shotgun pointed at the shelving. There are flames lapping all around the area he is in. In a flash, a Santa Muerte gunman who appeared to be dead, rolls over and shoots point blank at Dansberry.

The Policeman stumbles backwards but opens fire with his shotgun. He's goes down on his back.

The blasts hit the Santa Muerte thug full in the face and chest. It is a mess. Blood and body parts are everywhere. From a range of five feet, it is obscene how much damage two rounds from a Benelli shotgun can do to someone's face and chest. There is little of the face left and the chest is just a mass of blood.

After looking to be sure the Santa Muerte thug is dead, Dansberry flops back down and this time there is no movement.

Vlad's guard moves slowly toward Dansberry with his shotgun at the ready. "Dansberry, you OK?"

Dansberry doesn't get up but speaks from the floor. He is in obvious pain. "Maybe. Most of it hit my vest. But it hurts too much to move. Something is broken and something else is bleeding. I'll wait for the rest of the guys to arrive."

There start to be sounds from other corners of the hospital. Several patients, techs, therapists and nurses peek out. Everyone sees the fire and knows they need to get out. A doctor drags his arm as it bleeds down his frock. He has a small yarmulke or *kipah* on. His glasses are broken. He tries to help a patient who is leaning on him to walk.

Vlad's guard grabs a fire extinguisher and sprays the flames. They don't go out, but they are diminished considerably. "Any other fire extinguishers? If so, give me some help."

The Doctor with the yarmulke gestures around the corner. "There is a fire box and extinguisher there. Also over there behind that cabinet that is down."

People scurry to the extinguishers and use them on the fires. The room is smoky from the fires and the weapons fire. Everything is a mess.

Outside the police cars and a fire engine come to a stop. Armed officers charge through the door and take up defensive positions just inside. Once they see the danger is over they immediately move to help the wounded and clear the other rooms to be sure no shooters are left. There are still sirens of ambulances, more police and fire trucks on the way.

Vlad's guard checks on Dansberry as the paramedics load him on a gurney and watches as the rest of the folks are helped or gently lifted onto gurneys with white sheets over them. He then comes over to Vlad who has a medical tech looking him over and trying to put new drips, IVs and other crap back into his arm.

The cop's voice is low and sad. "Vlad, if I had realized he was going to shoot those folks, I'd have tried to do something."

"Don't apologize. I'm guiltier than you. It went too fast. I didn't have a chance to do anything either. I kind of feel that file clerk is my fault. I'm not at my best with all these drugs in me. I just didn't respond fast enough. GOD. I just didn't respond fast enough to save her."

Brookins peaks around the door frame to see Vlad and his guard. "Geez! The doctor orders a little bed rest and you even screw that up. You're hopeless. I'm just glad Sunny isn't here because there isn't anything you two can't make a bigger mess of."

Vlad shrugs at him but brightens up a little with the humor. Even the guard smiles a little.

Brookins can see both of them need a little something to get them out of their funks. "You know you guys are lucky we even got her. Traffic was just brutal out there. That line about Chicago only has two seasons, winter and construction really applied today. Even with the sirens we barely got through. Sometimes getting to where you want to go is such a pain it makes you look forward to purgatory. Heck, Chicago traffic jams might make purgatory look like a cake walk."

The guard agrees. "I used to work traffic. I used to recommend that people take their bikes."

Brookins chuckles at the response. "Sunny claims he knows an old guy he arrests every now and then who claims he was forced into a life of crime because of Post-Traumatic-Stress Disorder or PTSD caused by sitting in Chicago traffic so long he thought he was in a war zone. Sheila thinks it is probably just from breathing the gas fumes."

Both guys smile.

"Sunny has a friend with a five-year-son who was born in a taxi cab on the way to the hospital and was enrolled in kindergarten by the time his mother finally got to the hospital."

Both Vlad and his guard chuckle.

"You know Vlad, with the mess you and I always make, doctors are still trying to figure how something like you or me got into the gene pool. All they can come up with is they think there must not have been a guard on duty at the pool on our day. Because if we're around and people think things are going well, it is obvious they are overlooking something."

The mood in the room is clearly going up.

A military combat veteran like Brookins knows depression can set in quickly after a traumatic event like this one. Humor is a good way to get the shocked folks minds on another subject and moving forward. Brookins is good at reading people who need a little humor to lighten the darkness they find themselves in.

That said, Brookins is stunned at the damage done. He knows he better reconsider just how badly the Santa Muertes want to send a message to law enforcement types in America. They've killed more than their fair share of Mexican police and their families. Going after a Chicago Policeman with this type of vengeance is shocking. Time to realize this is open warfare and there doesn't appear to be any limit.

THIRTY-ONE

WHEN SUNNY GOT THE CALL ABOUT THE ATTACK HE hurried over to support Vlad. Brookins and he sit on chairs and watch the tech leave the room. Vlad will leave shortly for Cook County Hospital where he will be in a ward with reinforced windows and 24 hour/day guards. But right now they want to get the place cleaned up. There is bustling activity all around the smashed clinic. There are police, evidence techs, custodians and just shocked people trying to get things cleaned up and a full crime scene investigation. The cleanup crew is following the evidence techs so they don't damage the evidence.

Vlad, still a little shocked and shaken is glad he is joined by Sunny and Brookins who are just joining him for support. Sometimes just being there is enough support. They sit quietly in an oasis in the middle of turmoil.

Brookins breaks the silence. "The dead guys appear to be Mexican nationals, so we are initially assuming they are Santa Muertes. Ugly frickin' tattoos that aren't Chicago gangs and no ID of any kind. Fingerprints don't match anything yet."

"Lab says not in their database?"

Brookins nods yes.

"Damn. That means almost for sure they are Santa Muertes."

Sunny nods at his two friends. "You know Vlad, I have told you more than once, there is evil in this world. You guys who sleep in on Sundays don't listen to the ministers. You ought to listen. You ought to read the Bible. Most people refuse to believe there is raw, real evil in this world. But not believing in it doesn't change the fact there are evil people who enjoy doing evil things to innocent people. They enjoy inflicting pain on others."

Brookins nods in agreement.

Vlad looks around and gestures he gets the point.

Sunny continues. "It is an evil embedded from birth or at least at the earliest age. They don't just start doing these things when they are thirty. They did them in different forms when they were six. Think of a Pol Pot who killed how many million? Or Mao who killed sixty million or Hitler or Stalin. Look around at this clinic. Look at what those guys did to people who were just going about their lives trying to help sick people. We're here to stop evil. Remember, that's why we're cops."

Vlad uses the back of his arm to wipe his face as tears run down it. "They killed my nurse because she was here. That was all she did to offend them. She was standing by the front desk looking at medical records to be sure she was taking care of everyone the right way. That is all she did to offend them. The other nurse, the file clerk…all they did was come to work today. That was all they did. Get up, go to work, try to help people."

Brookins nods in agreement.

"You know guys, you're making sense. How else do you explain these drug cartels? They are evil and all they want to do is destroy people. How do we respond to people who don't have normal feelings? They don't care who they hurt or why. Their very reason for existence, their very job, if you can call it that, is to destroy innocent people with life destroying drugs.

Killing and maiming innocent folks who just happen to be there is just what they do. What is the answer?" Vlad speaks in an almost melancholy tone.

Brookins looks around to be sure no one else is listening. "Kill them. All of them. Period."

Vlad nods. "Remember that Vaclav Havel guy? He was the respected first President of the Czech Republic who died last year. He was just a poet and playwright. He wasn't a politician or a soldier. After his people pulled him out of the communist's prison, he was thrust into the role of their leader."

"Yea, big jump."

"He said something like the real test of a man isn't when he is doing what he wants to do. It is how he plays the role destiny hands to him."

Vlad contemplates the thought. "You're right. These guys are evil. We need to protect folks and get rid of these demons. Our legal system isn't designed to deal with pure evil. People who don't accept any constraints at all."

Brookins speaks quietly. "You know we've solved this stuff before."

Vlad reflects, "Yeah, in Afghanistan and Iraq, if you took a prisoner it got all political and turned into a big mess. Things this evil don't even qualify as people. They're demons. Some folks complain when Obama kills those radical Muslim guys with drones. I wonder what they want us to do. Invite them to talk over tea and crumpets? Kind of sanitary. Screw it. Kill the bastards before they kill innocent folks. They're more vicious than any animals by a mile. If we don't take prisoners, we don't have to leave the solution up to a political system that has already proven it won't do much about it. Or worse, the ACLU who most people feel is probably pro-criminal and pro-terrorist."

Brookins nods in agreement, "I didn't say anything about this. You didn't either." Brookins looks over to Sunny. "I know

Sunny won't either. This will never go beyond the three of us. Once you are ready to go, you can join Sunny and me. But for the sake of the honest folk who are just trying to live their lives in peace, we need to give them a solution. The system won't do it. It can't. We're trained for this stuff. We can offer a solution."

Vlad is in obvious pain, but the drugs are starting to take effect. He seems lost in the mayhem and destruction as he looks around. "You know the reason this stuff happens is because the guys who run Chicago and Illinois are so busy robbing the people blind and paying off their friends, they don't have time to deal with this kind of stuff."

Brookins nods. "Don't get into all that Burke stuff with me. We aren't South American death squads."

Sunny chips in. "The drugs steal their lives and Burke and his crooks steal their money and their future."

Brookins nods again. "I said, we aren't some South American death squad. The people get to pick the political crooks that run this place. They choose these crooks. It isn't our business."

Vlad looks a little wistful. "Yeah...I know. I know. What a frickin' mess."

THIRTY-TWO

IT IS JUST BARELY BEFORE DAWN AND SUNNY CARE-fully nods at Brookins, who is holding the Ithaca Mag-10 shotgun that Vlad prefers to carry. It isn't issue so it won't trace. One of those crime scene weapons that doesn't really exist anymore. Vlad bought it from a long retired police officer who moved away. That cop had taken it off a dead drug runner. They don't make Mag-10s anymore and this one was never really on anyone's records.

Sunny's weapons came from a murderer. It just didn't get handed in, so it won't trace to him at all. They both stand behind a ragged looking apartment building in the Little Village neighborhood. Both are in all black outfits topped with black balaclavas.

An informant said he saw three guys who only spoke Spanish and bragged about being Santa Muerte gunmen go into the building last night. Earlier, after a couple of beers, one of the three bragged to the informant they were leaving at first light tomorrow morning to have a discussion with some people who had cheated them.

It is very early the next morning and Sunny and Brookins are looking at the SUV the three have been driving. On the far side, out of sight, Brookins has already slashed the front and rear tires.

There is a lot of creaking as the old, wooden back stairs groan under the burden of three armed men coming down.

Brookins nods back to Sunny and they both flatten a little tighter against the wall.

The three come out into the near darkness without taking a really good look around. They look quickly but not at the angle behind them. It is too dark to see in those shadows. They step into the alley and check to be sure their car is still there. They have been warned that car theft of a decent SUV like theirs is possible. The SUV is here and they're happy and ready to go.

The Santa Muerte gunmen had been warned about how difficult parking can be in Chicago's neighborhoods. They were told it is so hard to find a place to park that some rich people abandon new Jaguars in the middle of the street with the motor running and hope the car is stolen. Then they can claim the insurance and just buy a new car. That is easier than finding a parking space in many of Chicago's crowded neighborhoods.

The gunmen aren't sure they believe the story. But America is a rich land and its people do weird things compared to the more down-to-earth Mexican citizens they are used to.

Without even a warning, Brookins who is still behind them opens fire with the Mag-10. Two go down without even getting a chance to turn around. Their weapons clatter onto the ground as the two crumble and collapse into the rapidly expanding pool of their own blood.

The third makes an incredibly fast turn toward the sound of Brookins Mag-10. His rifle is coming up and he is flicking off the safety as he turns. He doesn't even bother to sneak a peek in the other direction.

Sunny places a huge Sig Sauer P226 about a foot from the back of his head. There is no hesitation. He fires. At a foot the

Sig Sauer removes the entire front of the thugs face as the 9mm parabellum round comes out the front of his head.

The three are so obviously dead it isn't worth checking, but Brookins does anyway. Never too careful. Yes, they're dead.

Sunny and Brookins don't do anything to the bodies or the weapons. They are gone into the semi darkness with their identities covered by the black balaclavas. By the time anyone can respond to the shotgun blast, the two of them are long gone.

It is still just before dawn as they quickly drive away in a stolen truck. A mile farther south they turn into the alley where they left their unmarked Police car. Sunny jumps out and gets in the Police car. Brookins drives one more block and they put the truck back in the alley behind someone's garage, exactly where they took it from. He locks it up again. A nice exchange of vehicles. Whoever owns the truck will never even know it was gone.

Now they are ready and start driving back north. Brookins comments, "You did notice all three of those characters had AK-47s with the bigger magazine, didn't you?"

"Of course dipshit, you think I'm a crossing guard?"

Both laugh at Sunny borrowing Vlad's favorite one liner.

Brookins goes serious again. "You're thinking most of those Fast and Furious guns our idiot friends at the Obama Department of Justice managed to lose in Mexico were AKs and ARs with the oversized magazines?"

"Yep. And these guys were drug cartel guys who probably got the guns at a bargain rate."

"Well we didn't have an opportunity to check the serial numbers, although most would have already been removed, so we won't know. But I was thinking the same thing you are. They used those weapons to kill one of our border guards and a DEA agent. I sure don't want them to be able to kill one of our guys with them."

"Yeah, I don't think we can afford any more help from our friends in Washington. We can take care of our own business. Washington is just a road block to action."

"I'm with you."

The car falls silent as they drive with Sunny and Brookins thinking to themselves. Sunny is laboring in his conscience. Was this murder? The 10 Commandments are pretty doggone clear about GOD's view of murder. But Sunny and Brookins are law enforcement. Was this simply unauthorized law enforcement justice being done in an expedited fashion? Just post-partum abortions of morally non-viable fetuses?

In the Biblical Book of Romans, the apostle Paul makes it very clear, there is a reason the state bears the sword. Paul said it well, if you don't want to meet the state's sword, do good and you'll be fine. Sunny isn't all that sure that simply doing good will keep a crooked state like Chicago off your back, but now he knows he is playing semantic games with his conscience. The key is the state is expected to protect its citizens. Sunny and Brookins are the state's sword? Or is the Army the state's sword? These guys had come 2,000 miles to kill people Sunny and Brookins were sworn to defend.

Revenge? The equivalent to a military spoiling attack where you hit first to disrupt your opponent's attack? Taking out the trash? Would it have been OK to murder a Klu Klux Klansman when you knew for sure he was on his way to lynch some poor Black guy? Hitler? Stalin? Mao? The three greatest mass murderers of all time. Would killing them have been murder?

After the attack on Vlad at the hospital Sunny and Brookins emotions may have gotten the better of them. The attack at Sunny's house was probably justification enough. As Sunny drove the bullet riddled car with a badly wounded and bleeding Vlad sprawled on the floor, self-preservation was outweighing other emotions. But once they were out of danger, Sunny wanted to lash out at the murderers. He and Brookins had clearly done that this morning.

Sunny wondered, should he have played like an old West gunslinger and stood up to the thugs, explained why they had been singled out and given them a chance to defend themselves? Be sure they understood why they were about to die? Why? They certainly did not hold themselves to that standard of conduct? Drug Cartel gunmen weren't known for their chivalry.

Maybe consider it as something like preventive detention, but with no holding cell or Guantanamo Bay. It is just better to leave the body in the street to let the other guys know what to expect. As he told Jerry Katorski, this is delivering a message without using the post office. To the right people, bullet riddled, dead bodies carry a message all their own.

Sunny had never done anything like this before and was conflicted about the methods, but not the need to get these murderers off the streets. He had killed plenty of Taliban scum and al Queda murderers in Afghanistan, but this wasn't the same and he knew it.

He had even killed two Taliban fighters with his bare hands. They had been about to kill some little Afghan girls who were attending a girls only school. The text they were being taught was the Koran. The Taliban even opposed that. Sunny led the team to interdict the probable murderers. He needed to keep the advantage of silence for his team, so he couldn't use his weapon. His bare hands were more than enough. No guilt. They were about to be murderers. Evil dealt with appropriately.

The guy who slipped them the tip the Cartel gunmen were about to kill someone, probably a Warlord, owned a restaurant in the old portion of Little Village, Chicago's major area for Mexican Americans and undocumented workers. Sunny loved that phrase 'undocumented'. One of the better PC words. But he knew the guy. He knew the guy knew things cops didn't know. Sunny and Vlad ate in his restaurant when they were in Little Village. The guy had never steered them wrong. If he said they were about to murder someone. They were about to murder someone. Maybe Judge Leoni wouldn't buy the reliability of a known informant for a mobster, but nobody would have questioned his reliability for drug cartel gunmen.

Unlike the average Cartel member or gangbanger, Sunny has a conscience and it isn't crystal clear right now. He knows he is right, but it is still something close to murder. Justifiable murder? He may have avenged the murder of the personnel at Vlad's medical clinic...but...

Brookins looks at Sunny. "Second thoughts?"

"No."

Brookins looks at him for a little longer. "Don't worry, you're not going soft. I'm thinking the same stuff. You got a better idea, I'm all ears."

"Nope. Evil is evil and needs to be done away with." Sunny takes a moment to reflect. "You know they couldn't find a jury in Chicago or about any other city with drug and gang problems that would convict us. We'd walk. You know that."

"Yeah. If you were on that jury, would you convict some guys who did what we did?" Brookins reflects on his question.

"Nope."

"OK. Remember that."

Sunny sits there silently while he drives. "We're not Dirty Harry. We know that. But I just can't seem to get too worked up about taking out trash like those Santa Muerte guys. I know they are supposedly people, but I just don't see humanity in the lives they lead. We stopped them as they were getting ready to go kill some American citizen. Albeit a drug running, gangbanger, but still an American citizen who has not been convicted of anything, yet. Yet being the operative word."

Brookins nods in agreement. "Kill 'em all. In the Bible in the book of Roman's, thirteenth chapter, the Apostle Paul talked about a man's relationship with his government. Verse three roughly says if you don't want to have fear of authority, then do good and you'll be OK. In verse four Paul pretty much says if you do evil, be afraid for government doesn't bear the sword for nothing. We're the sword."

Sunny smiles that Brookins, also a religious man, quoted the exact same scriptures as Sunny had been thinking about. Of course, Brookins a hard core Bible reader had even quoted the appropriate chapter and verse.

Sunny looks thoughtfully over at Brookins. "You know, if we are after evil, we should start with Brennan Burke and his sleazy political buddies. They're ruining people's lives too. Refusing to educate kids. Looking the other way about open criminal activity. They have used taxpayer money to buy themselves power, influence and wealth while leaving the State of Illinois totally bankrupt. Stealing more money than these thugs, but doing it in a suit in front of some mentally deficient crook they put in the job. They don't call it theft. They call it legal fees. You think that might be expanding the definition a little too far?"

"You sound like Vlad. He was thinking the same thing. But that is way too far my friend."

Sunny smiles as he considers the thought. "Illinois and America would be better off without him and his self-serving crooks. They have destroyed one of America's greatest states. Did you read Vince Flynn's first book *Term Limits*?"

"No. I read the Mitch Rapp ones but wasn't that the one before Rapp came on the scene?"

"Yeah. It is a great book. You're right, it is his one book before Mitch Rapp became the hero. That is how his heroes started to clean up Washington. They just started taking out some of the worst of the actors with bullets."

"Don't get any ideas Einstein. People might thank us for both, but we have enough on our hands now. OK? Santa Muertes are killers and drug pushers. I think Burke is nonviolent although clearly a crook that is destroying the future of the citizens of Chicago and Illinois. There is a difference between violent criminals and just plain sleazy crooks. Even if it isn't very much. Let's see what the response is from this one."

"Yeah...just dreaming."

Both sit quietly and contemplate what they have just done. They hope it wasn't their emotions overriding their principles. Yet it is hard to think getting rid of three guys on their way to commit a murder is a bad thing. Sunny always liked to use the term post-partum abortion for these kinds of guys. They had never become viable moral fetuses, thus it wasn't murder, it was an abortion. Other guys use the phrase 'suicide by cop'. Same concept.

THIRTY-THREE

ALDERMAN BASS AND THE WARLORD'S LAWYER Leonard Bernstein, park her big SUV on the street in front of the Chicago City Hall. It is a no parking zone, but Aldermen ignore that minor technicality all the time. Most, but not all, Chicago Aldermen don't think the law applies to them. Why else would 32 of the 50 Chicago aldermen have gone to prison in the last few years if they thought they needed to obey the law? Another reason might be the citizens of Chicago don't like to elect really smart folks as aldermen. The dumb guys steal enough. Think of how much a smart guy could steal!

Bass' parking spot is right across Randolph Street from The Thompson Center, also called the State of Illinois Center or SOIC. The garish orange, faded blue and gun metal gray building is totally unique. It was designed by the famous architect, Helmut Jahn and renamed after former Governor Jim Thompson who put together the deal to build it.

It is another example of why the State of Illinois is bankrupt. The cost overruns were outrageous. In addition, state employees in the capitol of Springfield can stretch their paycheck much farther than they can in Chicago. So there is less pressure for ever higher wages. Once you put a giant building like this one right across the street from Chicago City Hall you immediately have every crooked Chicago politician maneuvering to get as many new patronage jobs for his ward workers as possible. The building ends up stuffed with unnecessary state employees who are really just more tax payer financed Chicago patronage workers for the machine.

Then to make it worse, immediately across LaSalle Street, kitty corner from Chicago City Hall is another totally rebuilt state office building with thousands more unnecessary state employees. The State of Illinois is broke. It hasn't balanced its budget since the last century. Its pension funds are the most underfunded among the entire fifty states. But these state office buildings are flooded with highly paid state employees.

For some of the workers, their only job is to dispense pin-stripe patronage to connected political hangers on. Big law firms get lucrative contracts. Many totally ineffective groups that do very little get big contracts to keep their politically connected employees paid. Oh well...it is what it is. It is Chicago and it is Illinois. There is a reason Illinois is ranked fiftieth of the fifty states for fiscal policy. Idiots.

Larenda Bass and the lawyer hurry across Randolph Street and try to go through the security check but there a guard is kind enough to remind them the Speaker of the House, Brennan X. Burke doesn't have an office in the Thompson Center.

Burke feels he is too important to share office space with the other three legislative leaders, the six state wide elected officials and the various state agencies. Besides he has so many questionable things going on in his offices, he wants them to be isolated from too many observers. He moved his offices across the street to the rebuilt state office building, named the Michael J. Bilandic Building.

The Bilandic building is an odd name for a building considering Bilandic is usually considered the dumbest man to ever serve as Mayor. In addition, he was never elected Mayor. He was selected by his fellow alderman after the real Mayor's death to finish the last two years of Richard l, the first Mayor Daley's final term. Honest people wouldn't think being popular with the Chicago City Council's notoriously corrupt and openly racist denizens a good thing. It is not generally considered a great character reference unless you are looking to hire a crook.

Bilandic was then not elected, after being slated by the machine, when he ran for Mayor because he had been such a disaster as Mayor. His entire legacy was insider politics, incompetence and being a loyal machine hack. He had been the Alderman from the first Mayor Daley's home ward, the 11th. A weird choice of a name for a major state building. Usually things are named to honor respected officials. But this is Chicago and getting respected means taking care of the crooks that run the place.

Almost as odd, one block east, the street next to the Richard J. Daley Cook County Courts Building was renamed for the presiding judge of the courts who had over one hundred of his court's personnel and lawyers who practiced there sent to jail. But he was smart enough to never turn evidence on anyone else. Especially the political guys. So a never-elected Mayor and a notoriously corrupt judge are honored in Chicago. This is how it should be in Chicago as seen from the eyes of the crooks that run the place.

Alderman Bass and the lawyer reverse their path and go across LaSalle Street. Again they are held up in security but eventually they get to the Speaker's office. Once there the staff informs her the check is still at the Comptroller's office across the street at the Thompson Center. The Comptroller's office is being difficult about releasing a check to a new community group with a nebulous mission and no track record. They refuse to hand millions of dollars to a minion of the Speaker of the House to give to someone they have never seen and know nothing about.

Bass and the lawyer then repeat their steps and go back across LaSalle Street, back through security and up to the Comptroller's office on the 15th floor. Bass is not used to the massive, wide open rotunda and looking down into an abyss that drops not just the sixteen floors but also past the elevators and down to the food court with its uniquely decorated floor leaves her dizzy. She is already very nervous and almost loses her lunch looking over the railing. Finally they arrive at the Comptroller's office.

The Comptroller of Illinois is one tough old lady who has been involved in Illinois politics since Lincoln was a State Representative. Of course in those days neither of them were Republicans yet, they were both still called Whigs.

The Comptroller's Chief of Staff, obviously a lady from the other political party as Bass and Burke is barely pleasant. She holds what looks like the check.

"We are not in the habit of writing bad checks to what appears to be a nonexistent community group to do just whatever it wants with that money? The Speaker of the House thinks this crap is OK, but we don't. What is this check for? Why is it being pulled out of a fund this is really nothing but a slush fund of federal stimulus money used by the Speaker? Do you want me to call some reporters to join us so you can explain to them and to me why you think you are entitled to this money? Illinois is bankrupt and people like you and the Speaker are the reasons."

The lawyer is as ready as he can be for this type of unexpected refusal. "You have no right to refuse to give us the check. It is a legitimate fund in a state agency and the money will go to a valued community group. Now give us the check and cut the crap."

The Comptroller's Chief of Staff just smiles a downright hostile smile. "You just said the Comptroller of the State of Illinois has no right to refuse to issue a bogus check from a slush fund account? In your dreams. Guess again. What do you think her job is?" She then tears up the check and throws it in the waste can.

Larenda Bass almost faints. She is gasping for air and feeling like a semi has just run over her chest. Even the lawyer is stunned. Both are speechless. Both of them realize what failing to get the check means. But Bass realizes it actually has a double meaning. The Warlord issue...yes. But she convinced Burke to give her $4.75 million dollars. The Warlords just may be dead. So be it. But more important, she has already committed part of the $750,000 dollars she intends to steal from the taxpayers. The contract is already signed. This is not good.

The chief of staff looks at them with a hard gaze. "If you don't mind, I'm busy. Could you feel sorry for yourselves elsewhere? You may not care about the taxpayers, but we do. Not move along, please."

The lawyer is about to start shouting but realizes it is a bad idea. He does not have any power here. All they can do is head back over to Burke's people and try to get them to intercede. They warned him the Comptroller was being a pain, but they hadn't quite prepped him for this. They rise, don't say a word and leave.

Bass is unstable on her feet and starting to hyperventilate. This is no time to put her over the edge.

Akile Fort has always told the lawyer Bass is their weak link. But weak or not, she is totally controllable so they have to just learn to deal with her. The Gangster Warlords have plenty of other allies in the Chicago political system, but none as totally in their debt as Bass.

Fort knows he can get Bass to do anything he wants her to do. She is weak and owes most of her political success and all of her personal finances to the Warlords. He even knows she has tried to hide some of her assets. He is well aware of those apartment buildings on the North Side. She isn't sharp enough to outwit the leader of the largest street gang in Chicago.

The lawyer decides this is not the place for a last stand...a knockdown, drag out fight. He will go back to Burke's office and then give Fort a call. They take the elevator downstairs to the food court to get some coffee or tea and give Bass time to recover. She will need to be sharper than this when they get back to Burke's office.

Once she regains most of her composure they take the escalator up to the ground floor to go back across LaSalle Street. Neither of them notices the young, attractive Latina, on the phone, who keeps watching them and follows them up the escalator. As they head for the door the young Latina follows them.

Just outside the door are several rough looking guys with gang tattoos in Spanish. They look like they might be some serious gangbangers or just plain bad characters. This is a group of the kind of guys your parents told you to stay away from. The Latina points to Bass and the lawyer and then turns away to go out another door.

As the lawyer and Bass reach the curb a big white van pulls right in front of them and stops. The side door opens. The rough looking guys come up right behind them, poke handguns into their backs and push them into the van. "If you say one word, you'll be dead right here. Am I clear?"

The lawyer nods and Bass almost collapses. The guys get them into the white van. A fellow inside the van has a large chromed hand gun in their faces. Several get in behind them and the rest stop to wait for a black SUV that immediately pulls up behind the van. Both vehicles are gone in less than twenty seconds.

Inside the white van the lawyer and Bass are gagged with duct tape and their hands tied with plastic pulls.

No one says anything until the van stops. The door opens and everyone gets out. They are inside a warehouse that smells of marijuana and charcoal smoke. Near them is also some big, cut in half fifty gallon drums and some mattresses in the middle of the floor. There are reddish stains on the floor near the fifty gallon drums.

The lawyer and Bass are pulled from the van and forced to stand facing a side wall near the van. The thug looking guys in the warehouse all seem to be speaking in Spanish. Neither Bass nor the lawyer understand Spanish so they can't follow the conversation.

Finally a man in a business suit comes up behind them, points a large pistol at the back of the lawyer's head and pulls the duct tape off his mouth. He speaks with a Spanish accent, but his English is still quite good. "Your friend and ours, a Mr. Akile Fort assured us you would be carrying a check for over four million dollars when you left the Thompson building. Please hand it to me."

There is a pause and the lawyer clears his throat to speak. "We don't have it. They wouldn't give it to us."

The man in the suit listens and looks around the room at his armed thugs. "I don't think you understand. That is not an acceptable answer. Please hand me the check and we'll send you on your way no worse than you are now."

The lawyer's voice goes up a notch. "No...I'm serious...they refused to give it to us. I swear it."

The man in the suit cocks the pistol and places it against the back of the lawyer's head. "Is that your last response?"

"I'm not lying. We don't have it."

The gunshot thunders around the room. It reverberates from ceiling to roof and back down. Most of the lawyer's head and face are splattered on the brick wall. His body slams forward with the force of the impact and what used to be him slowly slides down the wall to land in a heap.

Larenda Bass wets her pants and starts to blubber under her gag. She is so terrified she collapses in a pile on the floor next to the lawyer's body.

"Lift her up and hold her."

Bass is scooped off the floor by several nasty looking thugs. She looks pathetic. She is blubbering and her wet pants are dripping. She can't stand unless they hold her. Between the tattoos, the sweaty and not at all clean sleeveless t-shirts, the shorts that end mid-calf and the expensive basketball shoes, there isn't a single guy in the group you would want to meet in a dark alley. In fact you wouldn't want to meet these guys in a lighted alley. They hold her up to face the man in the suit.

"You do understand saying no is not an option, don't you?"

Unfortunately, Ms. Faust is finally meeting Mr. Mephistopheles.

CHAPTER

THIRTY-FOUR

INSANE JAGUAR GENERAL ARTURO ORTEGA SITS IN the back corner booth of a very nice Mexican restaurant on the Southern edge of Little Village. With him in the booth is an attractive but slightly matronly Latina wearing a wedding ring on her hand. She looks like the mother of several kids who is enjoying an evening out on the town with her husband.

They talk and laugh and Arturo toasts her for something or other. They clearly enjoy each other's company. He tells her another joke and they both laugh until they shake. Ortega knows a ton of jokes and he tells them well.

At the front of the restaurant there is a commotion. Ortega ignores it and continues to chat with the attractive lady until a group of four young, armed thugs push their way through the crowd and assemble in front of his table. The only thing that changes is Ortega's arm is now under the table. He does not even acknowledge the presence of the armed thugs.

All four of them are covered in tattoos and look like they are not totally comfortable in the restaurant or even in America in general. To an experienced eye like Ortega's, all of them look high on some drug. Doesn't really matter which one. It is enough to know they are not working with full decks at the moment.

None speak English and give orders in Spanish for Ortega to get up and come with them, now. The only phrases a non-Spanish speaker would recognize were Santa Muerte and "pronto" meaning fast or right now. A non-Spanish speaker wouldn't know what some of the other phrases meant, but clearly some of the language was not complimentary.

Ortega finally looks at them with close to distain in his eyes. "This is America. If you wish to speak to me here, I suggest you speak English." With that he goes back to chatting with the attractive Latina.

She looks frightened, but not terrified. She is tense but not shaking. He takes another bite of his meal and continues to ignore the gunmen. He is now eating with his left hand and the right remains under the table.

The restaurant patrons all run out the front door. The waiters and kitchen staff run both ways, the back door and the front door. Everyone looks terrified except Ortega.

The thugs are clearly frustrated as they are ignored. Several shout instructions again in Spanish. One fires several rounds into the ceiling for effect and makes a mess of the ceiling and the two tables near where he fired. Dust and small portions of the ceiling fall everywhere, especially on the gunman and the nearby tables. The ceiling dust all over the gunman makes it obvious he may be tough, he may be armed, but he isn't very bright. He is also probably high on drugs. All four of them point their weapons and keep shouting in a disorganized manner.

Finally Ortega looks at them again. He wipes his mouth with his cloth napkin. He then speaks in Spanish. It roughly translates to I'm at dinner. Why don't you go away and leave us alone? We'll talk about this later.

Two of the thugs come right up to the table and lean down to get close to his face. They want to get into his face. Up close and personal. Their weapons are slung over their shoulders and turned to the side so they can give that close and personal attention.

Ortega continues to ignore them.

The older of the two who seems to be in charge yells what even someone who doesn't understand Spanish would know is an insult. In fact a long string of them. He is face-to-face with Ortega. If he were any closer their noses would be touching.

Ortega continues to ignore them.

The tattooed thug reaches over and places his hand on the Latina's arm. She stiffens.

All hell breaks loose. A shell from the SIG Sauer P226 below the table explodes through the table top and lodges in the heart of the thug with his hand on the Latina.

Before anyone can even react, Ortega grabs the other thug by his greasy hair and slams his face into the table and jams his SIG Sauer into the guy's ear. The dead Santa Muerte gunman slowly slides off the table and drops to the floor. He leaves a trail of blood and gore on the table cloth and it runs in a messy line across the table cloth down to the floor.

At a range of six inches, the big 9mm bullet made a mess of his chest and came out the back. It is a very gory picture. No one is wondering if he is just wounded. He is dead and they know it.

Ortega's Spanish is almost spit out of his mouth. "I've been sitting here with my arm below the table and none of you even thought to check if I had a gun in my hand. You arrive high on drugs. Amateurs! You could never work for me. Also, you never put your hand on a better man's wife. Never."

The other two Santa Muerte gunmen don't know what to do. They just stare at the dead body on the floor and the SIG Sauer in their friend's ear.

The Latina casually takes a napkin, dips it into the water in a glass and wipes the blood off her arm and off Ortega's arm and the side of his face also. Her attention, the touching and rubbing, to remove the blood on Ortega is affectionate, very spouse like. She then takes a sip of water from a different glass and looks at the two thugs with a now very calm expression.

Their weapons are generally pointed at Ortega, but the gunmen are back on their heels. The leader is dead and his right hand guy is bent over a table with one big ass pistol stuck in his ear. Things start to look like a draw.

The two drift slightly in the direction of the table. Their movement is not obvious or fast, but they are getting closer to their cohort whose face is smashed into the table and his fanny is stuck up in the air like a prisoner in jail getting ready to make a whole bunch of new friends. He looks awkward, but not really scared. His eyes look like a dangerous thug trying to figure out his next move.

Ortega tells the gunman with the SIG Sauer in his ear, "Drop your AK-47, now."

It is hard to do with his face smashed into the table and his legs spread eagled behind him trying to keep himself from falling over. He slowly manages to get it off his shoulder and prepares to drop it.

The Latina reaches over and takes it from his hand. She checks to see if the safety is off and then points it at the other two before they realize what she is doing.

In one fluid motion, too fast for the gunmen to react, Ortega stands up. It knocks the table over, but it doesn't completely fall because of the Santa Muerte gunman's face smashed into it and the edge is resting on the dead body on the floor.

"Sweetheart, please leave by the back door, now. I'll call you later."

The Latina still points the AK-47 at the frozen pair, turns and walks sideways to the back of the restaurant. She never breaks eye or rifle contact with the two speechless thugs. Pretty or not. Maybe a little matronly like a mother of several kids or not. She sure seems to know what to do with an AK-47.

Ortega continues to speak in Spanish. His deep voice sounds like rolling thunder from the heavens above, or more probably as it applies to these inept mercenaries, the hell below. His huge and heavily muscled arm has a vice like grip on the third guy's head. The SIG Sauer stuck in his ear does not waiver in the slightest. The gunman can't move without losing his head and he knows it.

"OK. What would you like to do now? Should I kill all of you or let you live? You started this, not me. Your call."

The three remain silent. The two, clearly underlings, are speechless. The junior Santa Muerte gunmen are hired killers and not afraid to kill or fight, but they are not decision makers.

This standoff shows there is a very big difference between hired muscle and hired brains. These guys are obviously hired muscle not hired brains. Their level of experience or perhaps their level of intelligence, doesn't give them any idea of what to do right now in the real world of the here and now. If they are told to kill someone, they do it. But they are mindless thugs, probably high on drugs, sent to serve as backup, on a mission that has just gone terribly wrong. They have moved quite close to the table but they simply can't decide what to do.

More experienced killers wouldn't have gotten so close that they would lose their ability to maneuver. More experienced or smarter killers would have probably just started shooting and figured the rest of it out later. But as high as they look, they aren't thinking clearly enough to act expeditiously.

Without any warning Ortega throws the gunman he is holding and the table at the other two. They all stumble. They stupidly have given up any room to maneuver. They are too close to charge or run and way too close to fire. The table has blocked their ability to bring their AK-47s back down to a height where they can use them.

In little more than a flash, Ortega continues to shove the table at them, the three are pushed backwards and two go down with the table on top of them. The third Santa Muerte gunman is knocked sideways and he stumbles, but doesn't go down.

Arturo Ortega looks him right in the eyes. It is the last thing the Mexican gunman sees this side of hell. Without a moment's hesitation Ortega shoots him twice in the head and the heart. The thunderous sound echoes around the low ceilinged restaurant. It is deafening. The 9mm parabellum rounds make a total mess of his face and chest.

The guy's eyes go blank as his mind starts to realize he is dead. He doesn't fall immediately. He sways and acts like he wants to do something. It takes a moment for his brain and his reactive senses to realize he is dead and there is no longer a controlling impulse to tell the body what to do. The instant after death leaves the body's reflexes in a state of flux. They think they should do something but nothing is telling them what to do. Eventually the dead killer's body collapses in a pile on the floor.

Ortega has a powerful knee on top of the table to keep the two other Santa Muerte gunmen pinned to the ground. One is face down and the other is on his back. One is disarmed and the other's weapon is stuck under his body. They are helpless.

"I asked you what I should do. You didn't answer. Last chance."

The two make the mistake of taking a moment to think. Ortega places his SIG Sauer on the forehead of the guy he had been holding. He takes a moment to focus on his eyes. Before the man hadn't really shown much fear. Now, knowing two of his fellow gunmen are dead, he knows what that SIG Sauer is about to do to what little unscrambled brains he possesses.

The epitaph is delivered in Spanish. "I gave you a chance. If your friend hadn't touched my wife all of you might have survived. You made the call."

Another thunderous sound billows through the restaurant. The low ceiling makes the room into an echo chamber. It is deafening. There are blood and brain matter all over the floor and the table. The other Santa Muerte killer has blood and body matter splashed on his face and shoulder. The rest of him is under the table so remains clean.

Arturo Ortega pushes the SIG Sauer into his waist band and grabs the last thug by the scruff of his neck. He yanks him to his feet and knocks the AK-47 out of his hands before he can even get it into a usable position. He smacks the young guy across the face with a backhand that would stagger a moose. He then knees him in the gut and drops the guy who is gasping for breath and only semi-conscious.

He then methodically stomps on the gunman's hands, arms, legs and feet. He grinds the man into the floor. He breaks virtually every bone in his body. But he carefully avoids hitting or kicking him in the head. He is trying to leave him alive and maybe conscious.

Ortega grabs him again by the back of his neck and throws him against the wall. As the smashed body slides down the wall to settle on the floor he is hoisted up again and tossed against another wall. Without an ounce of mercy but with the precision of a surgeon Ortega dismantles the hired killer.

Ortega may have meant to leave him alive as a message, but he is clearly getting carried away. There is no chance the guy will survive the beating he is taking.

There is blood on everything and everywhere. There is blood all over Ortega's face, arms and shirt. His eyes are cold and his motions measured. He methodically destroys the lump of flesh on the floor. Despite his intentions of sending a message and leaving the Santa Muerte thug dismantled, but alive, he was just too mad at them for having the nerve to touch his wife.

He is an Insane Jaguar General and expects to be treated with respect. But to treat his wife disrespectfully, right in front of him, is an insult beyond his ability to forgive.

Ortega leaves the four messes on the floor. He walks over to the bar, bends over the sink and carefully washes off as much blood as he can. There is so much blood on his face, hair and arms he could almost be mistaken for an Aztec priest in the middle of a ritual sacrifice. The blood on his shirt has to stay, but the rest is removed.

Next he picks up the three AK-47s still there, puts the safeties on and checks the four gunmen for IDs. None have any ID and only a few things like some cash, knives and a set of car keys in their pockets. The cash turns out to be several hundred dollars.

He takes the cash and walks to the office door and uses a switchblade to pin the cash to the door. In the distance he can hear a police car's siren starting to come into focus. He hears it and in no rush, walks to the back of the restaurant and then goes out the back door.

THIRTY-FIVE

IN THE LIMITED LIGHT JUST BEFORE DAWN, A UNI-formed Chicago Police Officer uses his big Mag Light flashlight to look down the embankment of the North Branch of the Chicago River at two bodies floating right near the edge. The big Mag light is so bright it is easy to get a good view of the bodies.

One is clearly a White man wearing what looks like an expensive suit. The other is a Black woman who also appears to be well dressed. Neither seems to have much of a face left. Despite their apparently nice clothes, they are still unquestionably dead. Since their bodies aren't bloated and don't look like they have been fed upon by critters, it is a good guess they haven't been in the river all that long.

Sunny SunWarrior comes up behind the officer and offers him a cup of hot coffee. Together they look at the bodies. "How ya' doin' Markowicz? Anything to go on yet?"

The uniformed officer keeps looking down. "Not yet, Sunny. No clues other than what you can see. The divers should be here any moment. No abandoned cars in the immediate area. We'll see once the guys fish them out."

An hour later the sun is up and there is the beginning of what looks to be a very pleasant day. The water soaked bodies are in the process of being loaded into an ambulance. There is now a big crowd around Sunny and the several uniformed officers watching. No one is speaking.

There is a reporter, really a stringer for *The Reader,* a free local newspaper trying to get one of the officer's attention. Sunny walks over just to be friendly. He always tries to be pleasant to reporters. Beside, at this hour, if the guy is out doing his job, it behooves the police to show him a little respect for his effort. Never know when you might want a little cooperation from one of them.

"Nothing yet. White guy, fancy suit with no face and a Black lady, nicely dressed and no face either. We'll have to use fingerprints and hope for the best. The gun shots made a mess of their entire faces, including their mouths, so dental records probably won't be very helpful. Wish I could tell you more, but that is all we have at the moment."

"Thanks Sunny. I'll follow up. We don't get a lot of bodies swimming in our part of the Chicago River so I suspect we'll want to do a story."

Sunny gives the reporter his card. "Give me a call later. I'll tell you what I know. Of course it will be off the record, but it'll give you something to work with. If you hang out at the morgue you might get the news before I do."

As Sunny drives back to the station to start his report he drives by a Dunkin Donuts and at this early hour he is loath to pass up one of their mouthwatering fritters. He had to hurry to the river so he missed his usual fritter and mug of tea to start his day. It is just hard for Sunny to skip a fritter.

As he prepares to pull in to a parking spot he passes an alley and notices it is full of trucks sitting there with their motors running. He can see signs identifying the first couple as leased by the City of Chicago Hired Truck program. He doesn't get out of his car. Instead he dials his cell phone.

Mason Huntley is getting ready to leave his apartment and go to work when his cell phone rings.

"Huntley."

"I know who it is dipshit. I just dialed your number."

Mason certainly knows the voice. He responds in a similar vain. "Sunny, so good to be insulted by you this early in the morning. I hope you have something important to help me get over my feelings of rejection and diminished self-worth. By the way, I hope Vlad is recovering quickly."

"You bet your sweet ass I do. Grab your camera and try the Dunkin Donuts over here on Halsted. If these trucks are still here when you arrive, that will mean they live in this alley. There isn't any City construction anywhere near here."

"Oh great!"

"At least they show good taste hanging out at a Dunkin Donuts. Thanks for asking about Vlad. He'll be better if he gets smart enough to quit running around in front of guys with loaded guns. I don't know. He may never get that bright."

"You're GOD sent. Thanks, I'm heading that way as we speak."

"By the way. Nothing yet, but we just fished two stiffs out of the Chicago River an hour ago. White guy and a Black lady. Well dressed. Not in the river very long. Hard to ID with their faces blown off. You'll want one of your guys hanging around the morgue for this one. I just have a gut feeling these two aren't nobodies. Remember dipshit, you didn't get any of this from me."

"In polite company I wouldn't even admit I know you, let alone that we have these endearing, early morning chit chats."

Sunny chuckles at the put down. "Remember, Vlad and I are in the first row when you get your Pulitzer. Out." Sunny hangs up and keeps driving.

His cell phone immediately rings. "Sunny. Markowicz. Oh shit! That Black broad we just fished out of the river. It is, well maybe was, Alderman Larenda Bass. The political heavyweight on the South side and close pal of the Gangster Warlords. Burke's Consigliore for the Black machine wards. That Larenda Bass."

Sunny is stunned. By their clothing he had guessed they weren't just tourists caught in the wrong place at the wrong time. He had met Bass so he knew what she looked like. That was how badly the bullets had damaged her face so that Sunny didn't recognize her. "Oh no...This looks like a hit and it is right in the middle of the Warlord, Jaguar and Santa Muerte feud. Give the gang crimes and narcotics guys a call."

"Will do."

"Oh shit! Something else. Do you think this had anything to do with the killing of those four Santa Muerte wannabes at the Mexican restaurant in Little Village last night?"

"Good point. I'll try to tie it together and I'll get back to you."

"Thanks." Sunny hangs up and pulls his car over to the curb to sit and think a moment.

He dials his cell. "Brookins. Can you pry some of your donut eating compadres away from the coffee machine to get a couple of heavily armed guys to meet me by Arturo Ortega's apartment buildings?"

He listens a minute and laughs. "Don't give me that crap you have a real job, not just hanging out with Vlad and me. If you were any good at your job that dipshit wouldn't still be in the hospital recovering from being used for target practice by an army of incompetent death squad wannabes."

Sunny laughs more as he listens. "Don't forget that crossing guard isn't around to cover my back right now. He couldn't find an airline stewardess to do it so he designated you. About equal value in a shootout. Now no more lip, get them guys and go. Out."

As Sunny drives his cell rings again. "Sunny, it's Markowicz again. The white guy is Leonard Bernstein, the Warlord's top lawyer. He is very connected with the Chicago political structure. He is one of the boys. One of the real big boys. Major donor and always at the big meetings for the heavy duty fund raising stuff. What he was doing with Bass in the river is anybody's guess so far. But at least we know who it is, or was."

Sunny pauses as he thinks. "I'm on my way to talk with an Insane Jaguar General. Has to be an overlap with the shootout at the Mexican restaurant and the death of the Warlord flunkies. We're guessing the dead guys in Little Village were probably Santa Muerte guys and the killers of Bass and Bernstein probably were Santa Muerte."

"Makes sense."

"Maybe we're right. Maybe we're wrong. I'm not sure what just yet, but I'll bet a Dunkin Donuts fritter they're related. Let the guys know I'm on my way to Little Village. OK?"

"Sure, Sunny. But screw the Dunkin Donuts fritter. You want to bet with me then we're talking Ruth's Chris or Gibson's. I'm not a cheap date."

"Up yours. I'll go up to a Lou Malnati's deep dish, but that is my limit."

"You're on. Can't beat their pizza. Good luck. If I hear more you'll be one of the last to know."

Sunny laughs at the macho insult. "Thanks...out."

Sunny redials his cell to get Brookins. "I'm going to swing by our old buddy Jose La Boca's corner on my way over to Little Village. I need some more info and he is my best source. Take your time, but know where I'm at in case I need you. OK?"

"We'll take our time getting to Little Village and we'll drift closer to Jose's corner just in case. Out."

Sunny's police cruiser moves fairly slowly by Jose La Boca's favorite hangout. He is the captain of this corner and it is his job to be sure the drugs are circulated, the girls arrive at the right address at the right time or just jump in the car. It is also his job to know who the girls are seeing to be sure they are treated respectfully. Jose is never above letting a John know how to treat a lady respectfully when she is under his protection.

It is early for La Boca to be there, but it is worth taking a chance. He is their best source for information in the Latino gang world. He always seems to have a handle on the Insane Jaguars and was good at picking up rumors about what was going down with the Santa Muertes who were vacationing in Chicago at the moment.

His corner is empty, but farther down the street than normal Sunny sees Jose La Boca leaning against a taco truck nibbling on a breakfast taco and sipping a hot cup of coffee. He is having an animated conversation with the young and well-rounded but even better endowed Latina running the truck.

Sunny comes to a stop right in front of the truck. He charges out with his gun drawn and grabs Jose. The coffee and taco go flying against the side of the small truck.

"You didn't need to pull that BS on the vacationing college kids, jerk. Now there is all kinds of heat and it is your fault. Turn around and spread 'em." After Sunny pats him down, Jose puts his hands behind him so Sunny can slap a pair of handcuffs on him.

Jose leans his shoulder against the taco truck and smiles at the Latina. "This is my old friend, detective dumb ass. He's a real jerk. Trust me, you don't want to know him."

Sunny pistol whips Jose across the shoulder and knocks him to the ground. By hitting his shoulder he didn't hurt him but it looked like a nasty swing. He then grabs him, drags him to the back seat of the cruiser and shoves him inside.

The Latina looks petrified. Sunny looks her right in the eyes. "I wasn't here. He wasn't here. That clear?"

Her eyes are wide as saucers and she nods yes.

"OK." Sunny hops into his car and the tires squeal as he pulls away from the curb.

Five blocks away Jose sits up. He scolds Sunny with humor in his voice. "You son of a bitch. That was a great taco. Why couldn't you let me finish it? I'm hungry in the morning. Besides, if I'd had five more minutes I'd have gotten laid."

Sunny laughs at his complaint. "I didn't really think you'd be out this early or I'd have brought you some breakfast and I'm not here to serve as your personal pimp wise ass."

"Early? Yeah. I was hopin' you'd come by. Stuff to talk about. By the way, the word on the street is Vlad is doing much better and you guys are really pissed at the Santa Muertes trying to take the two of you out. I think that is the rumor you would want?"

"Yep."

"What you probably don't want to hear is the Santa Muertes are still after you guys. They plan on leaving your dead bodies behind as a calling card."

"Yep. By the way, Vlad told me to say hi and give you a kick in the ass from him."

Jose chuckles. "Hey, I'd cover my ass for protection but it is hard to do when my hands are cuffed behind my back?"

Sunny stops the car and goes around to the back seat to take the handcuffs off. "Anything else? How about the take down at the Little Village restaurant yesterday or the day before that disaster that looked like a Warlord attack on the Jaguar apartments? By the way, have you heard anything about the deaths of Alderman Bass and some scum bag lawyer named Bernstein? We just fished them out of the river first thing this morning?"

"Whoa sheet. Bass? No! She was the Warlord's political front lady. Man, she was big political cover. Even we did some campaign work for one of her dumb ass lackeys in the last election."

"You guys worked for Bass?"

"Yeah. Man we're connected you know. The vote fraud in those precincts! They voted half the dead bodies in Burr Oak Cemetery. I think most of Juarez votes in Chicago. Some guy kept complaining and kept calling your cop buddies and the state's attorney and nobody showed up. Nobody. We just kept stealing votes and he kept hollering. We finally threw him out of the precinct. Pain in the ass. This is Chicago. What did he think we were there for?"

Sunny laughed. "Yeah, Burke has told the FOP they had better not show up on election fraud stuff. The State's Attorney? She's his doormat. She isn't going to send someone out and piss off Burke. She knows who butters her bread."

"Yeah. Didn't hear anything about Bass being dead. Bernstein? No loss. Didn't know him but heard of him. Another crooked lawyer. Too bad they didn't get ten more of 'em. I hate dealing with lawyers. But that is big news. Give me some time to ask around. Anything or leads you can give me I can use to trade for more info?"

Sunny thinks for a moment. "Not that much yet. But their faces were missing. Shot in the back of the head. Probably 9mm rounds. Made a mess. Marks showed their hands had been secured and probably duct tape used to gag them. They were picked up on LaSalle Street in front of the State of Illinois Building. Had just been in to meet with some of Brennan Burke's flunkies. Apparently they thought they were supposed to pick up some state money Burke had promised them."

"Money for what?" Jose is incredulous. State money to subsidize gangbangers. How was he going to get in on that?

"Who knows? But you know the state is broke so the comptroller wouldn't give them the check and they were pretty disappointed about it. One of those inside things you can use to look in the know, Bass wet her pants before they shot her.

My guess is they shot Bernstein first and she got upset. But the big thing was the taxpayer check Burke was giving them for whatever reason."

"How big a check?"

"Almost five mil. A lot of payoff or hush money, whatever it was."

Jose La Boca just shakes his head. What does he need to do to get in on this stuff? He knew the guys running the place were crooked. He helped them be crooked. But passing out $5 million dollar checks to political hacks and gangbangers is just too much to believe. He knows Sunny knows stuff. He believes him. But this is almost too stupid for even Illinois' government. Almost he thought. But with the two last governors in prison... well maybe business as usual. He looks back at Sunny. "Thanks, I should be able to trade that for some more info."

"Thanks. Anything on the others?"

Jose looks like he is ready to explode with this new information. "Yeah. Big! The Santa Muertes sent four guys to take out Arturo Ortega. That is who was in the restaurant. They think he hasn't been very cooperative in their feud with the Warlords. Probably right."

"Ortega...whoa!"

"Yeah, Ortega has put on the street for his guys to keep low and don't get in the middle of someone else's fight. If his guys have personal reasons for wanting to help the Mexicans, fine. But don't get into it unless they feel they have to. He didn't do the Mexicans any favors."

Sunny nods in agreement. "That is our impression too. Maybe we're wrong, but Ortega seems to be playing it close to his vest. He isn't looking for trouble as far as we can see. "

"I hear Ortega thinks it was the Mexican's own fault for making a bad business deal. Thought they got greedy. Stretched 'em too far. Not his or the Jaguars problem. Ortega is big enough nobody can tell him what to do if he doesn't want to listen. So the Mexicans wanted to make an example of him. Cut the American guy down to size."

"Whoa. Ortega did that on his own? He must be as tough as he looks. Did you hear what a mess he made of them?" Sunny looks impressed. That was no minor fete of arms.

"Heard some of it. He took 'em apart. Killed all four and then used a switchblade jammed with money and nailed it on the restaurant manager's door to cover the damages, pay for his dinner and still left a serious tip. Kind of old fashioned, yeah?"

"Yeah."

Jose looks like he is thinking for a moment. "Not sure this is true, but heard he was fuming because he was having dinner with his old lady and they may have insulted her or something. Don't know. But Ortega is not a man to mess with. He is old fashioned about women. He's protective of the Putas who hang around his worthless thugs. Almost like he makes his guys act like gentlemen. He's kind of Catholic. It's kind of weird."

Sunny nods in agreement. "I have some experience with that. I've seen it firsthand. I think what you're saying is right. How about the Jaguar's apartments?"

"That was some seriously bad shit. Run like a military operation. Don't know much. Don't have good lines into Black dudes. Not my types. Jaguars are pissed. Apparently some Santa Muerte guys were there too and they were all killed. They Mexicans are real mad. Looking for a way to respond. But that was a well-run military operation. What has the Jaguars thinking is they have apartment buildings nearby. Would have been easier to hit. But they weren't. The difference? Weren't any Mexicans staying there. Has the Jaguars trying to read the tea leaves."

"You know something weird our evidence techs picked up. It appears the Warlords left something behind, probably a bomb. When the first Jaguar or Mexican backups arrived on the scene after the fire, the bomb blew 'em up. Almost like those Muslim terrorists try to do in the Middle East. Hit 'em and then take out the first responders also. That was a sophisticated operation."

Jose thinks about the second bomb idea. "Yeah. Not what you expect from the thugs who drop out of Chicago's shitty schools. We got tons of guys to recruit from, but they are rarely very bright or educated. Why do you think they get into drugs and violence? They're dumb shits without any ability or motivation to get real jobs."

"I suppose."

"You know half the kids in Chicago's schools drop out without graduating from high school? Gives us plenty of losers to pick from. Some try to do something else, but who other than us wants to hire an uneducated loser with an attitude?"

Sunny smiles at the thought.

"Can you picture some of these dudes walking in for a job interview?"

Sunny chuckles at that thought.

"Got their hat on sideways, peach fuzz on their face they pretend is a beard and their underpants sticking out of their jeans. They can't talk worth shit, walk funny and show up late for the interview. Then they're pissed no one wants to hire them. Dumb shits. That is what I got to work with. I'd just as soon shoot a couple of them to the keep the rest of them on notice. "

"Yeah. I don't usually think of it that way. But Brookins kind of explained that to me the same way the other day. His wife calls the Chicago, Harlem, Detroit, Milwaukee, DC and LA schools the up-front and personal face of institutional racism."

It is obvious Jose is considering that concept. "Yeah. She's right. My Priest talks about that stuff. He is always on the young girls to keep their legs together and quit havin' babies when they aren't married and the father has more tattoos than IQ points. Tells the guys to pull up their pants so we don't have to look at their underwear all the time."

"I agree."

"He says the kids just end up in jail or dead. So might as well save they selves the grief of havin' kids. He is tough on tellin' these kids about gettin' married, actin' adult and showin' some responsibility for their lives. He's an old school Priest, man. Real old school."

Sunny smiles. Ortega regularly surprises him. Now it is Jose. "You go to church? Aren't you afraid lightening will strike you down when you walk in the door?"

Jose laughs. "Yeah I am, but the Priest is good about takin' my confession and keepin' the lightin' bolts at bay. C'mon, I'm not that bad. I graduated from high school. I was an OK student. I even read newspapers. I watch something other than cartoons on TV. Hey, I've even got a library card."

"Stranger things may happen, but you are right there at the top of the strange heap. But, thanks. I'll tell Vlad you're glad he's in the hospital so he'll kick your ass again when he gets out."

"Up yours. Hey, drop me off South of here OK. I was out early hopin' to catch you and cause I got a guy I got to see."

Sunny nods yes. "No problem. Thanks. Big help. If I hear anything more you can use to trade, I'll arrest your ass next time. I'll even try to get you a dinner for your trouble in addition to the usual."

"Done. I don't care what they say. You're not as bad a guy as everybody says."

Both guys laugh at the friendly insults.

CHAPTER

THIRTY-SIX

SUNNY PARKS HIS UNMARKED POLICE CAR IN FRONT of the buildings where they have met Arturo Ortega in the past. The marked police cars pull up right behind him. The officers get out and they are all well-armed.

"Guys, please just wait here by the cars. Brookins! Don't walk around more than a few feet so you won't get lost. OK? Just wait here."

Brookins and the other officers spread out a bit, but chuckle at Sunny's friendly insult. Behind his back, Brookins quietly flips him the bird.

Sunny keeps his hands in view and walks up the front walk between the two buildings. His badge is in his left hand and it is held high. He is less than half way when two Insane Jaguars come out to meet him. Ortega is not with them. "I need to see Arturo Ortega. It is important."

The two Jaguars look at each other and finally one answers. "He isn't here."

"Fine, I understand that. But it is really important. Really important! I am sure one of you has his cell number. Please call him and let him know it is extremely important that Detective SunWarrior talk with him. I'll go where ever he designates and I'll come alone. Or I'll bring some of our muscle with me if he prefers."

The two Jaguars again look at each other but don't look confused. The older one nods to the younger and walks back toward the building. He pulls out his cell phone and dials. He speaks very quietly. He listens for a moment and then turns back to Sunny and hands him the cell phone.

"Meet me at the Skate Plaza on the North West end of Piotrowski Park on 31st Street in ten minutes. It is OK to bring the big Black guy, but no one else."

"Done. See you in ten. I'll only bring Brookins. He's the big Black guy."

Sunny turns back to the Jaguars. "Thanks. He wants to meet with Brookins and me. I'll leave the other guys here so you can see they aren't going with us. OK?"

Both Jaguars nod in the affirmative.

Sunny signals for Brookins and the other officers. "All of you stay here except Brookins who is coming with me. Make yourself comfortable, but stay alert. Ortega said he would only meet with the two of us. I trust him, but not some of his friends. Don't fall asleep but don't leave here until you hear from us."

They get into Sunny's unmarked car and head South and West to Piotrowski Park. While he drives they chat.

"You know Sunny, our little thing about dealing with evil may not be necessary. They're doing a pretty good job killing each other off without our help."

"Yea. I've been noticing that myself. Nobody even guessed those guys we did were anything but more of the gang feud."

It only takes a couple of minutes. They make a quick circle of the area by the Skate Plaza to be sure there is no one lurking around. They park and get out.

As soon as they walk toward the concrete Skate Plaza Ortega appears from behind some of the bigger chunks of concrete. Sunny signals they see him and walks to the semi-concealed spot. He reaches out to shake Arturo's hand. "You remember Officer Harold Brookins?"

Ortega nods he does and then shakes Brookins hand also. Ortega and Brookins shaking hands looks like two heavyweight wrestlers getting ready for a bout. These are two seriously, powerfully built guys. "Just being careful."

Sunny looks around. "Am I guessing correctly those four Santa Muerte muscle weren't at the restaurant just to buy you dessert?"

Arturo smiles at Sunny's description of his recent encounter with some of the Santa Muerte amigos. "Astute observation." Ortega nods and looks around also.

"You did one hell of a job on them. Four to one. Not bad work."

"They were high on drugs and a bunch of amateurs. It was an insult they only sent four guys and four losers to boot. That is why I sent them a message. If they can't do better than that, they are going to have a lot of problems."

"We just fished Alderman Larenda Bass and the Warlord lawyer Leonard Bernstein out of the river first thing this morning."

"Yeah, I know."

"How did you find out so fast?"

Ortega gives them another smile. "You forget. I run this place. I usually know before you do."

Both cops nod. "Yeah, probably so. Anything you can tell us?"

"Nothing beyond the Cartel was mad they didn't deliver the cash the Warlords owe. They got carried away. Thought they'd get the money and went loco when they didn't. They weren't planning on killing them, it just happened. Those Santa Muerte guys are crazy. They don't think straight. They have no strategic vision."

"What more should we know you're not saying?"

Ortega gives a deep throated chuckle. "I'll have to let you know later. I just agreed to meet so you'd know I wasn't ducking you. Keep your eyes open. Some big shit is about to unfold tonight."

As Sunny and Brookins drive away both try to figure what the warning about tonight means.

"You know Brookins I still can't figure him out. It is like he knows everything before we do. I don't know who his connections are, but they are deep inside."

"Yeah. With his reputation it doesn't make sense he is so cooperative. But I asked one of the gang crimes guys about what we were seeing with Ortega. He wasn't surprised. He described him like a big old grizzly bear. If you leave him alone he'll usually leave you alone. He usually doesn't go out of his way to find trouble. But like a grizzly he can turn on you when you are totally unprepared."

CHAPTER THIRTY-SEVEN

IN THE DARK, THE WARLORDS ARE INVISIBLE. THEY are all in black and have carefully selected positions that give them over lapping fields of fire. Good cover and concealment. Open lines for withdrawal at the proper time. Clear lines of communication so their cell phones won't get blacked out. This looks like an ambush set up by a Marine Gunnery Sergeant. Well maybe by a Lance Corporal, but it is precise and well thought out.

Mustafa's stock has risen even higher after the massacre at the Jaguar apartment. Akile Fort realizes Mustafa is right about the need for planning and precise execution. Fort absolutely loved the plan to have his guy take out the first Jaguars who arrived on the scene. He was excited to see if this trap would work as well as the last one.

All of the Warlords were trying to figure out who took out the three Santa Muerte thugs the other morning. No one would admit anything to Akile, Mustafa or Jaron. Via another alderman, Mustafa had one of Speaker Burke's flunkies, a cop named McGuire, check with the Chicago Police Gang Crimes Unit Lieutenant and all he got was the case was unsolved and it was still an open case. But the police were guessing it was the Warlords because of the well-organized operation, almost a military style assassination. Who else could have been involved in that precise a take down? It wasn't a very active investigation. Why? They were drug cartel gunmen from Mexico. Who cares?

Burke's flunky, McGuire, followed up with the city beat reporters from the *Tribune* and the *Sun Times,* as well as the Chicago News Bureau, a group of independent reporters and got similar observations. Nobody knew anything for sure, but they were all impressed at the precision of the hometown team, the Warlords. It is amazing how quickly a consensus about some news event can be formed.

All of the Warlord leadership were enjoying having the police, the media and just about everyone else talking about how well-organized and well-trained the Warlords were. But they still weren't so sure the Insane Jaguars hadn't pulled something and just let the blame, or credit, fall where it may. It was obvious Arturo Ortega wasn't exactly rolling out the welcome mat for the Mexican cartel gunmen. Nobody, especially the Warlords, really knew what happened.

To set up this event, Mustafa had used the oldest trick in the book. He had one of his guys pay big money to a high priced Latina hooker for drugs and sex. The guy didn't actually use the drugs to be sure his head would be clear, but he had gotten the Warlords money's worth in the sex department.

After they had finished a series of kinky, painful and unique maneuvers guaranteed to piss off the hooker, the guy ran his mouth about their big stash and the meeting at the safe house tonight. He would be back tomorrow to celebrate. He talked like a fool high on drugs and his ego. She took the bait right to her pimp who took it right to the Santa Muerte gunmen who are demanding information from anyone and everyone.

The Warlords are well drilled and know exactly what each man's role is to be. Most, but not all of the street lights have been knocked out. They wait quietly with their night vision goggles giving everything an eerie green glow. They check their weapons and make sure their extra clips are still full. Then they check their fields of fire and then they just wait.

Four SUVs roll to a slow stop on the dark street. Not even their running lights are on. They move silently and even when the doors are opened they remain totally silent. The inside lights have been shut off so they don't go on when the doors open.

Each vehicle disgorges five heavily armed Santa Muerte Cartel gunmen. The twenty spread out into an arc around the front of the building. They aren't worried about the back side, since it leads into a dead end courtyard. There is only one way out. The very dark street makes them feel invisible.

The Santa Muerte leader is thinking this is a nice group of buildings. A smart move by the Warlords to use a better neighborhood. The courtyard is enclosed and well-maintained. There are bushes and even a neat little yard. No one would have expected this to be a Gangster Warlord safe house. The Cartel gunmen check their weapons again. They advance in their arc with their weapons at the ready.

Every movement is followed in the night vision goggles. It almost looks like green daylight the way they can follow the twenty Mexican gunmen. All they need is Mustafa's signal. Every weapon is aimed and fully loaded.

The first rounds hit from out of nowhere. None of the Santa Muerte thugs are looking behind them and are completely unprepared to be fired on from behind. Twelve of the twenty go down in the first barrage.

What they don't notice is three of the Warlords are assigned the task of taking out the tires on the SUVs. Once they complete their mission by hitting those, they turn their weapons on the Cartel's men.

The Santa Muertes turn to return fire and the Warlords duck out of the line of fire. They pull off their night vision goggles and hunker down to avoid the first wave of bullets. Several of the Cartel gunmen rush back to the SUVS and get set to make a run for it.

From the hidden doors of the apartment gangways three Warlords emerge from what is now the blind side of the Cartel's men. The all hold several lighted Molotov cocktails. Without any hesitation they heave them at the four SUVS.

The Santa Muertes try to start the SUVs and pull away. But the tires are shot out and driving quickly on the rims of such big vehicles is almost impossible. But now the slow moving SUVs are engulfed in flames from the Molotov cocktails.

As the Cartel gunmen try to get back out and take cover, the Warlords, now minus their night vision goggles use the flames to give them great lines of sight. The flames give a backdrop to the Santa Muertes and every one of them is highlighted. The overlapping fields of fire leave every Cartel gunman being fired at from a minimum of two directions at once.

The last few try to run. Run to where? The Warlords have every angle covered. There is no escape for the Mexican killers turned targets. The fight is over in less than one minute. Every Santa Muerte is down and the bodies are all visible in the flames.

On command, the Warlords rush to the fallen bodies. They aren't worried about any hostile fire. They quickly count off the twenty bodies and make sure all are dead. A few extra bullets to the head and heart assure the body count includes all twenty.

Then the guns and extra ammunition are collected. The bodies not burning in the stationary SUVs are searched for anything in the pockets. That was all and on Mustafa's signal, the Warlords disappear into the night.

As they hurry away, Akile Fort can't keep himself from smiling. Another big victory over the invincible Santa Muerte Cartel. These Mexican killers built a very tough reputation on innocent bystanders, unarmed women and lowly drug addicts. They were big on killing the unarmed families of police and Mexican military personnel. They aren't so tough when they face a smart and disciplined marine like Mustafa. The Warlords are keeping their honor intact and loving even moment of it.

The 911 Center just received its first calls moments ago. This is a middle class, mixed race but minority dominated neighborhood. This is not the kind of area that needs to make many 911 calls. The police and fire are dispatched instantly.

In a matter of minutes the police have arrived. The SUVs are burning and they leave those to the fire department. The police keep a safe distance from the SUVs in case they explode. But with that much light they can see bodies scattered all over the ground. They move slowly to be careful of secondary explosions.

The morning news report the deaths of twenty Mexican nationals. None appeared to have been in the country legally. At the moment none have been identified and the assumption is they won't be without significant help from the Mexican government who is onsite and fully cooperating.

It is generally assumed they were Santa Muerte Drug Cartel gunmen. But what they were doing in a lake front, very middle class, non-Latino neighborhood just off South Jackson Highlands is not obvious. All of their cars, big SUVs had been torched and each gunman had been shot numerous times. Some had the marks of execution style shootings to the face and the heart. The only weapons found were a handful in the burned out SUVs. The police have no answers just yet.

The various Chicago Media outlets report the death toll. First from the apparent gang attack on two Latino gang owned apartment buildings in Little Village earlier this week that left 29 dead. Now this apparent example of gang land extermination of rivals adjoining the affluent South Jackson Highlands neighborhood, leaving 20 dead. These two are the worst death tolls since the Al Capone-led St. Valentine's Day massacre in 1929.

Of the 49 killed in the two major skirmishes, 43 were Latino. Unofficial sources say of the 43 Latino's killed, at least 31, probably several more, were undocumented. While almost ten young Blacks, assumed to be Warlords, were also dead, the media found the Mexican angle more interesting and played it up. Dead Black kids in Chicago is almost a daily event. Really not that newsworthy. Lots of dead undocumented gunmen, now that is a real story.

The city is in an uproar and Latino community leaders are absolutely up in arms demanding an increased police presence in their communities.

Some more radical elements in the Latino community think the military precision of the strikes show the U. S. Government is involved and has sent in Special Operations Units, intentionally murdering undocumented workers to strike fear in the greater Latino community. They believe it is a governmental attempt to intimidate Latinos in America and suppress their rights. They seem to forget to mention the guys were armed and probably Cartel thugs.

When told of the somewhat radical comments about the U. S. Government's involvement, an Illinois State Senator from Effingham, Wayne Simmons, who had served as a member of the Special Forces in the past said, "They are idiots and should quit saying such stupid things. The media should also quit covering idiots saying idiotic things."

A spokesman for the Department of Defense says there is absolutely no truth to the statements in any way, shape or form. American soldiers do not operate within America's borders.

With the various other murders this week, including a powerful, gang connected South Side Alderman, a gang connected political insider Chicago attorney and several gang members, the apparent death toll in what looks like a gang war, is well past fifty bodies in just one week.

The Mayor and the City Council are screaming for answers and telling people to be careful to avoid areas where gangs may congregate. Unnamed police sources concede the three major attacks were accomplished with absolute military precision. There are no reported observers to either incident. Police continue to request assistance from any possible eyewitnesses.

Lieutenant Dornan looks at Sunny with a hard expression. "Do you have any idea how much heat is coming from City Hall?"

With a mischievous nod and an angelic expression he appears to be thinking. "Are they concerned a bunch of the dead guys were ghost payrollers and now they don't have anyone to fill their empty precinct positions?"

If the Lieutenant wasn't used to Sunny's irreverent behavior he would have lost it. "Actually one of the guys killed at the apartment ambush was listed as an employee of the City Council Finance Committee. We couldn't find anyone who had ever met him but he had ties to Alderman Candyass Maldonado. Do you believe this shit?"

"Yeah. I love it. The guy is illegal but Candyass has him on the city payroll."

"You know Sunny, your warped view of the city's elected leadership is not appreciated. Remember they may be well known to be crooked jerks, but you and I work for them. Have you got that clear?"

Sunny chuckles at Dornan's kidding about the Chicago City Council. Both of them know in just the last few years 32 of the 50 Aldermen have gone to jail. Another, the 33rd was indicted just last month. Most people think the couple of Aldermen not indicted are actually FBI informants. It has to be true because they are some of the biggest crooks. If they weren't informants there was no way they'd be this side of a federal prison.

Dornan can see Sunny smiling and knows what he is thinking. "Now wipe that shit eatin' grin off your face and get serious. We have killings to solve and you're a detective, wiseass! A sorry frickin' excuse for a cop, let alone a detective, but you are supposed to be our expert on the Gangster Warlords. Remember?"

"I've got feelers out to folks who know a little about the Warlords as individual guys. I'm trying to figure out if they have a guy, maybe a leader, who is ex-military. Remember, I did this crap in Afghanistan. I know what an ambush is. I did them. These have all the markings of military operations. This is over the top for a street gang. I'm working angles."

"At least you're doing something to earn your paycheck for a change."

Sunny playfully reacts like Dornan just gave him a head slap. "These ambushes seem to be the work of a competent military guy or else the Warlords have imported extra help. That is the best angle to get things moving. It is a bloody mess, but they are clearly getting the better end of this fight so far."

"Why are you standing around wasting my time? Get out of here and find out if the Warlords hired former CIA black ops guys as mercenaries, unemployed Russian Spetznatz, Mujahedeen, aliens from Mars or whatever crazy excuse you have come up with. Go!" Dornan chuckles at his directions and points his arm at the door and shoves Sunny toward it.

Sunny mockingly salutes.

"Get a good night's sleep because as of tomorrow you are on this case 24/7 for the rest of your life or until you get an answer. That's probably the rest of your life. If you aren't back with answers by tomorrow afternoon, you aren't going to be getting much sleep in the very foreseeable future. I'm going to borrow Purcell's cattle prod to motivate you. Now go!"

Sunny chuckles at Dornan but pauses a moment and gets serious. "Lieutenant…this may sound like an odd question, but I'm serious. Any political feuds in the Chicago machine? Bass and Bernstein were cogs in the big corrupt machine. Any reason anyone would want them dead? Like that dead school guy we dragged out of the river the other day, were there any open investigations on any of the other dead guys? Ask around to the political guys by the superintendent. Anything they haven't told us that would shed light on this case?"

The look on Dornan's face makes it obvious why Sunny is a well-respected detective. All the macho kidding aside, that just might be the $64,000 question. This is Chicago. Dornan tells himself, don't be naïve, this is Chicago.

Dornan speaks quietly to Sunny. "I'll ask. They close open investigations if the guy in question does something like die. A closed investigation avoids anything they don't want on the street from getting there."

Sunny smiles. "You're catching my drift." With that Sunny waves goodbye and heads for his car.

Dornan is well aware in a city as notoriously corrupt as Chicago, there are lots of conspiracy theorists. Some still claim the city's first Black Mayor, Harold Washington was actually murdered. It wasn't really a heart attack, it was poison. Some called Harold's death an assassination. With his charisma he was changing the dynamics of Chicago politics. The Blacks were becoming ascendant and the old White Irish like Burke and his faction were concerned about losing power, patronage and of course, money.

For the first three years of the Washington administration the Chicago City Council was a war zone of racism called "Council Wars". The 29 Machine Aldermen, 28 White and one

Latino versus the 16 Black Aldermen, four non-machine Whites and one guy who could read the results of Washington winning his White majority but liberal ward. The funny part is all of the Black Aldermen were machine loyalists but didn't dare support the machine as years of Black frustration at the Machine's racism boiled over in the Black wards. 29 to 21 and three years of bloodshed to keep the city's first Black Mayor from controlling the process.

Chicago was nicknamed "Beirut by the Lake". The Mayor had a veto and the White guys didn't have the votes to override. The open racism, greed and corruption boiled over on a daily basis. Chicago was the national example of Democrat racism on graphic and open display. There were zero Republican Aldermen, but they were, as usual, still blamed for part of the trouble by the White Democrats who needed to deflect some of the blame for their racism so openly being displayed by their own people.

The White Irish Democrats in charge went way too over the top as they tried to destroy a legally elected mayor, just because he was Black. The personal attacks on Harold Washington were unbelievable. The nastiness almost unheard of. Right down to the horrendously demeaning, but often displayed painting of Harold in a ladies nightie done by a supporter of the "Machine".

Dornan thought of the racist 29 Democrats who did everything humanly possible to destroy a Black man who had made the decision to stand up to them and fight. A great group: 'Fast' Eddie Vrdolyak went to jail; Patrick Huels, the Alderman from the Daley family ward was forced to resign amidst a scandal; The mobster's guys, Vito Marzullo and Fred Roti, who went to jail; Brennan Burk's alderman, who went to jail; Jim Laski from the ward next to Burke, went to jail; Lovable old George Hagopian, who went to jail; Dick Mell, the father-in-law of jailed former Governor Rod Blagojevich, who made Blago's career; Old Anthony Laurino, who went to jail; and Pretty boy Joe Kotlarz, who went to jail. Dornan knew why people thought those guys might have been capable of anything.

It is beyond any reasonable doubt that Fred Hampton and the Black Panther Party leadership were murdered in their apartment while they slept. The then Cook County State's Attorney, Ed Hanrahan was a stalwart in the White Irish arm of the party. The White Democrats were very concerned Fred Hampton, who was running food kitchens and preschools under the Black Panther banner, was getting to be too mainstream, too respected and was turning to the traditional tool of power...elected politics.

Hampton had the nerve to ask what Black citizens were getting for their slavish devotion to the Democrat party. Demeaning welfare? Ruined, crime and drug-ridden neighborhoods? Destroyed families? Never rebuilt neighborhoods left over from the Martin Luther King assassination riots? Terrible schools? Life in the most segregated major city in America? No real political power? Hampton had gone way over the line and even put out feelers to Republicans?

Next thing anyone knows he is murdered in the middle of the night by a White, Irish, Chicago Democrat political insider. It was murder, don't let anyone kid you. Yet the State's Attorney who murdered Hampton was not going to indict himself or even empanel a grand jury to investigate himself. Then Hampton's dream came true. In the next election virtually every Black Ward and suburban Black towns voted Republican and Hanrahan was ousted and replaced by a Republican who served for eight years until he in turn was defeated by a young, pre-mayor, Richard M. Daley (Richard II).

Anyone who lives in Chicago for very long has their own conspiracy theories about the long in power Chicago Democrat Machine. But Dornan thinks what makes this salient today is because this mess started as another attack on Black Chicagoans, albeit Gangster Warlords. The minor technical point they are violent, drug running gangbangers is often over looked. The White Irish power structure might not mind a gang war between the Blacks and the Latinos. Racism is a real element in the Chicago Democrat machine strategy. It keeps White voters, who in other towns and states have long ago gone Republican, in line and behind the inept and corrupt Machine candidates. They are terrified the politicians aligned with the gangs will take power. Burke's guys quietly allow folks to think it is the Black and Latino politicians who have close ties to those dangerous gangs. The Machine White guys aren't worried it will affect the Black and Latino voters. They'll stay Democrat. If Burke and his guys want to keep the power, influence and all that money without a fight, they need to keep their opponents battling windmills.

Dornan just shook his head as he remembered the City Hall Latino political operative, Marco Morales-Simon, who was convicted of corruption but didn't turn evidence on other City Hall insiders, so he was allowed to drive himself to prison. Somehow, on the way, he got lost and ended up somewhere in Mexico. But to be sure he stayed in Mexico and kept his mouth shut, his family received $40 million in Chicago contracts. Of course no one thought it could possibly have been a payoff for keeping his mouth shut and getting lost in Mexico. The guys mentor and buddy, former Alderman Ambrosio Medrano, who served time in the mid-1990s was just indicted again. Dornan knew the Chicago guys didn't tend to change their spots.

Another example, the political big shot, real estate developer and a leader of the Chicago Public School system who they had just recently fished out of the Chicago River after what some claimed was a suicide.

Dornan remembered there had been that investigation into something like half a million of missing school board dollars that was dropped when the guy's body was found.

Dornan turned to go back to his car. He just kept thinking, was Sunny right this whole thing had something to do with a feud or maybe an internal power struggle of the Chicago Machine? He doesn't really want to even think of the option that all of this stuff isn't random. Were the Cartels paying off anybody in Chicago to get most of their drugs in without trouble? Was the problem of Sunny and Vlad grabbing millions of dollars of the Mexican/Warlord pact an accident that wasn't supposed to happen? After all, it was an accident, not part of a major investigation. As long as they kept the drugs in the Black and Latino neighborhoods...Dornan decides not to go there. Next thing he knows they'll be calling him some kind of crazy racial conspiracy theorist. Dornan would be made out as the murdered Black Panther, Fred Hampton reborn.

Dornan has a wife and kids to think about and doesn't need to commit police career conspiracy suicide.

CHAPTER THIRTY-EIGHT

SUNNY ENTERS COOK COUNTY HOSPITAL AND TAKES the elevator to the psych floor. As he gets off the elevator there are Chicago Police and County Sheriff's Police all around. It looks safe if the folks who want to kill you don't have RPGs or mortars or attack helicopters. This isn't Afghanistan. That is something Sunny appreciates.

Sunny has been stretched to the limit, working too hard, recovering from his wounds in the attack at his house, his best pal almost killed and worrying about the gang feuds that need to be stopped. He is just plain exhausted. He is also worried the political guys know things he isn't being told.

He doesn't like sleeping at County Hospital but knows having police protect both Vlad and him is a good idea. They have real people out there who really do want to kill them. Still he misses Sheila and doesn't sleep well in a hospital bed in a psych ward. The ward has reinforced windows and doors. It is also set off a little distance from the rest of the hospital. It is a very safe area and well protected. But Sunny would love to go home. Might be a bad idea, even if it was just maybe for this one night.

Sunny sits back in the chair by his bed and his mind begins to drift. This conspiracy with the Santa Muertes and the ties to Burke and the drug train right out of Mexico and Fast & Furious guns and he is swirling in everyone's conspiracy theories of what is actually happening. These theories aren't new. He has heard them all. Many times.

Doesn't matter now. Sunny needs some sleep and he should let this stuff go for a few hours. The Police Department doesn't want him to sleep at his own home, but he needs to restore some sanity. Sunny leans back in his chair and thinks about his own bed.

Sunny sneaks out without telling the guards and he returns home. He misses Sheila and this is as close as he can get for the near future. His home allows him to sleep in his own bed and that is so much more restful.

His home is still a little worse for wear after the attack. Sheila and he are going to need a few days of serious R & R to get the house repaired and to decompress.

The City of Chicago offered to pay the deductible on his home insurance to repair the mess. Of course his insurance isn't all that excited to cover the major repairs. They are having a hard time seeing the Santa Muerte Cartel as a natural disaster. Oh well. He'll worry about it later. He just needs some rest without the dreams or maybe more accurately, the night mares.

He senses something. It doesn't wake him, but it alerts him that he needs to concentrate. The Afghanistan Special Forces Sergeant's instincts aren't dead. There is a sensation of something evil in the room. It is like an evil cloud in enveloping his home. Something is dramatically wrong. Then the explosion rocks his world. He is under attack.

He is almost thrown right out of his bed. The entire room lights up like it is filled with flood lights. There are flames everywhere. The outer wall of the bedroom starts to sag. He can't hear himself think through the sounds of C-4 blasts. Then the entire front end of the house collapses.

He can't believe he is still alive. There is smoke, flames and flying objects all over the room. He grabs his personal SIG Sauer from under his pillow and rolls onto the floor. He has kept several night lights on around the house just to make it easier for him to get around in an emergency. With the explosions the electricity goes off and all of the lights go black.

What is happening? He starts asking unaskable political questions and now this! Did someone in the city government sell him out to the Santa Muerte Cartel? Burke? Leoni? Stu Black? Who else knows he is asking the unaskable? Who besides Burke cares? Is this something bigger?

He can hear the ceilings collapsing and see most of it because of the flames and the bright lights shining on his house. He finally realizes there are trucks surrounding the house with their high beams on. It seems there are gunmen standing in the truck beds and they are now firing at his home and indirectly at him, since they don't know exactly where he is.

More explosions rock what is left of his house. It leaves him disoriented. He is awake but can't get his mind around what is happening to his home. He can see the flickering and sparks shooting from the electrical outlets that have been torn apart by the explosions. He assumes the electric cables have been laid bare and he will need to carefully avoid them.

Shocked, disoriented and bruised from the falling ceiling and apparently other things that have flown around the room in the explosions, he still knows he needs to get to the basement. He doesn't have a safe room or anything like that, but his basement has thick concrete walls and he has stocked it with equipment he will need. There is plenty of ammunition, flashlights, night vision goggles and body armor. Then he realizes he doesn't need the night vision goggles with everything burning down around him.

Bullets seem to be flying around him. They tear through what little is left of his house's walls. He is certainly not paralyzed by fear or anything like that. He knows what he needs to do and is going about doing it. He doesn't bother to fire back since he is blinded by the lights and can't see who or what he is shooting at. He also doesn't want them to know for sure he is alive or where he is.

He needs to get to the basement to use it as a fortification until the Police respond to the 911 calls he is sure have already been made by neighbors all up and down the street. They will respond immediately to 911 calls about an attack on a fellow officer's home.

If they are this brazen to attack his home again, he worries they have made another attack on Vlad at the Cook County Hospital. After the last attack on the small standalone recovery unit the University of Chicago Hospitals operated, the Chicago Police Department wasn't going to take any more chances. They put Vlad on the top floor of the Cook County Hospital, in a corner room in a ward where the windows are covered by mesh. It is essentially a psych ward room, so it is well designed to be sure it can be protected from the irrational behavior of an occupant or someone wanting to get at an occupant.

There are plenty of Chicago Police and Cook County Sheriff's Police all around Vlad's room and the hospital floor. Sheriff Elway has been very helpful by assigning experienced Sheriff's Police. Sunny thinks the Sheriff has gone way beyond the call in being sure Vlad is safe now and that Sunny had been safe when he was sent to Cook County Jail by Judge Leoni. A very fine effort.

While all of the precautions would make an attack difficult, it doesn't seem to scare the Santa Muertes away from Sunny's own home they know probably had extra protection. Sunny realizes Vlad isn't his problem at the moment, his life is. He'd better get back to worrying about himself.

As an experienced police officer and Special Forces veteran of heavy duty training and close in combat in Afghanistan, he has more than enough practical experience to avoid panic. But that doesn't keep him from being flat out nervous. He is in too exposed a position to properly defend himself until help arrives. He knows help is on the way by now. He just needs to hold the Santa Muerte gunmen at bay for a few minutes, at most. Easier said than done.

He crawls on his stomach. There are flames above him and they are scorching his back and legs. He knows the Santa Muertes haven't entered the house yet because there is still too much indiscriminate firing with rounds flying everywhere. He hugs the floor. The shots seem to be too high and are going over his prostrate body.

Suddenly the entire house is rocked again. It feels like something big, like an RPG, has been fired into the house's core. Maybe the round hit the brick fire place or what was left of a brick supporting wall. It has hit something strong or it wouldn't have exploded. He realizes he has been hit by flying something. He assumes it is chips of brick broken loose and turned into shrapnel by the RPG.

Then he hears it or really doesn't hear it. The shooting stops and that means the Santa Muerte Gunmen are pouring into his house to be sure he is dead. If he is still alive, he knows they will want to grab him as a prisoner.

The one thing he is sure of is he has no intention of being taken alive. As a Comanche Warrior he has read plenty about what they did to their prisoners. He wouldn't even let Sheila read that stuff. She would have been up all night for weeks with nightmares. It wasn't just the brutality. It was that they enjoyed inflicting that kind of pain and suffering on another human being. They took pride in how long they could keep a prisoner alive to maximize the sheer human agony.

If they were surrounded and cut off, the cavalry told their troopers to keep their last bullet for themselves. Never let themselves be captured alive.

He didn't even want to think about what the Cartel might do to him. He had read reports of their barbaric treatment of Mexican Policemen they caught. Even more barbaric treatment of the families of the Mexican Policemen they grabbed for vengeance and intimidation. This was vengeance for $4,000,000 dollars. They would be real pissed.

That stuff was why Tiffany Burroughs-Rea had recommended he get Sheila out of town and hidden away some place safe. Heck, the Cartel treatment of just regular people who they tortured and killed with great regularity to maintain the climate of fear and maximize the level of intimidation was well beyond the pale. No point in imagining what they would do to him. Someone they were really upset with.

He knew he wouldn't get off as easy as that lawyer Bernstein or Alderman Bass. They just had their brains blown out. Based on the comments made about Bass there hadn't been a lot of brains to blow out. But that sleazy lawyer, Bernstein probably had plenty to spatter all over the walls.

Why guys like that so willingly sold their souls was more than most cops could comprehend. Money was nice. But how do you go to confession and face your priest with that kind of blood on your hands. Then Sunny realizes guys like Bernstein don't go to confession. They don't believe in GOD. A GOD. Or any GOD. They believe in themselves. The here and now. The almighty dollar. The pleasures that can be bought with enough money.

The posse is on their way to save him. Of that he is sure. But what he isn't sure about is if they will make it in time. It doesn't look like he will have the several minutes they will need to get to his house.

The Captain had been right. Sleeping at home, even if it was pretty much a secret, is turning out to be a very bad idea. He slithers around what had once been a corner and yanks open what is left of the basement door. He throws himself down the steps, rolling as he does it.

The temperature is brutal. There are burning embers dropping on the floor. He crawls through them. It hurts. They are burning for real. He doesn't have on anything but a sleeveless t-shirt and his underwear.

His eyes hurt. His chest and back hurt from rolling down the basement steps in the midst of the fire. The smoke is making it difficult to breathe or even see much. He tries to take deep breaths, but can't without gagging.

A laundry basket full of dirty clothes explodes into flames. He remembers he had done some work on the car the girls took and had gotten some grease on his jeans. They were in the basket. The grease ignited just like hot grease exposed to flames will every time.

He sees the lock for his stash of weapons and ammunition. He always sleeps with the key around his neck. He reaches for it. It isn't there. What? How? He always puts it on when he goes to bed. It has to be there. He desperately feels all over his neck and chest. Nothing. He can't get into the cache. He is trapped.

The foot falls are getting closer. They are just over his head. The floor is creaking and embers are breaking off and falling all around him. He can't figure how they were standing up and moving around in that heat. Their weapons must be almost too hot to touch. Maybe they are smart and wear gloves. But he doubts they have worn fireproof suits. How are they breathing?

Steps resonated at the door to the basement. He can hear them starting down the stairs. He aims his SIG Sauer at the point where the stairs twist a little so he knows they will have to slow and bend. That is why he rolled down them to avoid being exposed at that juncture.

Here they come. He will die fighting. No more time to wait for the cavalry to come and rescue him. He prepares for a fight to the death. He isn't going out alone.

The legs show at the bend. He fires. They don't seem to be hurt. The legs are red! Why are they wearing red clothes? Fire retardant suits? Then he sees the bodies and they are almost serpentine. They look like demons. Their eyes glow right through and out of the flames. They stare right at him. The smoke swirls all around these red demon like creatures. He almost empties his magazine of 9mm rounds. Nothing seems to hurt them.

He grabs for a knife he keeps next to the locked door. They slowly come at him. They hold their fire. They want him alive. They jump on him. He stabs and tears at them. He knows they want to subdue him alive.

Don't be taken alive! Don't be taken alive! They are fighting him, but he isn't giving up. He has kept one round in his SIG Saur. It is in his hand. He aims it at his head.

Sunny explodes into wakefulness. He is lurching every which way with a hand that does not hold a knife. Nor is his own SIG Sauer aimed at his head. There aren't any demons all over him. He is numb and drenched in sweat, but at least his house isn't burning. Or at least he isn't in his house, so he doesn't know if it is.

He is in the room next to Vlad's at Cook County Hospital. He is surrounded by competent guards. The attack has been as real as the small light on in the corner of the room. But... Sunny needs to step back. He needs to stay focused. It doesn't matter who the bad guys are if he loses it and can't help arrest them.

He thought he could hear the sound of a nurse making her rounds. She was probably heading into Vlad's room to be sure he was OK and also to check his vital signs. Vlad was probably holding her hand or something else. He could be a real gentleman and usually was, but he knew his charms and he worked at it.

Sheila thought Sunny was a pervert? He is at least a one-woman man. Vlad is a legend. He rides his big Harley Davidson down on Rush Street and in the hot areas in Lincoln Park and Buck Town with his leathers and his fake, reinforced Alexander the Great helmet for head protection. He even wears his shades at night. He may not have had Sunny's physique, but he was still a well-built stud.

Vlad got away with it by always treating the ladies respectfully and never talking about his exploits. Vlad does not believe in discriminating. He loves White girls, Asian girls, Black girls and Latinas. He loves women but he was raised by his parents to be a gentleman. The problem is no one anticipated the sexual revolution. But when it exploded on Vlad he did not shy away. Yet if you listened to Vlad you'd think he was celibate and studying for the priesthood. Half the nurses had probably begged for the chance to be his nurse! Whatever.

This sure beat being buried under a pile of demons. Oh well. He's alive. Soaked in sweat and his heartbeat running like a humming bird. Actually that wasn't much. After what he had just dreamed, a normal person would have a heartbeat of 1,000 beats a minute and then a terminal stroke! Sunny is in great shape. But, he has to get hold of himself. He can't let this stuff get to him.

CHAPTER

THIRTY-NINE

THE POLICE DEPARTMENT DECIDED TO KEEP SUNNY and Vlad at the County Hospital Psych Ward for safe keeping. Sunny was expected to come and go while investigating the gang war, but he needed some place safe to rest and eat. Of course Superintendent Purcell, with a chuckle, told Sunny the psych ward seemed a fitting place to stash him. That would have been OK if the Captain and Lieutenant Dornan hadn't so readily agreed with the appropriateness!

The Police Department was keeping a watchful eye on Sunny's house. First to be sure to see if anyone came by looking for him. A Gangster Warlord, a Santa Muerte Cartel gunman or an Insane Jaguar would look out of place in Sunny's neighborhood. The second reason was just to be sure it wasn't vandalized.

As a dietary assistant brings Sunny his breakfast an old friend sneaks in the hospital room door right behind her. In his hand is a Dunkin Donuts bag spilling over with fritters. If Sunny had been worried about his heartbeat last night, it is nothing to the thrill of seeing more fritters than he can eat. There were normally no guests allowed in this essentially maximum security hospital room, but Sunny got a special waiver for Terry.

Former prosecutor, now FBI mole, Terry Hake has an ear-to-ear grin on his face. As soon as the lady delivers Sunny's breakfast tray and leaves the room, Terry carefully checks to see if anyone is listening outside in the hallway and closes the door.

With an impish smile and a conspiratorial whisper, Terry lets go. "You aren't going to believe this! We're announcing the indictments from Operation Greylord tomorrow. One hundred of the dirt bags are going to be indicted tomorrow. Three of the presiding judges will be indicted. Thirteen of the leads you gave me are on the list. I got Fromm's permission to give you a heads up. But, obviously, no talking until tomorrow."

Sunny is so excited he is ready to jump out of bed and hug Terry. "Fantastic! Hey, did you get the guy who retired down in Arizona who let the mobster hit man off?"

After a pause Terry has a sad look on his face. "We have kept it fairly quiet. With all your partying around with the Mexican drug cartels you have been too busy to hear. The guy talked to us on the phone. Agreed to come back up for questioning and hung up the phone. Walked into his bedroom, got a pistol off the closet shelf, sat down on his back patio and blew his brains out."

Sunny is thunderstruck. "Talk about knowing you just got caught and deciding you really didn't want to have to face the music. Whoa!"

"Terrible. Hey...we had him dead to rights. He would have gone to jail and lost his pension. From a human perspective, I couldn't be sorrier. But he should have thought of that before he let the mobster walk. He returned a known killer to the streets."

Both sit there in silence a moment.

"Did you get that bastard Leoni after he sent me to County Jail for two weeks for calling him on his fix?"

With a rather sad look Terry shakes his head. "They made a decision to not indict Leoni. We had him solid on at least three different cases. There are several guys I know took money because I gave it to them or like Leoni and yet they chose not to indict them."

"What? They took money from you and they didn't get indicted? Did you screw up the hand off or something?"

"No. They chose not to indict them. They're not going to indict the Presiding Judge, Harold Commerton either."

Sunny is flabbergasted. "What am I missing?"

"Somebody higher up made the call. Maybe they turned state's evidence? Maybe they agreed to testify in front of a grand jury? Don't know. But the DOJ decided not to indict a bunch of guys we all know for sure are dirty."

"Whoa? If you decide not to take them down, at least don't leave them on the bench."

"I agree. Maybe they think they've been scared straight. Maybe some of them had big friends. Don't know. But a bunch of guys, including Commerton, the Presiding Judge, the dirtiest one of them all, will get off scot free. Can't explain."

The look on Sunny's face says it all.

"Here is another interesting point. Every one of the judges we are about to indict had been found qualified or highly qualified by the various bar associations in Crook County. What does that tell you about the supposed watch dogs?"

"You're kidding!"

"The Presiding Judge, Commerton received a 98% favorable rating from the various bar associations. Guess we know it is not just the political guys who have been covering up the corruption for all of these years."

"That sucks. But you know as well as I do there are a ton of sleazy lawyers in Crook County in addition to the political leadership of the county who like the system as is."

"Yeah...but let's look on the good side. This is the biggest cleanup of a judicial system in American history. At least we're getting more than 100 of the scumbags. That is more indictments than the other 49 states added together."

Sunny nods. "We get 100 of the crooks and we know we just hit the tip of the ice berg in the Crook County Courts. Sort of leaves you a little ambivalent, doesn't it?"

"Actually it does."

"But think about it, there is some good news. Now that it will be out in the open I can quit bad mouthing you to all of our friends. You go from turncoat jerk to hero. That will be nice."

"It'll be nicest for my wife. This has been toughest on her."

"My wife is taking the brunt of this crap we're going through with the Mexican Drug Cartel and all of these politically connected street gangs too. She is off hiding out somewhere. People would be amazed at how closely woven into Chicago's political fabric the street gangs are."

Terry smiles about the gang reference to the political structure. He had seen plenty of it in the courts also. Too many gangbangers, thugs, drug pushers, drunk drivers and just general losers getting a break from crooked or politically influenced judges on the bench.

Sometimes it would be the Crook County State's Attorney taking care of some ward committeeman's political workers. Or even worse, some political insider showing off his clout by getting some sleaze ball off. The reasons didn't matter, it was the results that frustrated the guys the levels below the political superstructure.

"Actually there is a second reason I'm here."

"You mean you didn't come to my hospital hideout just to wish me well?"

"Not just that. When we do the press conference tomorrow, do you want to be there? Remember nobody outside of our little group knows you are involved. Do you want to go public or just know the FBI and your government will be appreciative for at least the rest of the week?"

Both chuckle at the reminder that gratitude is often a fleeting thing. Memories aren't always very long. Sunny just sits there and thinks and thinks and thinks. He is obviously troubled by the situation.

Terry laughs. "Geez, sorry, I didn't mean to take up your whole day! I'd love to have you there, but if you want my advice, I'd not be there if I were you. We will rub some seriously powerful people the wrong way. We're sticking a cattle prod up the fanny of the Chicago political and Chicago legal establishment. They'll be mad."

"Oh yeah. It is so rare that anyone ever really challenges these guys. They have always viewed total control of the courts as a prerogative of their political power. Hey! Make you a bet!"

"What?"

"When they try to clean up the mess, the number one defender of the status quo will be Brennan Burke."

Terry smiles. "You're wrong. The number one defender of the status quo will be the Chicago and Cook County Bar Associations. This will reveal they have been compliant in the corruption. This is a real cattle prod where the sun don't shine for them. It demonstrates their bar association ratings weren't very good and maybe not even honest."

Sunny thinks a moment. "I think you've got me there. But the number two defender will be Brennan Burke. Who has made more judges than him?"

"Number two? OK. I agree he will be number two. When you're the chairman of an institutionally corrupt party, controlling the judges is mandatory."

Both guys sit and think a minute.

"You know we cops have seen so much of this stuff. It drives you crazy. You know 12,000 cops will be cheering you on. Not that it will make your life easier after this."

"I'll never be able to practice law here again. I'll always be watching my back. I'm through with a normal life. I volunteered for that. You're a cop. You have enough enemies. Adding the entire political power and legal structure of Chicago and Crook County to your list of enemies may be more than you and Sheila need."

Finally Sunny looks up. "GOD bless you Terry for what you've done. You know it is something we both dreamed of. But you're right. This is more enemies than I need. We both know somebody big, well over our heads, is protecting a bunch of additional judges we both know are crooks. So we don't even know for sure who are friends and who are foes. I don't need to add people I don't even know as enemies. A cop watching his back side is tough enough. But having guys big enough to get crooks at this level off might be dangerous. Thanks. Good luck man and I'll love watching you on TV."

Two old friends sit in the hospital room and smile. It is fun to win. Especially when you have taken on and defeated some of the biggest of the big crooks in Chicago. For Sunny, it is necessary to remember that sometimes discretion is the better part of valor. Terry has done a wonderful thing for the citizens of Crook County but will pay for it for the rest of his life. Sunny has other battles to fight.

"Hey, is your drill sergeant welching on my Ruth's Chris petite filet?"

Terry cracks up. "I'll talk to him, but I think you're screwed with Fromm. He's a cheap bastard. He took me out to celebrate at Lou Malnati's, not a steak house. But I'll make you a deal. I'm good for it. Once this is done we'll both bring our wives and make a night of it."

Sunny looks like he just won the lottery. "You are a man of your word. I will remember this to my dying day or next week whichever comes first!"

Both laugh.

"You know, Terry, we aren't through. You know there is far more corruption in the justice system here in Chicago and Cook County. Neither the Attorney General, Laura Burke or the Cook County State's Attorney will do any follow-up. They'll be mad we've shown everyone what a pair of machine hacks they are. Two more enemies. Plus the influence of some of these big ambulance chasers and PI fixers hasn't been trimmed all that much."

"True, but not my problem. Once we "out" me tomorrow, there won't be one guy in the machine who will speak to me again. I've done what I can do. Someone else's problem now."

Sunny just sits and smiles for a while. It is nice when the good guys win one. Knowing the price Terry Hake has paid and will continue to pay is a sobering thought. But no one ever said being the good guy is going to be the easy road.

Once Terry is gone Sunny calls Brookins. "Hey. It's Sherlock Holmes calling Dr. Watson."

There is a long pause before Brookins answers. "Who is this again? Some delusional inmate of a mental ward?"

"Thanks. You may have a point there though. But I need you to pretend you're a policeman for a minute. With the military precision the Warlords are now showing, we need to figure out who is their tactical genius. That will open some doors for us. Who do you know who knows enough Warlords to be able to look into finding that fact for us?"

"Not sure yet, but I know some folks I can call. I'll get back to you. Where you going to be today other than sitting on your fanny reading some great Brad Thor and Vince Flynn novels and eating bon bons with the crossing guard? You've finished the

Joel Rosenberg series already, I hope for your sake Thor or Flynn have a new one for you. Of course I'm assuming they taught you to read in the juvenile detention center you grew up in."

"Up yours! But I'm going over to his room right now. Out."

CHAPTER FORTY

SUNNY IS NOW DRESSED FOR THE DAY AND WALKS into Vlad's room to see how he is doing. Vlad is half-reading the paper and half snoozing. The drugs keep him from being all that sharp part of the time. "Rise and shine. Hit for fifty and we'll airborne shuffle five miles this morning."

Vlad flips him the bird and goes back to reading the *Wall Street Journal*.

For the first time since the ambush a few days ago, he carefully looks at Vlad. He has a bunch of tubes attached and lots of bandages. They are everywhere on his legs and arms. The burns from the Molotov Cocktails haven't healed yet. At the neck of his hospital gown, Sunny can see the massive bruising on his chest where the bullet proof vest took the hits. Not pretty. His left arm has a cast on the wrist. Add the stuff on his face where they had to put in a few stitches to take care of some nicks and scrapes and in general he looks like death warmed over.

Actually he looks down right terrible. He looks like the losing gladiator from Russell Crowe's great movie. Maybe even a little like Boris Karloff in the movie *The Mummy*. He isn't sure a good-looking guy like Vlad would want to be compared to one of the all-time great movie heavies who made his name playing ugly, scary characters. But, that said, he really looks like a serious mess.

All of the monitoring machines near his bed cluck and tweet and mumble. They flash various lights and read various bodily functions. All in all, it is not a pretty picture.

He had really rallied to help when the Santa Muerte Cartel attacked the University of Chicago recovery clinic. Of course having a bunch of well-armed murderers standing in the front entrance way of your recovery hospital swearing they won't leave until you're dead will tend to get the adrenaline flowing in any person, let alone a hard as nails Army veteran and Chicago Police Detective. But that had taken a serious toll on his system.

"You have any valuable information for me this morning?"

"Stay out of the stock market and don't buy U. S. government bonds." Vlad flips him the bird and goes back to reading the *Wall Street Journal*.

"Any observations of real merit?"

Vlad flips him the bird and goes back to reading the *Wall Street Journal*.

"Nice to see you too."

He sets the *Journal* on his lap. "I was thinking about how effective the Warlords have been from a military point of view. You and I are both vets. We understand this stuff. Gathering the intelligence necessary for proper preparation of the battle-field is tough. Plus setting up viable ambushes is an art form. Someone has to be leaking them information about the Cartel's actions and whereabouts. The ambushes are just too well pre-pared and executed. Not spur of the moment operations."

Vlad pauses for a moment. He is still sedated and it takes some effort to produce lengthy thoughts and then convert them to words.

"The Warlords have an insider with the Cartel or the Jaguars. Figure out who and you break a big portion of the case. Is it possible the Jaguars aren't happy about the Mexicans coming on their turf and acting like they own the place? Don't look at it from the Cartel's point of view. How do their actions affect the already established pecking order and the local lay of the land?"

With that Vlad flips Sunny the bird, picks up the *Wall Street Journal* again and goes back to reading.

Sunny smiles and shakes his head. "Yeah, I was just thinking of that myself. Thanks." He turns to leave.

Vlad looks up again for another thought. "It isn't that we are being asked to take out some bad guys. That is part of our job. We're prepared. We've done it before. But we are now being asked to take out some very dangerous bad guys. It isn't just that they are capable of taking us out also. Unlike us, they will enjoy taking us out and they'll make it as painful as possible."

Again Vlad pauses to restructure his thoughts. The sedatives clearly affect him.

"They enjoy murder and mayhem. That is the difference between them and us. We are both dangerous also. We've both killed guys as cops and as soldiers. But for us it is a calling to protect folks, make the world safe for democracy, a better place for our families and the neighborhood kids, apple pie, baseball, hot dogs, motherhood and all that stuff. For them, it is what they love to do. They like to hurt people. Don't forget that."

With that Vlad again returns to his *Wall Street Journal.*

Sunny nods in agreement.

Vlad decides to give one last piece of advice. "The early bird may get the worm, but the second mouse gets the cheese. Don't be a hero. Call for backup before you stick your head in the mouse trap to get a bite of the cheese. Brookins still has my Ithaca Mag-10. Don't let him waste an opportunity to put it to good use."

Vlad lets an impish smile show in the corners of his mouth as he flips Sunny the bird again. "Now get out of here and leave me alone to recover from the traumatic mess you have made of my life. You got me into this and it will cost you a Ruth's Chris filet mignon with sides to get off my S list. Start saving your nickels and dimes, I intend to enjoy the meal."

Vlad returns to his *Wall Street Journal* and playfully ignores Sunny.

Oh well, might be a good idea to take the blame for his shooting. Actually many shootings! Sunny's home was damaged, but Vlad's apartment building got burned to the ground. Luckily he had USAA insurance like most military vets so he came out OK. But having everything you own burned in a bonfire set by a Mexican Drug Cartel always leads to a few sobering thoughts.

For one of Chicago's most legendary gigolos, every now and then Vlad did a good job of putting things in perspective. He was right. As Sunny leaves the room, two uniformed Cook County Sheriff's Police join him to escort him to his car in the garage.

Sunny gets in his car, offers thanks to his guards and he is gone.

Almost immediately his cell phone rings. "We are dumber than cow dung." Sunny can tell the voice is Brookins.

"Speak for yourself. But of what do you speak?"

"We didn't remember, or maybe we didn't know, but we should have checked to know that Alderman Bass chaired the Special Events, Culture and Recreation Committee for the Chicago City Council. She had a pretty decent budget but not a big staff that anyone knew of. I asked a guy at The Hall who helps us some about it.

"OK. So?"

"She had a bunch of ghost pay rollers working for her committee. Nobody ever saw them. But my guy said the word on the street was she had a bunch of Warlords on her ghost payroll. She never released her broken out budget info, just the gross totals. That is how they cover up the ghosts."

"This is interesting info, but I'm not sure how it applies to our investigation."

"We should have thought about it. She was a Chicago Alderman. What are they best at other than pleading guilty and negotiating a plea deal? Maybe squirreling away ghost pay rollers on the public payroll? That is how they keep their lackeys in line and doing their political work. Right?"

"Yeah. So? This isn't much more than I could get from any other doughnut aficionado"

"So anyway, our guy gave me the name of her lead guy. A sharp guy named Mustafa was her lead guy who came to City Hall once in a while to take care of things for her. I think Vlad told me he is the guy you met at her office. He must be a Warlord."

"OK. Vlad and I met Mustafa when we met with her about one of her guys shaking down Vlad's main squeeze. Seemed very efficient. So?"

"Efficient? How about military efficiency? Mustafa was a Marine!"

"Whoops!"

"It was on his job application. He got extra points for veteran's preference because he checked the box. He was a lance corporal in a rifle unit. Honorable discharge so he must have done a decent job. Infantry unit, so that means he knows tactics and commo. He works out of her ward office."

"This is making sense."

"Our source told me he is the guy who organizes the Warlords and some other street gangs to do political work for Bass and the party all over the South side. He has friendly relationships with a bunch of the other gangs. Very well organized guy.

Get my point? He has to be the big shot we're looking for. You should go visit him."

"For once in your life you've done a decent job. Now you're finally making sense. I'm on my way."

Sunny pulls into the parking spot next to what used to be Larenda Bass' ward office. There are other cars around and the office is still bustling along. It is awfully active for the office of a dead person. Parked in front are two trucks that have Chicago Hired Truck Program placards on the doors. Behind them are two smaller Chicago Department of Streets and Sanitation trucks.

Without making it obvious he looks around to see if there is any security. There are two guys who could be guards to his left. They are carefully a little less than a block away and at an angle that allows them to see behind the four trucks. They could be on someone they didn't want there in a matter of seconds.

Across the street just inside the front door of a barber shop are two more young men in black and crimson. They have magazines and phones in their laps but they're not reading. They are a little too obvious and clearly armed. The other problem is the taxpayer financed trucks keep them from having direct sight of the front door, but they have an unobstructed view of the street and the other approaches. They are in good back up positions.

On the front stoop of an abandoned apartment building down the block on the right another two guys are sitting and smoking. They could just be stoners except their field of vision to the office is just way too clear. Besides they are too alert for stoners. They can see behind the trucks as well as all other approaches.

Sitting on the running boards of both Streets and Sanitation trucks are guys in City of Chicago shirts and they have cell phones in their hands.

Sunny is impressed at the excellent security. Clearly whoever is inside does not want to be surprised and has plenty of muscle to be sure nothing happens they don't want to have happen. Most of the security is fairly well hidden. Not too obvious.

The parked trucks add security by making it hard for an observer to get a view of who is coming and going. All four trucks are partially loaded and the City of Chicago Streets and San employees are keeping a watchful eye on the already loaded material. On the whole, fairly impressive security remembering this is the office of a dead person who doesn't need protection. Remembering he is dealing with gangbangers not soldiers; all in all it is good security.

He parks and prepares to go in the front door. Just as Sunny steps to the door it opens and three guys in City of Chicago shirts walk out carrying boxes that are well packed and heavily taped. Sunny holds the door for them and steps back to let them by. He then walks in. The lobby of the office is full of Gangster Warlords in their well-known black and crimson running suits, Chicago City employees and unknown guys who must be from the Hired Truck program. The receptionist Sunny remembered is there in jeans and a sweat shirt. She is directing all of the packing efforts. Boxes are packed and stacked by the walls.

When Sunny comes in everything stops. Everyone looks at him. No real hostility, but clearly people trying to remember who he is and what will he want? The receptionist is very pleasant and comes up to him.

"Can we help you please?" She seems to sincerely want to help. She seems to be searching her memory banks. The guy looks familiar. In a ninety plus percent black ward not that many big White guys come walking in. Especially a guy like this who looks self-confident and in control.

The only large number of Whites in the ward are in a gentrifying section right on the edge toward the neighboring Hyde Park and Kenwood neighborhoods. The area where Vlad's girlfriend lives. Solidly gentrifying neighborhoods with a good mix of updated older homes and buildings and good quality filler homes built on what used to be vacant lots or abandoned buildings.

"I'm Officer Ross SunWarrior. Is Mustafa here?"

"Oh yes, officer. Good to see you again. Sorry, I should have recognized you but I've been a bit distracted. Mustafa isn't here at the moment but he'll be back this afternoon. He is taking care of some final matters for the Alderman."

"Do you mind if I inquire what matters?"

The receptionist gives him a funny look. "Her funeral and internment."

"Ooops, sorry. I should have realized that."

"The Alderman grew up in Arkansas so she didn't have family in Chicago. Mustafa is taking care of everything. Many of her constituents, who just loved her, wanted to have a chance to say goodbye and thank you. The memorial services will be at Trinity United Church of Christ."

"My fault. Sorry. I'll stop back this afternoon. Could you please let Mustafa know I'll be back?" He hands her his card.

"Certainly, but is there anything I could help you with?"

"Not really. It isn't anything major. It can wait until this afternoon. I just wanted to talk with him."

"Certainly. I'll be sure to let him know you'll be back."

Sunny nods to the guys working away packing boxes and leaves. They are courteous and nod back but keep on working. Sunny wonders if they even realize they are breaking the law by doing private work on City time? After all this is Chicago and City employees view their political patron as their employer, not Chicago's taxpayers.

Once Sunny is gone Mustafa comes out of the inner office. He takes Sunny's business card from the receptionist and carefully examines it.

"I wondered how long it would be before they came looking for me. Didn't take too long. He must be brighter than average."

He looks at the guys working at cleaning up the office. "We better pick up the pace and be sure nothing of the important stuff is still here by this afternoon. I'll wait until we are sure he is gone and then I'll go a little distance to be sure no one is tracking us and call him on his cell phone."

The secretary and the group of guys nod acknowledgement of the directions. It is clear Mustafa is in charge.

Mustafa gets to the door and turns back. "Reverend Jeremiah Wright will come back to preach the funeral service. You know Alderman Bass loved him. It will be a beautiful service. The Reverend sure can bring the house down with a personalized, powerful funeral oration. I'm looking forward to seeing him preach again."

Just as Mustafa is about to leave the door opens and a frazzled looking woman enters. She is nicely dressed but looks like she is afraid or mixed up or at least disturbed. "I need to see Alderwoman Bass!"

Mustafa is polite as he holds the door. Just as he starts to close it three of his outside guards barge in the door. All three have weapons in their hands and look like they weren't more than a few steps behind the nicely dressed lady.

All three guards look at Mustafa. He nods back and all three quickly put their weapons out of sight. He nods again and they turn and go back outside without saying so much as a single word.

The woman is stunned. All three guards had looked like tough characters and they were armed. It is obvious from the look on her face she isn't sure what to say or do.

Mustafa walks over as the woman looks warily at him. "Good morning, Ma'am. Is there anything we can do for you?"

She still looks a little stunned and isn't sure if she should speak to a guy who could direct armed thugs with nothing more than a nod.

"I'm sorry you seem worried. Is there anything we can do for you?" Mustafa asks for a second time.

"Who are you?"

"I'm Mustafa, Alderman Bass' assistant. Can her office be of service to you?"

She is still wary but realizes she came here for a reason and might as well try to explain. But first she still wants to ask for the Alderman. "Where is our Alderman?"

Mustafa has a sad look on his face. "I'm sorry. I guess you hadn't heard, Alderman Bass is deceased."

The woman is shocked. "When?"

"Just the other day. We're in the process of cleaning up her office for her."

"What happened?"

"It doesn't really matter. A personal issue. I deeply regret she is no longer with us. But we are her staff and can be of assistance."

The nicely dressed woman finally gets up the nerve to talk about what brought her to the office. "We have been seeing drug pushers on several corners near our homes and want to ask the Alderman to get the police to increase patrols in our area."

Mustafa looks sincerely interested. "What is your address? I am sure we can speak to the police for you." After Alderman Bass' assistant writes down her address, Mustafa guides her to the door. "I'll speak to the police today. Sorry for the inconvenience."

As soon as she is gone Mustafa gestures for one of the Warlords to come to him. He hands him the slip of paper with the lady's address. "That is right by Roosevelt's corner. Be sure he is more careful. Also be sure someone watches her house. If she gets noisy again, have someone she hasn't seen before pay her a visit to explain the facts of life on the streets. Then break a few of her windows and key her car to finish the message of what a snitch can expect. We don't need some dumb busybody making trouble by being a snitch. Clear?"

The Warlord nods he understands. "I'll head over to Roosevelt's now. As much product as he moves, I always figured he must normally be sharp. I am sure this was just a mistake." With that he is out the door.

Mustafa smiles at his workers. "OK. Enough entertainment. Get your lazy butts back to work so we can get the important stuff out of here pronto."

CHAPTER FORTY-ONE

HEARING FROM MUSTAFA IS GOING TO BE IMPOR-tant. If he isn't the guy they are looking for, maybe he'll give Sunny a hint who it is. Mustafa will be a loyal Warlord, but might say something by mistake. He'd see. After all, based on recent events, he would be feeling somewhat immune.

Akile Fort had just walked on a murder and torture rap, so a guy like Mustafa wouldn't feel threatened. But maybe the death of Larenda Bass and Akile's scum bag lawyer at what was assumed to be the hands of the Santa Muerte Cartel might get him in the mood to talk. Lieutenant Dornan told Sunny that Leonard Bernstein was a bit of a miracle worker in the Cook County Courts getting Warlords and other scum bags off with supervision, fines, restitution or minimal jail time. Dornan told him about several cases that reminded Sunny of the open corruption he had faced with Judge Leoni. A lot of cops and prosecutors felt there was more to the lenient sentences than just Bernstein's effusive closing statements. Sunny had hoped Terry Hake and his team might have the evidence to indict Bernstein. But now that he was deceased, beating a dead dog didn't seem worth the effort.

Besides, in this gang confrontation, there were plenty of dead bodies to go around, yet so far, the Warlords had gotten the better end of the Cartel. This was Warlord turf and they knew the ground better. But if that makes the Cartel mad enough, they might bring more gunmen and bigger guns from Mexico. The border is so porous that getting the gunmen and guns to Chicago isn't an issue they would need to worry about.

The Warlords have handled themselves well so far, but it is a street gang made up of poorly educated, young thugs, not a paramilitary unit. How many well trained guys could they really have? In addition the heavy artillery, communication skills and sophisticated tactics they would need for a prolonged confrontation were not minor impediments.

The dead little old grandmother's 911 call and Sunny's response is why all of this happened. Just as he is thinking of the Warlords as plucky underdogs putting up a great fight against the evil Mexican drug cartel he remembers the dead grandmother and her grandkids. He thinks of the folks who have died from the drugs the Warlords have distributed. His old friend, Des Moines Detective Tiffany Burroughs-Rea's and her informant, KeShawn Okambo. They had pulled off appendages and cut off his body parts. Plus the neighborhoods that are intimidated into seeing and hearing nothing by these thugs. Oh well, he thinks if they'd just kill them all, both sides, they'd just save society the trouble. Brookins is right. Evil is evil. There can't be any compromise with evil. There is only one solution to these guys. But for the time being he thinks he'll just let them supply the solution to each other.

As Sunny thinks about all of this his cell phone rings. "Sun-Warrior, start talking or quit bugging me."

"Do you guys still want the front row at my Pulitzer ceremony? Forget the apple fritters. I'll throw in a Ruth's Chris petite filet on the *Sun Times* tab. But if you want to avoid being on every connected scum bag in Chicago's hit list, I'll do you an even bigger favor and not mention your names. But if I cover for you, you'll owe me big."

"Huntley, will you ever learn respect for the guys who put your sorry ass on the map?"

"Look, I'm willing to sink to the level of talking to a known reprobate like you. You're lucky. How much more respect can you expect from a man who surely is about to be named the top investigative reporter in America?"

"OK. OK. Enough self-promotion. What did we just accomplish?"

"Sunny this hired truck thing is so much bigger than anything you and I realized. It will be a multi-part story. The first installment runs Sunday and will be splashed all over the front page. We have traced at least forty million in stolen money! We think that is just the start. At least 380 tons of stolen asphalt!"

"Good start."

"Part of the program was run by a Chicago machine-connected ex-con. The guy went to prison for stealing millions of bucks in quarters from the toll highway authority and then they hire him back to help run a forty million a year program with almost no supervision."

"Sounds like something Chicago would do."

"A bunch of the trucking firms have mob connections and give big campaign contributions. You know that also means they lend campaign workers and facilities to help the machine stay in power. At least two of the crooked trucking firms seem to be owned by guys connected to the Insane Jaguars. If this story were any bigger it would be front page in London. Heck it may be front page in London by the end of next week."

"Is that all you got? Come on, this is Chicago. What's a few million bucks to pass around to our friends?"

"All I've got? Try this we uncovered a bunch of fake minority ownership stuff. Connected guys put their mother's and sisters or just a trusted Black employee in charge of companies so they got minority owned business preferences. You know Chicago knew about it because they got expedited minority preference OKs. I have pictures and license plate numbers of so many trucks sitting doing nothing, but still getting taxpayer money, that we can't even run them all."

"OK, but I'm not overwhelmed yet."

"Plus the program's executive director is a former Hispanic Democratic Organization guy with a record who it appears is, or at least was, an Insane Jaguar. He is another of Victor's guys. That is who they had running the whole thing. A forty to fifty million dollar a year program run by two ex-cons. Talk about no supervision."

"OK. I'm almost impressed. Almost. When do I get the petite filet?"

"Ah, come on. Give your old pal a pat on the back."

"Would a kick in the ass suffice?"

"You have no heart. With some help from you. Not much help. Begrudging help at best. I break the biggest story of the year and you can't even say, 'good job Mason'?"

"Not as bad as your usual job Mason. I'll give you that."

"You're hopeless. By the way how is Vlad doing? I heard he is recovering pretty well."

"Honestly? If it weren't for his vest he'd be dead." Despite Sunny's banter, for the first time there is a catch in his voice.

Mason Huntley doesn't say anything. He can tell it is better to just let Sunny go.

"If he hadn't been trying to be nice by offering to get out of the car and check things out instead of me, we'd both be dead. He told me to stay in the car because he knew I'd be upset if the house was messed up, so he was just trying to spare me seeing the mess. The only reason we made it was I was still behind the wheel. If I'd gotten out and been wounded, I might not have been able to get back to the car and then couldn't have driven us out of there."

"Wow."

"But that said, hundreds of young single women in Chicago have been sending me thank you notes. They were overjoyed to hear that Vlad will make it."

"Glad to hear it. Tell him I said hi and be sure he gets a copy of Sunday's *Sun Times*. It'll be a banner headline across the whole top of the page with photos of bunches of trucks you guys sent me to."

"I don't want to get all mushy and honest with you, but we really are glad you pulled this one together. Remember what I said? We're on the same side. We don't like these crooks either. There is no way we can get them screwed through normal city channels. You know the city will cover for them and the State's Attorney won't listen to us. She is a toady for Burke and we all know it. So we're glad to help you put them away."

"Hopefully." Mason is a little more dubious about the willingness of the Crook County Prosecutor to carry this case the way she should.

"Without you the Crook County State's Attorney wouldn't touch this even with a cattle prod up her fanny and we both know it. That's why we helped you. We needed to shine some light on these guys. Remember that old Senator from downstate Pekin, Ev Dirksen, used to say they'll see the light when they feel the heat. You're the heat!"

"That's my job."

Sunny is smiling to himself. "Thanks for your good work. Keep the heat on them. Now get your butt back to work tracking other criminals. Don't rest on your laurels!"

"Thanks. I'll talk to you later."

"Out."

Sunny hangs up his cell phone and just smiles. Corruption in Chicago is open and blatant, but the Illinois Attorney General, Speaker Burke's daughter, Laura Burke and the Cook County State's Attorney refuse to investigate. They know who put them in office, who paid for their campaigns and have no intention of rocking the boat. Every now and then guys like Sunny get to sneak around them. Usually working with a good investigative reporter. Sunny just feels something is going right. It is the good days like this that make the bad ones livable.

Gangbangers are having their numbers thinned. A crooked Alderman is dead although he would have preferred a trial to have the time to twist her tail and see what she might say to get a lighter sentence. Operation Greylord is about to break and send one hundred of the court systems crooked schmucks to jail. The Sleaze balls over at Building and Zoning will soon be exposed and indicted. Even the dozens of City Council ghost pay rollers are going down. Now the guys stealing millions in the Hired Truck program are about to take a dive.

Unfortunately, it is just scratching the surface. As Sunny said to Vlad the other day, nothing in Chicago is on the level. Nothing. Everything comes with a cost. Maybe the more accurate terms are bribe and payoff.

Sunny was just thinking to no one except himself, that even in Chicago, the belly of the beast as far as public corruption is concerned the good guys actually win them once in a while. Not often and only when they help of the media or watch dog groups, but occasionally is better than never. Now how do they get the epicenter of it all, Brennan X. Burke himself? Is there a prosecutor in Illinois with the courage to take on the big daddy of it all? Probably not.

CHAPTER FORTY-TWO

THE CELL PHONE RINGS AGAIN AND SUNNY ANSWERS. "SunWarrior."

"Officer SunWarrior, this is Mustafa from Alderman Bass' office. Sorry I missed you. Margarite told me you wanted to talk to me. What can I do for you?"

"I was sorry about the Alderman."

"Thank you. We have been very close. She meant well."

"Can we get together and talk for a few minutes. Strictly off the record."

A very long pause. Probably best called a pregnant pause. "OK. Where."

"Your choice."

"Based on where I am right now, how about Prince Asiel Ben Israel's restaurant on 75th Street? Do you know the place?"

"Oh sure. I know the Prince. He's the leader of the Black Hebrew Israelite Congregation and their International Ambassador. Good guy. Good choice for healthy food. Of course you've got to watch that healthy stuff. Too much of it will kill you. I've talked with him about their congregation in Dimona, Israel, out in the Negev. Look forward to it. See you there in ten minutes?"

"OK. See you in ten."

Sunny exits the Dan Ryan Expressway at 75th Street and quickly gets to Prince Asiel's restaurant. He parks and enters to see Prince Asiel himself talking with customers. The Prince, no longer a young man, but still very dignified, spry and well-spoken is a popular fixture on Chicago's South side, in the capitols of many African nations and of course, in Israel.

Prince Asiel sees Sunny, hurries over to him and gives Sunny a big hug and handshake. "Sunny, how good to see you. It is a pleasure to have you in our humble restaurant. Where would you like to sit and what can we get for you?"

Just then Mustafa enters the restaurant. He had been across the street watching to be sure Sunny came alone without any backup. He wanted to be sure he didn't walk into a trap. Prince Asiel sees Mustafa also and waves him over to join Sunny.

"Sunny, have you met my dear friend, the late Alderman Bass' faithful right hand, Mustafa?" Mustafa joins them and shakes hands with the Prince and Sunny.

"Actually we chose to add your wonderful food to a place to meet for a little talk. Is there any place we could sit for a while with some privacy?"

"Of course. Please. Both of you follow me." Prince Asiel leads them to a quiet, out of the way table. "Sit here. I'll have one of our staff here in a moment."

The two guys settle in as a waiter bustles around being sure they are all set and their food ordered. For the first time he looks carefully at Mustafa. He is one of those self-effacing kind of guys who doesn't draw attention to himself. He does not look like a leader of a street gang. He certainly doesn't have the personality of a gangbanger. He doesn't dress like a gangbanger. Maybe something more like a high school English teacher. He speaks in a very precise manner.

But then Sunny looks at the physique. This guy is in good shape. He may sell drugs, but he doesn't use them. He probably eats in healthy places like the Prince's regularly. He is lean and sinewy. Nicely muscled but not heavily muscled. The kind of guy who doesn't carry an ounce of extra fat anywhere. One of those virtually no body fat kind of guys. No question, he could have been a Marine rifleman. No question about it.

Sunny leans forward to speak quietly. "Thank you for joining me. This is strictly off the record. Just you and me. I need some info and I may have some that helps you also. At the moment, this is not part of a police investigation."

"I'm all ears."

"Mustafa, I know you're a Gangster Warlord big shot and I know you were a Marine. By the way, I appreciate your service. I know the Alderman had a friendly relationship with your guys. You probably don't know I was Special Forces in Afghanistan. "

Mustafa maintains a poker face but nods in acknowledgement. "And your service also. What do you want to know? I am not sure what I know that you might need."

"The Warlords have been doing an awfully good job of ambushing the Santa Muerte Mexican Drug Cartel. Home field advantage is a big deal. I remember that from my days. These ambushes look like the kind of thing a well-trained Marine would know how to set up."

Mustafa keeps his poker face.

"That said, we don't like the violence. The dead bodies are getting to be a little embarrassing for the Mayor and the Aldermen. From a police point of view, it is a little hard to get worked up over the deaths of a bunch of drug running gunmen, illegally in the country, up here to try to kill American citizens."

The poker face doesn't budge.

382 | SENATOR ROGER A. KEATS

"Remember two of those citizens they want to kill are my partner and me. My partner is still in the hospital and I've got a few new stitches and a bunch of nasty bruises under the vest my wife is smart enough to make me wear."

Mustafa nods. "I heard about the attacks. I also heard you aren't all that bad at driving a car with blown out tires and windows."

"Necessity is the mother of invention. At that moment, driving was not optional. It was mandatory I did the best I could with what I had. My old Special Forces training suddenly came back to me. Lucky for Vlad and me."

He smiles. "I think I understand your predicament. But I'm still not sure where I fit in."

"We aren't offering any deals. That is not the point of me meeting with you. Your guys own enough judges and lawyers you don't need our help there. But the Mayor is losing his sense of humor over the dead bodies being left in the street. We need to stop this stuff."

The poker face is still there. He doesn't bother to counter Sunny's assertions. They both know they are true, so they just keep moving on. "I understand the Mayor' point of view."

"From appearances we can draw the conclusion the Insane Jaguars don't seem to be in the middle of this. Some of their guys, maybe. But most of the action seems to be local guys wearing crimson and black and Mexicans who do not appear to be citizens."

Mustafa just listens.

Sunny pauses and looks carefully in Mustafa's eyes. "Do we need to get more active to bring this to an end or is this about to end on its own?"

Mustafa's eyes betray nothing. He continues to listen and think. "I don't have any firsthand knowledge of any of this. That said, the word on the street is the Mexicans are still pretty mad and thoroughly embarrassed. I doubt they will tuck their tail between their legs and crawl home in abject defeat minus some money they claim they are owed."

"Big money?"

"Big money. Based on their reputation I'd cancel any of your guys leave time for the near future. Maybe even for the longer term future."

"Bad news but how about the Jaguars?"

"The Insane Jaguars keep their own counsel. But on the street, it appears they do seem to have gotten the message that their only members targeted are those that choose to get involved in something that isn't their business. But, as I said, that is just the word on the street. I know nothing from a first-hand perspective."

Their food arrives and both guys dig in. The food may be vegetarian or Vegan or something, but whatever it is, it's certainly good. Prince Asiel's restaurant is a great spot for those who like healthy but still tasty food. Sunny was thinking maybe he ought to bring Sheila and let her spend a day in the Prince's kitchen. The Prince is rightly proud of his menu and would probably do Sunny the favor of teaching his wife a few of the recipes. It would do wonders to improve the taste of the Sun-Warrior family menus.

Both guys use eating as an excuse to remain fairly quiet. Both aren't sure of exactly what else they should say. They share a little friendly chit chat about military stories, Sunny's days with da Bears and as South Siders they both follow the White Sox. But in general, these are not guys with a lot in common. Mustafa finishes first.

"If you don't mind, there are a few last things I need to attend to for the Alderman's funeral and memorial service. I need to get back down to Trinity United Church of Christ on 95th Street to finalize everything."

"Will it be Reverend Wright or his replacement, Reverend Otis Moss who preaches the funeral service?"

"Reverend Wright was friends with the Alderman for many years and will come back just to honor his old friend."

Sunny acknowledges the answer. "I've heard both guys. They can light up a service pretty quickly. Old Jeremiah Wright got to be pretty controversial, but I've heard several of his sermons. He seemed to basically preach a biblical message of repentance and grace when I heard him. Seems to be a very pleasant guy. Met his wife. Charming lady. They've been married for like fifty years. I also remember he was a Marine. We military guys always have a bond. The rest of the stuff is up to him and GOD, not you and me."

Mustafa grins. "There is no such thing as was a Marine. We are simply no longer on active duty."

Both laugh at the military kidding that goes on between the services.

Mustafa stands to leave. "Thank you for the lunch and I'll be sure to keep your words in the back of my mind. If anyone asks for my advice, I'll deliver your message."

With that the two shake hands and Mustafa leaves. Sunny relaxes a bit and orders a refill of his tea. Then he intends to go down the street for dessert. The Prince's restaurant serves wonderful, healthy food, but he is a downright short on obscenely sweet and fattening desserts. The kind Sunny loves the most.

As long as Sheila isn't in town he might as well take advantage of it. Dessert and Sheila are just things that don't mix well. She just doesn't seem to understand that chocolate and peanut butter are gifts from GOD and are meant to go together.

Refusing to enjoy a gift from the good LORD himself seems almost to be a sin that would require a trip to Confession. So when Sheila wouldn't let him have dessert, out of guilt, he would attend Confession. Luckily his Priest agreed and penance was usually a trip across the street from their church to the ice cream shop for a large cup with a couple of scoops of ice cream for both of them. His Priest especially liked to mix the chocolate and peanut butter ice cream with some pralines and cream.

As Mustafa drove his car out into traffic to get on the Dan Ryan Expressway going south, he dialed his cell phone. "Jaron, it's me. When we hit the Mexicans tonight we need to clean up. We need to take the bodies and the cars and dispose of them in Indiana."

He listens as Jaron responds. "Not my idea. Comes from a friendly warning we should acknowledge. We can put them in the landfill there or the one just into Michigan off I-94. I'll take care of getting us in at that hour. We'll just leave the cars on the street in Gary with the keys in the ignitions."

Mustafa listens for a short while again. "Right. I hope the girl is ready. We have gone over what she needs to do plenty of times and paid her very well. Don't let her take any drugs before she goes in. She needs to be sharp and not blow her assignment. She does understand that if she screws it up, we'll kill her and her family? Any questions?"

Mustafa listens for another moment.

"I need to get to Trinity United Church of Christ to finish with Alderman Bass' funeral but I'll be over as soon as I finish. Be sure she understands we don't want to hurt her or her family, but...ultimately that is up to her and her performance."

CHAPTER

FORTY-THREE

ONCE SUNNY GETS INTO HIS CAR, HIS CELL RINGS. The number is blocked but he answers anyway. "Sun-Warrior. Have something important to say or mind your own business."

"Sunny, this is Arturo Ortega."

About then, Sunny wishes he wasn't such a wise ass when he answers his cell phone. He also is wondering how Ortega got his number. Then he remembers he gave it to him. If he is calling on the cell phone number it just might be important.

"Yes Arturo. What can I do for you?" He decides to just ignore his greeting. There isn't anything he can do to change it now, so just to keep on truckin' seemed to be the best way to handle it.

"Can you meet me for a talk?"

"Sure. Where do you want to meet?"

"Some place out of my neighborhood, but where I won't look out of place. Do you know Humboldt Park on the Near North West Side very well?"

"Of course."

"Meet me at the pavilion boat house. How long before you can get there?"

"Give me a half hour. I'm still South. A bit north of 75th Street. But I'm on the Ryan heading your way already. OK?"

"See you then."

Sunny slaps the police light on top of his car and pushes down on the accelerator. He will need to hurry. As he goes from the Dan Ryan to the Kennedy Expressway, for a change, the bottle neck isn't bad. He continues North and gets off heading West on North Avenue and takes the light off the roof. The light helped on the Ryan and Kennedy, but was a little too high profile here.

The police light on top of the car needs to go to lower his visibility as he approaches the large, two hundred plus acres of Humboldt Park. This is the North side. The park is such a pleasant place he is glad Ortega suggested it. This is the heart of the Puerto Rican neighborhoods. At one time it was a major institution in Chicago's huge Polish community.

Ortega's Little Village is the heart of the Mexican neighborhoods. It is the South Side. Both Latino so a muscle bound thug like Ortega wouldn't look out of place, but Puerto Rican gangs aren't allies of the Mexican gangs and especially the Jaguars. As a General in the Insane Jaguars, Ortega would not exactly be a welcome visitor. That is OK. They'll just keep a low profile.

Sunny pulls into the large parking lot of the well maintained, but probably one hundred-year-old building, overlooking a beautiful Jens Jensen designed lagoon. It is a scenic delight with a relaxing view of a lagoon and a great deal of natural fauna. A wonderful place to just meet friends and sit enjoying some beer. Maybe do a little fishing. Not a lot of fish, but you don't fish in a park to catch fish. You want fish, go to Lake Michigan. It is for companionship and a chance to drink some beer with your pals. A little male bonding. Or maybe some lemonade with your kids or grandkids. That is a wonderful way to bond. Kids remember going fishing for the rest of their lives.

There aren't any other cars here, but he figures Ortega parked on one of the inner roads that run through the park.

The pavilion has a large archway through the building to give a spectacular view of the lagoon supported by smaller structures on each side. The structure on the South Eastern end of the archway includes the men's room and some park district offices or maybe just meeting rooms. Ortega steps out the door near the men's room and Sunny walks over to join him.

They shake hands and Ortega leads Sunny back inside. They walk into a medium sized room off the main door. Ortega locks the door and they sit at what could be a table for kid's art projects.

Ortega opens the conversation. "Sorry to inconvenience you but the Santa Muerte guys are still pretty upset with me for killing so many of their guys. I thought I'd be respectful of their feelings and skip my favorite restaurants and go elsewhere for our meeting."

"Good thinking. I only like to fight when I have no other option. JESUS said something about blessing the peacemakers."

"The book of Matthew, the fifth verse. From the Sermon on the Mount."

As usual, Ortega surprises Sunny. "I don't think of you as a churchgoer."

"I was raised in Mexico, one of the most Catholic countries in the world. We went to church. We have some beautiful Catholic Churches in Veracruz. Remember vera cruz means the true cross. That is pretty Spanish, very Catholic and totally Christian. My parents always took me to mass." Ortega chuckles. "Knowing a verse doesn't mean I have to practice it.""

Sunny just shakes his head again.

Ortega looks around and out the window. "The Santa Muerte's don't respect the peacemakers. So we could fight about it, but for the moment I would like to continue to avoid that. We are still superficially their allies and that does have certain benefits."

Sunny chuckles at Ortega's mild mannered explanation of the simple fact the Cartel wants him dead and he doesn't want to endanger his friends right now. "No problem. The Cartel and the Warlords have the Mayor and his guys pretty doggone upset at the moment. They are too busy being mad at them to be mad at you right now. You're clear for today."

With a smile, Arturo responds. "Small blessings."

"Arturo, I want to give you a heads up. This has to remain confidential. Shortly they will announce the indictments of fifteen of the crooks in the Zoning and Building Department. They will arrest a bunch of them quickly so they can't run and hide."

"Good."

"This is what you'll love, your buddy Jerry Katorski ended up a hero. He is the guy who turned on his buddies and sold them all down the river so he wouldn't be indicted. I guess your kicking his ass scared him straight and he went from future inmate to prosecution all-star."

"Glad to be of service. I don't care if you shoot them all." Arturo pauses as he looks out the window. "Have you heard from your wife? I'd be worried if mine were gone this long and we were out of contact."

Sunny wonders how he knew they weren't in contact. "You're married? I didn't know that."

"Sure, why not? We have three kids, one is in college."

Sunny smiles at that response. "You never fail to amaze me."

"We went to the same high school in Veracruz where we both grew up. We started dating when she was fifteen. Her mother was opposed because I was older and a bad guy. I'm not that different from you. I just never had a judge send me to the Army to do penance and to clean up my act."

Sunny really has nothing to say. Insane Jaguar General, Arturo Ortega the blood thirsty killer running a major wing of one of Chicago's two biggest street gangs is married to his high school sweetheart and has three kids. One is in college. Truth can be stranger than fiction. But Sunny has a hard time seeing Ortega sitting at the kitchen table helping his kid with math homework.

All of this is just difficult to imagine. He even takes his wife out to dinner where unfortunately some Santa Muertes tried to kill them. But still, the guy has a wife and they go to dinner, without guards, at a nice restaurant. He remembers Jose La Boca say Ortega is a big tipper. Probably popular with the waitresses. Ortega knows Sunny's history and has a sky box at Soldier's Field for da Bear's home games. Will wonders never cease?

Ortega smiles as he sees Sunny speechless. "We're here for business, remember?"

"Yeah. What is it we need to discuss?"

"You found Bernstein and Bass' bodies already. Do you know who killed them?"

"We know they had ties to the Gangster Warlords and we think they were killed by some Santa Muerte muscle. Last place they were seen was at the State of Illinois building and some Mexican looking guys grabbed them there. Must have been pros. Picked them up right off the curb at LaSalle Street. The guys were fast and efficient. No much more than twenty seconds and they were gone. We're trying to piece it together from there."

"Do you want the rest of the story so you don't have to waste so much time digging it up?" Ortega almost has a conspiratorial gleam in his eyes.

"Are you a detective now?"

"I run the streets. Word travels fast in our world. I'll save you slapping it out of Jose La Boca."

Sunny is stunned at the mention of one of his top informants. Guys get killed for informing to the cops.

Ortega almost guffaws. "You think I don't know your sources? I assigned Jose to you to be sure you knew what was happening. Don't worry everything he tells you is true. He likes Vlad and you. He enjoys working with you guys. I didn't want you blaming us for things we didn't do. There are enough things we do you can be mad about. No point in getting pinched when we're innocent."

Sunny just shrugs his shoulders and smiles.

"By the way, he wishes you wouldn't interfere with his sex life. I sent her there because he has been too busy to find his own dates. But don't tell him I was pimping for him."

Sunny loses it remembering Jose's complaint about needing five more minutes. Both guys sit as Sunny keeps laughing and Arturo smiles at showing off some of what he knows. Finally they stop and Sunny looks at Arturo with an expectant eye.

"I told you I was trying to limit our exposure to the Warlord, Santa Muerte feud. We're businessmen. We don't go out of our way to cause trouble. We stick to our neighborhoods. We follow the Chicago rules. We even have some communications with the Warlords to avoid unnecessary problems. A little friction is unavoidable, but we try to avoid the big blow ups."

"Contacts with the Warlords?"

"Our CIA had contacts with the KGB. This is a business."

Sunny loves to listen to him. He notes Ortega said our CIA, not your CIA.

"Jose La Boca and Mustafa get together for some back channel information sharing once in a while. We try not to interfere with each other's business. There is plenty for everyone. What is that phrase, cooperate and graduate?"

Just like two bankers or lawyers getting together for a business lunch to discuss a loan or a case. Sometimes Sunny feels there is far more to Chicago's gang network and drug trade than the police or anybody else know.

"We work precincts for Speaker Burke's ward organizations and get signatures on his candidates nominating petitions. We contribute to his candidates. We are careful to pay taxes on our buildings and restaurants. We try to keep our neighborhoods from becoming such major blights the city's powers that be come after us."

"I guess that makes sense."

"We stay out of downtown. We run some legitimate businesses to make us acceptable in polite society. You leave us alone, we leave you alone."

Sunny knows of at least two trucking firms the Jaguars had interests in. "Where does Bass fit in? Why did Bernstein get waxed? Why did they come after you so openly?"

Arturo Ortega takes a long and hard look at Sunny. He spends some time thinking before he responds. "Bass violated the rules. She tried to get Burke involved in a drug war. She wanted to mix Obama stimulus money and State of Illinois tax money to pay off a drug debt. No one represented the rules better than Larenda Bass. But then she got carried away and this is what happens to folks who stick up high enough they need to be hammered back down."

"Hmmm."

"Rule number one is no matter what you see, hear, or do, you don't know nothin'! Especially you don't drag Burke and his pretty boys in their thousand dollar suits into street business. They know we're here. We work together with his guys. We don't deal with Burke directly. Don't make it obvious we know each other."

"As sleazy as Burke and his organization is, it makes sense they pretend to be solid citizens. Kind of like the mob in the old days?"

Ortega nods yes. "Rule number two is nobody knows the guys who are gone. Nobody admits they knew former Governors Ryan or Blagojevich, but you know everybody did. Remember the President said he only met Blago at a Bear's game. But then lots of pictures of them together suddenly appeared. There are too many pictures of everybody around. I didn't know Ryan. My wife and I vote in the Democrat primaries. Hey, I liked Blago. We supported him. Money and workers. We have precinct captains in what used to be his congressional district. He left us alone and we made sure not to embarrass him. My guys vote. We buy tickets to fundraisers. Sometimes we buy them in our mother's or grandmother's name, but hey, money is money."

All Sunny can do is smile.

"Rule number three is even if everybody in Chicago knows it, you still know nothing. Hear no evil. See no evil. Speak no evil. Bass knew that. She was an idiot. Break the rules and...hey, that is how it works on the streets. We don't break the rules."

Sunny decides to see how much he can learn so he intentionally looks at Ortega with the still a little unsure of himself expression. "OK, but I'm still not quite there."

"You and Vlad Kozak took millions of dollars of product from the Warlords who had it on loan from the Santa Muerte Cartel. That meant the Warlords couldn't pay back what they borrowed. Santa Muerte collects its debts. You know they kill anybody and everybody to make their point."

"I've noticed they try."

"They didn't get you and Vlad yet, but, I warn you, they aren't through trying. They haven't gotten Akile Fort yet, but they will. They have gotten some of his foot soldiers. My problem is some of the Santa Muertes are related to our guys. We have done some business with them so they just expect us to be their cannon fodder. I tried to stop that."

"With some success, yes?"

"Yes. But you and Vlad are still on the list to be punished. They need to make sure everyone knows never to mess with them. Dead bodies on TV deliver a message far better than the post office. They may live south of the border, but their business is north of the border."

"Didn't they try to, as you say, punish you?"

"Of course. But I let them know that was not going to happen. We have a truce."

Sunny wonders what a truce between a drug cartel and a cold-blooded killer is like. "I follow you, but I still don't see where Bass was involved."

"Akile Fort told the Santa Muerte's that Bass would get the money from Brennan Burke. They thought she did and then tried to stiff them out of their four million plus interest. The four million is cash, the interest in blood."

Sunny again shrugs. "What is Burke's role?"

"He was going to give Bass money from the State of Illinois and the Obama stimulus funds to pay off her debts. She is, excuse me, was the number one boss on the South Side. The Warlords were her foot soldiers and enforcers. They also generated a lot of cash for the party. Burke needed her to keep doing her job. The South Side is number one in carrying the whole ticket. In Chicago, Blacks vote and they all vote Democrat. Heck the way Bass and the Warlords worked a voter didn't need to be alive to vote and anyone who thought they could skip voting still voted absentee. The nursing homes vote 100% and that is 100% Democrat."

"Burke knew It was taxpayer money not political walking around stuff he was using?" Sunny queried.

"I don't know what he knew. He keeps his own council. Why would he care about taking tax money to pay a drug debt? He just cares about getting the vote delivered and the tickets sold."

"Excuse me Arturo. I can see through the window there are some guys sniffing around my car. Any idea who they are?"

Arturo looks carefully. "They aren't wearing colors. They don't look familiar with the terrain. I just looked down the road at my car and there are a couple more down there. Did anyone follow you here?"

"Damn it. I was in a hurry and wasn't paying attention. I should have been. Don't tell me these are some Santa Muertes. They'll find us eventually. Is there an exit we can use?"

Arturo pulls out a hand gun. "I would never box myself in. There is an exit, but on foot in the Humboldt Park area is not a good tactic for us. I left everything in the car. This is all I have here."

Sunny pulls his weapon to show it also. "I left it all in the car also."

"Let's bluff. We only need 30 seconds to get to your car. There isn't a prayer we'll get to mine. I have plenty of stuff in the back end but no way to get it."

"OK. Before they make a call for backup, let's go now."

As they go out the door, Arturo speaks over his shoulder. "I've got an idea. Follow my lead." He hustles out the door and down the steps. He starts shouting in Spanish and waving his arms. "Hey, that is my car!! What are you doing? Don't try to steal my car!"

Sunny thinks this looks like a pretty good bluff and just follows along. He pulls out his car keys and pops the door locks.

The two Santa Muerte gunmen are caught off guard. But it is obvious they are processing the faces from the memory of the pictures they were shown. They hesitate and pause just a little too long and that allows Arturo and Sunny to get way too close.

These are muscle not brains also. Brains wouldn't have let Arturo and Sunny close to within a few feet before responding. At the same time, both go for their guns. They don't have rifles but do have heavy duty hand guns. More appropriate for wandering around in a public park.

Arturo never hesitates. His old favorite, his SIG Sauer P226 is in his hand before either Santa Muerte is ready. Both are down before they are even ready to respond. Arturo quickly puts a final round in both of their foreheads. No point in leaving an enemy alive behind you.

Also, be merciful. Don't let them linger in agony. They are going to be on their way to Hell and it is courteous to speed their journey. There isn't going to be any Purgatory in these guy's afterlives. That was the decision they made when they hired on to the Santa Muerte Cartel.

He quickly retrieves their weapons and kicks them over to get their spare magazines also. Next in one fluid motion he aims at the other two Santa Muertes by his car.

The Cartel gunmen heard the shots and were quickly concentrating on who, what and where. One of them acts like he might be the brains for the other guy's brawn. He scans the area and the parking lot and picks up on Arturo. He doesn't see his own guys so he knows the who and the where immediately. He deduces the what almost as fast. Just in time for Arturo's first round to nick his leg. The guy jumps behind a car and signals for his pal to do the same.

The difference between a well-trained Special Forces soldier and a smart Cartel gunman then becomes quite obvious. While both Cartel gunmen concentrate on Arturo and their fallen compadres, Sunny sprints behind the parked cars and is almost parallel with them before they have a chance to wonder where the second guy is.

The brain's pal is down before he fires a shot. Sunny doesn't put an additional round in his forehead. He doesn't need to. He is Special Forces. They don't miss.

Now the brain is caught between a hidden Sunny to his right and an advancing Arturo to his front. Arturo is farther away, so he turns to find Sunny.

A trained soldier would know to never expose his flank. Arturo has now killed seven Santa Muerte foot soldiers. And he is supposed to be an ally! As soon as he gets to the body Arturo puts the bullet in the forehead and pops the rear door on his big, dark blue Lincoln Navigator SUV.

The only thing in there is a large gym bag. Just as he grabs it several bullets slam into the side of the SUV, the pavement and the big Maple tree right behind it.

Both guys look at where the bullets are from. They can see at least seven guys running their way with drawn guns. Luckily in a public park none are carrying AK-47s. Would make them too obvious.

Arturo grabs the bag, slings it over his shoulder and gestures for Sunny to run for his car. "This boat of mine is worthless if they chase us. I can run faster than it can accelerate, doesn't corner that great, we don't need the seat warmers and we won't be able to hide in something this big. Only helps if we are going off road. Let's take yours."

Both guys sprint back to Sunny's unmarked police cruiser. He pops this trunk and grabs a shotgun, some protective vests, an extra handgun and a bag of ammunition. It goes in the back seat. Arturo jumps in shotgun style as Sunny slams the car into gear.

Arturo chuckles. "Thought I'd let you drive. You outdrove them last time they tried to kill you so I figure you're on a hot streak. But remembering what happened to your last shotgun rider I'd appreciate it if you'd be a little more careful this time."

As soon as he does a circle and pulls out of the parking lot on to Humboldt Avenue, a pair of cars head straight at him. One is running right across the lawn with a Santa Muerte leaning out the passenger side window. He opens fire but his car is bouncing too much to allow for much accuracy. All he does is scare the crap out of a couple of families playing soccer and picnicking.

A car pulls out to block their way on Humboldt Ave. as they go to exit from the park on North Avenue and it stops in the middle of the street. Gunmen jump out and line up behind the car to open fire. They aren't great shots. Hand held pistols in the hands of drug runners from rural Mexico are not very accurate weapons.

Sunny doesn't even swerve. He heads straight for the car. The three gunmen realize he is about to ram them and dive out of the way. At the last moment Sunny pulls right to just nick the front of the car as he goes around it. He zips by but the Cartel car takes off like a spinning top. It spins left and skids into two of the gunmen who aren't smart enough to get well clear of the vehicle. Both are crushed and go down like bowling pins.

The third guy, a little smarter than his friends, threw himself behind a concrete and wood bench. As his car slams into the bench it crumbles but holds. The car is a mess. The bench is a mess. The two gunmen are at best, badly injured, but more than likely dead.

But the third guy is alive and lies behind the crumpled bench. He just about wet his pants, but he is alive. He makes no effort to get up and follow or shoot. He just checks his body to be sure all of it is still there.

Sunny zips right, zips left and then right again. He is out on North Avenue and moving at well above the speed limit. He cuts across three lanes of traffic and up an alley. He is moving parallel to Humboldt Avenue but at twice the speed.

Trying to move quickly on crowded Chicago City streets is like swimming against the tide with a hundred pound weight around your neck. Plus it is awfully dangerous and Sunny is a police officer sworn to protect the citizens. He decides to stick to the alley where it is safer both for him and for other drivers and pedestrians.

"Do you want to run or should we take all of them out?"

Sunny looks at Arturo. "You're a tough son of a bitch aren't you?"

"They'll kill us if they can. Two blocks up slam on the brakes, I'll jump out with my bag and one of your vests. You go one block farther and pull into the alley way by the big apartment building. The alley dead ends. Leave the engine running and both front doors open. You hit them from the side when they have to stop and I'll get them from the rear and the other side. You game?"

"Screw the bastards! I'm game!" Sunny hits the spot and slams on the brakes. Arturo is out before the car stops. Both take off in a swirl of dust. The dust covers Arturo's move so the chase cars probably never see him jump out.

In less than 30 seconds, two Santa Muerte cars charge right past Arturo as he hides behind a garage putting on his bullet proof vest.

Almost as soon as they are by him they also have to slam on their brakes as they realize they are about to hit a dead end. They don't realize stopping in the middle of an ambush is not a very bright idea. Of course they don't realize it is an ambush. They mistakenly assume Sunny didn't realize he was trapped either.

They make no attempt to look behind them because the dinged up police cruiser is sitting in front of them with the doors open. Immediately they scan the back side of the big apartment building looking for Sunny and Arturo. No one notices Arturo step out from behind another garage with an H & K MP5 machine gun firing 9 mm NATO rounds from a big clip.

The rear tires and back windows are gone before any of the Cartel gunmen even can look behind them. All four of them are hit, one is already dead. The driver of the trail vehicle throws

400| SENATOR ROGER A. KEATS

the car into reverse to try to back up and ram Arturo. Crummy cars with blown tires on cheap rims don't drive well with no rear tires. Arturo's next clip kills the driver and demolishes what is left of the rear end of the car.

All of the Santa Muerte gunmen are now focused on Arturo. Bad idea. Sunny steps out on their left side with Vlad's Ithaca Mag-10. The side of the front car is rubble after the first three rounds. Sunny ducks and reloads another three. By the end of this three, the wounded driver is dead and the other two thugs in his car are about there also.

Sunny and Arturo empty the magazines from their weapons into the two cars and the bodies on the ground. There were seven tough as hell and mean as they come hired gunmen in the cars as recently as less than a minute ago. No one said they were bright, just tough. Now there are seven dead bodies and they are a mess. After the final fusillade, everyone was hit by no less than five rounds. The driver of the rear car has taken sixteen rounds from Arturo's H & K MP5.

The new partners hurry to Sunny's beat up police cruiser, pull a quick 3 point turn and are on their way. Getting past the two smashed hunks that used to be Santa Muerte cars is a little tight, but bumping them out of the way is a small price to pay to be gone as quickly as possible.

Both can hear police sirens in the distance. Sunny knows for sure that standing next to a heavily armed Insane Jaguar General wearing a Chicago Police Department bulletproof vest, talking with a uniform cop he doesn't know, surrounded by piles of dead bodies was just not the kind of conversation that would come out well. He'd come up with something for Lieutenant Dornan later. Right now the better part of valor and smarter idea was to be absent from the scene.

Once they are South of Humboldt Park on Kedzie Avenue and clear of any pursuit, both of their hearts start to slow down a little. Arturo asks, "Do you mind dropping me off at the corner of 28th and Kedzie. I'll see if I can get my car back tomorrow. But I think I'll come with a few friends. Well-armed."

"That's a plan. I think our new little partnership has seen enough excitement for the day. Can I have the vest back? It is Vlad's and he may need it someday."

"No problem. I hope he needs it later, not sooner."

Sunny looks back across his shoulder again. "Why were you so sure that alley would take me into a parking lot that made a perfect ambush?"

Arturo laughs. "I should know, I own the building."

As Sunny progresses South to Little Village he thinks about his message to Mustafa a little earlier. The Mayor and the Aldermen are getting very thin skinned about all of the dead bodies being left in the streets. So if it was OK with Mustafa, could he please not leave them right where the little old grandmothers have to trip over them?

Now here he is leaving dead bodies and wrecked cars in the middle of a residential neighborhood by one of the most popular parks in the city. He is going to need to come up with something to explain all of this. Right now he doesn't have the story worked out but he will need to have it down pat before he faces Dornan or the Captain or GOD forbid, Superintendent Purcell.

Remembering the threats to his life, limb and posterior the Superintendent had made to be sure Sunny realized he needed to be back on the streets, he didn't even want to think of what hideous Comanche torture Purcell would come up with based on today's mess. Staying at the hospital under police and County Sheriff's Police protection was looking better and better just now.

The only survivor, the third guy from the car Sunny rammed, scared shitless and scraped up by the broken chunks of concrete from the bench that hit him, is smart enough to simply disappear. He has no intention of going back to Mexico or to face the Chicago Police. Trying to explain a failure of this magnitude to drug runners in Mexico was going to be beyond his vocabulary and he knew it. He would be a dead man walking if he tried to go home. Let them think he was already dead and he might have a prayer at survival. Luckily his family was no longer near the Cartel folks, so they should be OK.

He would take his chances here. He had cash in his pocket and grabbed the rest from several of his dead cohort's pockets. Then with his gun and extra magazines in his belt he melted into the city. He would catch a Greyhound Bus to California or Arizona. He had cousins in both places. They would know how to get him an ID card. Some back breaking honest work in the agricultural fields seemed to be his best option for the near future. Even if he didn't find a job, he would still be alive and he'd be in America. This could be OK.

The helpful Mexican Consulate in Chicago will never be able to figure out who three of the seven in the two cars are. The two from the car Sunny rammed in the Park and the four from the boat house give them six more dead bodies. Thirteen dead guys almost two thousand miles from home. Five of the dead would never be identified.

The dead bodies of his fellow hired muscle will be shipped back to Mexico to be buried by their families if they have any. The others will go to pauper's graves.

Hopefully, at some point, the leaders of Santa Muerte will realize this four million dollars just may be too expensive to collect. But sitting in a comfortable hacienda in the Mexican mountains, surrounded by sycophants who bluster about the incompetents running the operation in Chicago, does not give them an accurate picture of what is happening almost 2,000 miles away. Besides, lives don't mean very much to them. They can hire more. It is their machismo that counts.

CHAPTER FORTY-FOUR

JARON FORT KNOCKS ON THE DOOR OF THE HOME of the young lady who will be their bait tonight. Not yet fully recovered from the bullet in his leg, he still has an obvious limp and uses a walking stick. He knows the Santa Muerte guys have been away from home for more than several days on a testosterone loaded mission. They will be an easy target for a girl as cute as Brittany. She is part Black, part Mexican and who knows what else?

If Mustafa's use of a hooker to deliver the information to set up the last ambush is the oldest trick in the book, this one is a legitimate derivative of that and maybe should be considered oldest trick 1A.

Brittany is usually reliable but she has never done anything like this before. Jaron doesn't want to be embarrassed in front of Mustafa and his brother, Akile, so he is not going to take any chances that Brittany will get confused. She is loyal and well-intentioned but not the sharpest knife in the drawer. She has more boobs than brains. About normal for a girl who hangs out with gangbangers. No point taking a chance with the restaurant owner either.

He doesn't need to worry. Later at the restaurant, Brittany comes over to the table to take the Santa Muerte thugs orders. If her outfit is any more suggestive she can just skip the clothes altogether, jump up on the table and get to work right here and now.

Six seriously macho Santa Muerte gunmen sit at a corner table. They haven't seen Brittany before so all want to be sure she knows just how tough and macho they are. None speak much English and are quite happy to have Brittany use her mediocre, but understandable Spanish. Her Spanish language gaffes, almost always tie to some suggestively sexy mistake or mispronunciation. When added to their almost nonexistent English it leads to plenty of laughs.

They eat too much. They drink way too much. They talk too much. They leave way too big of a tip to impress their young waitress who seems to be falling out of her skin tight outfit. There is no question they want to see if she will catch their not very subtle hints. It was also a sure bet all of them want to see what their cute waitress looks like flat on her back minus that skimpy outfit.

When Brittany apparently catches their not very subtle hints and suggests she has several friends who aren't busy tonight, it all goes quickly. The gunmen will supply the drugs and the cash. Brittany will supply the apartment, the girls, the snacks and the booze. It appears to be a match made in heaven or for this group, more than likely, made in Hell.

Brittany is picked up outside the restaurant a little before ten o'clock by the spiffed up guys who have a nice new, big SUV and a clunker that looks like it had seen better days in the 1990's. Off they go to her supposed apartment to meet her supposed friends for supposedly a fun evening of partying, booze, drugs, snacks, music and whatever else seems natural.

No one is upset when they arrive and find only one of Brittany's friends. She explains the other girls are still changing after work and will be here shortly. She assures them it will be worth the wait. Her friend suggests they should get the night started off right with some music, some dope, some ice cold Negra Modelos and some munchies she has already prepared.

If they think Brittany's outfit is suggestive, compared to her friend's it was PG-13. The friend's blouse is cut to her navel and the cut is made to advertise everything inside it. It leaves so little to the imagination that taking it off is going to be almost irrelevant.

The friend may not be quite the honey Brittany is, but she is well within the range of good and knows how to advertise her attributes so well the guys don't really notice she is a few notches lower on the 1 to 10 scale made famous by Bo Derek. They are excited this looks like the beginning of a night to remember. It is.

The macho thugs light up the marijuana they brought and offer some to Brittany and her now introduced friend, Adora. Whenever Adora leans over, which she does as often as possible, her plunging neck line leaves nothing hidden.

All six of her guests have a hard time ignoring her flitting around among them. She tries the marijuana, enjoys it, kisses two of her guests, rubs against three more, gives everyone good looks down the front of her blouse and then heads for the refrigerator for a round of Negra Modelos. She assures them when their friends arrive, probably momentarily, they will have a night they will be dreaming about for a long time to come.

With Adora in the kitchen, Brittany keeps them looking at her so they won't pay much attention to Adora, the beer and the snacks. Each of the thugs takes an ice cold Modelo and a handful of nibbles. While Adora uses some marijuana and drinks some beer, she avoids the snacks. Explains they are bad for her figure. All of the thugs assure her she doesn't need to worry about that.

Only someone worrying about something bad happening will have picked up that Adora and Brittany take the beer designated by Adora but neither touches the snacks. No problem, girls need to be more careful about their figures than a bunch of hired killers, right? Who cares about the little stuff?

None of the Santa Muertes are worried about anything but who will get the first shots at Brittany and Adora. Then they will turn their attention to the late arrivals who they hope look half as good as the present options.

Before the arrival of Brittany and her horny gunmen friends, Jaron had used a needle to inject the paralyzing poison into the cans. Nothing was at all obvious when Adora opened the cans for the guys. Cold beer and cold cans. No one is looking too closely. The snacks had been laced with another drug not meant to kill, only to incapacitate.

Brittany and Adora carefully make the rounds of their guests with suggestive hints and blatant touches. Everyone's mind is on matters other than worrying about defending themselves. The music is blasting and the girls are well beyond suggestive.

Two of the thugs quietly lean back against the couch pillows and appear to be drifting in a marijuana and Modelo haze. Then two of the three sitting on the floor begin to get glassy eyed. The sixth is leaning on the wall closest to the bedrooms and hopefully closest to what will soon be some serious action with one of the hostesses. He feels the need to sit and slides down the wall into a puddle on the floor.

The last guy on the floor groggily looks at his friends and starts to realize something is wrong. The girls are still dancing and swaying and keeping the attention on them. He tries to get up but Adora kicks him in the chest and he goes back down flat on his back. The girls hurry to grab the weapons just to be sure no one recovers too soon and is still armed.

The fast acting paralysis agent works to perfection. Jaron has been worried about how his girls will do. He needn't have-they did magnificent work without a hitch. Brittany calls Jaron on her cell.

In two minutes there is a knock at the door and Jaron, Mustafa, Akile and six other Warlords come through the door. They are all in their black and crimson colors and have ear-to-ear smiles as soon as they see the six lying around in a haze.

Jaron hugs Brittany and Adora and introduces them to the rest of the Warlords. He makes a big point of building up Akile and Mustafa. He knows who he wants to impress. He makes sure Brittany and Adora get their fat envelopes full of cash and plenty of praise.

Then the Warlords go to work. Everyone's hands and feet are secured and duct tape is put across their mouths. The car keys for the SUV and the clunker are handed to Mustafa. Each also has a bag put over their heads.

One of the Warlords makes sure no one is watching as the bodies are carried out the back door and loaded into the waiting van. The six are dumped in a heap in the back.

As the Warlords prepare to leave Adora approaches Akile. "Since you're the boss, would you let me go with your guys?"

Akile looks her straight in the eyes. "These guys did some serious shit to four of our young guys who they trapped in the same way. You do realize we intend to return the treatment an eye for an eye? Right?"

She nods in the affirmative. "Some rotten bastard friends of these guys killed one of my best friends right at the beginning. We were friends since we were kids. I almost lived at their house. His mother was kind of like my real family. They were people I cared about. I'd like to be involved when you return the favor."

Akile looks around to see if anyone objects. No one is opposed. He then looks back at Brittany. "Do you want to join us also?"

Brittany seems unsure and then makes a decision. "I'm not real good with blood. I work in the Cook County Clerk's office and I really need to be there tomorrow." She gives a cute grin. "We may not work very hard, but we are expected to be there. Is it OK if I skip?"

"Of course, this is not a part you signed on for. Thank you anyway."

Brittany leaves and Adora takes off her party clothes to put on jeans and a baggy sweatshirt. She makes no attempt to hide while she takes off one set of clothes and puts on the next. For a very short time she stands there in the skimpiest thong underwear any of them have ever seen. The Warlords standing there appreciate the view. They aren't sure what point she is making, but whatever it is, it is OK with them. This just might be a fun evening after all.

Mustafa hands the keys to the SUV and the clunker to two guys who know to take the cars to Gary, Indiana where they will be left on the streets, unlocked and with the keys still in the ignition. They are wearing gloves so they won't leave any finger prints. One of the other guys is assigned to follow along and pick them up.

The seven lock up the apartment and get in the cars. Adora makes sure she gets in the big black SUV with Mustafa and another two of the younger guys. She tosses a gym bag in the back, then rides shotgun and has a smirk on her face the entire time.

The first stop is at a beat-up old store front building almost to the Indiana State line right off I-94. The six are unloaded and dumped in the middle of the floor. The room isn't well lit, but just enough to see what they need to see. Adora pulls out the bag of marijuana the gunmen had at the apartment and turns on a small CD player she brought. The lights are low, the music is quietly pulsing, the marijuana is good and the Warlords are in the mood for vengeance.

They pull the hoods off the Santa Muerte's heads. All of them are at least semi-conscience but none are mobile yet. They are probably aware of what is about to happen but unable to do anything about it. These are thugs and murderers. They never gave any mercy but suddenly they are hopeful they will receive some.

Two hours later the six are now dismembered corpses. There is blood everywhere including all over two Warlords and Adora. They were the ones who did the cutting. The scene is well beyond gross and disgusting to a normal person. Even two of the young Warlords blew their dinner twice during the cuttings.

But Adora, covered in and soaked in blood, has a look of pure satisfaction on her face. No one spent more time cutting on the Santa Muertes than she did. She spent time on all six of them. She carved marks, symbols and words into their naked bodies. She seemed to relish tossing the dismembered body parts into the plastic bags that were then sewn onto the chest skin of the dead killers. She was the one who collected the six right hands the Warlords were going to UPS to Mexico as a message about what had happened to their friend Rodney.

Every one of the Warlords looks at her with a look of bewilderment on their faces. She had gotten into it more than any of them.

Mustafa points at the Warlords. "Alright, I got clearance to drop them off at the landfill right off I-94 just into Michigan but we need to get moving. Put them in the plastic bags and get them loaded."

He then says to Akile. "We're set from here. Unless you just want to come along for the ride, we can handle the rest."

"Thanks, but you're right. I'll leave the rest up to you." Akile signals for Jaron to join Mustafa and him. "Mustafa, my brother, you have been brilliant. I cannot believe the schemes you have put together. You make me and every Warlord proud. We have avenged ourselves many times over."

With that he hugs Mustafa with a bear hug and he holds on for a long time. He then turns to Jaron but points to Mustafa. "Follow this man. You'll learn even more. And you also have performed wonderfully, my brother. Thank you."

With that Akile flashes all of the Warlord hand signals, waves good night and good bye to the assembled Warlords and he and his driver leave. They walk out into the early makings of a serious rain storm.

A blood spattered Adora comes up to Mustafa. She is naked except for the miniscule thong panties and looks like an Aztec priestess at a ceremonial bloodletting. "Is there a bathroom?"

Mustafa looks around. "None that work but there are bushes outside or a Port-a-Potty at the landfill."

"The bushes are fine. Don't leave without me." With that she gives him a kiss and runs out the door.

Mustafa watches her go. Considering what she has just been doing for the last two hours she comes across as almost an innocent kid. She certainly seems happy about having a chance to even her personal score with the Mexican killers.

Outside Adora stands in the increasingly heavy rain and uses it to rinse the blood off. The puddles around her feet run red with blood. Standing almost naked in the driving rain, she pulls out her cell phone and dials. She whispers into the mouth piece. Then she pulls out her sweat shirt and jeans and puts them on.

CHAPTER

FORTY-FIVE

THE ROADS ARE FAIRLY EMPTY AT THIS HOUR IN THE middle of the night. The driving rain makes visibility limited. No one in their right mind is standing outside in this down pour. Akile and his driver carefully exit going North on Stony Island Avenue to eventually turn West to where they are staying.

Out of nowhere, their big Lincoln Town Car is surrounded by four clunkers. At a small distance, a big, dark blue Lincoln Navigator SUV follows. The clunkers bump into the car and try to force Akile to stop. It looks like a bumper car game at a carnival or maybe more a demolition derby.

The cars slip and slide on the rain soaked street. It is now coming down so hard there is standing water at the curbs. Visibility is almost nonexistent. Inside the Lincoln, Akile and his driver pull out their weapons. "Don't stop! I don't care what happens, don't stop!"

The clunker's windows bristle with weapons sticking out and they open fire. The big Lincoln is damaged and takes some hits, but they keep going. They are struggling to get up Stony Island but the clunkers keep bumping the Lincoln.

In the initial gunfire a clunker was able to get just ahead of the Lincoln and struggles to stay there. The driver of the clunker regularly slams on his brakes and tries to force the Lincoln to stop but its giant engine overpowers the worn out brakes of the piece of junk. Besides all of the cars are skidding on the rain slick street but the big Lincoln Town Car is now in four-wheel drive and has a control advantage. That said the Warlords still can't break free of the smaller clunkers.

It is impossible to accelerate away from their attackers with the clunker bouncing along on their front bumper. The Lincoln is getting beat to a pulp but the driver is doing a good job to keep moving and avoid getting blasted with too many direct hits from the other clunkers. The gunfire he can't avoid.

As they get to Mosque Maryam at 73rd and Stony, Akile hopes to see some of the Fruit of Islam guards around the building. If they are there he can quickly exit Stony Island, blast right through the locked gate and hope for some help. Black guys versus Mexican guys. The Fruit of Islam would give him some help before they got a chance to ask what was going on. But no such good luck. In a driving rain storm, the Fruit of Islam guards are way too smart to be standing in the puddles getting soaked. The huge Mosque is completely dark and the area around the building looks vacant. No cars in the rain soaked parking lot.

Akile finds himself thinking about the last time he was there to hear a talk by Minister Louis Farrakhan of the Nation of Islam. It is a magnificent building and a perfect setting for the Minister to deliver his weekly messages. Some might call them harangues. On social issues and traditional values, the Minister of the Nation of Islam is actually quite conservative. Akile was surprised to hear his calls for strong marriages, respect for Muslim women and their role in society, careful upbringing of your children, religious education in conjunction with better general education and for men to behave in a manner Allah would be proud of.

Not the message he had thought he would hear. He was much more interested in a condemnation of White devils and a defense of Forts' efforts to bring down a White racist society that had always treated him unfairly. He had been forced to be a gangbanger by a racist society that didn't understand his need for respect. Using drugs and violence to undermine a racist society was fair game.

Unfortunately too many minorities were pulled into his web of corruption. His guys turned schools upside down, making it impossible for kids to get an education and a head start in life. But that was just collateral damage. Once he won his struggle he'd come back and worry about the lives he had disrupted. Too bad for now...he had bigger issues to deal with. He felt he was at war with the racist White devils or at least that is what he told those who asked him about his motivation.

Fort had found it interesting that the main room is divided down the middle with men on one side and women on the other. The building is a former Greek Orthodox Church originally purchased to be converted into a Mosque in 1972 by Elijah Muhammad. By the 1960's the Greek Orthodox and White population in general had pretty much disappeared from this part of the South Side. People are always surprised to learn the name Maryam is Arabic for Mary, the mother of Jesus. Most people don't expect the major Chicago Mosque and headquarters of the Nation of Islam to be named after the mother of the Messiah of the Christian faith. Oh well, an interesting tidbit he thought.

Then Akile thinks, what the heck am I doing worrying about Mosque Maryam while a bunch of guys are trying to kill me? He realizes things really do slowdown in life and death situations.

With no one at the Mosque he realizes there won't be any help unless he hits a police officer on routine patrol. The torrential rain has forced everyone else inside. Besides, any gang-bangers on the street here will be hostile to the Gangster Warlords. They'd be more apt to help the guys trying to kill him than help him. He is in trouble and he knows it.

His driver runs every red light without making any attempt to slow down. The clunker is still jammed into his front bumper. As they skid through intersections running with torrents of rain water, the isolation becomes more obvious. They empty several magazines full of shells at the clunkers. Maybe they hit them. Maybe they don't. His head lights and most of those on the clunkers are long since broken. It is too dark to tell if their shots are hitting anything. But the noise of the rain makes the thunder from the gun shots almost background noise.

Just as they approach the Southern entrance of Jackson Park that will lead to the Museum of Science of Industry, a bullet smashes through the front windshield, his driver yells and falls forward over the steering wheel. He has performed with great skill and courage and Akile intended to promote him as a reward. Won't be possible now.

The blood is all over the driver, the dashboard and some has splashed on Akile. But now rain comes through the broken front window and washes over Akile and the dead driver. He tries to get control of the steering wheel with his left hand. As he yanks it, the badly damaged Lincoln jumps the curb and is finally able to get away from the clunker that has stayed smashed into his front bumper.

He pulls off his seat belt and does his best to get behind the steering wheel. He grabs the just reloaded 9mm the driver had dropped and shoves it into his waist band. The seat is soaked and so is Akile. As he tries to accelerate, mud flies from the rear tires.

With a Herculean effort he manages to push the driver side door open and then pushes the dead driver out. But the dead man's foot is caught in the door and his other foot is still in the car jammed under the seat. He is being dragged through the mud beside the car. The dead driver twists the car door and it can't be closed. More rain pours in on Akile and the driver's body. Finally, as Akile kicks at the driver's foot, the body falls away on the muddy grass. One of the clunkers following behind runs over the mangled body as it lies sprawled on a fairway of the Jackson Park Golf Course.

Once the body is gone, Akile tries to close the car door but it won't close. It is too badly damaged and water just keeps pouring in the opening. One of the clunkers angles ahead of the Lincoln that is now so badly damaged it is almost impossible to steer. The car slips and slides on the muddy golf course leaving huge divots in the middle of the fairway. More bullets tear into the car and hit the driver side front tire. The tire blows and the effect pushes the car even farther in the direction of the clunker now aimed directly at Akile's open door.

The sharp pain in his side and leg make him realize he has been hit. Then the clunker smashes into the driver's open door. The Lincoln swerves, turns sideways and is now skidding along, being pushed by the clunker and a second vehicle that is smashed into the rear of the dead Lincoln.

The pain of a direct hit from a clunker shakes Akile's entire body. He twists with his pistol to defend himself and two rounds explode in the face of the clunker driver with blood splattering all over the front seat and windshield. The rain washes the blood down the dashboard onto the seat. It makes it impossible for Akile to see if he has killed the man. He just can't see.

The beautiful gold Statue of the Republic is now right in front of them. It is visible through the downpour glistening as the rivers of water run off its head and shoulders. The Lincoln and the two totaled clunkers jammed into its side and rear skid to a stop just at the curb of the circular drive that goes all the way around the famous statue. There are giant clumps of grass, mud and water thrown on the road way.

Akile drags himself out of the wreck. The driver of the clunker smashed into the Lincoln's rear falls out of the driver's side door. The pouring rain washes the blood off his face and chest and he lays there in a pool of muddy, bloody water. He is desperately hurt and looks up at Akile who calmly points his pistol in the guy's face and blows half his head off. He then shoots the guy in the shot gun seat. He isn't moving but no point in taking a chance. He might be faking.

Immediately he hobbles toward the big gold statue. Water splashes before his feet and he has to drag the leg that has been shot. Another of the clunkers bounces over the curb and straight at him with a wall of water driven before it. He dives left as the vehicle guesses which way he will go and guesses wrong by swerving right.

Akile rolls over and fires at the swerving car which then loops in a sharp circle and comes right back at him, pushing another wall of water before it. With strength he didn't know he still had, Akile makes it to the steps surrounding the statue. The clunker is right after him but hits the steps and bounces up like a hard hit ground ball, causing the driver to lose control of what is left of the battered and bullet riddled piece of junk as it comes to a sudden stop on the steps.

Akile smashes the window with a bullet and then jams his pistol in the window and puts a round into the side of the driver's head. Before he can get any farther two rounds tear into his back. He twists and tries to return fire but another bullet tears into his right forearm and he drops his weapon into a puddle of water churned by the torrent of rain hammering into it. Another round breaks his left leg and he falls on his face in a pool of water. Ripples rush out from him like a stone landing in the middle of a pond. He struggles to roll over onto his back and use his left hand to grab the 9mm in his waist band.

Just as he finally gets on his back a drenched Arturo Ortega steps on his left arm, pinning it to the ground. Arturo shifts his SIG Sauer P226 to his left hand and reaches down to pull the 9mm out of Akile's waist band. Arturo Ortega looks Akile Fort right in the face. Eye to eye. Water runs off Ortega and falls in Fort's face.

Akile's eyes light up with recognition. He knows who Arturo Ortega is. He has a pretty good guess why Ortega is standing on his left arm.

"You stupid bastard. You caused all this. Do you realize how many people have gotten killed because of your incompetence? How much money we have all lost? We had a good deal going but you and your stupid bitch, Larenda Bass have probably ruined it for all of us," laments Ortega.

Still standing on Fort's left arm, he places the 9mm pistol right against Akile's forehead and blows his brains all over the steps. The pool of water runs red with Fort's blood. Ortega puts a second round through his heart. He takes out a handkerchief, wipes his fingerprints off the weapon and sets it on Akile's chest.

As he looks around a soaked Santa Muerte Cartel gunman splashes through the water holding the AK-47 he used to destroy Akile Fort's arm and leg. He walks up behind Ortega and stops just short but within easy earshot.

In a heavy Spanish accent, the Santa Muerte gunman yells through the rain. "Senior Ortega, there is no one else alive but you, me and Carlos. We need to leave before the police come."

Ortega nods and splashed across the pavement as he returns to his big blue Navigator SUV. "Leave these stolen pieces of shit cars. You guys come and ride with me."

Carlos, an Insane Jaguar, is wounded...not badly, but is bleeding. He looks like a drowned puppy but does as he is told.

He gives Ortega the hand sign for the Jaguars and Ortega smiles, nods and gives the hand sign in return. As they walk to the car Ortega wraps his arms around each of their shoulders in a friendly bear hug. "Well done. He was as tough as we thought he would be. But...but he is dead and we are alive. That is all that matters!"

Once in the car, he tosses a small towel to Carlos in the back seat. "Use that to keep the blood from dripping all over. Push hard."

The Santa Muerte gunman climbs into the shotgun seat of the car and they pull away just as police sirens can be heard in the distance. The rain obscures everything as they quickly disappear on Lake Shore Drive going north. They follow the road right past the Museum of Science and Industry and keep going.

They drive off, very careful to stay within the speed limit and do nothing that might look suspicious. In the distance, they can't see the squad car stopped where the Lincoln and the junkers had jumped the curb and skidded their way across the formerly neat and flat fairway of the Jackson Park Golf course. The officer is looking at Akile's driver's body smashed to a mess after having been dragged and run over before he bounced to a stop and lay still in the bloody water and the mud.

CHAPTER

IT IS STILL DARK OUT, AS ORTEGA DROPS CARLOS AT the curb. He pulls right into the Emergency Room entrance overhang to allow Carlos to stay out of the rain as much as possible. With his arm wrapped in gauze, a soaked Carlos walks into the Saint Anthony Hospital Emergency Room on West 19th Street.

Carlos goes straight to the admissions desk and explains in Spanish he was hit by a stray bullet. He doesn't know who or what. He only knows he was talking with his friend when gun shots erupted and one nicked his arm. Perhaps it isn't that bad, but he can't be sure. That is why he is here. That sort of nebulous explanation of a gunshot wound is how a gangbanger pretends he is a good kid caught in the wrong place. The fact that he was out on the street in the middle of the night is a point that is ignored and he is not asked why he was out at that hour.

He hands the clerk his City of Chicago employee insurance card. He is listed as an employee of Alderman Maldonado. The entry clerk is very helpful and gets the forms filled out quickly. She can see he is hurt but it doesn't look life threatening so she does the paperwork before she has him taken back to see a physician. It gives her time to flirt with him.

The clerk gives Carlos an admiring glance. He has a good job with the City. If you overlook the fact they are soaked and have blood on them, his clothes look good. The clothe are state of the art fashion, fancy earring and jewelry. He claims he was shot while just hanging out so he is claiming not to be a gangbanger. Interesting guy.

It is a hospital emergency room so no one asks why he was hanging out, outside, in the middle of the night, with a buddy in a driving rain storm. The issue of what shooter would be shooting at soaking wet guys dumb enough to be standing around outside in a torrential rain storm never comes up. No one seems to think of the line, "too dumb to come in out of the rain." Carlos is supposedly another innocent guy standing around and hit by a stray bullet from who knows where. Being an employee of an Alderman immediately takes his injury out of the gangbanger category.

Carlos is looking pretty cocky despite the wounded arm. He thanks her for her assistance and offers to take her to breakfast after her shift ends and he is patched up. She is clearly thinking about it as he walks back with the nurse.

Farther east Mustafa just finishes dropping off the last of the Warlords who rode with him. The bodies are in the landfill. The Santa Muerte cars are long since stolen off the streets of Gary, Indiana. The Warlords are feeling very good about their eye for an eye treatment of the Mexican murderers. The rain storm has helped cover their actions this morning.

Still sitting in the shot gun seat is Adora. A least she has rinsed off the blood and cleaned up quite a bit. The rain gave her a cheap shower. She still has that smirk on her face. She has enjoyed this evening as much as any in her life. Now she wants to finish with a flourish.

Adora's face screws up like she is thinking hard. "Do you think we've got the Santa Muerte bastards to realize they are messing with the wrong guys and they should go home and leave us all alone?"

"I hope so. But I'm not sure they are that smart. Too macho. We'll see.

"When I get home I want to take a long, hot bubble bath. It will feel wonderful."

Mustafa nods as he drives.

"Do you want to join me? It is a big bath tub with Jacuzzi jets and all. I'll cook breakfast. We can swing by your place and you can pick up some dry clothes and things."

This is something Mustafa expected, but he isn't sure it's a great idea. She is nuts: blood thirsty, kind of quirky, downright kinky, an exhibitionist but with some pretty nice things to exhibit. She rubbed her almost naked body all over several of the Santa Muertes as they cut them up. She claims that is what they had done to his young Warlords when they cut them up. She said she just wanted it all to be even.

Maybe it isn't a good idea to stay at her place. He doesn't really know anything about her. He doesn't know if her apartment would be safe. He's tired and needs a rest, but...but?

He agreed with Akile they would stay out of sight tomorrow and just lay low. Get a little rest, relaxation and down time. So no one is expecting to see him tomorrow. All of the Warlords on the raid were exhausted from their long evening and morning of butchery, perversion and mayhem. Everyone, even a Gangster Warlord, needs a little down time.

The more Mustafa thinks about it, the more he realizes he isn't planning on doing much tomorrow any way. It might be a nice way to relax with a kinky young thing that has a cute figure. He has seen enough of it today to be interested in seeing even more, up close and personal. It could be a wild ride.

Besides she has a really quirky sense of humor and has been downright funny at times. It just might be worth a laugh or two to spend a little time with her. The Jacuzzi wasn't a bad idea either. He just feels it isn't a good idea, but...?

"Yeah. Thanks. Nice idea. Let's take some time to unwind. I've got some stuff at Alderman Bass' old office. We can swing by and I'll pick it up. Save us a trip to my place."

An hour later with dawn approaching, Mustafa parks his late model SUV a block and a half down the street from Adora's apartment. Finding a parking spot in any decent neighborhood in Chicago is a total pain. At this hour, with everyone home, he certainly can't get anything in front of her place. He had hoped to park closer because the rain has suddenly returned, big time! Oh well, if there isn't a parking place, there isn't.

They hold hands as they run through the driving rain to her apartment building's front door. They had pretty much dried out as they returned from the landfill in Michigan, dropped off the other Warlords and picked up clean clothes for Mustafa. Now both are thoroughly soaked again and their clothes hang on them as they drip on the floor in the entrance hall lobby.

He is shocked at what a nice building she lives in. Once they get to her place he is just as shocked at her very well furnished and immaculate apartment. The kitchen looks like it is on one of those cable TV cooking shows. He didn't know where she lived. He had never thought of it before. He barely knew her before today. All he really knew is she is a friend of Brittany's.

Never in a million years did he expect such a nice place here in the youthful and trendy West Loop. This is definitely not a gangbanger girlfriend neighborhood. This is affluent and upscale for the thirty-something crowd. But Adora is definitely not thirty-something. For the first time Mustafa wonders what Adora does to occupy the rest of her life. You don't live in neighborhoods like this if your only skill is cutting body parts off Mexican assassins.

Mustafa suddenly realizes Adora has to be a call girl. He doesn't mind. Living like this, alone, at her age? This is not the apartment for a receptionist at some big, downtown law firm. Oh well, everyone needs to make a living. Remembering what he does as a Warlord, Mustafa clearly doesn't think he has any right to judge another person's career choices. But looking at this apartment, whatever Adora does, she does well. This looks like it is about to turn into a wonderful day off.

Adora very carefully locks the door behind them, then pulls her soaking wet sweatshirt over her head and tosses it on the kitchen's tile floor. She is naked from the waist up and shakes like a cat trying to remove the rain from its body. Then she drops her jeans around her ankles and kicks them off. Somewhere she has lost her underwear. She is soaked and water runs off her hair and down her chest. Mustafa realizes again why he decided to take her up on her offer.

She is really a little odd, but there is just something about her. Mustafa can't quite place it. But they aren't getting married. She has offered herself to him...probably a thank you for letting her go along. She really has gotten into the revenge side of the action...strange for a girl. He has been awfully busy lately. Maybe a relaxed night in a Jacuzzi with a wild thing might help him get back on track to normal. No point spending so much time thinking about or rationalizing it.

No need to be anywhere tomorrow. She has a big screen TV and maybe a full refrigerator. Hey, what harm could it do?

With a sultry smile she comes over to wrap herself around Mustafa. She pulls his soaked shirt up over his head. "Coffee, tea or me? How should we start? Breakfast? A bath? Or just drop to the floor and get started right here?"

Mustafa and Adora are way too occupied to notice the bedroom door inch open.

CHAPTER

FORTY-SEVEN

THE NEXT AFTERNOON A STREET PAN HANDLER tries to break into a late model SUV parked under a deserted viaduct in the Englewood neighborhood. Because of the tinted glass he can just barely see something lumpy under blankets or something like that in the back end of the vehicle.

He looks around to be sure no one is nearby and takes a big lump of concrete broken out of the aged, collapsing viaduct. He smashes the back window, reaches in and pulls open the rear gate of the SUV. He hopes to find something he can take, use or eat. Just then he notices a foot protruding from under the blankets.

A short time later, Sunny is surrounded by other police officers, crime scene techs and at a little distance, a big crowd of onlookers. He looks a little depressed.

"I can ID the male body. This is definitely a guy I know. Maybe knew is correct. That is or was Mustafa from the late Alderman Bass' office. He was also a Gangster Warlord. But being in Englewood is not his normal turf. But I have no idea who the girl is."

Lieutenant Dornan of Sunny's detachment approaches. "Add Mustafa to finding Akile Fort's body on the steps of the Statue of the Republic in Jackson Park and Fort's brother Jaron in the park and you are looking at the demise of the key leadership of the Gangster Warlords. The lady's body with Jaron was identified as some Brittany somebody. Worked in the County Clerk's office and moonlighted as a waitress and...and whatever...other things she didn't do during work hours. Kind of messy."

Sunny looks at the body and says to Lieutenant Dornan. "Mustafa seemed to be a sharp guy. But this is the reason gangbangers don't bother to open IRAs. None of them will live long enough to need them."

Lieutenant Dornan chuckles. "I never thought of it that way."

Sunny just keeps looking at Mustafa's remains. "You know Lieutenant, the Warlords were clearly getting the better end of the fight until last night. One bad night and the big leaders are all gone. It will take a while for them to get reorganized."

Dornan nods. "Yeah. Probably so."

Sunny moves closer. "Is this the time to wipe the Warlords out? They are leaderless and I am sure confused. With no leader, we could really apply the heat and maybe destroy them."

Dornan chuckles. "Why? They'd just be replaced by another gang expanding in to fill the vacuum. The powers that be don't want these guys gone. They just want them to be easier to control and to keep a lower profile. The drugs won't go away. Hookers? Go away? Yeah, right. Nice idea but you won't get any support on that idea."

Another Officer faces Dornan. "Do you think this will be the end of the feud between the Warlords and the Santa Muerte Cartel?"

"Hope so. We'll see. But we are dealing with one seriously blood thirsty Mexican Drug Cartel with their honor at stake."

The Officer looks back at Dornan with a quizzical look. "Honor? Interesting choice of words."

Dornan smiles. "You've got a point there."

A spokesman for the Mayor's office approaches Dornan and Sunny. Both guys look at him because it is obvious he has something he wants to say.

The political guy looks around to be sure only Dornan and Sunny can hear him. "I've just been talking to city hall. You know all of these killings have been getting national press. It isn't good for the city. They've been taking to calling us the murder capitol of America. Is there anything we can say about this bunch so it looks less like an open gang war on the streets of Chicago?"

Brookins approaches and gestures for Sunny to come to him. Sunny is glad to not be part of this conversation so he nods to Dornan and heads to Brookins. This is a political decision to be made way over his head.

Brookins leans in to Sunny and speaks quietly. "Do you think we ought to have a chat with your soul mate from the shootout at the OK corral?"

"Ortega? The Humboldt Park attack?"

"Of course dipshit. I haven't seen Wyatt Earp or the Crystal Palace Saloon around here recently."

Sunny knows he accidently set himself up for that one so he just smiles and waits his shot to get even. "We've got to finish here and then let's head over to Little Village."

CHAPTER

FORTY-EIGHT

SUNNY AND BROOKINS LEAVE THE MURDER SITE in Englewood and drive north. Suddenly Sunny's cell phone rings.

"SunWarrior. Light me up, baby."

"Mason Huntley of the *Sun Times*."

"I know. I know your number. I'd know your voice even if you were calling from a prison cell or a whore house."

"Is that good or bad?"

"Neither. I'm a cop. We remember things, places and voices. As much as we talk I could imitate your voice so well your mother would think it was you. You know I know a lot she might not like. Don't forget I know her phone number and where she lives. So never piss me off!"

Sunny can hear the chuckle on the other end of the line.

"I've got some great news and some interesting news about what we have decided to call The Hired Truck Scandal."

"Don't keep me in suspense. I can't take the pressure. Out with it dipshit!"

"Just leading up to it. First, the Federal Judge will be Ruben Castillo."

"Whoa are you lucky! A great Federal Judge who knows plenty about corruption in Chicago so he won't be a softy like some of them. I really respect him for what he did when he was at MALDEF in the late eighties and early nineties. Before my time, but there was a lot going on then. Tough but reasonable. I think I remember he was a federal prosecutor before that. You just got a break. If you got one of the wimps the entire case might have fallen apart."

"You know it! We're overjoyed to have one of the top federal judges. Just thought I'd give you the good news. Since you are almost an unindicted co-conspirator, I thought you'd want to know."

"Hey! A co-conspirator is a bad guy. Vlad and I were the good guys. Remember?"

"Not really. When you're a world class reporting superstar like me, it is hard to remember the little guys who might have given you some tiny snippet of almost worthless help on the way up the ladder."

Sunny guffaws. "See if I ever slip you an exclusive again. But what was the second thing?"

"This is a real shocker. Remember the mobster slime ball involved, Nick "The Stick" Lecco?"

"Sure. He was a city employee, bookie and what all. Didn't he have a lot of say about who got what contract?"

"Yeah. Remember LoCoco loved to ride and was really a very good horseman?"

"Didn't know that. A gangster who likes to ride horses. Ride something else, maybe. Horses?"

"Well in the middle of a bunch of pro games, with all kinds of money riding on a ton of them, he decided to go for a ride."

"Strange."

"Even stranger, while he was all alone he fell off his nag and broke his neck. He's dead."

"A bookie goes for a ride, all alone, in the middle of an important day of work. He's an excellent rider but still falls off his horse and dies. Well that's Chicago for you. Can't feel all that bad about it. Besides he wouldn't have said anything in court anyway. Mobsters almost never talk. Especially in cases like this. Nothing violent so they know they won't get that much time to serve anyway."

"I know, but strange. It is being dismissed as simply an accident."

"Mason, this is Chicago. At least he died doing something he liked. Nobody cut off his body parts while he was still alive. He's lucky."

Huntley smiles at Sunny's response. "Thanks. You guys have been a pleasure to work with. Please let Vlad know the good news. OK?"

"Will do. Thanks. Out."

Brookins looks bewildered and shrugs to Sunny.

Sunny turns to Brookins. "Nothing you want to know. This is one of those where ignorance is bliss."

"Sounds like much of my life. Especially my sex life. I haven't got laid in what seems like a month."

"Dipshit. Your wife is out of town."

"Oh yeah. I knew there had to be some reason the dirty dishes and laundry were piling up."

Sunny laughs as he shakes his head. "Senile dipshit."

CHAPTER FORTY-NINE

BOTH LAUGH AS THEY APPROACH THE OFFICE address that is on Ortega's business card for Aztec Properties. They stop a block away and Sunny calls him.

"Arturo Ortega. May I help you?"

"Arturo, it is Sunny and Brookins. Got a few minutes?"

"For you, always. I'm tied up for about another half an hour. Then where do you want to meet?"

"Would it be OK to meet at Aztec Properties?"

"Sure. It will only take a couple of minutes to get back there. My Southern friends seem happy with me and the world right now, so we might as well be comfortable. That back alley driving and running around parks is a little too exciting for me anyway."

"See you there."

Sunny turns to Brookins. "We've got a half hour. There is a Dunkin Donuts. You buy the fritters and I'll buy the tea."

"Tea? What kind of wimp do I look like?"

"A big one. Get what you want."

The two sit at a table away from the window, but with a good view all around.

Brookins enjoys his fritter. "You know if Sheila were here we'd both get shot for eating these wonderful delicacies."

"Yeah, I know. So eat hearty. I bet she'll be home soon."

"Let's hope. If the Santa Muertes aren't mad at Ortega any more, should we be reading something into that?"

"That is what I want to know. OK. Time to go."

Just as Sunny and Brookins arrive at the front door of Aztec Properties, Arturo Ortega pulls his big, dark blue Lincoln Navigator SUV into the reserved parking space next to the building. It is a pleasant store front office. Clean windows. No graffiti. Sidewalk without cracks. A neat looking real estate office.

Sunny notices the SUV has just been washed, but the bullet holes from their park adventure haven't been repaired yet. With all the rain last night, who knows, the navigator probably got pretty dirty. No point reading too much into a car wash.

"Sunny and Brookins, nice to see you." Arturo extends his hand to shake.

They all shake hands and enter the office. Inside is quite nice but nothing extravagant. A pleasant Mexican motif to the decoration. Lots of bright colors. Several comfortable chairs around a table in the outer office. Nice Mexican-oriented pictures on the walls.

The two most prominent pictures are one taken from the very top of the seats of a live bullfight in the Plaza Mexico in Mexico City, the world's largest bullfighting ring. Plenty of color and action. Another great picture is of the magnificent El Castillo at Chichen Itza in Quintana Roo State.

Sunny and Sheila had visited Chichen Itza once and climbed up El Castillo during a vacation to Cancun. They loved Cancun, the food, the history, the miles of long, beautiful beaches, the iguanas and peacocks at the ruins of El Rey off Kukulcan Blvd. and of course their visit to the giant Mayan ruins at Chichen Itza.

They stayed in an old Army friend's time share at a place called Club Regina. Literally right on the beautiful, almost white sand beach. Great! Almost every night they had reenacted their honeymoon skinny dip in a triangle shaped pool that was almost part of the Caribbean. Their room's veranda opened on to the pool and they could simply step off the veranda into the water. With a set up like that, how could you not go skinny dipping at midnight? This time they were lucky and no one seemed to have caught them. If someone did, they were nice enough not to say anything.

Sheila's efforts at sun tanning by the many pools at the hotel, the Westin Regina which is attached to Club Regina had also attracted a bit of attention. Her body always did. The very limited coverage by her two piece swimming suit probably had something to do with the interest. Her voluptuous figure could bulge out of a tiny swim suit with the best of them.

Sunny suddenly snaps back to the here and now! Great memories, but he is in Chicago in the office of a General of the Insane Jaguars. It is time to get the blood flow to the right part of his body and pay attention.

A slightly matronly but still attractive and friendly Latino woman greets them as they come in. She seems busy with paperwork but genuinely happy to see them. Arturo walks over and gives her a kiss.

Both Sunny and Brookins are surprised but say nothing.

"Honey, please meet Sunny SunWarrior and Harold Brookins. They are the police officers I mentioned to you." The lady beams with a room warming smile and extends her hand.

"Guys, this beautiful lady is the love of my life, my wonderful wife, Alejandra."

They both cover their surprise at who the charming lady is and shake hands.

"Come into my office." Arturo leads them through the door to the back area. Inside is a spacious and very attractive office. A big desk with a comfortable chair. Several more comfortable chairs for visitors. A huge credenza behind the desk. Lots more colorful pictures of Mexico. All in all, the ambience is nothing of what you would expect from the office of a General in the Insane Jaguars. Besides, why does a big time gangbanger need an office anyway?

As he closes the office door Sunny stares at the big front windows. "Don't you worry about all of that window exposure?"

"No. It is bulletproof and the walls are reinforced."

Sunny and Brookins both think to themselves, this guy thinks of everything.

Sunny looks around before he sits down. "Great pictures. My wife and I have been to Cancun. She loved the place and especially climbing El Castillo at Chichen Itza."

"Beautiful. We go there some also."

Sunny is always amazed. An Insane Jaguar General and his wife walking hand in hand down the beautiful beaches of Cancun. Does he have his SIG Sauer in his swimsuit's waistband? Probably riding those convenient buses into town for nice meals, great margaritas and walking through the shopping bazaars buying souvenirs for his favorite drug pushing mass murderers. Ortega is unbelievable.

Ortega continues. "Sorry I was tied up. I was just at a meeting with three of Burke's ward committeemen who want to be Alderman Larenda Bass' replacement as the boss of the South Side. Amazing. These people do not have a working relationship with reality."

Both Sunny and Brookins think to themselves that is a serious indictment when it is a major gangbanger, drug pusher, cold blooded murderer saying you're the one who doesn't have a working relationship with reality. "Why you?"

"Who do you think runs the wards for Burke and his cockroaches? Patronage is limited. Hardly anybody in their right mind would volunteer to help that pack of slime balls. Who else can deliver the troops? Us and the other groups on the street. The money and the troops come from the government unions, especially the Service Employees International or SEIU, a bunch of leeches and us. The ambulance chasers kick in big money but they don't do any work."

Both cops laugh because they know it is true. Both of them hate lawyers anyway. So many of the Chicago Bar are ambulance chasing, criminal defending, and frivolous lawsuit filing sleaze balls. There is a reason the Crook County Courts are considered some of the most corrupt and plaintiff-oriented in the nation. Glad to see Ortega thinks the same about lawyers as they do.

"Then Burke shakes protection money out of the big businesses in Chicago. Those are the sources of Burke's power. He takes care of all of us except the business guys. They just give the money as part of a protection racket. They know he could treat them worse if he wants to so they try to buy him off. People think we extort money for protection. Compared to Burke the groups on the streets are a bunch of cupcakes."

The almost stunned chuckle that breaks from Brookins gives Ortega and Sunny a smile.

Ortega gestures expansively. "It is all what you can do for the other guy. How do you think my kid got his college scholarship? He has a legislative scholarship from our local State Representative. If I'm going to help Burke's crooks and idiots, they should give a little back also. Fair?"

Sunny's mind swims as he listens to Ortega. Ortega's grasp of the situation in Chicago is amazing. He guessed that all might be true but to hear it so openly from a major gangbanger is unbelievable. Plus he didn't call them gangbangers, he called them groups on the streets. Interesting. He also calls himself a businessman. Looking at the this office and his real estate hold-ings, he has a point. But a taxpayer funded scholarship for his kid's college expenses? That is another shocker.

"You know Sunny, if anyone made even a small effort to go after the vote fraud in Chicago, they would uncover so much they'd have a heart attack. The nursing homes. Oh my GOD! The fraud there is unbelievable. Absentee ballots. Oh my GOD! We vote so many undocumented folks even I get nervous."

Brookins nods. "It isn't very clean in my area either. But one of the unspoken costs Burke extracts from our union and the local prosecutors is they stay away from the polls on election day. We can wander in unannounced and say hello, but we don't respond to very many vote fraud calls."

Ortega nods in agreement. " The Cook County Clerk hasn't cleaned the voting roles for years and years. That lets them vote people who have officially been registered at an address for years and are thus above suspicion. Of course they moved away five years ago."

Sunny and Brookins look at each other. They always expected this, but to hear it from a guy who runs it is different.

"Most of my guys and the undocumented folks vote under the names of folks who have moved away. Then we take them to the next precinct, get the name we are to use and vote again. In neighborhoods like this they make almost no effort to verify the voter is who he says he is. Everybody is afraid they'll get yelled at for voter suppression. Also all the extra names make the turnout appear smaller than it is. That also covers a lot of the fraud. If the turnout was 95% folks would go crazy. But with all the names of folks who left or died years ago the turnout per-centage is artificially low. It seems to be normal not too big."

Sunny looks exasperated. "Arturo, how do you know all this?"

Ortega laughs out loud. "Who do you think runs the polls around here? We technically do it to help Alderman Maldonado since he doesn't have that many workers. You see, we work for free around the elections. The other folks want to be paid. Our only paid workers are the election judges. Free workers get the benefit of the system."

Sunny shakes his head but comes back to the point of their conversation. "Who is the next in line to be the boss of the South Side?"

"The couple of sharp ones who have some brains try to keep at least a little distance from Burke, so the only ones who want it are like Bass. Ambitious dimwits. Just like Bass. But helping these guys is the cost of doing business. The prosecutors, the judges, most of the cops and whoever else pretty much leave us in peace. We play by the rules and keep a low profile. We don't make waves. What do I care who Burke anoints as his new consigliore? Doesn't mean anything to me."

Ortega gives Sunny a wink. "Sunny, you guys need to learn to leave us alone. If you hadn't filched that idiot Fort's stash, this would have never happened."

Sunny ignores the wink and thinks a moment. "I just assume you know about Akile Fort and his right hand guy Mustafa?"

"No loss. Fort caused all of this mess. If he hadn't gotten so greedy, 60, maybe 75 folks would still be alive. Damn idiot. Gang wars always end badly for everyone involved. We're just businessmen in what is almost a family business. Most of our kids on the street come from broken homes or worse. The crappy schools leave them uneducated. We're their family. That greedy bastard Fort got some of our family killed for no reason other than greed. We should avoid violence. It is counterproductive. Just stick to what we do."

"Maybe I shouldn't be surprised at your response, but...I don't know. I expected you to be concerned."

"Since when does a Jaguar General feel bad over the death of a stupid thug and drug pusher like Fort? The guy wasn't smart enough to become a business man. Mustafa had the potential to be more, but I guess not anymore."

How candid can a guy be? It is as if he thinks he is immune. Ortega clearly fears no one in Chicago. Certainly not Burke's power structure or the state and county prosecutors. What does he know that Sunny doesn't? "Is it over? The Cartel got everybody but Vlad and me and maybe should I include you?"

"I'm OK. I took care of business with the Mexicans. But you're forgetting the big issue, the four million bucks. They don't have that yet."

"Isn't that their loss for doing business with an idiot?"

"Maybe. But do you want to suggest that to them?"

Sunny and Brookins chuckle as they get the point.

"The leaders of the Cartel are living in beautiful haciendas, really armed compounds, in the mountains of Northern Mexico. Some live on our side of the border in Arizona and Southern California. The border is easy to cross so they can live where they want. Whenever they move it is in armored convoys surrounded by sycophants. They have killed how many thousands of Mexicans, Americans, Columbians, Peruvians and Bolivians? Who do you think is dumb enough to deliver the message they should just write off their four million dollars?"

Sunny and Brookins chuckle again. They love to listen to Ortega.

"OK, they wiped out the Warlords. They've made a big point. I'd guess the way to make them happy is something like at least one more very big, very public, and symbolic something. They are still out the money, but their machismo would be intact and then maybe they go home happy. "

Both Sunny and Brookins consider that option.

In a conspiratorial manner Arturo offers some advice. "They're packing their bags for the trip home. Keep your heads down for a while longer so you don't become their big public splash."

Both guys nod. Good advice. "What would you do if you were me and the Chicago Police Department?"

Ortega cracks a huge grin. "I'd give up and sue for peace. Throw yourself on the mercy of the Insane Jaguars and let us police the town for you. We'll cost less and we won't be so inhibited in getting rid of the riff-raff on the street. We'll do away with petty crime and street people. The town will be quieter and safer."

Sunny and Brookins absolutely lose it. They are almost falling out of their chairs laughing.

Brookins quits laughing first but can't wipe the huge grin off his face. "The worst of it is I think you've convinced me. But I've got the same problem. No one to deliver the message to the Mayor, the Aldermen and Burke."

Arturo smirks. "Don't worry. I can do that for you also."

Both of them lose it again. They realize Ortega probably does have better access to the folks running the town than they or the average citizen.

"Arturo I love you. I can't tell you how much I have enjoyed getting to know you. We better leave you and get back to work. If you're right the Santa Muertes aren't quite done yet and want something big. We better start trying to figure out what they'll do."

Arturo nods. "Don't let this stuff make you bitter. Bitterness only hurts you, not the other guy. Keep moving forward."

Arturo rises and leads them out of his office. He speaks with a friendly smile. "You know if you or the superintendent need help keeping things under control or anything else, I'll be here."

Sunny and Brookins say their goodbyes to Alejandra. She couldn't be more pleasant. Then they walk out the front door toward the street. It is a very pleasant day now getting ready to turn toward evening. Ortega joins Sunny and Brookins walking all the way to their car where the three guys shake hands.

Ortega tells them one of his hilarious jokes and has both of them laughing up a storm as they get in their car and drive off.

Senior Insane Jaguar General Arturo Manuel Ortega walks slowly and majestically back toward his office in the heart of his kingdom and doesn't pay any attention to anything. It is good to be king. He just enjoys the approaching evening and the comfortably light breeze.

It is way too late when his mind snaps back to the here and now to realize that three guys have just stepped out from the side of the office building armed with AK-47s. They all open fire within an instant of each other. There is the thunder of mayhem rolling around them everywhere. Ortega is immediately hit with 20 or 30 bullets. Who can count? He tries to pull his SIG Sauer but is dead before he can bring it to bare.

A fourth gunman steps around behind the others, yanks open the office front door and throws in two hand grenades. The pins have already been pulled and the explosion is almost immediate. Alejandra never has a chance. At the start of the gunfire she had pulled a pistol from under her desk. No point. Didn't help her at all. The office becomes a brilliant ball of flames. Because the windows are bullet proof and the walls reinforced, the explosion never gets past the front wall. The noise is deafening, but the hand grenades only destroy the inside.

The Santa Muerte gunmen walk to Ortega's body and empty magazine after magazine into his lifeless form. Hundreds of rounds riddle his corpse. This is serious overkill. The blood and body parts are everywhere. This is a message being delivered in about as public a forum as there is short of doing it on the corner of Michigan Avenue and Water Street, right in front of the Fox News studio.

The fourth gunman walks into the real estate office amid the smoke and fumes to make sure Alejandra is dead. He empties a full magazine into her also. No need. Two hand grenades have done more than enough damage. She is literally blown to bits and emptying a magazine into her is another case of overkill. He then pours lighter fluid on the floor and tosses a match in it. The flames explode into the air and engulf the building. Even more overkill maybe, but when you are delivering a huge, very public message without bothering to use a postage stamp, a few extra bullets and a blazing building are good for adding emphasis.

CHAPTER FIFTY

SUNNY AND BROOKINS INSTANTLY RESPOND TO THE call from the 911 dispatcher. They know the address. They just left there five minutes ago.

Brookins has Vlad's Ithaca Mag-10 in his hands and Sunny has the city issue Benelli shotgun. The scene is straight out of Dante's inferno. Behind them more police sirens wail. A crowd starts to form at the edges but no one gets very close. Smoke billows from the burning real estate office and Ortega's big blue Lincoln Navigator is also in flames.

Sunny is almost in shock. He has a hard time recognizing the mass of blood and body parts. The clothes, the shoes and the Sig Sauer are all he recognizes. His knees give out and he sits down on the sidewalk next to the bloody mess that used to Arturo Ortega's human form.

Brookins drifts back to the real estate office but he knows Alejandra isn't going to be in need of any of his assistance. He can't get very close because of the flames.

Sunny straightens his uniform and nods to the other folks entering Superintendent Purcell's office. Sunny has recovered his composure as he prepares to enter the office. These last weeks have been almost as rough as his tour in Afghanistan. He still can't believe this has happened in Chicago. Sure, Chicago is the murder capital of the world, but...even knowing that...this has been horrendous.

Superintendent Phil Purcell sits behind his impressive desk in his big office. In front of him sit Sunny SunWarrior, Harold Brookins, a still much hobbled Vlad Kozak and Lieutenant Dornan. Behind them are the First Deputy Superintendent, two lawyers from the City of Chicago's Law Department and a lawyer from the FOP. Next to the Superintendent's desk is the Cook County State's Attorney.

This is a meeting of the minds of the folks in charge. As it ends, Purcell signals for Sunny to remain there.

The other people file out, but Sunny goes over to face Superintendent Purcell.

"You know Sunny, you are a master at getting in the middle of things. Especially things folks outside this department don't want to deal with. Do you really think anything is going to come of all this information you have given us?"

Sunny is hesitant to speak. "Do you really want me to answer, sir?"

"No, not really. We all know the State's Attorney will bury all of this. Her investigation won't find anything they don't want found. It is her responsibility to be sure none of this ever gets out on the street. Burke doesn't like his dirty linen being aired in public. Why do you think she is State's Attorney? Previously she spent 13 years as the assistant State's Attorney in charge of the public corruption section. Do you know how many investigations she did during those 13 years?"

There is silence.

"Zero. Not one investigation in Chicago or Cook County in the entire 13 years. Nice try, but don't hold your breath waiting for something to happen."

Sunny looks a little hopeless and shrugs.

"Sunny this is Chicago. The most corrupt city in America. You and I got into this for all of the right reasons. We were those idealistic guys who think they can make a big difference. We were fools. But we can make a small difference. Never lose sight of the fact you moved the ball forward. Burke and the political guys in charge will ignore small advances. But he has no sense of humor if you try to move the ball too far. Be careful of these guys. You know I have your back. But I don't run this city."

CHAPTER

FIFTY-ONE

SUNNY IS PREOCCUPIED WITH HIS THOUGHTS OF the meeting with Superintendent Purcell and his excitement that Sheila is finally home. They had a wonderful homecoming last night. They probably didn't get more than a few hours sleep between the two of them. An early dinner at her favorite restaurant and their long awaited chance to make up for lost time. When he left a bit late this morning Sheila was still in bed. Sunny leaned over to kiss her goodbye and she whispered he had truly reinforced the accuracy of her affectionate nickname for him: pervert.

The sky is overcast and a medium drizzle blankets everything in a subdued haze. He parks his car in his driveway and relaxes for a moment as he thinks about the day. Because of the rain and clouds at dusk, it is fairly dark except for the garage light. For some reason, the porch light isn't on, but there are lights coming from the back of the house by the kitchen. He guesses Sheila having been gone forgot to turn on the front porch light.

Because he is running late, he called and left a message to let her know roughly when he would be home. She was probably at her favorite market getting some more GOD awful vegetables to feed him. There is a smile on his face as he thinks of Sheila working hard at cooking some unbelievable healthy meal that always seems to taste like three-day-old dried toast. He knows he will never tell her that her cooking sucks. She is a wonderful wife with many thoroughly lovable traits and funny idiosyncrasies, plus she has great tits; so why sweat the small stuff? Their home is always immaculate.

Sheila teaches at their local Catholic grade school three days a week. They like to treat it as additional monies for their tithe and until they have kids of their own it gives Sheila all the kid face time she needs. He loves her humor about the problems when the kids have given her more attention than she wants. Sheila is not the kind of person to let the truth interfere with a good story and some of her misdeeds at school belong on the Comedy Channel. Her great points have always overshadowed her total failure as a cook. Sunny couldn't ask for a more loving wife. After all, no one is perfect, but Sheila lives well within that zip code.

Finally he opens his car door and climbs out. He hunches over and pulls his rain coat tighter to avoid getting rain down the back of his coat. He is especially dressed up today because of the meeting in the Superintendent's office and the follow-up with some of the local press. Mason Huntley had been there and asked some great questions.

Just as Sunny straightens up to hustle to the porch a man who looks remotely familiar steps out of the shadows. With the limited light, rain and overcast skies he can't get a good look at his face. The guy is hunched over to keep the rain off his face and from running down his back. But Sunny thinks it might be McGuire, Speaker Burke's driver and all around flunky. The voice is familiar.

"Sunny, I've got some information for you. This applies to your meeting with the superintendent. I can't talk to you where anyone could see us. Can we talk a moment? This is real important."

Sunny tenses and under his rain coat carefully puts his hand on his gun. He is trying to get a better look to be sure the guy is McGuire. He doesn't seem hostile so Sunny relaxes. Maybe some last piece of information to reassure Sunny the Santa Muerte Cartel have had their vengeance and gone home to their strongholds in the Mountains. Or better yet he had heard about Sunny's meeting with the superintendent and might be coming forward with information about Speaker Burke. All of the corruption swirls around Burke and maybe, just maybe McGuire's policeman conscience is leading him to give Sunny some information. Nothing threatening except making him stay longer in the rain.

He isn't sure who it is, but might as well listen. No harm in listening even if it is in the rain. "Sure. What've you got?" He looks toward the kitchen lights to see if he can see Sheila.

He is distracted and before Sunny can respond the man pulls a Steyr GB 9mm pistol from his waist band and opens fire.

EPILOGUE

FACT TRULY IS STRANGER THAN FICTION. YOU JUST can't make this stuff up and make it any more interesting than real life in Chicago. All of the political corruption stories are basically true and are close to the real events. Most characters are based on real people. These guys really do not have a working relationship with reality. Sadly, University of Illinois Professor Dick Simpson's published research really proves, based on indictments and convictions, that Chicago and its political machine are the most corrupt in America. It is impossible to have been part of the Chicago Democrat Machine and not know that on a daily basis you are working with crooks.

Of course Sunny Sunwarrior, Sheila, Harold Brookins, Stephanie, Vlad Kozak and their friends are fictional. But they are composites of real folks. If I made real people the heroes of the story, their careers in Chicago would be over. One police lieutenant publicly admitted to being a Republican and his duty assignment was moved to the far end of the city where he had to work with a politically powerful alderman who did not appreciate his political choice. Hopefully not, since he is a good cop, but admitting he is a Republican probably was a career ender.

The metropolis of Chicago is in Illinois which is a problem. State government in Illinois, totally dominated by The Chicago Democrat Political Machine, is no longer functional. In the story I mentioned Illinois raised its income tax by 67% and yet the state's budget deficit increased! True. Where else could a government raise taxes by 67% and still end up deeper in the hole. Where Chicago and Illinois are concerned, fact is stranger than fiction. You can't make this stuff up.

Most clean government observers would agree, the Cook County State's Attorney has been fairly represented. She really did head the public corruption unit and not investigate. Her former boss didn't' do anything about public corruption either. I think the characterizations of the Attorney General and Cook County State's Attorney are quite accurate. In the most corrupt city in the most corrupt state, both take the position that public corruption isn't an area they'll spend much time investigating. But if not them, who?

It is impossible for any elected official in Chicago to not know about the corruption that splashes all around them. While some try to act, they are a very tiny minority. There is really very little they can do anyway. As long as the voters of Chicago prove, as they do every election, that corruption and incompetence aren't something they care about, what can a reformer do?

Many fine investigative reporters for the *Chicago Sun Times, Chicago Tribune, Chicago Reader,* stories from the former Chicago News Cooperative that usually appeared in the *New York Times* and of course Fox TV News, Chicago report the shenanigans. Fine columnists like Steve Huntley at the *Sun Times* and John Kass at *The Tribune* as well as investigative civic groups like the Andy Shaw-led Better Government Association or the Lawrence

Msall-led Civic Federation all regularly have written or reported stories that document the corruption and incompetence. Everyone knows about it, but the voters continue to elect the very people the good government folks have pinpointed as crooked. With that kind of corruption tolerant electorate the various governments do nothing to stop the corruption.

For those who might think the story exaggerates the ties between the Chicago Machine and the city's gangs, you may want to read some recent research. Start with a wonderful article, "Gangs and Politicians in Chicago: An Unholy Alliance" by David Bernstein and Noah Isackson. I simply change the names to protect the guilty.

Corruption isn't limited to the old Irish dominated white guys. The corruption in the Chicago Machine refuses to be racist. Just about every ethnic group is well represented. No one is excluded based on their ethnic or racial heritage.

Just recently a former and a sitting Crook County Board member were indicted. The sitting guy is Black and a former alderman. The former board member is Latino. One of the Latino guy's mentors was convicted on a cocaine charge but was still allowed to drive himself to prison. He forgot to use his map and ended up in Mexico! The Mayor's office breathed a sigh of relief. He has stayed there for years and no one seems to be able to find him. Of course his family has received $40,000,000 in contracts to help him stay there. I didn't make that up. My imagination isn't that good.

The State and Cook County Chairs of the Mayor's party are widely considered to be influence peddling crooks. The *New York Times* has been especially brutal on the pair. Michael J. Madigan is the State Chairman and is also the Speaker of the House and his daughter really is the hear no evil, see no evil and speak no evil Attorney General. He has been Speaker for 30 years (yes 30) and has presided over Illinois' total collapse as a fiscal entity. But despite his obvious total incompetence at governance, it has had no effect on his ability to control the political process.

One of Speaker Madigan's innovations is something called "Member Initiatives" where he simply gives all of his members and himself, millions of taxpayer dollars to do with as they see fit. No oversight. This is way past congressional earmarking. This is free money for their buddies with no strings attached. Some media has uncovered huge levels of corruption, but the Speaker doesn't care. Alderman Larenda Bass getting the money could easily have come from a member initiative or Stimulus funds.

The corrupt politicians and power brokers in Chicago are so inbred that when they leave they appoint their relatives to replace them. There have been cases where both the father and the son were aldermen or ward committeemen and both went to prison. You can't make this stuff up any better than the real truth.

The long running abuse of the University of Illinois' admission system did generate huge headlines and a cover-up investigation chaired by a politically connected lawyer. That led to blaming the University. Like an extortion case where the victim is blamed for the crime! The then president of the university, a first rate guy and educator I knew, a former dean of the Michigan Graduate Business School, the top ranked business school in America, had to resign as the scapegoat. By far the biggest abuser of the system was the Speaker of the House who never even bothered to testify at the hearings. The story of an insider trying to get his kid in when he is near the bottom of his high school class is a true story. I simply change the names to protect the guilty. By the way, despite all of the political heat from Chicago Democrats, the university refused to admit the politically connected student at the bottom of his class. I am told the kid finally decided to grow up and has actually become a solid citizen?

Some will question the story of Judge Leoni sending Sunny to jail and the Sheriff protecting him while he is there. True story. The sadly pathetic story of pulling a political insider, under possible investigation for misuse of school funds, out of the Chicago River after a possible suicide is true. Emblematic of the regular misuse of public funds. The guy apparently used at least some of the funds to fly to Copenhagen to support the Chicago 2016 Olympic bid. With his death, suicide or murder, who knows, the investigations essentially stopped. As usual, I simply change the names to protect the guilty.

We sent over 100 judges and court personnel to jail during Operation Greylord and the follow up Crook County Court investigation, called Operation Gambat. The corruption was so open that in a Mob murder case where the "hit man" was identified by two eye witnesses, the Judge still found him innocent.

The Operation Greylord and immediately followed by the Operation Gambit scandals were actually worse than I portrayed them. The suicidal judge was true, actually two of the apparently guilty judges committed suicide. A truly sad end, but... The Head Judge and several others were never indicted and no one knows why. The favorable Bar Association ratings for the crooked judges is true.

For decades the Cook County courts have been a national laughing stock. But, in all fairness, there are plenty of judges who ignore the corruption, the influence peddling and sloth and serve the people who elected them in an exemplary fashion. I want to carefully say that, because some of those judges are the very people who told me what was going on. They want the courts cleaned up as much as we do.

Terry Hake is a real person, a first rate guy and a true hero to those who care about justice. I did take extensive liberties with his personal actions. Terry paid a personal price for doing what needed to be done. The story of the judges taking off big chunks of summer for golf and sun tanning is also true. The story was broken by a combination of Andy Shaw's Better Government Association and Fox News in Chicago. I simply change the names to protect the guilty.

As bad as the courts are, you should try to get your corporate property taxes corrected without paying off the folks in charge. According to the *New York Times,* Michael J. Madigan, the State Chairman of the Democrat party, who also happens to be the Speaker of the House (For the last thirty years! Yes, since 1982!), apparently has made millions of dollars using his clout. He's not the only one, either. Just in the last couple of years, the Speaker has shifted over one billion dollars (yes billion, that is not a misprint) of assessed valuation from his clients to the individual home owners and has yet to be investigated.

The Crook County property tax system is actually different from the other 101 of Illinois' counties. It is a guarantee when Crook County has a system that is different from everyone else's that it wasn't set up to simplify the process or improve the ethical standards. But the Chicago Democrat Machine controlled legislature refuses to fix the broken system because it benefits them. Fact is stranger than fiction. You can't make this stuff up.

Crooks are shocked when they get indicted. Their question is, why me? What am I doing different from everybody else? Think of jailed Governors Ryan and Blagojevich's reactions to their indictments and convictions. When they get caught they are just mad because they got caught, not because they did something wrong.

Even the reformers get coopted. The private company who administers the tests for hiring police and fire department personnel has been charged with fraud. They were brought in because the city was considered too corrupt to hire its own employees and these guys were the folks who would clean things up. Fact is stranger than fiction. You can't make this stuff up.

In the area of housing and inspections, Vlad's lady friend being expected to make a payoff to get her occupancy permit for her beautifully rehabbed home and Vlad having to protect her by going over the inspector's head sounds farfetched. Even though Jerry Katorski is fictional, the scandals he portrayed were deeper and broader in their scope than presented here. Both stories are true. I simply change the names to protect the guilty.

The Hired Truck scandal was actually bigger and really was broken by accident by a hard working *Chicago Sun Times* reporter. I just didn't have the hundreds of pages it would have taken to cover it more thoroughly. Nick "The Stick" LoCoco was real and he did die when he fell off his horse. The rest were, in my opinion, fairly represented. There were mob ties, gang ties, fake minority contractors and all of that. I simply changed the names to protect the guilty.

Walmart was a true story and some gutsy African American Aldermen did stand up and faced previously unheard of levels of retribution from the city's government and private sector unions and the Chicago Federation of Labor. The attempted recall of Wisconsin Governor Scott Walker was a minor skirmish compared to the war declared on the brave aldermen. I was personally active on that issue and also helping a challenged alderman. Mayor Daley who supported Walmart helped the threatened Alderman.

The abuse and open corruption at the state and city pension funds sent a bunch of folks to jail. Some of them were huge political heavy weights. Those investigations also led to the suicide of Governor Blagojevich's Campaign Chairman as he prepared to leave for his term in jail. One of the many pension scams was the first chink in the armor of Governor Blagojevich who is, as you know, in prison as you read this story.

Other examples of how the pension system is used by insiders was when the Chicago controlled legislature really did enact a very specific amendment to allow a Chicago political insider and lobbyist who really did work a grand total of one day as a substitute teacher to qualify for a six figure pension from the Teachers Retirement System for the rest of his life! He will receive millions of taxpayer's dollars in benefits from the already bankrupt fund. He was making well over $200,000 dollars a year when he spent the one day as a substitute teacher. He kept his old job and still makes several hundred thousand dollars a year. No repercussions. Yes, union officials are really allowed in the pension funds. Is it hard to understand why the State's pension funds have the largest unfunded liability of any of the 50 (or is it 57?) states? I didn't use names to protect the guilty.

Unqualified City inspectors with union ties and still in their teens being paid big money to hold safety jobs? True. One convicted inspector was rehired to a new city job only a week after his conviction! His new salary? $78,000/year for doing clerical work! You can't make this stuff up.

"Pinstripe patronage" includes but is not limited to the millions of dollars in political insider legal business and bond business that is passed out. A well-respected judge told me it was a scandal how often judges had to give unrequested continuances because the government's lawyer missed the court call. In a case involving legislation I passed, the school board lawyer missed three straight court appearances and lost the case for lack of representation! It was an open and shut case. The School Board only had to show up to win. The judge actually called the Chicago School Board's chief attorney to ask her to get the lawyer to show up. But he still didn't. He was not disciplined and still got paid.

The Council Wars Era in the early years of the Mayor Harold Washington administration was still another racial blight on the reputation of the most segregated big city in America. It was embarrassing and demeaning and Washington received a great deal of well deserved credit for the way he handled the situation. I don't think Harold was murdered. As a friend, I well knew his appetite and the foods he enjoyed. He gained close to 50 pounds as Mayor and he was no longer the trim young man of his WWII pictures. He loved the job and lived it to the hilt. I think his zest for the job and the fun part of it killed him. RIP to my old friend.

You can do your own research on the murder of the Black Panther's leadership. I say Fred Hampton and the rest of them were murdered by the then Crook County State's Attorney. A lot of people agree. I'll defend that assessment anywhere and anytime.

The political power brokers feel free to act like old style bosses and are so petty that when a major candidate for the opposition political party was caught campaigning in a public park in Chicago the Ward Boss sent three Chicago police officers, in uniform, to tell him if he didn't leave he could be arrested. Interestingly, the Ward Boss's candidates for Governor, Pat Quinn and Attorney General, Lisa Madigan were campaigning in the park at that exact time. A public park in the heart of the Puerto Rican neighborhood, filled with thousands of folks at a back to school festival organized by a mega evangelical church was off limits if you are a Republican. Hubris. Fact is stranger than fiction. You can't make this stuff up.

Many like to blame former Mayor Richard M. Daley for all of the problems. No question he turned a blind eye to the corruption around him. But he was the Cook County State's Attorney during Operation Greylord and he worked in harmony with the Federal prosecutors. That took real guts. And he was also more innovative than any previous Mayor. When you look at the strides the city made during his tenure, it is impossible to not recognize his achievements as Mayor. Chicago had started to reverse its massive population loss under Rich from 1990 to 2000. But as the unending drumbeat of corruption in the early years of the 21st century rolled on, the population began to decline again. Chicago lost another 7% in the first decade of the 21st century. If he had retired a term earlier, before the recession started and never gotten himself involved with the 2016 Olympic bid, I personally think he would have retired a revered figure.

Da Mayor was not and is not a crook. He is a very likable guy who is a decent, church going family man who loved being Mayor of Chicago and did a great deal of good to somewhat compensate for the bad. He is a product of and part of the Chicago Political System. His family's business was running Chicago and he inherited that business. Unfortunately, he believes in the system he inherited and believes its flaws are less than its virtues. He is wrong.

When a tourist or uninvolved resident looks at the well maintained lake front parks, the spectacular skyline, the huge new assortment of rental and condominium residences downtown, the rebuilt theatre district, the South Loop, the West Loop, numerous other reclaimed neighborhoods and the beautiful gardens they tend to overlook the open corruption, street violence because they didn't see it, massive debt and theft by the folks in charge.

Many like to say da Mayor sold out to the real estate developers in his dealings with them. Maybe, but if he did, da Mayor and the citizens of Chicago clearly got the better end of that deal. Presidential Towers that anchors the move into the West Loop is a perfect example of corruption that helped the city but cost the taxpayers dearly. The Godfather of that deal was former Ways & Means Committee Chairman Dan Rostenkowski who, like so many Chicago politicians, went to prison. Presidential towers should have been enough on its own, but he was so crooked they didn't need the Towers to send him to the Big House.

I feel it is fair to say of da Mayor's administration, with the tax money they didn't steal, they did a good job running the city. Of course it might have helped if they hadn't run up so much debt and had put some money in the bankrupt pension funds.

The new Mayor, Rahm Emanuel, is a longtime political henchman of Mayor Daley's and Presidents Bill Clinton and Chicago's own, Barack Obama. He also took now jailed Governor Rod Blagojevich's and previously jailed Ways and Means Chairman Dan Rostenkowski's old congressional seat. Those of us who followed Rahm's career were impressed that Rahm is the first machine Democrat congressman from that seat to not go to jail in half a century (Give him the benefit of the doubt. He is still a young man and there is plenty of time for him to follow in his predecessor's tradition.).

In between Rahm's years as a power player, he took a few years off after the Clinton administration and before Congress to make multi, multi-millions of dollars as another Washington insider peddling influence. He also made a ton of money as another hear no evil, see no evil and speak no evil Freddie Mac Board member in the middle of the housing, mortgage and accounting scandals that eventually pulled the American economy down into the quagmire. The taxpayers are out over $150 billion dollars and counting on Fannie and Freddie. Yet there has not been one DC indictment for all of that fraud. Chicago isn't the only place where politically connected the prosecutors turn a blind eye to corruption.

Maybe with established credentials of being a successful influence peddler, brutal machine insider and enforcer and with the proven ability to ignore obvious corruption all around him, Rahm Emanuel may make a pretty good Chicago Mayor.

His attempt to bully Chick-fil-A was classic Chicago. Time will tell if he grows into the job.

No one has ever been any better at intimidation and obfuscation than Rahm and the Illinois Speaker of the House, Michael J. Madigan. In Chicago or Illinois, if you choose to stick your head up, expect to have it cut off. If someone dares to mention there are a few problems in a city where 32 of the 50 aldermen go to jail, the response is always to attack. A 33rd was indicted in February of 2012 but is not in jail yet. The rule for Chicago machine flaks is to never respond to questions about your flaws. If need be, make up some flaw of your accuser and immediately attack him or her. It is standard operating procedure in Chicago and due to the overlap has now become standard in Washington DC.

If you think I'm unfair or too tough on the crooks in Chicago, look up Professor Dick Simpson of the University of Illinois at Chicago. He is a former Chicago alderman now back in the academic world. He is clearly a card carrying member of the progressive wing of the Democrat Party and his analysis isn't any different than mine. Just more analytical. Simpson is a good and decent guy even if we might differ quite a bit about politics.

This has been a great deal of fun to write. I loved living in the Chicago area for almost my entire life. This is absolutely the most interesting place in America to open a morning newspaper or see the TV news and find out who just brazenly stole what.

It is hard to visualize anyone who has been part of this totally corrupt machine being elected to anything outside of Illinois. Someone who supported jailed Governor Rod Blagojevich 100% of the time. Everybody should know about it, but... Chicago and Illinois are governed by folks who from a governmental point of view, truly do not have a working relationship with reality. And they have gotten away with it for years. That is why Illinois is bankrupt beyond the ability to save it and

Chicago is heading in that direction. Yet the leaders have become millionaires on the ride down. I am afraid it is totally entertaining but actually a sad final chapter on life in what was once a great city and what was once America's boom state. All empires come to a sudden end...

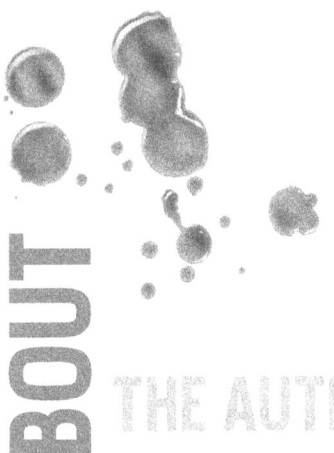

ABOUT THE AUTHOR

ROGER KEATS HAS BEEN AN ILLI-nois Senator in three different decades in America's legendarily most corrupt City and State. He served amidst two gover-nors, 15 fellow legislators, 100+ judges and court personnel and countless government employees who ended up in jail. Chicago has 50 Aldermen and recently 32 have gone to jail! No one knows Illi-nois' corrupt politics and politicians any better. He has been honored by the Illinois Conservative Union and was an honoree for Black History Month in 2009. No one has been a more suc-cessful reformer, working with diverse groups and challenging the corrupt leadership of both parties. As Barack Obama's pred-ecessor in the Senate said, "I'm not sure who hates Roger more, the Democrat or Republican leadership." Roger even acted as a "mole" to catch corrupt state employees. He is also a retired Army Lieutenant Colonel.

After four decades, he finally got so tired of fighting the cor-ruption in Illinois that he and his wife retired to The Hill Country of Texas.

www.ingramcontent.com/pod-product-compliance
Lightning Source LLC
Chambersburg PA
CBHW071631260626
47170CB00001B/60

* 9 7 8 0 9 8 8 3 1 9 4 0 0 *